THE HEAD THAT WEARS THE CROWN

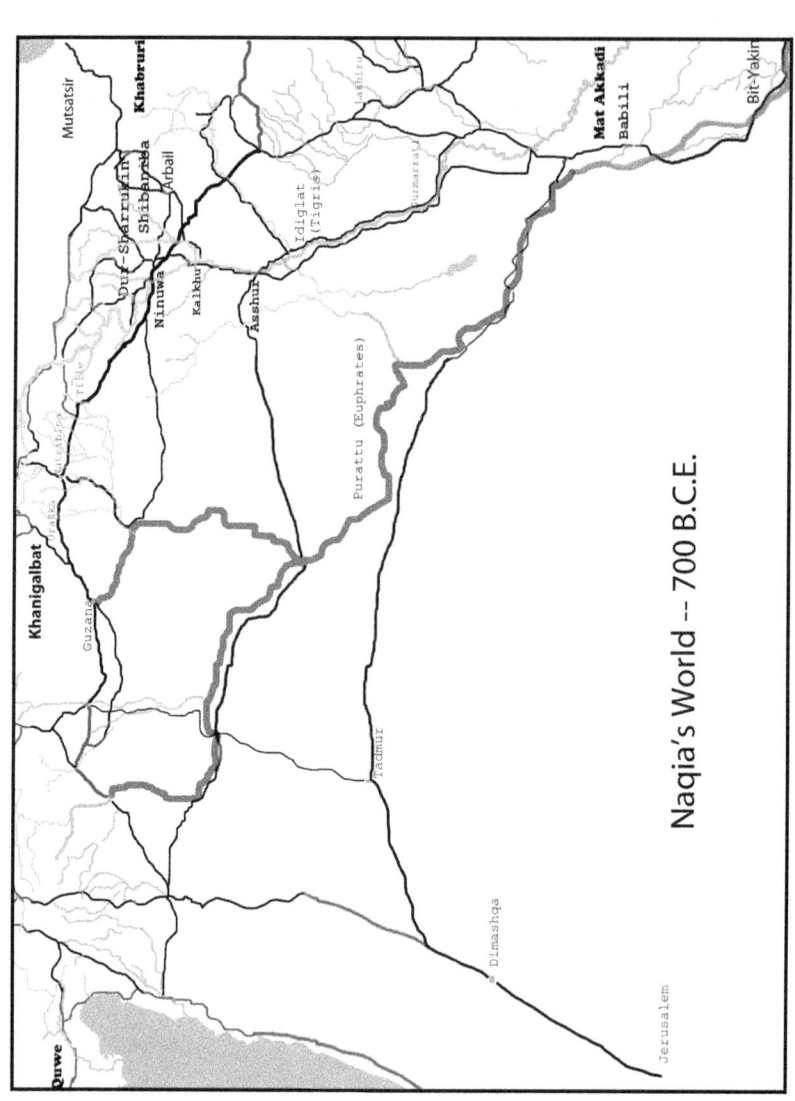

THE HEAD THAT WEARS THE CROWN

by

JUDITH REINKEN

This edition first published in New Zealand in 2020 by
Beulah Press
PO Box 27
Ōmāpere 0444
ffms@farmside.co.nz

Copyright © Judith Reinken 2019

ISBN 978-0-473-51100-5

All rights reserved. No part of this publication may be reproduced, transmitted, or stored in a retrieval system in any form or by any means, without permission in writing from the author.

Dedicated to those
producing the
State Archives of Assyria
series

Preface

In 701 BCE men and women uprooted from their professions as poets, musicians, dancers and administrators were taken from Jerusalem eastward to the land now known as Iraq. In this book I imagine their story. I have included among them a woman known to us from official archives as Naqia, later titled Zaqutu, who was wife to the king Sennacherib, mother of his successor, Esarhaddon, and grandmother to Asshurbanipal.

It rarely happens that past events we have known are confirmed anew. Archaeologists have over many years been unearthing in the Middle East large collections of texts written in cuneiform on clay tablets, some from Asshurbanipal's own library. Several texts include details of the activities of the Assyrian king, known in modern times as Sennacherib. The text of some of the documents details the assets offered by the king of Judah to persuade the army of Asshur to spare the city of Jerusalem.

In one account Sennacherib's scribes write: "In addition to the former annual tribute, I imposed on them more gifts owed to my rule ... together with 30 talents of gold, 800 talents of silver and select antimony in small blocks and large blocks of stone, couches inlaid with ivory, boxwood and all kinds of valuable treasure, he also sent his own daughters, women of his palace, male and female musicians after me to Nineveh my lordly city."
(This quote is from the Chicago Prism, another cylinder adds more furniture and fabrics, tools and weapons.)

In the Hebrew Bible we know today we read:

> "In the 14th year of the king Hezekiah, King Sennacherib of Asshur came up against all the fortified cities of Judah and laid hold of them. King Hezekiah of Judah sent to the king of Asshur at Lachish saying, 'I have done wrong, turn back from me; whatever you impose upon me I will bear,' and the king of Asshur laid upon King Hezekiah of Judah payment of 300 talents of silver and 30 talents of gold."
> (II Kings 18:13-14)

The events described here are mostly historical; most of the characters are real people known to us from the ancient texts. The roles of the women in this story are based on contemporary assessments of the cuneiform tablets from the 7th century BCE. Details of the religious observances are also based on ancient sources, many of which are older than the time of this story.

Yet this is a work of imagination, of fiction, despite the historical background. But perhaps it will bring those long ago times to life.

In this book I imagine for Naqia origins in the west and a passion for engaging the artists who carved the friezes of the grand palaces that the kings built. I imagine the scenes they depict as being Naqia's own choices. The illustrations in this book are based on photographs published in the multi-volume State Archives of Assyria published in Helsinki under the direction of Simo Parpola and his many colleagues.

The cover, drawn by Rachel Brand, shows the queen herself. All the book's illustrations have also been drawn by Rachel Brand except for the 'reconstructions' of the city of Asshur.

Contents

Book One: Naqia Becomes Zaqutu

Chapter 1	3
Chapter 2	14
Chapter 3	19
Chapter 4	34
Chapter 5	44
Chapter 6	56
Chapter 7	69
Chapter 8	76
Chapter 9	84
Chapter 10	93
Chapter 11	103
Chapter 12	109
Chapter 13	115

Book Two: Intrigue

Chapter 14	125
Chapter 15	131
Chapter 16	137
Chapter 17	140
Chapter 18	150
Chapter 19	157
Chapter 20	160
Chapter 21	174

Book Three: Patricide

Chapter 22	179
Chapter 23	190
Chapter 24	193
Chapter 25	196
Chapter 26	203
Chapter 27	207
Chapter 28	211
Chapter 29	218
Chapter 30	228
Chapter 31	231
Chapter 32	239

Book Four: Ishtar's Revenge

Chapter 33	247
Chapter 34	256
Chapter 35	268
Chapter 36	274
Chapter 37	280
Chapter 38	285

Genealogies

Sennacherib — Tashmetu
└ Nadim-Shumi

Sennacherib — Zaza
├ Arda-Mulissi
├ Shumu-Etli
└ Sharrani

Sennacherib — Naqia/Zaqutu
├ Esarhaddon
├ Shaddati
└ Shibanu

Sennacherib — Tebua

Judah's Royal Family

Akhaz — Abijah
├ Qat — Khizkiyahu/Hezekiah
│ ├ Naqia
│ └ Pele/Manasseh
└ Zekar
   └ Abiramu

List of Characters
Other than members of the royal families

Naqia's Household
    Annabel, handmaid to Naqia
    Uribelit, handmaid to Naqia and Ahat-Abisha
    Ataril, devotee of Ishtar, chief eunuch to Naqia
    Amat-Baal, chatelaine in Kalkhu
    Shebna ben Shaqed,
      sometime counselour to Qat, tutor of Esarhaddon, spy for Naqia

Sennacherib's Household
    Aram-Suen, third man
    Suen-Akhu-Utsur, Grand Vizier
    Sulmu-Bel, general (turtanu)
    Addati, chatelaine in Ninuwa
    Shezibanni, chief steward of Dur-Sharrukin, husband of Abby

Esarhaddon's household
    Shemahu, physician of Kilizi
    Hussani, charioteer
    Bel-Emuranni, general (turtanu)
    Inurta-Nadi, Grand Vizier
    Remutu, Eshara-Hammat's chatelaine

Other Characters
    Nikkal-Amat, chatelaine of Ninuwa Central
    Ruradidi, eunuch to Nikkal-Mat
    Aplaya, chief eunuch to Arda-Mulissi
    Baya, Prophet of Ishtar at Arbail
    Banba, son of Abiramu, governor of Dur-Sharrukin
    Zakir, ashipu (shaman, healer)
    Ben-Zakir, dog named after Zakir
    Yesha and Yoldah, foster-parents of Naqia

Principal Gods

Ishtar, high goddess of Asshur
Asshur, high god of Asshur
Shamash, the Sun, god of justice
Marduk, the Hero, victor over chaos
Nabu, scribe of the gods
Ea, the god of wisdom
Suen, the Moon, god of truth and purity
Adad, the storm god
Mummu/Mulissu, the mother of the gods,
Nergal, god of the underworld, of the dead
Ereshkigal, goddess of the underworld, of the dead
Anu, the head of the gods
Tammuz, consort of Ishtar
Gula, goddess of healing

Assyrian Calendar Months

Nisan [Spring New Year]
Iyyar
Sivan
Tammuz
Ab
Elul
Tishri [Autumn New Year]
Marchesvan
Kislev
Tebet
Shebat
Adar

BOOK ONE

NAQIA BECOMES ZAQUTU

Chapter 1: Journey to Urakka

Naqia, not yet thirteen years old, sat astride the mule. In the full afternoon sun the heat beat down, not even her thick shawl offering protection. The fat old mule had mange too. Naqia's legs itched and she fretted as the mule fell further and further behind the caravan. The wind swept sand into her face and she kept her eyes closed as much as she could. Then she fell so far behind she no longer heard anything, no shouts from the soldiers herding the women along. Alarmed, she raised her shawl and peered ahead.

She could no longer even see the immense baggage train, mules plodding, stretched out across the horizon. She couldn't make out the shrouded figures of the hundreds of women who formed part of the booty Sennacherib had exacted from Jerusalem. All she could make out was the  standards—the sun-disks of Asshur—glinting, and the sun reflecting off the heavy armour some of the soldiers wore. The mule may have sensed her alarm and began shuffling along, faster and faster, bringing her up closer to the others.

Suddenly she did hear them, shouts and then screams drifting back from the vanguard. Her mule plodded on towards the caravan. Feeling a wind behind her, Naqia lifted her shawl to look. Arab camel-riders were pouring off the hillside towards the baggage train. She saw the soldiers shove all the women into a clump and form a circle around them.

The mule is taking me straight into the raid. Should I get down? she wondered. *I wouldn't be able to get up again and those bandits would grab me and take me away* ... As if another person lived in her head she heard, *Take you away? Rob you, rape you and leave you for dead in the desert.* Dread seized her as she realised they'd see her as soon as they looked back. She covered herself with the shawl and bent forward along the mule's back.

Sensing her fear, the mule stood fast. Soon no sound came from the caravan. Peering behind her, Naqia saw nothing but bare windswept sand, red-gold reflecting the light. She'd freeze to death after dark. *They'll abandon me here, no food, no water, not even a blanket. Dropped by the wayside, left for dead.* She choked on sobs of self-pity.

Then she heard shouts and a woman's high-pitched scream. She squinted, trying to pick out what was happening. A raider had dragged a woman off to the side, his arm tight about her waist. He flung her to the ground and grabbed both her feet, parting them as he shoved his knife towards her face. Riveted, Naqia watched as he knelt between her legs, dropping his knife to push her shoulders down as he began to thrust himself into her.

Naqia tried to kick the mule to turn her around, but it plodded forward, intent on joining the rest of the mules. As she came nearer Naqia saw one of Sennacherib's soldiers jump behind the Arab, grab his hair, and pull his head so far back she thought it would come off. Instead the soldier's stabbing knife sliced across the Arab's neck. Blood gushed forth all over the raped woman. Naqia, revolted, felt vomit rising in her own throat. Her hands went numb and she fell forward on to the mule's neck. She remembered none of what followed.

Naqia remained in a coma and, together with three other women, was abandoned by the soldiers at a small village called Urakka. By the village gate stood a rough hut formed of sticks and mud. At noon in midsummer there was little movement. The few inhabitants stayed within their walls, no travellers passed along the road.

Naqia woke to the silence. *Where am I? What's happened to everyone? Is this the end?* Her questions hung in the air until she noticed a woman peering into the darkness of the windowless shelter. In a quavering voice Naqia asked if it were her cousin: "Abby?"

"Peace to you, Naqia. Oh, it really stinks in here. You've been sick again and ... oh, I'll have to try and get some clean straw."

"Straw, Abby? What's happened? Where are we? Why am I in this prison cell? Where is everyone?"

"Gone. Here, well this is Urakka, a tiny place, and poor. We were left here because we got too sick to continue all the way to Ninuwa. They wouldn't let you inside the wall because you were so much sicker than we were. You might have had a demon, you know."

"Sick? I remember nothing. So you were sick too?"

"I was sick too but I am better now. The other women got better too, but they've been taken into the headman's hut—as servants, would you believe? But you and me, I think they hope we'll die."

Naqia, alarmed, reached out for her cousin but Abby backed away. Naqia's head ached and she felt rebuffed. *Even Abby fears me.* Then Abby put down the food she was carrying and came over to crouch beside Naqia's bed of straw. Naqia took her hand and Abby held it.

"Naqia, we aren't really welcome here, but I don't think you'll die. I have to fetch all our water and even beg to get us some food. But look here, they let me take some milk from their goats and even this pottage of crushed millet."

Naqia wrinkled her nose and frowned. Still disoriented, she asked, "What day is it? Do you know?"

"End of the month. They're fasting, that's why they gave us food. Take it."

"You look perfectly healthy." Naqia inspected Abby's face which had grown thinner during their journey. She noticed that her clothes were stained and dusty which made her wonder. Abby had always been so particular about her appearance. Uncertain, she asked, "Was it you I heard laughing last night? Was I dreaming? I thought I heard you."

"Yes, you did. I was flirting by the fence, teasing that young gate-keeper. Don't worry, he was just a little kid and anyway, the headman of the village came out and gave the boy a dressing down. They're still afraid we'll pollute them. And you, you've been off your head with fever. You seem to be frightened almost to death whenever you wake up."

"I have been, ever since ..."

"Ever since?"

"That attack, the raiders, the ... the rape and then ... Oh, Abby, all that blood."

"What blood? Are you raving? You don't feel that feverish."

"Not raving, I want to forget." *That knife sinking into the man's neck. The blood spurting all over, on the soldier, on that poor woman he was trying to ... I wasn't imagining it. It's like I was doing it, like the soldier, like I was killing the man and I got all spattered with blood.* "Maybe you didn't see."

"I have no idea what you saw. Was it the raid? We just crouched under the wagons and kept still. Now, Naqia, you must drink this."

"You're saying I stink, but what's in your hand? It smells off to me."

"Goat's milk, and it's not off, it's still warm from the goat. It's going to be hot again today and, believe me, it's you who really stink. I'll fill a water-jar to give you a bath."

"Wait with me while I drink this and try to keep it down."

Naqia ate and drank and felt somewhat better. She put away the rest of what Abby had brought and started to turn over, but Abby gestured her to stop.

"My dear, I ought to take your clothes off. Can you sit up?"

Naqia propped herself up and let Abby remove her clothes. She sighed and asked, "How long have I been here?"

"Seven days. This just a tiny way-station along the main road from Kharranu to Natsibina, a crossroads. When you are able to move we will have to make our own way to Ninuwa somehow."

"Will you know the way? And what about water?"

"I don't know the way but it's a road. There must be streams along the way. There's one here and that's why they have any food at all. Everywhere else is parched. The village boys who go to get fodder for the king's horses and mules have to traipse way off into the hills."

"Is that what I was hearing this morning? The chattering? It wasn't a dream?"

"No, it was real. But they don't have anything to say when they come trudging home at night. It's a hard life here."

"How long is it since we left home? How long have we been gone?"

"We left on the seventh of Tammuz and tomorrow's first of Ab, so it's three weeks. Now, let me wash those sores on your legs."

With a damp cloth Abby started to wash Naqia's legs. The sores oozed yellow pus, staining the linen wrapped straw. Naqia drew her legs away.

"Abby, stop, no more!"

"See here, I have to wash you and I ought to put cloths soaked in vinegar between your legs. I'll have to beg for it, offer them something. A ring maybe."

"You have to use our jewellery? But, Abby, if there's no one looking after us couldn't they just take all our things?"

"Well, no, there were two soldiers here, you know, to guard the horses and mules and, I suppose, us. I asked them to make the villagers give us food, but even they weren't always given food. It's a really poor village. Now those guards have gone for some reason. But if I go to the river where the women are washing someone may help us."

Naqia dozed while Abby went for help. In her half-doze she remembered her mother, Qat, reassuring her that all would be fine. *Fine? Is this what she meant? Was she just lying to me?* As Abby appeared in the doorway Naqia started awake.

"Abby, I don't understand why we're not looked after. Are we so unimportant?"

"Ah. I'll see what I can do. But, Naqia, help. Let me clean these sores without you moaning."

"Oh, now the straw is wet as well as soiled. Filthy, smelly and horrid. Will we ever get out of here?"

"I heard a bit of gossip at the riverbank. Women were muttering about more travellers interfering. I think that's what they were saying, it's a funny dialect they have. Remember the last town, Guzana?"

"No. Really I remember nothing nothing that happened since, since that ambush."

"Oh, the ambush. Let me see. Guzana was after that. A crossroads we passed. Well, the man I flirted with last night told me a new draft of mules is coming. The king's expected. He's been on campaign in Shubria, they say. "

"So what? He won't pay any attention to us."

Abby shrugged. "Let me clear all this stuff away. I might get some clean straw."

"I can't stand up, don't let me fall."

"Naqia, you really have to."

"I'll try, I will. But I can't stop crying. It's like that song, you know. 'Oh that my head were waters, and my eyes a fountain of tears'. Now I think I know what that means. Abby, I am sorry to be such trouble. I suppose you have to barter with the villagers even for straw."

"I do. I guess the straw is intended for king's mules not for his women."

"It's a bitter thought. I'm grateful to you for staying with me. I know you might have been able to get away."

Naqia stood leaning against the dirt wall of the hut while Abby sorted through the pack of clothes for something to cover her with. Abby frowned as she looked up at her cousin. "Get away! Where to? On my own? Not a hope."

"Couldn't you stay in the headman's house? With the others? If you did I'd just die here in this hovel."

"I won't desert you, but I am going to get some straw, somehow."

"If the king comes will, you …?"

"I'll get some more straw."

Abby returned with a bundle of straw and some news. She tidied away the old damp straw into a pile outside the opening and spread the new straw on the ground inside. When all was straightened up she came back and sat beside Naqia's pallet.

"Naqia, no one knows whether the king is coming but those mules are for him not us. We'll still be in this awful place after the new moon, I imagine. And it'll be hotter yet. "

Naqia's whole body shivered when she caught sight of Abby's face. It was as though Abby's courage had suddenly failed. *If she gives in I really will die, why not?* "Abby, what's happened? You look so sad. Why?"

"They've forgotten us, or someone's reported us as having died. But we've both recovered now, even you. We'll end up sold as slaves I expect, or worse."

Naqia looked through the doorway to the empty road and the dirty straw piled up beside it. *That's frightful. Slaves? It can't be possible. Oh …*

She straightened up her back and asked, "Worse? What do you mean?"

"Don't you know? A female slave brings a price of at least half a minah of silver. As a maiden, as long as you're in good health, you'd fetch twice as much. That's a fortune to anyone from a small village like this."

Naqia began to cry again, trying to get control of herself, but groaning with sickness and fear.

"Don't moan, Naqia. It doesn't help either of us. At any rate no one would pay for you in your present state. Your clothes are filthy and you still smell really terrible."

"You're no comfort, Abby. I …Why did they leave us behind, like worthless trash?"

"We got sick. What don't you understand?"

"Do you suppose they want me to die? Maybe the king doesn't want to marry his son to me. If I die he gets out of it without breaking the treaty."

"So why did he make the treaty then?"

"My mother, you know. Qat made him do it. As she always does, getting her own way no matter how the rest of us feel."

Abby stopped and spread her arms out. "Your mother? You can't be that naive. That's ridiculous. How could she? You know Sennacherib is really the lord of all Judah. Your father hides in his room and Qat—fine, she's Queen Mother, but of what?"

"Oh, Abby, I wonder. If she'd wanted me to get to Ninuwa safely she'd have sent an escort—you know, our own troops. If she meant me to marry the king's son she'd have given me ..." Naqia's voice quavered and then gave out. Her misery seemed to rise up to strangle her.

Abby took her hand and squeezed it. "Stop crying, Naqia, please just stop."

"I've no status, no different from you other temple women. If Qat cared there'd be spies on the lookout, they'd notice we've gone missing."

"Her? Send spies after you? You believe that?"

"No, but she did say ..."

"She'd say. That's easy, say anything she would. Do? That's something else. Anyhow, what'd she say?"

"Just that I'd marry the king's son, be able to help her. That's what she told me."

"I don't believe it. I mean, she may have said it but she must have known it was nonsense. Look, we temple women never had a high opinion either of her or her nosey spy-master."

"You mean Shebna ben Shaqed?"

"We were a bit afraid but never very admiring. You ought not believe her no matter what she told you. Look, I'll go now."

"Why must you go? What if someone comes for us?"

"No one'll rescue us. All we're worth is what we can make men think we're worth. I'll try to find some more vinegar."

Naqia dozed, fevered dream images flickering, a young woman skipping through a garden, toes hardly touching the earth; blood splattered against a smooth stone wall, dripping until dried by the hot sun; a hand piercing her chest to rip out the liver; a bliss of emptied self, body only a husk sucked dry by a mighty spirit. She woke drained and empty.

That midsummer day, the last day of Tammuz, everyone fasted. Stopped along the main road the king, draped in grey mourning garments, listened to his messages from Ninuwa. He tapped his foot, his eyes wandering over the low hills, dusty and brown.

They hadn't been able to find any shade when they made camp and the early morning sun promised discomfort. He always hated the monthly fast when on campaign. Riding, whether on horseback or in his chariot, gave him appetite. Now he could hear his stomach, rumbling, sorely missing breakfast. By the first watch he thrummed with impatience for the day's end. Then, as his servant began reading the next letter from the capital, he jumped up and began pacing the width of their camp.

> To the king my lord, your servant Gallulu. Good health to the king my lord! May Nabu and Marduk bless the king my lord! Concerning the tribute levied upon the western lands about which the king my lord wrote to me, all the furniture from those places arrived safely. The king my lord asked after the male and female musicians. They have arrived. Dancing women, too, arrived by barge to Ninuwa on the twentieth day.
> Na'id-Ilu sent to your servant asking for a receipt for 387 dancing women. Only 384 women, not counting the musicians, arrived at the city gates. Na'id-Ilu also asked me to write to him as soon as the daughter of the king of Judah reached the city. She has not come into the city. I asked Nikkal-Amat, chatelaine of Ninuwa Central. No women have been received in the household of the mother of the king my lord.
> The king my lord may say: "Why does the guard Gallulu wait so many days before writing to the king my lord?" The barges carrying the women were very heavily loaded. I waited for the next lot of barges to see if the missing women were on them. The next lot of barges carried no women. So I have written to the king my lord. May the king my lord not be angry with his servant!

Furious, the king sent for the governor of Natsibina. "Listen to this! Did you know about this? Why didn't you audit the tribute? Days later! It's a week! The Judah woman, the daughter—can't remember the name. She's missing, together with three dancing women. What's happened? Stolen? How? Who's trying to make trouble? Well?"

"The king my lord is right to be angry. On the fourteenth we received notice from Guzana that the horde of women given you by the king of Judah had been sent ahead. But those women didn't come here—they went south through Singara to Balatzu to the barges because they were so many. The king my lord knows that country is an empty place. No one who escapes there survives. I expect the messenger from Kharranu later today with the monthly toll report. The king my lord may wish to wait here. We'll find out who has passed through Kharranu and Guzana before nightfall. By tomorrow your chariot horses will be rested."

"Oh, all right then. But I need to do something or I'll break the fast. Get me a fresh horse."

The two men made their way to the stables. Natsibina was a main staging post and the stables were well-fashioned and clean. The governor stopped at the door to let the king precede him, bowing as the king passed.

"Which one would you like, my lord the king? "

"The black stallion with the white blaze. He'll be good. I can head for the hills for some hunting. Until it gets too hot."

The governor nodded. "I'll have the guard alerted to come and stable the horse when the king my lord returns. We'll transfer the king's regalia to the next horse you'll use. You won't need all that for hunting."

Shortly after midday, discouraged by the summer's heat and the absence of game, Sennacherib returned to the garrison. At the gate a guard grabbed his knees, kissing his feet, gibbering with excitement. The king brushed the gabbling soldier off and led his horse to the stables himself. At the stables he found the governor waiting for men to saddle his own horse and fit it with his regalia. Sennacherib came up behind him, touched him on the shoulder.

"Where are you off to? I found no game but I am well. You can be happy."

"Oh! The king my lord should know, the missing women have been found. My messenger stopped to water his horse at Urakka. They asked his errand so he told them. They said, 'But the women are here. Their guards left them at Urakka, too ill to travel. Three dancing women almost died but they are well. The king's daughter, she is not well.' They said no herbalist from Guzana had come. Now I have ordered my herbalist Sama-adi to accompany me to Urakka. I hope my lord the king approves."

"Yes, I do. Urakka? Never heard of it. How far is it?"

"The king my lord should know, not far. Three hours, perhaps four."

"Give me your horse. I've nothing better to do—I will ride with the herbalist."

Naqia dozed fitfully, still damp with sweat and hollow inside. As she lifted her head to call out for water she realised it was late afternoon; the doorway showed the long shadow of the hut. Before she could try to use her voice she heard the sound of hoofbeats, very near. She stopped breathing to listen. Men's voices, angry and excited. *Perhaps they've come for me.* She heard Abby's lovely, high-pitched voice begin a greeting and then stop abruptly. Naqia could make out only murmuring. An old man's voice, tremulous, rasping with a thick accent.

The sound came closer as the man drew nearer until he stood at the doorway, peering into the darkness within. "My lady, are you awake?"

"I am thirsty. Please may I have water? Abby? Who is this?"

"It's a herbalist by the look of him. That satchel he's taking off obviously has some things in it."

"Girl, you go and get me a goblet and a spoon. Go!"

Naqia, fully awake now, bristled with indignation. *Who does he think he is, smelly wretch?* She found her voice and it came out much stronger. "Look you, she's no servant—she's my cousin. You have not even told me who you are. I've been ill but I still ought to know who you are."

"Just take this. I've mixed it for you."

"I won't. Who are you? What is this?"

"My lady, I am Uballitz, the herbalist. You must ..."

"I won't. Not until you've said what's in it."

As the herbalist grabbed at Abby's wrist to pull her over to him, Naqia turned away and hid her face under her shawl. In rough Aramaic the herbalist gabbled at her. Naqia heard Abby agree and felt Abby take the shawl off her face. The herbalist summoned her back to his side and gabbled something Naqia couldn't understand. Abby nodded. "Naqia, I can translate for you. You have to take this. He's ... The king's here, outside. He sent this man to you. He's sent for another one, too. What's the matter? What do you want?"

Naqia sat up, shaking her head, her lips pursed tight. Abby took her shoulder to shake her into replying. Naqia grunted, refusing, but then opened her mouth. "He won't tell me what it is. I won't take it unless I know."

"Really Naqia this is no time ... "

"I won't."

Abby turned to the man. "Sorry, Uballitz, she knows about medicines; you must explain."

With her back to the door, Abby didn't see the approaching figure, but Uballitz did. He fell flat on his face on the filthy floor. Naqia pulled the shawl back over her head and face as waves of nausea rose and fell. She felt so limp she feared she'd faint away and disgrace herself. She choked down some bile as she heard a firm, deep voice order both the old man and Abby to get out. His large body blocked the light from the door of the hut but even in the dimness she knew he'd removed his turban. She could smell the perfumed oil he'd been anointed with, and leather, and the sweat of a man who'd just ridden far. She shrank deeper into the bedding and tried to wish him away.

He came right up to her. "Let me see for myself. Are you the daughter of Judah's king?"

"I am, my lord. May my lord the king pardon my wretched state. I have been ill."

"I am Sennacherib, king of the world, king of Asshur, king of all the lands. You should not have suffered this indignity at the hands of my faithless servants. Tell me what you desire in recompense, whatever it may be."

Naqia was stunned. *What should I do? 'Don't be afraid,' Qat said, 'and don't humble yourself. They are men and not gods.' But he—he does look like a god.* She stared at him and voiced her thought without thinking. "My lord, you are like a god. How can I deserve any recompense from you? I do not understand anything. I don't even know where I am. That man wanted to make me drink his potion, but there's no one I can trust."

"There, there. You can trust me. I'll stay with you until the proper healer arrives, I've sent for him, but so late in the day ... no moon to lead them. No one will harm you. I promised your father to marry you to my son Arda-Mulissi. He will be king after me and you shall be his queen. No one's going to hurt you."

Chapter 2: The Story of Adapa

Sennacherib stood just outside the wretched hut while he waited for the second herbalist. As he watched, the villagers sent a bed and generous amounts of clean bed-straw for Naqia's hut and as if by magic clean linen drapes covered the walls and now lay over the girl herself. Incense burned in one corner to drive away the stale smells.

The king came back in. At a loss what to say or do he sent for a stool to sit on. Beside her pallet he let himself down with a sigh. *What shall I say to her? She's so little, she looks so young. Maybe she would like a story.* "My daughter, do you know the story of Adapa?"

"No. Is it a true one?"

"The scholars disagree. Because it's a story about a sage, each tells it his own way. Maybe all are true. I'll tell you mine." The king saw her smiling hesitantly. Lowering her head a little, she looked up at him from under her eyelashes. "You are so small and you look so young. Have you a strong spirit?"

"A strong spirit? I don't know." She covered her mouth but then asked, "Adapa, who's Adapa?"

"A man, a special man. Ea made him to be perfect, to be like Ea, immortal. Don't you know? Ea? Ea, the wisest of all the gods, created Adapa to be his likeness among men."

"I see."

"Adapa had all understanding, he could perceive the design of the earth's creation. He knew how everything came to be as it was."

"I know all about the creation of the world and all."

"Don't interrupt. Such knowledge derives from Ea, and Adapa is the sage who passes it on."

"Sorry."

The king took a deep breath and, hoping she would obey and keep quiet, he continued. "Adapa knew exactly how to do everything the gods love because, having been given long life, he had learned all rituals. He could keep his hands clean and his deeds blameless.

He made the ointments for the gods, he oversaw all the bakers, he provided all the bread and water for the temple of Eridu."

"Eridu?"

"Don't you know? It's the oldest city south of Babili—you have heard of Babili?"

"Of course."

Sennacherib frowned. *She must know. Her father collaborated with the rebel prince of Bit-Yakin, Marduk-Baladan, when he styled himself 'King of Babili'. Otherwise I'd not have invaded Judah and squashed that king. She must know, that's why she's here. If I hadn't come near to defeat I'd not have made the treaty. No, not a defeat. The king of Judah capitulated. The rest of his women and his treasure are safely in Ninuwa now.* He shifted his weight on the stool and started to clear his throat, but words didn't come until she prompted him.

"My lord the king? The story?"

"One day Adapa set sail from the Holy Quay of the New Moon; he set out to catch the fish the gods love. The wind blew every which way and Adapa's boat drifted. With oars he tried to steer his boat upon the wide, wide sea. Adapa sailed across the wide ocean and the South Wind blew as hard as any wind can ever blow. You do know about wind?"

"Oh yes. We came from Dimashqa to Tadmur. Nothing but wind. So hot and dry. Abby says that's why we …"

Sennacherib put a finger to his lips, reminding himself to stop asking her questions. He didn't want to hear the answers. He brought his face so near hers that she must have sensed his annoyance. She reached out to his hand and said, "The king my lord knows, of course."

Still scowling, he returned to the stool and again made her wait a moment before resuming. "As I was saying, the South Wind blew so hard it tipped Adapa's boat over so he'd fall into the sea and drown. Any other man would have despaired, but not Adapa. Ea had given him all wisdom, you see. He knew the spells for everything, even for breaking the South Wind. 'South Wind,' he cried out, 'withdraw from me all thy venom. Stop this wildness or I'll break thy wing!' No sooner had he opened his mouth than the wing of the South Wind broke. See my fists? That's how he broke the wing with his great fists clenched.

"So, no more South Wind. As you know, it couldn't go on for long without someone noticing. The great god Anu called to his vizier, 'Why has the South Wind not blown over the land these seven days?' The vizier answered him, 'My lord, Adapa son of Ea has broken the wing of the South Wind.' Anu was very angry. He stood up and shouted for the gods to fetch Adapa. 'Let them fetch him hither!'" The king stopped as Naqia sat up, smiling. "You like this bit?" he asked.

"Oh, I like how you can do that. Be the god and give the orders."

"I see. Now Ea, having all wisdom, knew at once what would happen so he took hold of Adapa to mess up his hair. See like this. He made him put on mourning clothes, just like these fast-day tunics I'm wearing. Yes, a ragged linen tunic, ash-stained and dirty. He gave him instructions. So. What do you suppose he advised?"

"You tell me. I'll keep my mouth tight shut."

"Well, he told him, 'Adapa, my son, you'll be summoned before Anu the king of the gods. You'll take the road up to heaven and there you'll approach the gate of Anu. Tammuz and Gizzida, the gate-wardens, will be standing by to watch you approach and they'll challenge you. "Man", they'll say. "Who are you in mourning for?" Ea explained how the gatekeepers, hearing his reply, would glance at each other, they'd nod, they'd come before Anu to announce him, they'd put in a good word for him. Ea gave him more advice, warning him, "As thou standest before Anu, if they offer thee the bread of death, don't eat it. If they offer thee the water of death, don't drink it.' But he also said, 'When they offer thee a garment, put it on. When they offer thee oil, anoint thyself.' Ea insisted Adapa should do exactly as Ea told him." The king stopped telling the story when he saw Naqia shake her head and put up her hands. He couldn't tell whether she wanted more or wanted him to stop.

"Do you like this?"

"Can I ask a question?"

"Of course."

"The king my lord ... can he explain why Adapa can be dressed but cannot eat?"

"I can and will, but first hear the story."

The king went on to describe how things came about just as Ea had spoken. Then he stopped and looked at Naqia. She was sitting up and looking straight at him with a smile across her face. *I think she's flirting with me!* He smiled back with a wink and continued. He told how Anu judged Adapa, how Adapa acknowledged his wrong-doing and how the gate-wardens whispered in Anu's ear,

The Story of Adapa

commending Adapa. "Their words soothed Anu. Ea's trick worked, Anu's wrath was appeased."

The king patted Naqia's hand and continued. "Ea's wisdom, you see, is very great. Ah, but Anu's heart is very great. Let me tell you what happened next. Anu gave judgment. He said, 'Why did Ea choose this worthless man from all those in heaven and earth to disclose to him the whole plan of earth? Why so distinguish him, why give him such fame? No mere man should have such power. Tell you what, fetch for him some of the bread of life. Water of life too. He can be one of us.' And they did, they put bread and water before Adapa, but Ea had said not to take any food from them. He put on the garment they brought him. He anointed himself with the oil. But he didn't eat the bread or drink the water. So, Naqia, do you think Adapa did the right thing?"

She nodded and pushed out her bottom lip. The evening light streamed in through the doorway showing him the soft, moist pink flesh inside her mouth. If she opened her eyes wide a man could get lost in them. A twinge of envy of Arda-Mulissi struck him. He shook his shoulders and drew a breath.

"No, Anu looked at what Adapa had done and laughed in his face. Asked him why he'd refused. Told him he'd now missed his chance to be immortal like the gods. 'Ah, perverse mankind!' he said."

Naqia shook her head and started to speak. The king saw and invited her to do so but stopped smiling when he heard her. "No, wait, I've heard a different version. God was very angry at the wise serpent, the one you call Ea. So mankind has always to serve ..."

"You know the story then? Why didn't you say?"

"The king my lord is telling a different story. Not the one I know."

Sennacherib laughed and took another look at her expression. Lively she looked now, and, yes, intelligent. *Maybe she is older than she looks.* "Ha, you're a clever little one, aren't you? You'll run rings around my boy. But you're right. There are many versions of the story. I know one where Anu gets angry at Ea. Anu says, 'Of the gods of heaven and earth, as many as are, who would ever give such a command? Who would dare make his command exceed the command of Anu?' In another version Adapa looks all over the whole heaven, sees its awesome size, realizes what a little thing he is."

The king felt relaxed and looked at her closely. In the evening light he saw her enthusiasm. It reminded him of his own appearance, his hair messed up where he'd shown how Ea had messed up Adapa's hair.

She seemed eager to hear more and asked, "Will the king my lord tell me what happened to Adapa?"

He didn't reply. Seeing the cluster of men escorting the healer along the path to the door, he rose, brushing off his clothes and composing his face. He turned to Naqia in the doorway to answer her. "By refusing the bread of life and the water of life Adapa brought ill upon all mankind. We get sick and we suffer and we die. The healer has come to see that you will not, at least not right away, sicken and die."

"You said you'd explain why Adapa didn't take the bread!"

"Another time, daughter, another time."

Setting the goblet on the floor, the newly arrived herbalist knelt beside the pallet. He took the girl's hand gently to hold it between his own. "I know you have had fever. I know you are beginning to feel better. If they do not die, everyone feels better after a week. But everyone also has pain, pain in their belly and pain in their head." He looked to see whether she heard, whether she understood. "Yes. Now this wine has powerful spells on it, spells against pain. And I have put poppy in too. You know about poppy?" The healer saw her frown. "Not too much—no, I don't put in too much. Very bad."

She nodded but asked, "Spells? What have you said? Whom have you invoked?"

The herbalist rocked back on his haunches. "My lady! I only invoke the gods of the king my lord. I ..." He seemed unable to find words to defend himself against some horror of which he stood accused. Slowly, mumbling, he chanted in a foreign language:

> "Ereshkigal opened her mouth to speak,
> saying these words to Namtar her vizier:
> 'Up, Namtar, knock at the gate of the palace of justice,
> bring forth the Great Gods on their thrones of gold,
> sprinkle Ishtar with the water of life.' "

Hearing the man's chant, the king came back into the hut. The herbalist was struck dumb for a moment. Then he bowed his face to the ground to make obeisance. "My lord the king!"

The king reassured the healer, "The lady Naqia has just heard the story of Adapa. She has been dressed and anointed. She wonders whether she should drink. There's no need for your obeisance now. Just heal this girl. And Naqia, he offers you the water of life not the water of death. Drink! Look at me, that's right."

"I do not wish to bring ill upon the king my lord, so, gladly will I take this goblet. I must sit up though." She turned to the healer.

"My lady, I will help you up."

"Thank you. If you have judged the amount correctly I shall sleep now through the night."

Chapter 3: Lessons in Etiquette

So deeply did Naqia sleep that she heard no sounds. The king dozed beside her bed until men called him away. She hadn't heard the troop of men and wagons that had trundled into the village in the middle of the moonless night. But just before dawn, trumpets blowing outside startled her out of a deep and ghost-ridden sleep.

Abby stood in the doorway, calling. As Naqia opened her eyes she caught sight of two young girls waiting with large pots of water, one of them steaming in the fresh morning air. Such a sweet herbal smell rose from the hot water that she wished she could plunge straight in and wash all over. Itching scabs reminded her that such a plunge might hurt.

Abby grinned and showed what she carried. "Look here, the king has ordered new clothes for you. See, a cotton tunic, plain. Not really new. He had to go to a lot of trouble to get anything here. He wants you to attend him for the meal."

"What kind of meal? Is it like the New Moon feast we have?"

"No idea. I'm hungry enough to eat anything."

"Abby, but it might be bad stuff."

"Whatever it is we'll eat it. Now, sit up so I can get you undressed."

"Why are you so cheerful? What's happened?"

"You wonder? These two serving maids—they're called Annabel and Uribelit—belong to you."

"To me?"

"That's right. Because I'm your cousin, he'll give me a post in your household."

Surprised and a bit puzzled, Naqia asked, "Household?"

Abby was so smiling and optimistic, pointing to the doorway where the new maids were hanging a large swathe of linen to shield Naqia's bath from the passers-by. She turned back to Naqia and observed, "Maybe your mother was right, you know. So forget about your sickness, forget the smell, forget your worries, everything. It's going to be all right. You'll have quarters in Ninuwa Central until the king's son moves into the Succession Palace. Then you'll live with him."

"Quite a change then, from a stinking hut with mud floors and filthy walls to some sort of palace. What's Ninuwa Central?"

"I've no idea. I'll ask the girls. It's where they originally come from."

Abby got Naqia ready and went outside to ask the two girls about Ninuwa Central. She considered not telling Naqia right away but thought better of it.

"Well, Naqia I've found out. Not quite as good as I thought."

"So, tell me."

"Ninuwa Central is the central shrine, a temple of Ishtar. Not like our temple. It's very rich. Especially now. The king's mother has put all her wealth and property in the shrine to be managed there."

"Well, Qat does the same at home."

"But in Ninuwa the chatelaine, Nikkal-Amat, has got so much power that she could make the king marry Zaza, her own sister. That Zaza is the mother of the crown prince, the one you'll marry."

"Why is this bad?"

"Well, you see, Nikkal-Amat controls everything. All the wine sales, all the slave sales, all the women with dowries offered to the king—ones from Asshur as well as well as any captives taken in battle or paid as tribute, like me and the other temple dancers.

"Annabel and Uribelit are daughters of temple women. They were at Natsibina, sent from Ninuwa Central. They say that because Nikkal-Amat controls so much of the trade throughout the king's lands, she can do whatever she likes. All the women living and working in the temple complex do whatever she wants—or else ... punishments"

Naqia wondered, *What has all this got to do with me? I'm going to have a household and servants. But now we're headed for this place, where this woman rules. Punishments?* "Or else what?"

"I don't like to say ..."

"You must tell me."

"She tortures them, puts things, gourds like, inside them ... you know, between their legs."

Naqia shivered.

Abby sighed. "I shouldn't have told you. Would that have been better? But I thought, we can't pretend." Abby bit her lips. She sat down beside Naqia and took her hand.

Naqia looked her in the eye and shuddered. "She ... she violates them?"

"Yes, and other punishments. Like she'd keep the women waiting in difficult poses or she'd strip them in the midst of the courtyard with everyone looking on."

"Oh no. Abby, do we have to go there? Both of us?"

"Seems so."

"And you said I didn't have any worries! I mean to say."

"We'll stick together, look out for each other."

Naqia stroked Abby's hand. She knew her cousin hadn't wanted to tell her the news and she also sensed Abby's own dread. "Abby, you know you could get away. We could write to your father, to Zekar. He could pay, you know. Buy you back from the manager woman. You could go home."

"Me? Why?"

"Wouldn't you want to?"

"Want to? No, I wouldn't. But what you said ... about buying me back. That was another thing. Nikkal-Amat runs a trade in virgins. She buys and sells them. That's why she terrorises the palace maids and their daughters, like Annabel and Uribelit."

"So?" Naqia's puzzlement left her bereft of further words. Abby just shook her head, her eyes shut tight. Naqia knew that though her cousin feared for her own future, she also dreaded what would happen to Naqia.

"Don't cry Abby. But why wouldn't you leap at the chance to go home? We could manage."

"Thank you, Naqia, very brave and generous. I'd never be able to live with myself. Besides, look, how could I be a temple woman after this? Or one of the dancers? Imagine how furious Qat would be. She doesn't want me or any of Zekar's other daughters to stay in the West."

"I see your point. Nothing matters to her except securing power to Pele, making him Crown Prince. No one else counts."

"Yes, she chose which women would go to fill Sennacherib's quota. She sent away anybody that might get in the way of her schemes. Of course she doesn't want Pele to have a child by any of Zekar's daughters. Qat wouldn't think twice about me being tortured if it suited her purposes."

Naqia nodded and let out a deep sigh. "Her purposes? I guess she wanted to get rid of me too. I've been really naïve, idealistic. Dreaming instead of thinking. 'Be very careful,' that's all she said. No, she said, 'Use your wits.' Yes, I'm sure she knew all about Ninuwa Central. Shebna, her spymaster, makes sure she knows everything."

Bathed and about to dress in the clean cotton tunics laid out for them, they looked up to see Annabel bringing a gift from the king, an alabaster jar with rose-scented ointment, a rare fine oil, to anoint them. With their own antimony they darkened their eyes. After putting on the fine lapis lazuli necklace from her father, Naqia walked to the door of the hut and out into the space in front of the village gate. She stood briefly to look around.

Inside the gate, staring at the king and his companions, a group of people had gathered. They looked poor—poorer than anyone in Judah. No one made any sound at all, not that she could hear. Along the peeled logs that formed the wall of the village stood a few soldiers looking bored and tired. *Probably hungry after their fast.* She could smell the horses and mules but couldn't see them. *They must be around the corner of the village wall.* A rough table stood in the cleared space in front of the gate and at it sat the king, dressed in a bright clean tunic and draped in a stole richly embroidered with antelope and lions in a delicate green forest glade. She stared, startled by the beauty glowing there amid the squalor of the surroundings.

The king's entourage stood beside him on each side. Naqia, leaning on Abby, moved towards them slowly. Naqia tried not to look at her feet, yet at each step her legs scraped against each other; the sores began to ooze. She made Abby stop, letting the maids walk a few steps in front until they too stopped in the centre of the open space. A mist seemed to fill her head, and Naqia swayed on Abby's arm.

The king commanded, "Send someone for a stool you fools. Look, the princess may faint."

Naqia stood still as if frozen. Abby leaned towards her and whispered in her ear, "Naqia, you have to say something."

"Me? I can't think of anything."

"You must."

"My Lord the king, uh, your humble servant thanks you for your generous kindness to me and … to my cousin. I wish also to thank this village and those who tended me in my illness. Uh … Abby?"

"Thank you, my lady. The king my lord, and your servants, we are grateful to the gods of the king for their … for bringing us to you. May all the gods of the king bless the king and may Suen and Shamash bless the king our lord."

A sigh went through the crowd, relieved that the correct words had come forth. Naqia sat and looked around. Then trumpets blew again. Men came forward with trays of cooked food and beakers of wine. First they served the king and the governor. While other officials, even the chariot driver and the third man of the king waited, a man offered food and wine to the Judaean women.

Naqia felt embarrassed at such honour. When the yeast smell from the new loaves of bread came to her nose she smiled as she reached out to take the loaf and a handful of dates. She ate greedily at first but soon her chewing slowed. Her mouth was full when she felt the sores on her legs ooze more pus. She swallowed the whole mouthful in a gulp.

In Judaean slang, so the girls attending them wouldn't understand, Naqia told Abby what was happening. As soon as she got back on to her feet the white tunic would be stained. Embarrassed to the point of tears, she couldn't manage to eat any more. She felt the eyes of the villagers condemning her. Abby patted her and sent one of the maids to fetch Naqia's shawl to wrap around the girl's waist. They let it fall behind the stool so she wouldn't be sitting on it.

As Uribelit was standing behind Naqia, fastening the embroidered shawl about Naqia's waist, Sennacherib came over to the Judaean women to introduce them to his third man, the person who rode beside his chariot driver. Taller than the king, dressed in light armour, the eunuch wore a rather grim smile. The king told Naqia, "Aram-Suen speaks the best Aramaic in my company. My daughter, you want instruction. I will let him stay with you today and tomorrow, to instruct you. I must visit stations along the river to the south, but the day after tomorrow we will all proceed to Ninuwa. Now, daughter, you do not sit in my presence."

"My lord the king, I am so ashamed. I beg you on my knees for your forgiveness. I do need instruction. I don't know how to behave."

"You cannot make a proper obeisance and hold the shawl too, my daughter."

"But my lord. What have I done wrong?"

The king turned to Aram-Suen, "Make sure you tell the lady Naqia how and when to make obeisance."

Aram-Suen nodded to the king, but he still frowned as he regarded the two women. He did not seem happy to take charge of Naqia. She thought, *He thinks I'm just a child. He's asking himself whether he's been demoted to nursemaid.* She noticed his brow becoming smooth again as he turned to face the king.

"My lord the king, I will try. Now, my lady Naqia. What do you want to learn?"

"Oh, Aram-Suen, everything."

"And the first thing?"

"What was that verse the king recited when I was kneeling before him?"

"A refrain from the story of Ishtar. Let me think how to put it into Aramaic. 'When through the first gate he had made her go out, he returned to her the breech-cloth for her body.'"

"Is it a bawdy song?"

"No, not at all. It comes from a tale about Ishtar. She descends to Ereshkigal, goddess of the dead, but Ereshkigal forces her vizier to send Ishtar back into the world of life."

"The first gate? What was that?"

"The first of seven. But no more of Ishtar. The king says you need to know how to behave. Come over here to the pavilion, we have some woven mats for you to sit on or lie on. I'll sit on this stool where I can lean against the posts."

"You will need to know about Asshur. From the beginning in Asshur's city, 'the Inner City' the god who is every god, Asshur, has set his king to reign over the world. The king is Asshur's earthly agent. A king has to keep all the peoples of the world doing their proper work just as Asshur keeps all the gods in line."

Naqia nodded. "So, when the king took those gods, Bel and Nebo, from Babili, does that mean those statues weren't just plunder?"

"Plunder? I wouldn't use that word. Tribute, yes. And you may call the god Bel, but our name for him is Marduk. And you pronounce the other Nabu, not Nebo. Now the taking of those statues, I don't know what you heard, but we took the gods' statues to punish the men of Bit-Yakin.

"You see, if any men rebel against the king he has to punish them. It was to punish the rebels of Bit-Yakin. Often rebels challenge our rule over Babili. At the moment his wife, Tashmetu, keeps things quiet in Babili, but those people are still ... well, restive. They don't like being ruled from Ninuwa. That's why the king is in such a hurry. He has to rest the army up here and also keep a tight rein on the southern forces, his other army. I see Abby is taking all this in. And you, Naqia?"

"Please go on. I want to know everything."

"Everything is a lot. Has my lady something more to ask?"

"Yes, though it's hard to say. I'm interested in all that about the armies the cities and the gods, but I need to know simpler things. Where do you fit in? How, in a correct way, do I address you? Wait, let me continue. I don't understand where I am. I mean where I fit in. If I want something, how do I ask for it? If I don't want something, how do I say so? Wait, listen, I don't want to give offence, but I don't know how ... how to get what I want."

"My lady, you are ... well, you are beautiful. Perhaps, if you wanted, you could make a man do anything."

"What has that to do with it? And besides ..."

"Oh, I know you've been sick. It hasn't changed your appeal, your face, your hair, and you are exotic, too. You look straight at people. Women here, well, they look down more than you do. No one will think you show false modesty, but ..."

Make a man do anything? "Do you mean that I would give offence if ... well, if I have insufficient modesty?" *Abby says we're slaves. But she says all we are worth is what we can make a man think we're worth. What am I worth then?* "But what if I'm expected to say something?"

"My lady I will try to help you. You want to know how to address me?

To understand where I fit in? I am not one of the king's magnates, I do not govern a province or hold high office in his government. I have honour and great wealth because the king trusts me, but I rule only my personal household and the village the king gave me for myself. You see, a eunuch like me gets given grand estates because, without heirs, our lands revert to the king. I am not your lord but I am not your servant either. Since we both serve the king you may call me brother."

"Why do you call me 'lady' then?"

"Aha. You're to marry the king's son who'll be crown prince, then you will be my lady. I am being polite now because ... Yes, Abby?"

"Aram-Suen, if I may call you by name with propriety, are you then a brother to all the king's servants? To the slaves?"

"It's hard to know how to answer. Either of you could easily become very powerful, or you could drop into obscurity. In either case, I am the king's slave, as are both of you. Oh, I could buy my freedom, many times over. But why would I? To serve the king is my life."

"Could I buy my freedom? I am betrothed, but could I become free? Would I have enough money?"

"I look at you, my lady, and I see that necklace of lapis lazuli, I see wristlets of gold and the silver bells on your ankles. You could pay your price many times over. My lady Naqia, I have to say this. What would your life be afterwards? Who would offer you passage to a place beyond the king's lands? What would you do there? Abby my sister?"

"So, Aram-Suen, you are telling me and Naqia that we are not free, we are slaves. I get that. But we are frightened. We have no protector, we'll go into Ninuwa and be ... well be under the control of someone who ..."

"Yes, Abby, that's true. But neither of you is without protection as long as Naqia is destined for the Succession Palace."

"My brother? Is that right?"

"Yes, Naqia, you can address me as brother."

"No one has told me anything about the man I am supposed to marry."

"He's still a boy, really, but he's older than you. Good-looking, healthy. He needs ... well, maybe he will learn from you ... restraint and discretion. It often happens in marriage, the couple grow more alike."

"But will I have to do whatever he asks? Like a slave? I don't feel comfortable. I mean, suppose he is unstable? And he orders me to do something ... well, something that's not right. I'm just a slave."

"Not quite. In Ninuwa you can ask the chatelaine or the king or the husband, whoever, for anything you want. If you phrase the request properly."

"What do you mean?"

"It is courteous to ask so that the person you ask can readily refuse you."

"And?"

"We are civilised. The same courtesy should be shown to you, you should be allowed to refuse a demand made of you. If anyone refuses a reasonable request, of course, the aggrieved person could complain to whoever ruled them—headman, magistrate, governor, even the king. Anyone who asks something unreasonable, about them a complaint could be made too."

"What if—I am not sure I know how to phrase this correctly—what if the king is unreasonable? I mean, is it possible? What would happen then?"

"Yes, well. Although the whole world must submit to the king and no one on earth can interfere, the king is a servant too, servant of the gods. Anyone with a grievance against the king can pray to Shamash, the god of justice."

"Are the other gods then not just? Why only to Shamash?"

"My lady, those questions are too hard for me. Ask me something simple."

"Aram-Suen, the king told me a story. At first I said I didn't know it, but later I realised maybe I did. A different version. Are all the stories different here?"

"That's not a simple question! I don't know your versions so I can't say."

"Do you know any stories about husbands and wives?"

"Of course, and so do you, I'm sure. You know how Ut-Napishtum's wife encouraged him to aid Gilgamesh in the quest for the plant of immortality, and surely you know how Ninhursag first cursed her husband Enki for eating their progeny and then healed him, bringing the great gods into existence."

"Yes, I've heard those. But no stories of mortal men and women?"

"No, I don't know of any."

"Well, I had better hear more about the gods, the ones the king obeys. A person with a grievance prays to Shamash, then what?"

"It's not that simple. Don't you know the story of Etana and the eagle?"

"No, I don't think so. Maybe under another name? Can you tell it?"

"The first king of Kish went on a quest into the high mountains to make a shrine for Adad, far up high, and a fine poplar tree grew in the shade of the tower."

"Adad? He's the god of storms and battles?"

"In a way. Anyhow in Etana's poplar, in the top, an eagle settled.

Lessons in Etiquette

At the bottom of the tree lay a serpent. So high up both could see all the game in the woods, better hunting than my lord the king has had these past few days."

"Is this an old story? A poem?"

"Old, yes, a poem and partly about a husband and wife. I can recite it to you.

"One day the eagle spoke to the serpent, saying: 'Come, let us be friends. We'll be hunting partners, you and I!'

"The serpent opened his mouth and spoke unto the eagle saying: 'Evil is anyone who breaks friendship in the sight of Shamash. By such evil you would grieve his spirit, doing an abomination before the gods, a forbidden thing. We'd better be on our guard. Let us swear an oath by the nether world.'

"Then, before Shamash-of-the-fates, they swore saying, 'Whosoever transgresses the boundary kept by Shamash, let Shamash deliver him as evil into the hand of Nergal-the-slaughterer. Whosoever transgresses the boundary kept by Shamash, may the highlands deny him entrance, may the stray weapon go straight towards him, may the sun-rays of Shamash cross over to ensnare him.'

"Once they had sworn this oath they went up into the highlands. Day and day about each kept watch over the movements of the game. When the eagle caught bulls and asses, the serpent ate and withdrew, letting his young ones eat. When the serpent caught mountain goats and gazelles the eagle ate and withdrew, letting his young ones eat. When the eagle caught wild boar and bison, the serpents ate. When the serpent caught other kinds of wild game the eagles ate. The young of the serpent grew fat from the food, the young of the eagle became full-grown.

"But after the eagle's young became full-grown the eagle plotted evil in his heart. Indeed, in his heart he plotted evil: he determined to devour the young of his friend! The eagle opened his mouth to his young: 'The young of the serpent I shall eat, I myself. The serpent will harbour his wrath, so I will ascend and abide permanently in the heavens. Were I to come down even to the treetop, only the king himself could save me!'

"Yes, you have a question?"

"So that's why the eagle makes its home in the topmost crags of the mountain. I get it."

"Don't interrupt, please, my lady. It makes it hard for me to remember. The point of the story is what comes next. Do you want the rest?"

"Yes, please."

Aram-Suen went on to tell the outcome. The serpent appealed to Shamash, keeper of their oath, and received advice on how to trap the eagle. He had him hide inside a fresh kill where the eagle would join the other birds at the carcass. The eagle went for the best part, the fatty coating of the guts, where the serpent lurked. So the serpent seized him, took all the feathers off his wings and cast him into the pit, just as Shamash commanded, 'Pluck him and cast him into the pit that defeats life, that he may die there of hunger and thirst.' The eagle opened his mouth saying to the serpent, 'Have mercy upon me and I will give you a gift as it were the gift of a bridegroom!' Yes, my lady?"

"Gift of a bridegroom? What does that mean?"

"Don't you have that in your country? When a man marries?"

"Women bring their dowry, it remains theirs even if they're widowed or put aside. Men sometimes pay a bride-price, but not always. Is that the 'gift of a bridegroom'? Why is that special?"

"The bride-price isn't special, no, and it's paid to the family. But the gift of a bridegroom is different, a present for the bride. Like her dowry it's hers for always."

"Aram-Suen, if there is no dowry ... like for me ..."

"My lady, I cannot discuss such matters with you. It's not for me to say."

"My brother, I almost want to weep. I am not free, as you have told us, and I don't know anything about what I am bound to, and you won't tell me. I have to imagine it's because I won't like what I hear. And I don't want to cry ..."

"Do not weep, my lady, and do not be afraid. I think you are most threatened by what you don't know. That's always worse than being threatened by what you do know. All I can say is that you do not appear to me to be quite as helpless as you may think."

"Thank you, my brother." Naqia swallowed hard and clasped and unclasped her hands. She looked around and then turned to Aram-Suen. "Please go on telling us the story."

"In the pit the eagle stays; the serpent won't let him out because it would violate Shamash's ordinance. The wise serpent knows if he let the eagle go, Shamash would put him to die in the pit instead."

"So the eagle stays in the pit?"

"Yes, and then he prays to Shamash for rescue. Abby?"

"What a rogue!"

"Well, yes, he points out that if he dies in the pit no one will hear about the punishment Shamash has in store for oath-breakers. If Shamash lets him go he will proclaim that truth to all."

"Is Shamash taken in by that?"

"That's another story. I must stop story-telling, here's our evening meal."

For two days Naqia soaked up the eunuch's training. On the evening of the second day the trumpets sounded. The king returned in a good mood. Khanigalbat Province had proved peaceful and loyal, the road to Magrisu smooth and well-stocked, able to carry the army all the way to Asshur in autumn.

That last evening in Urakka, Naqia and the Judaean women lodged with the village headman's women in a small room opening off the central courtyard where the king's men ate. In Naqia's opinion the headman's home was hardly more luxurious than the hut they'd stuck her in when she'd been sick. The corner where the women washed themselves felt damp and smelled of mould. A few stone flags had been placed around the centre of the room where they could sit or kneel to reach the baskets of food. Naqia struggled to keep her face expressionless, not wanting to show her distaste.

Abby stayed with Naqia but the other two dancers had to entertain the men. Without music, and with only two performers, their dancing limped sadly. Naqia blushed for the crude quality of the show while Abby fumed at the coarse shouts of the men. After they retired for the night the little maids boasted to them of the entertainment offered at Ninuwa Central. Naqia fumed.

"So Annabel, first they have gourds shoved up them and then they dance with such delicate grace. Wonderful dancers indeed." Annabel muttered some foreign words under her breath, but Naqia got the message. You just wait and see what they'll do to you, you pert little miss. Naqia looked at the cumbersome wrappings around her legs, and huddled in a corner where she could whisper her misery to Abby before they slept.

Everyone woke early on the fourth day of the month, the king ready to set out for Natsibina. Fresh horses from Katmukhi snorted at the gate and ample provisions lay strewn about. Abby watched them unpack wine-skins, fruit and fine cakes. Six horses stood waiting but only one chariot. Standing close by, ordering everyone about, Aram-Suen paid no attention until she stepped behind him and tapped him lightly on the shoulder.

"My brother?"

"Yes, Abby, what can I do for you?"

"What arrangements have been made for us? Are we to ride with you? Will you leave us here?"

"Is that a joke? My lord is thoughtful and kind. He wouldn't leave a goat here if he could help it. You can ride, can't you?"

"Of course we can ride. But, if Naqia has to ride I must bandage her legs. The fat mules—she's so small—they ... Her legs are still ..."

Khanigalbat · Urakka · Natsibina · Kharranu · Guzana · Tille

"Abby, you should start saying 'my lady Naqia' if you don't want to give offence."

"Thank you, but can you get us some large swathes of linen? Now? I'll need a bit of time. But we'll be ready to ride with you, um, mid-morning?"

"Don't try to flirt with me, Abby. That's also a bit offensive. I'm third man to the king. I'm always on guard against any danger to the king. But I do sympathise with you and with the lady Naqia's situation. I will let the driver oversee the baggage loading so I can go look for some cloth for you."

Once he'd found cloth Abby set the maids to work. All four sewing as fast as they could produced two sets of bloomers to wrap Naqia's thighs. She could walk, with a sort of waddle. They made sure the felted fleece stayed tied around her thighs inside the trousers. The girls looked shocked as Abby rocked with laughter at how comical Naqia looked when she walked across the plaza, but Naqia laughed too. Their merriment attracted so much attention that Sennacherib himself came out to see. The soft woollen fleeces wrapped around Naqia's thighs made a strange-looking bulge under her tunic, but she still laughed as she waddled. When she saw the king coming she dropped a curtsy and bowed her head.

"Get up, my daughter, we will be travelling in the dark at this rate. Aram-Suen, are you ready yet? Let's get these women mounted and be off. Get the guards to lift Naqia on to the smaller horse; Abby can have the stallion. You'll ride next to me. The maids can go in the chariot with the baggage.

"Naqia, daughter, we normally ride swiftly and go on all day, exchanging horses at midday. Today, however, we are going only as far as the governor's fort at Natsibina. My own horses are there. Call out if we go too fast for you to manage."

"The king my lord is very kind. If you made me travel further on a mule, I'd cry. But I love horses. This mare and I will be friends I promise you. She already likes me, see, when I stroke her. She's a lovely mare."

It was midday when the king and Aram-Suen reined in their horses and signalled to the others to stop. Aram-Suen sent the chariot driver off to get water for them and their mounts. He himself circled the roadside nearby and looked about him without hurry. When he was satisfied, he returned to the king.

"My lord the king, we can stop here for water. The women can dismount if they need to. It is safe here. My lady Naqia?"

"My brother I am fine and don't need to dismount. Abby?"

"My lady Naqia. That's how I have to respond. What about your legs? How are they?"

"They itch, but it's not hurting. The scabs have stayed on. You're a genius. I look funny walking, and I'll need your help taking the things off or putting them back on."

"Do you need to ... now? There's that hillside and a stream trickling along beside the track."

"No, I'm fine. You?"

"I'm not hurting."

Aram-Suen approached them. "My ladies will you take refreshment?"

"No, thank you, my brother. But is Abby now also a lady?"

"She is here and now. After all, I do not know what she will become." He smiled at his own wit, before adding, "There is fruit as well as water and wine."

"The water or wine would bounce inside me, my brother, But fruit is good. Abby? Will you have some?"

"Yes, thank you." The eunuch sent the maids to bring fruit. After he had gone Abby whispered to Naqia, "I think I am beginning to get some idea about things. Do you notice how when the king rides in front Aram-Suen hurries after him, he rides close beside the king and registers every detail of the countryside we pass through?"

"Yes, I have seen that. But I am looking all the time too. Whenever we pass by a watercourse the land goes from pale green to brown. Where the early harvest has left the fields bare the wind lifts puffs of dust that drift past from the hooves of the horses in front. That's when I put my shawl over my mouth. So they're in front protecting us I suppose, but I'd rather be unprotected."

"Don't complain. This is the best time we've had all month. And think of the chariot driver and the maids who are coming behind us, four sets of hooves for them. All of us have our mouths closed. No one will be saying much."

The chariot clanked behind them and no one even tried to speak as they moved into the low hills that divided the streams feeding the Kharmish. In the middle of the afternoon they topped a ridge where breezes cooled the air. Sennacherib dismounted. He went off in one direction with Aram-Suen close beside him. The chariot driver lifted the women off their mounts and motioned them to go in the other direction, sending the maids scurrying after them. They found a patch of shade under a large shrub whose leaves scented the air with a sharp but pleasant smell. Abby lay on her back peering at the sky through half-closed lashes. She sighed, at ease and happy. "How nice. We're having an adventure, not a nightmare."

"I cannot be so optimistic. What comes at the end of this lovely journey?"

"Look here, I'm confused. What's wrong with you?"

"What's wrong with me? Physically? Look, I'll stand up. I'll put on these stupid sandals. Yes I can walk. Look I can go around the bush. I can even jump, see? The bandages stay on."

"So you can keep the bandages on. But your problem? Tell me. What's on your mind? You're obviously feeling much better. So what's wrong?"

"I am too young to marry—I haven't even started to bleed. Among all those women I'll have no protector. Everyone will make fun of me, pick on me, make sure I get punished. So, I can appeal to the king, can I? How? Once we're inside it'll be no use."

"The way he's treating you, you've already appealed to the king. I can tell even if you can't. Look here, tell him how you feel. Tell him the truth. The worst that can happen is he'll laugh at you." The king's party arrived earlier than planned at the governor's fort. As they passed the grand pavilion set out for their feast, Naqia and Abby were ushered into the women's quarters for a proper bath. Naqia clapped her hands with joy. Instead of a tub the women used a sunken pool lined with bricks. Once the maids had ladled cool well water into it, Abby and Naqia splashed and played in the water. As they moved out of that room the chatelaine handed each of them a new tunic.

"You are our king's daughter, my lady, so these are our gift. But now, what do you want us to do with those things you took off your legs? They are stained and smelly and you won't want to carry them with you, will you?"

"My sister, you are very kind. My maids will wash these. Abby?"

"I will take them and the maids will clean them up. My lady Naqia must have them for riding tomorrow. Otherwise we cannot ride with the king, I mean with my lord the king."

The chatelaine peered at Naqia, covered with the nearest cloth. "My lady Naqia? How...?"

Naqia replied by lowering the cloth. "My lady, I will show you. You see? I rode such a fat mule, her hide lumpy with sores and mange. Weeks of it."

"Very well, your maids can take these to the river.
But now, you two, the governor has asked you to sit with them at meat tonight. I'll show you the way."

Naqia followed her along the corridor to the centre of the atrium.

This place is more like a house although there is such a maze of storerooms. They keep the women's quarters at a pretty far remove it seems. The main courtyard here and a good sized hall off it. Well, here we are. I'll make the obeisance the way Aram-Suen wanted it. Oops. My stomach has cramped. I suppose I'm nervous. It's my first test.

Chapter 4: Naqia Confides in the King

Here I am, perched like a little mouse, next to the king himself. I'll show him I can behave properly. If I just watch the governor's wife I can imitate her every gesture. Oh no, that's not going to work. She keeps handing her husband little morsels and putting them into his mouth. She isn't really getting much to eat. I suppose she'll make up for it later. And the king doesn't need my help. He's quickly taking whatever he wants and stuffing it into his mouth. Maybe they aren't particular here about table manners.

"My lord the king, I have been listening carefully to what people say, trying to get better at understanding. I'm not that good at Aramaic. But, now everyone is so busy eating there's not much conversation. Is it permitted for me to speak to the governor directly?"

"Yes, my daughter, you can certainly speak as you choose here."

"My lord the governor, I have not heard any music for so long. Aren't there people to play for us, sing us your songs? I hope I have asked correctly, making it easy for you to refuse."

"My lady, that is a perfectly polite request. But may we not hear your songs first? Will you sing for us?"

"Me?" Naqia looked around the table. More than ten strangers, many of them important-looking, reclined or squatted around the low table. She turned to the end of the table where Abby sat eating happily and talking with Aram-Suen. In her Judaean dialect she asked, "Abby? What should I say?"

"My lady Naqia, I'll try to speak for you." She turned to the governor. "My lord the governor. We have brought no instruments, not even a drum."

"My ladies, all I have to do is clap my hands and my steward will oblige. Just wait a minute and you will have a zither and two timbrels. Now, will you ladies stand and play for us? Yes and sing too."

"My lord the governor, we will."

Abby came round to Naqia's side and they moved a little way off, still behind the king and the governor. She whispered, "Naqia, shall I play a lively tune?"

"No! No joke songs. No love songs either."

"What then will you sing of?"

"No quick timbrels. Sadness, death. Give me the zither and I'll start the chords. Now?"

"I see where you're headed. I'll strum and you chant."

"Emptiness, vain striving, despair." She segued into a sweet sad melody. She sang of the futility of all men's labour, of how the generations come to birth and then to death. The sun rises and it falls, the moon likewise. The wind moves first one way and then another. Streams run endlessly into the sea but never fill it. Every new sight turns out to be the repeat of an earlier one. There is nothing new under the sun and everything which seems important in the present moment will turn to dust.

As soon as Naqia's sweet high voice died away Abby stilled the slow beat. A different silence hung in the courtyard. Not for lack of thought but for awe. She who looked so young and sweet had brought to each of them a sense of their own smallness.

The king reached out for Naqia's hand to place her beside him. "You sing beautifully and your words are wise. You expressed how Adapa felt when Anu showed him the greatness of the heavens. Now, daughter, eat and drink. We start early tomorrow and may not arrive at Tille until late evening. Eat, drink and rest." Turning to the governor, he asked for music. "The lady Naqia has shown herself generous. You should give us some songs of your people."

At daybreak they mounted. Not until the middle of the day, when the heat became overpowering, did they dismount. Fresh horses were nowhere to be seen but their own mounts could go no further. As they saw no well nearby, Aram-Suen strode off in pursuit of some herd boys he had spotted. The maids lay in the shade of the chariot and slept. The others sat close around the chariot to wait for the third man's return. Naqia sat cross-legged, half-turned to the king who leaned against the chariot driver. Abby walked apart from them to get out of sight of the king, leaving the two of them.

The king turned to Naqia and asked, "Are you thirsty, my daughter?"

"No, my lord, thank you."

"But where are your smiles? Let me see your face. Is it only the futility of life that saddens you, then?"

"No, my lord. I cannot smile for you."

"Are you weary of riding?"

"No, the king my lord cannot know …" *Oh dear that doesn't sound right.* "I assure you, that I am just flustered. I don't know how to tell you. It would be lovely to go on like this … forever."

"I can see that you are hot and sunburned, but your words are earnest and yet you do not say what troubles you. You are troubled?"

"Yes, my lord."

"How can I reassure you if you say no more than that? Our journey will end in three days. You will be at home then."

"Oh my lord, I cannot …" *Some home, but I mustn't cry. I'll stop my mouth, I won't say it. I'll just take a few deep breaths. He is being kind.*

"My lord, I cannot imagine how I can find a home …" *Oh dear he will be offended.* "My lord, but …" *now, don't moan …* "the women's … it's no home for me." *I can't say it, even if he asks me.*

"Naqia, daughter, what better home for you? I see you full of dread but don't know why. Tell me."

I'll just keep my mouth shut until I can speak calmly. I must say something. "My Lord, it is not yet with me as is the way with women. I will be afraid and I will be alone and I won't ever be allowed …" *I must keep calm, I can't say I don't want to lose this closeness, being with him. What can I say?*

"Allowed what? I am sorry but you must say what you mean."

"My lord, please …" *I have to answer him, I'll have to change the subject.* "Uh, you never finished telling me about Adapa."

"You are stalling me. Adapa is the first priest, mortal like all priests, not allowed the gods' food."

"Who does eat it then?"

"The offerings? We do, unless we are priests."

"And the priests, what do they eat?"

"Rations donated to the temple for that purpose."

I haven't fooled him, I can see he doesn't want to do this. "What do the temples look like? Have they couches and tables?" *Ah, that's better, he's smiling. My naïveté charms him.*

"We deck our temples with as much finery as we can to honour the gods. And so, of course, each temple has much wealth. Ninuwa Central, for example, has a huge fortune in precious metal and jewels."

"Huge? Are there so many temples like that?"

"Many temples, yes. The gods live in their hallowed places, answer prayers and give wisdom."

"In Ninuwa, then, how many? I mean, I've heard about Ninuwa Central. So it's not the only place?"

"It's the biggest, the richest, the most powerful." The king stopped when he saw the distress on Naqia's face. He asked her, "Now what have I said?"

I'm about to give myself away. I must not look so dismayed. He can see how disgusted I am. "My lord ... I want to tell you the truth ..." *How can I tell him about gourds being stuffed into girls as punishment? If only ... he's getting more impatient and irritated, I have to go on.* "If only I knew ..."

"The truth? You want to be allowed to know the truth? Like Ea? You want to be a god then?"

"My lord, I am miserable because, well, because I don't know what's going to happen."

"You must look me in the face, my daughter. I will tell you. You are promised to my son. I do not go back on my word. I have some notion of your character, you are honest. You must understand that I am obliged to be honest too. Like the moon you seem to me a mixture of purity and prudence, so say plainly. What do you want me to do?"

I can't answer. I don't know ... "I don't know." *Now I've done it. He thinks I'm joking, I'm being funny, or he's mocking me. I can't tell. I must ask him ...* "Can you not find somewhere I can be safe until I am old enough to marry?"

"Well, my daughter, I see that you are serious. I'm thinking. Ninuwa Central is safe. Now please don't start crying. I think I understand. You want to be somewhere else though. Somewhere safe." The king closed his eyes while Naqia waited.

Well, I've said it. I wonder what he thinks of me now?

The king patted her hand. "And you want to know, yes, I saw you peering over at my dispatches this morning. Hmm. You could read them—you didn't wait to hear the scribe read them out to me."

"Yes, that's right."

"You were asking about the gods, too."

"Sorry to interrupt, but, yes. Aram-Suen told us about Shamash, how he enforces the oaths of friendship." *Is it proper to speak to him this way?*

"Friendship?"

"Yes, like between the serpent and the eagle, and I wondered why the eagle felt he could beg Shamash to release him. See, if Shamash did release him then his oath-breaking wouldn't have been punished. So what could the eagle then say to others about how Shamash enforces the oaths taken? Aram-Suen said he couldn't tell me those things, being a soldier, not a scholar. Can you not explain?"

"My dear, I too am a soldier rather than a scholar." Sennacherib thought for a moment. *Perhaps Arbail would be better?* He turned to Naqia and smiled. "I see what you're getting at. I see and maybe I understand. Now, I hear the horses coming. Stand up, lady."

Though she felt she might not be able to get up and walk, she stood up. Her stiffness showed in the grimace that twisted her mouth.

"You're stiff, are you? Well. I will consider your request. You are a strange picture just now."

Naqia tried to smile but her sores had started to hurt. She stood awkwardly before the king. Aram-Suen took in the scene as he rode towards them to report. He suspected she'd wangled some gift from the king. To make light of it he asked if she wanted a spread of gems to ornament her hips. Her smile faded, her shoulders drooped. As if sorry to have flustered her he added, "Just a joke. It's the third gate. When Ishtar returns to the world of the living she retrieves her girdle of gems at the third gate."

They ambled on foot over the top of the hill and down to climb another one until they reached a well with three or four rickety huts clustered about it. Boys drew water for them and for the horses, but the rest of the villagers hid from their sight.

"My brother Aram-Suen, why don't they come out?"

"My sister Abby, they are afraid. We might be robbers."

"What have they got we'd want to take?"

"I suppose they think we'll take their goats, their garments, their children. Anything we could find that we might be able to sell."

"How awful."

In Tille at evening the townspeople, expecting them, met them along the road, cheering and bearing torches to light their way into the town. No bath house here, but the mayor offered banter and wine to compensate for what he lacked in furnishings. The villagers spoke a dialect Naqia had never heard; Aram-Suen said they used the old style speech of Asshur.

The travellers, so weary they left the dinner tables before the others finished, tumbled into their sleeping quarters unwashed. They stumbled out at sunrise to break their fast and found a true feast.

Out of some hidden storehouse the people of Khanigalbat brought dried fruits and soured milk, ground millet cakes and a sweet honey-cake new to Naqia. The villagers laughed to see the girl in the odd bloomers stride forward to grab another cake before the platter passed her by. "Ishtar!" they called out.

Sennacherib exchanged a wry glance with Aram-Suen as he took Naqia by the shoulder. "My daughter, we are ready to set you back on your horse. The journey you want never to end goes on. Come."

Holding his hand in one of hers, skipping to match his long stride, she held in her other hand, clasped to her breast, the cake she'd just taken. Aram-Suen laughed at the sight of them. Laying a finger on the cake, he joked to the king that his little Ishtar had truly got an alluring breastplate.

From Tille the road bent south to Ninuwa, but the king's party continued east to the river. As they rode beside the small tributary stream from Tille, tears of self-pity formed in Naqia's eyes. Their journey would end. The king would drop her, somewhere, maybe under the rule of that vicious chatelaine Annabel so hated. To die alone and far from home seemed sad but sweet; they'd all be sorry they had sent her away.

Aram-Suen commented, "You are like Ishtar, then, my lady. I'll lift you off the horse now."

"I don't understand."

"Don't you recall? Didn't you hear the villagers calling out the name of the goddess when you walked to the table? You looked like the goddess, wearing those funny things. Ishtar leads the king in battle wearing leg armour, as you do."

"Aram-Suen, can you not tell me more of Ishtar? May I ask that?" *I don't know why they laugh at my questions. The king does too. And where is he? Oh, he's summoning Aram-Suen and motioning for us to go the other way.*

Abby and Naqia, walking stiffly now, made their way to a place over a small hill where they would be hidden from all eyes. Abby stopped, looked around, and then approached her cousin with a stern expression. "Naqia I have to undress you." As Naqia winced and shuddered Abby stripped the coverings off. She smiled up at Naqia, "Those scabs have almost healed. What's the matter?"

"I'm afraid I'll be sick again. Terrible pains in my belly."

"You don't seem to have a fever."

"It's just cramps in my belly. I'm not going to vomit."

"Fear and worry. Look here, I don't like the sound of Ninuwa Central either. Here's Annabel coming to take your riding garments to wash them, but she's bringing clean ones." The serving maid hastened towards Naqia, and Abby challenged her. "Annabel, what are you doing? We won't need those now. We're finished riding, may the gods be praised. But don't you sneer at me."

"Oh, my lady Abby, I was ordered to bring the clean things."

"Why? Who ordered?"

"We're not heading down-river. He, Aram-Suen over there, says we're crossing over and riding on towards Tamnuna. That other man is the king's real chariot driver."

"Annabel?"
"Yes, my lady Naqia?"
"Your arm, it's bruised."
"My lady, that other surly lout won't be coming with us now."
"You poor thing, that's why you hated that chariot."

Annabel looked away, but reached out to hand over the garments.

Naqia turned to Abby. "Dear Abby, come and help me with my bath. I'm feeling much better."

"I am glad. You girls go and get the rest ready."

As soon as they had gone Naqia smirked. "We aren't going to Ninuwa."

"No? Then where are we going?"
"That I don't know but I told the king, like you said."
"About the torture?"
"No. Not that. I couldn't."

Across the river they left the green irrigated valley and rode through scrub lands. To the northeast rose steep hills where, though the ground looked dry, wells dotted the trail. The party made slower progress as, being away from the main road, they found no fresh horses. Yet eight hours from Tamnuna they arrived at the huge fortress of Dur-Sharrukin.

"Now, my daughter, I will take you down off this horse for we have finally come to a place where I can entertain you, in my own palace. My father built this place so he would feel safe if the Mannaeans and the Urartians banded together to attack Asshur."

"It certainly looks safe with those high walls. But elegant too, all those gateways carved and, oh, the friezes. They are beautiful."

"You like those, do you?"

"Oh yes, my lord, yes, those carvings are beautiful.. But where are all the people?"

"Look upstream. At this time of year everyone tends their orchards and gardens near the river. This place, because it's not on a trade route … few people live here year round. It's a refuge, not really a home."

"Where's your home then? In Ninuwa?"

"Not a simple question my dear. Once Asshur's kings ruled from Asshur but that site, an isle in the river, it became too crowded. As the realm grew my ancestors founded new cities. Look south. The old kings ruled from Kalkhu, north of Asshur. We now call Asshur the Inner City because it is at the centre of our kingdom. My father wanted his capital even further north, nearer to the trade routes east and west."

"Did you learn to … I mean your father, he showed you how to …" *Oh dear, I must be polite …*

Naqia Confides in the King

"How to what?"

"How to be king. You see, I've been thinking about you ... you're not at all like ... like what I expected. Don't laugh."

"I'm not mocking you, daughter. Tell me what you expected."

Now I'm for it. But, so what, I'm going to tell the truth. "My father doesn't go about much. I ... I suppose I imagined you sitting high on a throne, with crowds of people shouting praises at you and ... well, you seem used to travelling such distances. From what you were saying to Aram-Suen it seems you spend days and days ... "

"My daughter, sitting on a high throne all day looking at throngs of worshippers, wouldn't you be bored? Of course you would. So would I."

I suppose he's right, and he's being kind. Letting me hold on to his arm. I wonder. Was my father bored like that? So bored that he let Qat run everything? Bored so much he didn't seem to care about his daughter, or even about his son Pele? "Was my father bored do you think? His kingdom was small and he didn't go about much. Is that why ..."

The king turned to Naqia and searched her face. Her questions had irritated him before, but now he seemed to be merely puzzled. "Why what? You seem to be very innocent of affairs. In your father's house, didn't you hear of what was happening?"

"My lord, I was hardly ever there."

"So where were you?"

"I ... well my mother wasn't ... she didn't like me I suppose. I learned medicine with another woman, a wise woman. She was learned and kind. And that's all I did until they sent for me to form part of your tribute. I was never important enough to be involved in their affairs. Oh, I heard. I went into exile with the others when you besieged the city. But my mother—and really all the temple women—they cared only about dowries and position for themselves."

"What did you care about?"

"Learning about the medicines and foods, learning the ways of the different nations and their gods. I love our music and poetry and the stories of our ancestors. And now, well ..."

"So you didn't want to come? I am asking because I want to know, don't be shy."

"My lord, that's like me asking you if you liked being king. You can't help it. No more can I."

The king put his hand over Naqia's to comfort and reassure her. After a few moments she looked up at him with soft eyes. The thought of love crossed his mind. "Kings love. I do and my father did too. My father loved battle—he never sat anywhere for long. He built this place but never used it."

"And you've brought me here so I can be safe?"

"No, we'll be here only for one night, but you will be comfortable."

"I'm perfectly comfortable if I have only you and Aram-Suen to behave for."

Naqia's smile faded and her whole body grew tense. The king touched her shoulder. "I see that you've thought of another worry." *I wonder if she's a bit mad. Every time she starts to be charming she stops herself. But she showed such aplomb at the governor's feast at Natsibina.* He turned to ask what was wrong.

"My lord the king, I would like to be shown, with my women, to our quarters."

"Of course, my daughter." Relief softened his countenance. *A young girl who feels a need to make her toilette is not mad, just a bit awkward socially.*

The party took their evening meal alone, only the steward—Shezibanni, a widower about the king's age—ate with them. Abby sat next to the king, making the story of their journey to Urakka into a comic tale.

"As far as Dimashqa Naqia had a pony and the rest of us rode on wagons—no pain, even fun. The road from there to Tadmur was no fun at all. We could have gone further and faster without the mules. They drank so much of what little water we had, and they were so slow we missed the relays."

"My soldiers, didn't they look after you properly?"

"Well, you know. They didn't look after themselves any better. So it's not their fault. The Arabs attacked. Didn't you hear? How we missed the relays? Got held up in Kharranu? No water? Everybody getting sick?"

"Some I heard. Yet you are cheerful, making jokes. I wonder you are not resentful."

"My lord the king, as I'm sure you and my lord Shezibanni know, misfortune looks funny, once it's over. Naqia?"

"My brother Shezibanni. This is such a lovely meal and such nice wine. Thank you so much. My brother, I am trying to learn about things here. Aram-Suen has told me I may ask questions if I am properly polite, but I don't know always what's polite. Am I right? I address you as brother?"

"Yes, lady. I see you wondering. I do not call you sister because you come here as daughter to the king."

"I hardly know what it means. No one ever tells me anything about the king's son, where he is or what he is doing and I hardly like to ask about such things. Can you tell me more?"

"Everyone's title derives from the king, every slave is known by the person he serves, or she serves."

"Yes?"

"If you called me 'my lord' it would say I governed here. The king himself governs here. So you used the correct form."

"Oh."

The Governor smiled at the girl. "Is it hard then, learning these things? Is it different in your country?"

"I have to think about that. Yes, different. It's hard to explain without seeming, well, superior. In my own country I belonged to myself, here I belong to the king. Because of him ..." *Oh dear now I'm blushing, I mustn't let myself go ...* "If I did a stupid thing in my own country no one but me, only I, would suffer. If I misbehave here it might reflect on him. I don't want to embarrass him."

The king stopped eating and turned to Naqia. "I hear what you whisper my daughter. Let me reassure you. I can easily endure what shame you are likely to bring upon me."

Oh dear, now I'm sweating as well as blushing. I'll have to laugh along with them. But what if the king thinks I don't want to belong to him. He might think I have been complaining. I'd better make sure I always have a joke handy whenever I'm put on the spot. And he's still watching me. I'll ask him. "Where are we going?" *That sounds too fond ...* "Tomorrow, I mean. In the long run only the gods know where we are headed."

"Tomorrow we'll ride to Shibaniba and on to the crossing of the River Zaba, a ten-hour ride, with fresh horses at Shibaniba. I heard your earlier question. You are anxious to meet your betrothed? I will bring you to Arda-Mulissi at the right time. Shezibanni? You've made the arrangements?"

The steward bowed to the king and reassured him. "I've also made sure you'll have new mounts across the Zaba. Even so it's a long day's ride for them, coming from Imgur-Illil."

"Good. The lady Naqia is a fine rider, she and her women have been good travellers, uncomplaining and sweet-tempered. We'll be tired when we arrive. And, Shezibanni, you've sent on ahead?"

"Yes, my lord. The messenger has not returned but you should be certain of a favourable reply."

The king winked at his steward and they both laughed.

Why is that funny? And Abby doesn't get it either. "My lord?"

The king laughed again and addressed the steward, "Quite so. The mistress of Arbail will see her advantage."

Naqia, mystified, touched the king's arm to get his attention. "My lord, who is this mistress?"

Chapter 5: Naqia is Given to Ishtar of Arbail

The next days passed like a dream. At Shibaniba the king had a haruspex kill a sheep. He surprised both Abby and Naqia by insisting they watch the whole thing. For Naqia it was another strange thing she didn't want to get used to. Back at home priests dealt with carcasses out of sight below the men's quarters; women never saw the offerings being slaughtered. Here the royal party looked on and it appeared to be required. Naqia shivered at the blood spurting out the ram's neck. *That's just it, what I saw that day.* The horror of the blood spurting from the neck of the raider rose up in her and made her dizzy. *Oh dear, I will pass out. I can't watch.* She closed her eyes and held on to Abby for support.

But even with her eyes shut tight her mind still showed her the raider's neck gushing blood. She shook her head to rid herself of the sight, but the smell of the ram's blood turned her stomach. As the priest's knife slashed the abdomen, and the guts and stomachs burst forth, she tried to turn away but felt the king's hand on her chin, turning her head to the altar. She saw the diviner take the liver and place it on a hollowed out stone, chanting in a strange tongue. Aram-Suen whispered that they always used the ancient tongue of Babili for omens, and the diviner would ask the god's forgiveness in advance for anything he might have done wrong. Only then would he beg the god to come and stand inside the carcass.

Naqia steeled herself to peer forward at the liver, staring as the diviner explained to the king what each groove meant, how they read the channel, even how healthy the sheep had been. Though she raised her eyebrows at the thought of Shamash, the god of justice, the very Sun himself 'coming down' or 'standing' in the sheep, she found herself drawn in. The king grunted and said, "You will like that," but added nothing more. Still, he seemed pleased.

The route they took left the hills, skirting irrigated farmlands until they reached the ford over the Zaba. Even with the summer drought the water flowed swiftly, deep enough to wet the bellies of their horses and the men's cloaks. Naqia's breeches were soaked through. On the other side of the river the king's servants brought them fresh horses. With no delay they mounted and their wet clothes dripped over the new mares. Abby came over to attend her, to help her off with her clothes, expecting that water would have soaked her menstrual rags.

"No, Abby, no need. The bleeding has stopped. And I really don't need these riding things any more, but I've come to like them. It makes me look obvious, an outsider. I find that comforting somehow."

"We'll just go on now to the next resting-place. I'm glad you're better."

"This trip is one I am really enjoying. But, at the next resting-place. Well …"

When the party stopped for some food Naqia whispered to Abby, "I need to talk to the king."

"Naqia, be careful."

"Oh, I'll be careful." *I'll just tiptoe over to where he is lying down to rest. I can whisper in his ear. He says I can't shame him.* "My lord?"

"What? What now?"

"You said before that you saw how honest I was and …"

The king nodded.

"I didn't lie to you, not then, saying I wasn't a woman yet. Since then, though, I am a woman. Does it make a difference? In Arbail, I mean?"

"No, don't worry. Shamash has given the oracle; to Ahat-Abisha you will go, and there you will stay until you marry."

The king's reverence when he spoke of Arbail and the Lady Ahat-Abisha, High Priestess of Ishtar, seemed at odds with the appearance of the temple itself. The king had earlier described to her huge temples with great riches. In cities, main centres like Ninuwa, Asshur, Babili, the king and his magnates worshipped Ishtar in public ceremonies. Her magnificent sanctuaries there reflected her importance. Ishtar held the "_me_", all the aspects of the great gods belonged to her, the rituals for the major feasts and fasts celebrated her exploits.

Though Ishtar's sanctuary in Arbail was older than any of the city temples, it sat in a small compound, housing few people. Its walls stood high, but were formed of plain wooden stakes rather than stone. Gardens, orchards and vineyards surrounded the temple enclosure but no people could be seen at work in them. The countryside felt hushed in silence as though the sheep themselves were too awed to bleat.

The king's party stopped outside the gates, they dismounted and waited in silence until the gates opened. Out came a heavyset woman dressed in an un-dyed woollen robe, long-sleeved, her single ornament a moonstone worn upon her brow. Naqia started as Sennacherib's hand pressed her shoulder down hard until she joined the whole party in an obeisance. As she looked over at him, wondering at the king himself kneeling on the ground, she saw the woman Ahat-Abisha dwarfed by a halo of light. As she stared the light became a shape, a huge goddess shape she could recognise, a ferocious spirit, wise beyond reckoning. Beside her she heard the king whisper, "Agushea."

Aram-Suen took Naqia's hand and placed it in the lap of the priestess, he herded Abby and the two girls in behind Naqia. Only then did the king break the silence. He spoke about a minute in a strange language.

"My lady Naqia."

"Yes, my brother Aram-Suen."

"He has given you now. You call her 'Mother.'"

"Given me?"

"You have been sacrificed to the goddess, to Ishtar. You are hers now."

"Forever?"

"That's up to the goddess."

Without a word, the king and Aram-Suen, leading the spare horses, turned to ride away. Tears welled up in Naqia's eyes. Not even a goodbye, dumped outside the gate like a piece of useless baggage. Eyes half-shut she stumbled along behind the Mother into the temple enclosure.

Polished stones underfoot, shining whitewashed brick walls of the small houses, and a true fountain bubbling in the midst surprised her. Everything looked bright in the glow of the evening sun. Nothing but the sound of water splashing broke the silence. A young man led Abby and the two maids into one of the houses but the Mother took Naqia's hand to make her sit beside her on a smooth white bench just outside the entrance to Ishtar's sanctuary.

Silent, her palm held in the Mother's, Naqia gazed about the courtyard. Benches like the one they sat on flanked each doorway, smooth on top but carved with fantastic shapes on the upright panels. *It's as if they showed stories*, she thought. Gazing from one to the next, she tried to read them, hardly breathing as she concentrated.

"Daughter, you belong to Ishtar now. You will learn to worship the Goddess, you will learn our secrets, our mysteries. We keep much silence here but absolute silence outside these walls. We do not speak of the mysteries, ever. You will come with me into Ishtar's presence, you will bind yourself to her."

What is all this now? I didn't expect this. He didn't even ask me if ... "But I don't know what it means." *I'm not in Ninuwa Central but maybe this is worse. It's a hidden, secret and maybe dangerous place. And why not talk about it?*

"Naqia, my daughter, you need not worry. You will learn what it means."

"I? I ..."

"Lift your head, Naqia. Look at me. Take some deep breaths, I don't want you to faint."

I've been offered to the goddess, as a sacrifice? All of me? I'm to be bound to a goddess I don't even know? What if I refuse?

"Naqia?"

"What if ... what happens? I mean what happens to me? Is it my body? Or my mind. What if I refuse?"

"Well, daughter, I don't think you can. You were the king's, and will marry his son, but he has given you to the goddess. And not only your body, your mind is also hers now. So is your will. Don't be so frightened. You can stop shivering. Do look at me please."

"I see you are smiling, I can see you mean to be kind. Please don't take offence. But ..."

"Speak up. This is not an ordeal."

"May I ask questions? Will you tell me how to ask properly?"

"Of course. I'm laughing because the king has told me you like asking questions. That's why he decided to bring you here."

"You'll teach me how to ask properly?"

"There is discipline here. I decide. You'll get one answer each day, so you should think carefully before speaking. But first you must devote yourself, make your own vow. The king says you read Aramaic. Here is a writing tablet for you."

In Jerusalem the Goddess inhabited no separate temple; her women lived in Yahweh's temple and she stood—well, the sacred tree did—in the courtyard. Moreover, there only the Queen Mother was dedicated. Here in Arbail both men and women served the Goddess. *And now me,* Naqia thought. *I suppose ...* here her thoughts halted. Feelings welled up from her stomach, tightness in her chest stopped her breathing. *Alone! Abandoned!* She bit her lip so hard it started to bleed. As the priestess led her inside the warm salty taste on her tongue brought her back to herself. *Abby says we have to make our own way.*

In contrast with the brightness outside, darkness shrouded the inside of the temple. The door faced east so little light shone through at evening. A small lamp burned in front of a massive statue, carved stone overlaid in gold leaf. Naqia could make out the gigantic eight-pointed star pricked out in relief overlaid with silver behind the cylindrical turban crowning the head of the goddess. Even in the dimness the jewels around the circumference gave off sparks of reflected light. The eyes of the goddess, source of all spiritual knowledge, deeply graven, loomed as dark holes. What little light glimmered in through the door disappeared into those depths, reminding the worshipper how Ishtar embodies Ereshkigal, the Dark Mother, as well as Mulissu, the source of life and nourishment. The ears and nose of the goddess appeared enlarged, that she might hear and know all. Huge forearms, held uplifted from her sides, supported hands with elongated fingers.

Naqia gave a start and drew breath sharply as her eyes travelled along the body of the statue. Ishtar wore bloomers! At a closer look she could make out greaves, maybe of leather. Teeth still gripped on her lower lip she felt the bloomers still cloaking her legs because—being vain—she thought of Tille, of the people calling out 'Ishtar'. Shamed, she wiggled bare toes on the stone floor. *I brought this on myself.* As her eyes travelled up from the lion that formed the pedestal of the statue she sighed. *Oh, Goddess.*

The priestess put a parchment into Naqia's right hand. She stood a little behind her and spoke. "Naqia, here's a lamp so you can read the vow."

> I belong to Ishtar of Arbail. Oh Lady, let your father Suen be before me. With Shamash the great sun at my right side let the sixty great gods surround me. From your golden chamber in the midst of the heavens watch me that I do not slip. Keep me from shame. Give me faith. I will praise you; when daylight declines I will hold torches. Place me between your arm and your forearm.

"Mother? What now? Where are you?"

She felt rather than heard the stillness that followed her question. Heaviness filled her and her head stayed bowed, her eyes on the floor. From somewhere behind the statue the Mother brought out a dry wafer made of some sort of meal and a golden beaker with water in it. Naqia pointed to her dusty feet and soiled bloomers but the Mother thrust the wafer towards her mouth. As she opened her mouth to protest she felt the wafer thrust in and tasted its powerful sweetness. Blinded by tears she took the cup the Mother placed in her hand. Obedient, she drank the cool water. When the beaker was empty the Mother took it and left it on the floor in front of Ishtar's statue. She pushed Naqia in front of her towards the door.

The sun had nearly set. The moon, nearly full, rose above the hillside, large and yellow. "A very good omen, child," the Mother reassured her.

Now her fate was sealed. Naqia would stay in Arbail. Like the other temple women from Judah, however, Abby remained the king's property. Only a week passed before the Mother summoned both of them to let them know that Abby had been given to Shezibanni, the steward of Dur-Sharrukin, as a wife. Naqia's mouth dropped. Ignoring the High Priestess, she grabbed Abby's hand as if to protest. Abby showed more presence of mind. She made an obeisance to the Mother and gave thanks.

"Abby. It's terrible. What if you don't like him?"

"I did, in fact, but so what?"

"I don't suppose I can argue. But the maids and I must get together a dowry of some sort."

"Thanks, Naqia."

With her maids' help and stores from the temple Naqia got together a small collection of clothing and a few ornaments to supplement Abby's own possessions. The Steward had sent a small wagon to collect his bride.

"Naqia, I must leave today, but I will write to you whenever I can."

"I do hope you can. Now, my dear cousin, I want you to have my necklace. Aram-Suen said it would buy your freedom. If you need it."

"No, Naqia. It's yours and you must keep it. Like Ishtar."

"You've been listening to my lessons!"

"A little. I have to learn things too. You keep it."

"Yes, when through the fifth gate he made her go out, he returned the chains for her neck."

Naqia raised her head and moved to embrace Abby. Abby patted her back and smoothed her hair. As she met her cousin's eyes Naqia realised that Abby was glad. She wanted to go away for that new life. A wave of envy passed over her. Abby always knew how to do things and get things and, she thought, *I am so helpless. And now I will be all alone.* "Abby, I don't know how I am going to manage. And you, you are sure you'll know what to do?"

"Of course. I am looking forward to it."

"Yes, you are sure and confident. But then you always were. Me ... well, here I am, hesitant, weak in every way, and this discipline. It is really hard for me."

"But ..."

"Yes, I get to ask one question a day."

Naqia watched as the small wagon rode out of the gate and into the distance. *Left out, left behind. I am baggage too, but no wagon comes to collect me.* When Abby was no longer in sight Naqia turned and went back inside. All she wanted was to hide herself in a dark place and grieve. No shred of her old life remained.

As the days passed Naqia began to learn the ways of the temple and the lore of the Goddess. The Mother called her in to report on her progress from time to time.

"Naqia, if you prove worthy you can become an initiate. You have begun well, serving the goddess."

"The mysteries, may I ask now? Senn ... uh, the king my lord, he wouldn't tell me anything about you or about Ishtar. Is that why? Because they are mysteries? I mean, when I asked Aram-Suen about Shamash he would talk about it. He told me and Abby a story—well, part of a story about the serpent and the eagle. But he never finished it. Did he stop because it comes to be about Ishtar? Would the king my lord have let him finish the story if it did?"

"Everyone knows about Etana and the eagle. And yes, the story tells of Ishtar, in the seventh heaven where the eagle comes bearing Etana. But that is not part of the mysteries. The king our lord respects the mysteries, certainly. But also, it seems, he doesn't know much of them. And knows he does not know. A wise man."

"Mother?"

"No more, you've had the one question."

To remind herself she took out the writing tablet she now kept to hand. On it she wrote 'Agushea', the name the king uttered at Ahat-Abisha's appearance. Nothing escaped Ahat-Abisha. She stood beside Naqia to read the tablet.

"You want to know about the name? She is Ishtar as a daughter of Suen, the moon, the god of purity and prudence; the basic arts of civilisation form Ishtar's breech-cloth as well as her other adornments. Where did you hear that name?"

"The king said it when he ... when you came out to us. You wore a sort of nimbus, a light following you. We bowed when we saw you, and that's when he said the name."

"Ah, that means either you or the king, or perhaps both of you, have been granted Ishtar's favour. I will warn you though. If you have been chosen by the goddess for favour it may not be a cause for rejoicing— the goddess can be terrible, to you or to the king or to both of you."

I can't ask anything more today. "I mean to work hard, really hard,

Naqia is Given to Ishtar of Arbail

so I can measure up ..." *I wonder if I've showed her ...* Naqia stared at the Mother but knew not to ask anything. *Have I let her know how deeply I love the king?*

Every time she remembered the Mother's words a warm glow filled her belly; she and the king had been blessed by the Goddess. Both of them had seen that vision. Still, she set herself the task of repeating 'the king my lord' twenty times each hour so she wouldn't forget her manners and refer to him by name.

She needed little from the two maids so she sent them to work for Ahat-Abisha. They returned each evening to comb her hair and set out a bath, chattering merrily about their adventures.

"So, Annabel, you are happy here,"

"Oh, my lady, happy is too little a word.

Everyone here is ... is kind to each other."

"Not like Ninuwa Central?"

"My lady, look at you now, your hips, your breasts, your face.

My lady, in there they might be kind to you."

"Why me?"

"Oh well, you are beautiful."

"And you, Uribelit? Are you also happy here? Like Annabel?"

"My lady, just like Annabel. But it's not just your beauty. You are clever. And the king likes you, favours you ..."

"Yes, I see, And here everyone acts kindly. Favoured by the Goddess, everyone seems beautiful and clever in her eyes. Is that it, do you think?"

"My lady, we don't know such things. If you think it's the Goddess it probably is."

Never before had Naqia lived so much alone. She missed Abby's advice and desperately wanted someone to confide in. The long hours she spent on watch at Ishtar's feet left her mind open to fantasies of glory but also prey to agonies of loneliness. By need or instinct she began to talk to the Goddess. *There's no one here who really cares for me. I've never had anyone really, who cared for me.* As if she heard those words she stopped herself. *Well, at home—choking on a lump in her throat—I had Yoldah, uh, and Pappy, my foster-parents sort of. But they were teachers, not friends. And Abby, she's left me too. But I'm no more than a piece of baggage abandoned on the way.* The Goddess loomed over all, unmoving and unmoved.

Bitterness would grow and fester inside her. At first she resented Abby abandoning her. Soon her focus shifted to Qat, a sense of her mother's betrayal forming a hard black stone inside her. It softened only when she looked up to the Goddess's breastplate and felt love streaming forth. Of course, she thought, *as Mulissu she is mother of*

Asshur, and his consort as well. All love flows out from her midst.

Naqia's loneliness began to subside as she became immersed in her training. Each disciple of the mysteries memorised tablets: every poem, every prayer, every rule. So long had Ishtar been worshipped at Arbail that stacks of tablets accumulated everywhere. In Naqia's first weeks seven disciples studied alongside her, two men and five women. They'd been there from childhood, but only now were some leaving to assist at public rites all over the kingdom, as far as Karkhemish and Tsurru. The man going to Tsurru—well, the eunuch going—had been twenty years initiated. He would found a temple to introduce the new rites in the latest city Sennacherib had taken over and put under the rule of Asshur. The Mother spent most of her time with that eunuch; the other disciples kept out of their way.

At the next new moon the older disciples left. Only one man, Ataril—a boy really—remained for further study alongside Naqia. He knew the Akkadian signs of Babili but could hardly speak Aramaic, much less read or write its letters. He helped her learn the signs, and in return she taught him letters and how to read Aramaic.

He told her about Etana and the eagle. Twice the eagle tried to get Etana up to the highest heaven, but the grafted-on wings didn't work. Then, the third time, Etana came before Ishtar and she gave him the medicine that would enable his wife to bear a son. In that story Ishtar was remote, but in the temple enclosure Naqia felt the goddess close as well as powerful.

Though Naqia felt she needed to swallow the new knowledge in great gulps, she sometimes choked on the paradox and complexity. The great gods acted as one in the council, Anu presiding. That she understood, but also his being the single emanation including the whole. She found the concept difficult to swallow.

"Ataril, it's awful. I don't see how it works."

"If you look here, look at the sacred tree in that fresco on the wall. Here in the topmost branches, Anu. In the trunk Ishtar; Nergal and Ereshkigal in the roots. You see how each branch represents a divine emanation from Ishtar."

"But the crown of the tree, Anu, is he an emanation too?"

"Yes."

"What about Asshur then, which branch is he?"

"Naqia you are so simplistic, mundane. Asshur and Ishtar are one."

"But he's a he and she's a she!"

"They are one. Haven't you seen the Mother's seal? Look here's a letter ready for the post rider. See the star? It has sixteen points, that's Asshur and Ishtar as one being. Sometimes the engraver shows a bit of one out of line with the other and then you know for sure."

Naqia is Given to Ishtar of Arbail

"Yes, now I'm looking at the tree, and I will try to digest all those contradictory elements. That's the picture, and you keep talking about the tree. And its mystery. But, Ataril, show me the tablets. Show me where it's written."

"Haven't got any tablets about the tree."

"So there's none here? Or none anywhere?"

"No one tells it. Gilgamesh cuts down that date palm for Ishtar, but then, is that the one? Ishtar sacrifices her children, but, well ..."

"Ataril, don't you think that's horrible? You know, the king made me watch ... it was for the decision to send me here I realise. But I saw ... it sickened me, even that sheep. Its guts spilling out. I saw it like the blood flowing from the Arab's throat."

"What Arab?"

"When we were on the road. I'd been left behind the caravan on an old mule and I saw the raid. And one of the bandits started to rape a woman and the soldier pulled back his head ... cut his throat ... the blood flowed all over the woman and ... I was so sick."

"And that's why it bothers you to see Ishtar towering like a giant over the children, knife raised?"

"Yes, that's horrible too. She's been rescued but in a fury she sacrifices the children anyway."

"Some people say Tammuz is the same as the children. Ishtar and her sisters ..."

"Sisters? What sisters?"

"You've seen the friezes Naqia, Don't you really look? A eunuch serves Ishtar. The sisters are her other aspects. All of them attend to Tammuz at his departure, following him into the wild."

"She and those sisters, then, so they are all one. Is that the one? I mean is it Ishtar as all of them who mates with Tammuz and then gives birth to him? As a story it doesn't make sense."

"Sense? What Ereshkigal does in the underworld? She gives birth to all the gods—you've learned the chant."

Naqia's distaste for the story made her screw up her lips but, looking across at Ataril, she relaxed into a smile. In him she'd found what she wanted. He enjoyed being the knowledgeable one, the one to tell her things. With him she could ask more than one question a day. As that month drew to its end she found she now had a friend too, someone who cared for her, someone for whom she wasn't a mere 'daughter to the king'. He smiled when she squealed with joy at receiving a letter from Abby. She grinned back at him as she broke the seal, promising to read it to him.

"May I read it after you? Then we'll see if you've taught me anything."

"Yes, but I'll read it first. Ooh! Ah! Oh dear!"

To my cousin Naqia, your servant Abiramu, wife of the Cup-bearer of Dur-Sharrukin. Greetings from both of us. May all the gods bless your sleep and your waking, keep your steps safe and bring you joy and honour.

How do you like my new style? And this lovely fresh new parchment? I can requisition a whole goat if I need to! I haven't bled and so I expect to give my husband the son he has been so anxious to produce. His former wife gave him three daughters and, in my view, not very lovely ones. He's not so young and not particularly handsome, as you know, but I love him. He is good to me and lets me have my head. I must tell you of Ninuwa. We have just returned from a week there and I took one of our eunuchs and explored the whole place.

Well, you'll be lucky. The Succession Palace is new, in the latest fashion—that's like in Babili—and has two baths, one of them large and set within a little garden. No one occupies it at the moment so I walked through all the rooms. The prince's quarters open off the inner courtyard but they're quite plain—no carving, no decorated plaster. I imagine they must have had some tapestries.

The king's palace is a gloomy place. He's not in Ninuwa, off somewhere in the field. I looked around but the furniture is all shrouded in linen and it feels like a tomb. They say the king's mother is so pious she just about lives at the Ishtar shrine and neglects her own household. Zaza, the queen, wasn't there either. She has lands upriver in Ukku where she and Arda-Mulissi go in summer.

The Ishtar shrine now. I didn't go there, since married women are kept out unless they have been devoted to Ishtar of Ninuwa as maidens.

Some bad news. I tried to locate some of the other women from Jerusalem. There are no women of Judah in Ninuwa, none. My eunuch says they all died or were sold off. I wonder what really happened.

I'm looking for news of you and the others at Arbail.
Write soon.

"There you go Ataril. See how well you can read it. But try not to move your lips."

"It's awfully colloquial Aramaic."

As Ataril slowly read Abby's letter Naqia felt proud. She had accomplished something. Ataril could read all the dispatches now. He finished and she said, "You are doing well, not as slow as you were before."

"Thanks, Naqia. Here's the parchment. And it's a new one. Is this the first letter you've received?"

"Sadly, yes."

"No letters from your old home? You boast about how everyone in Judah can write."

"Yes, well, I suppose nobody cares much about me." *I will not cry.*

"Your parents?"

The tears can stay in my eyes. I'm not going to cry. "Ataril, your father sends you clay tablets in every other pouch. You still belong to your own people even though you serve Ishtar the same way I do. It's different for me." *How can he understand?* "My father is unwell, so my mother runs things, does all his work. She corresponds with many merchants and governors. Shebna ben Shaqed, you'd call him the vizier, probably lets her know how I am—if it matters. Maybe not, but he keeps spies, paid informants, everywhere."

"But not in Arbail!"

"So maybe they don't know where I am. Let's get on with memorising the tablets."

Chapter 6: Naqia is Initiated

At summer's end, the last days of Elul, they undertook a three-day fast. In the second day of the fast they heard hoof beats and went to look. Naqia jumped up and down with pleasure as she sighted the king's insignia on the chariot. In defiance of protocol she ran out the gate toward the chariot. "The king my lord!" she shouted again and again.

The chariot driver pulled up. Aram-Suen jumped down to help the king step to the ground. Naqia rushed forward, arms open, putting them around his neck as he lifted her up to kiss her. "Well, my lady. I can see at once you are very well indeed, the Mistress of Arbail has given you health. But not yet much discipline." He set her down. "I must be greeted and invited by my sister, not by you."

Chastened she returned to the archives where Ataril smirked. "I can almost hear our Mother telling you off. She'll be hard on you this time, you wait and see."

"I couldn't help it, seeing him excited me so."

"Naqia, how can you be so foolish? You are betrothed, taken."

"So? Why does that make you blush? Are you ashamed for me?"

"The king won't love you, you'll be his son's wife. I wonder at the way you throw yourself at him, out in the open."

"Throw myself at him? Don't be such a prude. I love him, you complain. But that's proper, isn't it? Surely everybody's supposed to love him? Me, you, Ahat-Abisha?"

"Naqia you never understand anything complex or ambiguous."
He turned to the lectern and began reciting the next tablet.

> O Father Ea, let not thy daughter be put to death
> in the netherworld,
> Let not thy good metal be covered with dust
> in the netherworld,
> Let not thy good lapis lazuli be broken up for stone
> by the stonemason,
> Let not thy boxwood be cut up into the wood
> of the woodworker,
> Let not the maid Ishtar be put to death in the netherworld.

Naqia turned to him and joined in.

> Father Ea answers the Vizier of Ishtar:
> 'What has happened to my daughter! I am troubled,
> What has happened to Ishtar! I am troubled,
> What has happened to the queen of all the lands!
> I am troubled,
> What has happened to the High Priestess of heaven!
> I am troubled.

Annabel knocked on the door post to get their attention. "The lady Ahat-Abisha wishes you both to attend her and the king. They're in her quarters."

They put the tablets aside and followed the maid. Naqia looked at Ataril's solemn face, feeling her heart sink as they waited at the entrance of the Mother's courtyard where she and the king faced each other, voices raised. Naqia and Ataril couldn't help hearing the king's impatient voice..

"No, I've not been fasting. Last year at the fast the seer reproved me saying, 'Is one day not enough for the king to mope and eat nothing? For how long still?'"

"Yet you name today an evil day. One should not even think on an evil day. Wait, at the new moon it will be auspicious."

"Sister, I cannot wait for the new moon."

"Brother, you make far too much of your urgent needs. Your treaty obliges you, you say. Yet you won a great victory, triumphed over all the little kingdoms in the west. Why be afraid? For one maiden? You can't wait? Unbelievable."

Both the scorn she showed and the king's mildness shocked Naqia. One look at Ataril's face told her that he also was spellbound.

To their surprise the Mother wouldn't give in.

"You will fast. You will wait or you will not see the girl at all. On the 28th day we clear the temple. We'll bring in the wooden ladders. On the 29th we will draw the curtain, take down all the jewellery of Ishtar and remove her from the lion. The king my brother stands inside Ishtar's realm now. He knows the ways of the Goddess. Naqia will take part with us in the descent and ascent."

"But Sister …"

The Mother stood to prophesy, looking straight into the king's face, arms raised and held straight out from her shoulders, hands pointing to the ceiling where the eight-pointed star, Ishtar's emblem, glowed as her words poured forth.

> "The word of Ishtar of Arbail to Sennacherib, king of Asshur. She summons the gods her fathers and brothers, she sets out for them bread and from a flagon of water she gives them drink. Hear the words: 'In your hearts you say, "Ishtar is slight", and should you go to your cities and districts and eat your bread there you may forget these words. But when you drink from this water you will remember the promise made in the name of Asshur, that Naqia belongs to me.
> As if I did not give you anything, Sennacherib! Did I not bend the door-jambs of Asshur, and did I not give them to you? Did I not vanquish your enemy? Did I not collect your haters and foes like butterflies?
> As for you, what have you given to me?' Ahat-Abisha, Mother of Arbail, prophesies this."

Sennacherib fell on his knees. His sister reached forward to pull him to his feet. She smiled, and to Naqia she looked pleased and a little mischievous.

"My brother, you have offered Naqia to Ishtar. No one but the Goddess can release the child to you."

"As you say, Sister. I shall keep the fast from now and I will observe the new moon at Kalkhu."

She ordered him, "Return on the second of Tishri. Then Ishtar will speak by one of her prophets. Now, here they are."

"They?"

"Naqia and her teacher, Ataril. Come in."

The king pointed at them without greeting them at all. "He's her teacher?"

"He is. Naqia, speak to the king your lord, tell him you are safe in the care of the goddess."

"You have trained her well. She now makes a proper obeisance. But I want to hear from her lips."

"My lord, ... I am happy the king my lord is well. I am well also." *I mustn't get sick to my stomach. A hundred questions and can't ask even one! I'll shut my mouth. But I can look at him. Maybe his face will tell me something. But no, he just looks fierce.* "I hope my lord the king's son is well."

"Oh, my sister. That's wonderful. You have done a great job here. How well-behaved, how polite! My lady Naqia, I am sorry to be laughing at you. But the changes in you are impressive too, not just funny."

"I hope my lord the king is happy with the changes. He may laugh if that is his will."

"Pardon me, my lady Naqia. Notice, not my daughter. I no longer call Arda-Mulissi my son. Both of us must wait upon the gods. We will see what omens the new moon brings. And you, you rest secure in the arms of the Goddess. As Abisha reminds me you are the Goddess's property, not mine. But, we shall see what Tishri brings. May Ishtar, Suen, Shamash and all the great gods bless you. Now, I have seen you and you may leave us. Sister?"

"Go, children, as the king your lord commands."

The two novices returned to their study. Naqia was too nervous to stand at the lectern and just paced back and forth in the small space.

She stopped next to Ataril. "Ataril? Don't just stand there. Say something."

"Naqia, we are here with stacks of tablets to memorise. But ... I've no idea more than you have what's going on. And here no one will gossip to us. So I'm just left staring off into space."

"We've learned so much, why doesn't that help? I don't know. When the moon first becomes visible, it portends wellbeing. Or does it?"

"If it wears a crown at its appearance, and if it makes its appearance on the first day."

"Do you know what the Mother meant, about taking her off the lion?"

Ataril shook his head and gestured towards the lectern. "You'll see. You know Ishtar links to the moon."

"Come on, Ataril. I know the words. She's the warrior, Agushea. I know that."

"Well, then, you know that being the daughter of Suen, the moon, gives her sublime wisdom and purity since he's the god of contemplative wisdom, understanding and prudence. You've seen the carving where a woman offers wine to the gods. She's the Ishtar of wisdom, she's veiled to symbolise chastity. She guides Gilgamesh in his quest for wisdom."

"Yes, I know that. She lives beside the sea of knowledge, I know, but that's Apshu, where Ea lives."

"She's daughter of Ea too. She's daughter of the moon, that's chastity. Descent into the darkness makes everything possible. At the same time she's daughter of Ea, that's wisdom."

"I can chant the hymns and lists of attributes perfectly well. But each time you speak of the mystery I feel … Well, I feel as if I've stepped into a fast-flowing stream that might sweep me away. I don't want to hurt your feelings, Ataril, but I need more solid ground. And I know that Ea gives her all the arts of civilisation. So let's recite the fourteen _me_, the arts of civilisation."

"Naqia, you have learned the names of the _me_ but not their elaboration. Until you have them all in order you'll not be taught the new ones."

"The new ones? The women's arts of allure and music?" *I shouldn't have asked. What'll happen now? They'll send me back. I've tried so hard, all for nothing. I wonder if anyone in Jerusalem would want me. Probably not. I'm a reject, no good even as booty. Ataril's trying to get my attention. I wonder if Ataril would want me. I wonder. Would he even think of such a thing?*

"You look worried. Is it the women's arts you fear?"

"Not fear. But perhaps I cannot learn." *I don't mean that … I feel as if I'm drowning. As if there's no hope for me. Poor Ataril, but he's no good.*

"You can learn. I mean it. You love the wisdom, but Ishtar is not only Ea's daughter …"

"Oh, Ataril. It's not my memory. I can never get hold of it. Forever chaste and yet also the bride and then the Mulissu, the mother from whose breasts milk gushes forth."

"But you do know, don't you? No, I'm not teasing. You know that's why the king's son, the one meant to succeed him, suckles from an Ishtar priestess—it means he's been fed from the breasts of Ishtar."

"So what? Then all of a sudden he's no longer the king's son." *And I'm no longer the king's daughter.*

"It's not usually like that and of course it's not simple. Ishtar is the weapon, as well, the rainbow Marduk uses to slay Tiamat, or so we say in Babili."

Naqia fumed. The contradictions weren't just irritating, they left her feeling lost and bereft. "Ataril, that's the sort of thing. Now it's Ishtar, but before you said it's his penis he uses."

"Look at the tree again, Naqia. Well, the trunk is Ishtar, the rainbow and the penis, all the same thing. Remember the new moon of Ab? Then we sang a hymn about Ishtar in a destructive aspect. I think you resist certain aspects of the Goddess because you want her to be like you."

"No Ataril. That's unfair. I think you bring up first this bit and then another contradictory one just to annoy me."

Ataril sighed and looked as if he would begin to laugh. He tried to reassure her that she would soon grasp what the tablets celebrated. "First learn all Ishtar's aspects. Let me hear you recite the portions of each of the fourteen *me*."

"It's hard to get them right, in the right order."

"So, just visualise her. Look at the ornaments, starting at the top and moving down."

"Ah, I can do that. The crown, then. The shape of a walled city—that's about control, shepherding."

"Don't forget the high-priestly divine kingship, the first of the *me*. Think of all the gods, too, not just only Ishtar. They carry the sceptre and staff. With the rod and line they measure out the sacred space, making the city. Or the temple. Now, go on."

"Yes, the ornaments. The necklace, the small beads? That's it, the priestesses and the royal women."

"And the priests too, all incantation, all libation. Don't forget the knowledge."

"I can see her, striding forth in all her ornaments. The necklace separates head from body. But my head is too small to hold the ideas. I suppose that's where she gets truth and the power to move between the below and the above—aha, so also oversight of the underworld. Then comes the double strand of beads, the long ones, they must be the cutting and piercing weapons. But then they're also make-up and clothes."

"And hair-dressing. See, you get it. And love-making. Watch my hands—the arts of allure."

"You don't have to be vulgar. Men always want one aspect."

"So? You remember."

"Kissing the phallus and prostitution. I really don't see why they're not part of the alluring breastplate."

"The singing is the enticing part, the music, the instruments, the wisdom of the elders."

"You might as well add flattery and the prostitutes, slander and the tavern bringing them in,"

"It's all described as speaking truth. It makes me laugh too, you know. It's a bit ridiculous."

"Yes, I can laugh too. You're really good, you know. You can chase my despair away." *But that doesn't mean he'd want me for a wife. He knows I don't have the women's arts.*

"Now, be serious. Go on. The gold bracelets on hands and feet. An assortment. Think of them having all the different emblems."

"But they don't. How could they? Art of the hero!"

"The hero needs treachery, plundering. Needs lamentation and rejoicing. They're all opposites on the bracelets. Rebellious deceit and kindness, travel and secure dwelling. Just remember bracelets give opposites, they go over the two hands and feet, left and right."

"I'm glad to be getting to the end of the list. At the sixth ornament it's part of the second of the _me_. Bother. It doesn't work."

"No, no. The tools, not the one using them. So, crafts for working materials, the eleventh _me_. Cleverness, too, a perceptive ear, looking after the sheep, fear and dismay. Care and craft go together."

"So the breech-cloth? The royal robe? It gets all the rest of the arts?"

Ataril began to recite the whole list.

"Wait, you're reciting so fast you're blurring the words."

"Power of fire and kindling strife, labour and decision, family and soothing of the heart, procreation and giving good counsel. There. When all of these are gone she's left naked. When she's gone all civilisation and even life itself is gone."

On the third day of their fast Naqia, reeling with hunger, drooped on the bench outside the sanctuary. As the Mother sat down beside her she murmured words of sympathy and took her hand. "Well my dear, you have been keeping the fast as the rites demand. You will have deserved the feast. Now receive answers to many things you have not asked. Two weeks ago, just before the full moon, the chief eunuch to Arda-Mulissi wrote to the king. He asked—no he demanded—you to be handed over to your betrothed. The prince has turned sixteen, you see, ready for marriage. As it happened the king refused, told the eunuch to find some slave to give to Arda-Mulissi if he couldn't wait.

"A monstrous insult, you realise. The king hasn't yet named Arda-Mulissi as his successor, hasn't handed the Succession Palace over to him."

"And so?"

"Our father made certain of the succession by putting Sennacherib into the Succession Palace as soon as he married—well, as soon as he married Tashmetu. She produced the king's eldest son who rules in Babili with his mother. Next Sennacherib brought Zaza, our mother's choice, into the Succession Palace. There she bore Arda-Mulissi. When you weren't given to him right away, Arda came to think the king meant to disinherit him."

"But—" Naqia began.

"Shh. Arda has rebelled."

"Rebelled?"

"There there, stop shaking. Yes. He brought his entourage to Nikkal-Amat, chatelaine of Ninuwa Central, thinking to take you from there.

So he would have if you hadn't persuaded the king to bring you here. Nikkal-Amat is his aunt you see. Thwarted, Arda forced his way into the old palace—not into his mother's wing but into the king's quarters."

"I see you think it's serious. Why?"

"Rebellion."

I can't think, I'm so cold and hungry. I don't want to think about it. But Ahat-Abisha is calm and soothing. She's saying ...

"You belong to Ishtar, you are safe. The king wanted to make sure you'd not been stolen."

"What? Stolen?"

"There was a scene, between Nikkal-Amat and the king. I've heard the report. I'll tell you."

And Naqia listened to the story.

"When Nikkal-Amat realised what her nephew had done she dispatched him to her summer palace in Zibia. He'd been gone only three days before the king appeared at the gates of Ninuwa Central to request an audience. Nikkal-Amat received him in the vestibule of the temple of Ishtar of Ninuwa.

'My lord the king, I trust you are well. I am well, you may be happy.'

'I am well, sister, but I am not happy. You know why. What is the matter with your nephew? How dare he invade my quarters? And—where is he?'

'He is not here, my lord, I assure you.'

'That's not the question. He has transgressed, you know that. Even were he truly Crown Prince he would have no right to my women. He has violated the obedience he owes me, I will clip his wings.'

'Clip his wings?' She shrugged and the king realised she knew she was impervious, that he could do nothing to her. She taunted him. 'You are the wise serpent now? You'll cast your eldest son into the pit?'

'I remind you, Nadin-Shumi is my eldest son. Have you forgotten that? Your little favourite, Arda-Mulissi, let him offer himself for restitution or else.'

'Or else what? What will you do?'

The king thought she had moved beyond propriety. He couldn't punish her directly, she had too much power and wealth, she could finance a rebellion. So he threatened her. 'I will divorce his mother and disinherit all her sons.' He watched, delighted, as her face fell.

'Divorce Zaza? Is that how you honour Shamash? You'll go into the pit Shamash provides sooner than Arda will.'

'I have consulted Shamash; my oracle is favourable. The pit waits for you, you eater of the young of your friend. I have many ears in this city.'

'You'll get no help from me. Let your ears tell you where your son is to be found.'"

Ahat-Abisha smiled at Naqia. "The chatelaine turned her back on him, very insulting, but she is like that, goes her own way and never worries about behaving properly.
"The king tells me he was quite pleased and summoned his vizier to begin proceedings against Zaza. 'I'll see she marries a grateful governor, someone ruling a province far away, Quwe,' he said.
"Now, Naqia, you say nothing. Aren't you curious? That's funny. Don't you want to ask?"
"I know you'll tell me, Mother."
"Of course you want to know what has happened. The king hasn't returned; he set off to capture Arda-Mulissi—they say the boy headed east to the Mannaeans. They're wrong, I think. I believe he'll go south towards Elam."
"I can ask more? Why would the king return here?"
"To offer his son as a sacrifice to the goddess."
"A sacrifice?"
"You wonder? Yes. A sacrifice, his very life, to slake the appetite of the Dark Sister."
It's not just empty poetry, to offer his own son. "Will he do it? Will Arda-Mulissi be offered to Ishtar just like a ram?" *Oh no, how sickening. No blood, let there not be any blood..*
"Yes, if the Goddess wills it."

Faint with hunger, Naqia followed the other devotees of Ishtar into the dim sanctuary; dizzy and reeling, she joined them at the wall. From the chant she knew what to expect. Ishtar determines to leave her throne and descend to the underworld. At each gate the keeper strips off some ornaments; the *me*, civilised life, disappears bit by bit. She shivered to see Abisha stand in the doorway, as if at the entrance to the netherworld. She joined in the chant where Ishtar threatens to destroy the gate separating life from death, but the dark sister, Ereshkigal, though frightened of leaving the gods below to join the gods above, tells the gate keeper to admit her.
Naqia continued chanting with the others until she felt herself turn pale, until her lips grew chill at the point where Ereshkigal fears the coming of Ishtar. The fear seeping into the earth from the underworld gripped her. The impulse to live slackened, a wish to join the dead seemed to replace the need to mourn them. No chanting passed such cold lips, but she watched as the elderly eunuch went to the Goddess and climbed a short ladder to remove the bejewelled turban. Naqia's

own head swelled and grew light. As the pendants left the ears of the Goddess she felt her own ears tingle. The coldness moved from her lips slowly down her body. Her breathing slowed and each breath grew more shallow.

As the Goddess lost her necklaces, breastplate and girdle of jewels Naqia stiffened, still standing but unable to move her limbs. Mist seemed to flow into her mind, she knew she'd not be able to shift any weight from foot to foot or move an arm. So she stayed stock still while they stripped the Goddess of bracelets and anklets, even at the last 'gate' when they took off her breech-cloth. Eyes fixed open, Naqia stared at the naked Goddess, beautiful and terrible. Then—not because she willed it but as if it had been forced out—she shrieked. Next thing she knew she chanted with the others the command of Ereshkigal: "**Go Namtar, lock her in my palace! Release against Ishtar the sixty miseries!**"

The recital of the miseries complete, the worshippers moved into the middle open space of the temple. Weeping they bewailed the sterility forced upon the world of the living with Ishtar's departure. Bulls, asses and men, none copulate. The great gods send to find out what's wrong and the weeping of the women intensifies. Naqia found no voice left. With the knife she carried she slashed at her arms, willing blood to fall to the earth, to slake the thirst of Ereshkigal, appease her so that she would release the Goddess. Entranced, neither the sight nor smell of the blood affected her. Her mind registered only the tickling sensation of the blood on her arms.

Meanwhile the chant described how the servant of the great gods distracts Ereshkigal by demanding the water of life. With a mighty curse she threatens him—takes from him his honour—but, subject to the great gods, she orders her vizier to release Ishtar. With horror Naqia watched the ritual frenzy. She stared as Abisha used her knife to castrate Ataril, watched him offer himself and his blood to distract Death, to save Ishtar, to restore the world of the living to health.

Naqia dropped her knife. Her whole body drained of feeling, she fell back into trance, dreaming perhaps, but she knew each step of Ishtar's return. Each part of her body felt the ornament fall into place. Fully conscious, she shook with a bitter chill, lying flat on her back in front of the statue of Ishtar in the temple, which blazed with light and rang with hymns to the Goddess:

> Praise Ishtar the most awesome of the goddesses,
> Revere the queen of women
> She is clothed with pleasure and love
> She is laden with vitality, charm and voluptuousness.

> In lips she is sweet; life is in her mouth
> Her figure is beautiful; her eyes are brilliant

Naqia felt life returning, felt herself become the beautiful goddess

> With her there is counsel
> The fate of everything she holds in her hand.
> At her glance joy is created
> Power, magnificence, protecting deity, guardian spirit.
> She dwells in and heeds compassion and friendship
> She owns all that is agreeable.
> Be it slave, unattached girl, or mother - she preserves her
> One calls upon her; among women one names her name.

Naqia heard herself join in the refrain, chanting Ishtar's name with awe as, in stanza after stanza, they celebrated the Goddess's power over all the world. She didn't feel any pain, though each arm still oozed blood. She felt only a transport of joy, as if the well-being of the whole world oozed out with her blood. Dancing out of the temple with the rest of the worshippers, Naqia looked around, surprised to see the world outside the same.

After the feast Ahat-Abisha came to invite her into her own rooms. Naqia responded to the Mother's look in a single word, "Yes." She needed no other words, as if all questions now found answers, a single answer, Ishtar herself. At the centre of the earth was Ishtar. Throughout all the heavens. In the breath of every thought. She gave birth to the world and all its gods. As the Dark Sister she sent all into nothingness.

Naqia's trance had led her away towards Ereshkigal. In the bottomless abyss lay Ishtar, source of all being, stripped naked. Unleashed, her dark sister roamed freely sowing destruction and death. *Down there*, thought Naqia, *I have been with her in death*. The ascent of Ishtar, the resuming of the emblems, those *me*. The image filled her mind, the Goddess, her gory earrings swaying, and the smell—the smell of blood. Sickened now, she swayed and swallowed. Those earrings! She felt the mother's hand on her forehead and the memory of the fresh blood gushing faded. Poor Ataril!

Ataril's sacrifice drove all other thoughts from her mind, she went to him. "It's the second day now. Let me see how you are. Last night the new moon wore a crown so you have no fever. My poor dear. Do know I love you. You will be Ishtar's forever, now that you have given your manhood."

"And you? You understand now? About the ascent and descent?"

"Yes. I do now."

"The earrings of lapis lazuli, the pendants, they are—"

"Shh."

"So, you?"

"Perhaps I am surplus to requirements. I don't know what the king my lord will do. I look at these scars—I actually cut myself. That would have been unthinkable three or four months ago."

"Your face always shows what's in your heart. Ishtar rules us both then. For better or for worse."

"I hope she keeps us together. You know I actually wondered if you would be willing to marry me. But now I've been sent to change your dressings."

"You?"

"Well, they ordered Annabel to do it but she seemed horrified and I knew I could do it better. Uncover yourself, there's no shame any more."

Gently Naqia removed the pads from his groin, putting drops of oil on the blood-encrusted wounds. She lifted the dressings and sniffed. She replaced the linen and pulled the breech-cloth over him, sitting beside his pallet, the cool stone chilling her backside. "Good, there's no pus. You'll heal in no time."

"You're quite a good nurse, I see. As usual you underestimate yourself."

"Maybe. I did study the healing arts, you know. Ataril, did you ... did you dream? I mean, so you can remember."

"Yes."

"I did too. I felt as if I might shrink into ... well, into almost nothing. All my being felt like a tiny seed, a lentil maybe. And although my body felt like a hard little bean thing all my feelings expanded. I ... it was as if suddenly everything had come clear. And swallowed up in love ... as a little bean-thing I got drawn into the goddess, through the navel. I went inside and ... I think I may understand the contradictions. Everything all dark and cold but at the same time bright and hot."

"Naqia, thank you. I know it's hard to tell those things. Hold my hand and I'll tell you mine. It is hard. I did dream."

Poor Ataril. He can't say what happened. I suppose his feelings are too strange. Or too strong. Or maybe too painful. I wonder.

"Not at all like yours. Bliss at the beginning and pain at the end."

How would the pain have felt? Worse than cutting one's arm I imagine. The knife slashed, I bled, but I didn't feel any pain at all.

"It started with swelling. I filled up with ... sex. I couldn't see or hear anything but I kept getting bigger. Maybe I thought I'd explode. Just when I knew I'd burst open and all my soul would flow out into ... well, then I saw the Goddess's vulva, glistening and red, opening to me.

An explosion and I only ... well, I didn't know. I heard shouting and music and felt people moving all about me but I lay still."

"Yes."

"You went into the navel, I went into the vagina. But ... after. I wanted to die for her ... I felt like the Goddess drew me down, down to hell. We'd mated and now I would take her place hanging from the tree."

"But Ataril, do you still want to die? A dream, you say. But is it still real?"

"A dream, I'm happy to say. I am Ishtar's now to do with as she chooses. As she herself is chief eunuch of the gods, I shall serve her."

The two devotees remained silent for what seemed like an hour. Naqia looked over at Ataril and rejoiced in their closeness. She could depend on him to understand her. *Life will be different for us now.*

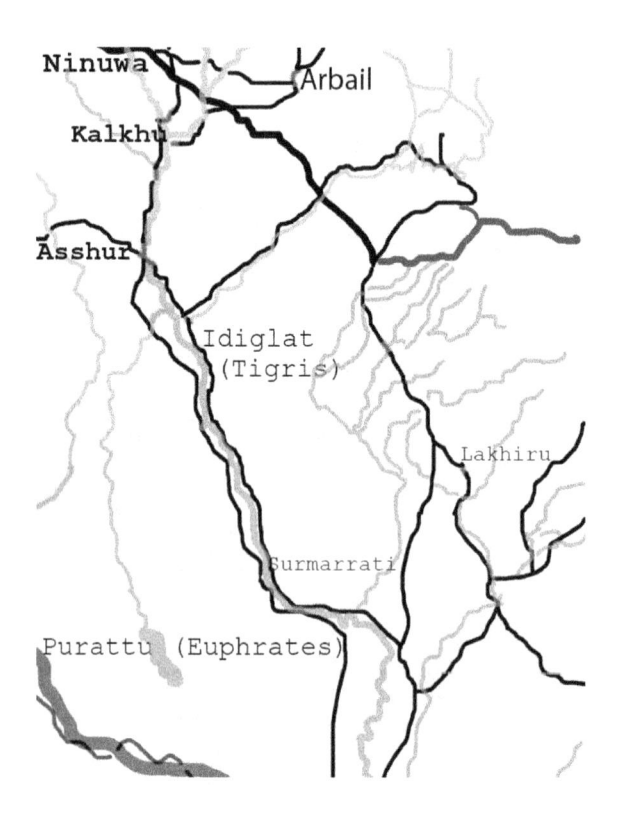

Chapter 7: Naqia Leaves Arbail

While Naqia observed the ritual of Ishtar's suffering and renewal Sennacherib set off south after Arda-Mulissi. He failed to find him but he met other successes. Many of the king's magnates hated Babili and feared Nadin-Shumi's accession to the throne in Ninuwa. They were prone to favour Arda-Mulissi. Luckily the chariot army under the king's general stayed loyal. They arrived from Balatzu at the Inner City, Asshur, where the chief treasurer and his army linked up with the king's forces and those of the chief cupbearer. They headed downriver to Sinni, unsure whether the southern army would fight on their side. The king had sent his first-born son to rule in Babili. Sennacherib's first wife, Tashmetu, was a noble woman of Babili; she ruled in fact. While her influence remained strong Babili remained loyal to Asshur.

But Babili was riven by factions and Sennacherib refused to placate them. Many in Babili still seethed with resentment at Sennacherib's father who had taken their chief gods and removed them to the Inner City, making them obviously subservient to Asshur. Now, however, Tashmetu and all the important men of Babili refused to side with Arda-Mulissi, perhaps hoping Nadin-Shumi would ascend the throne of Asshur instead. In Babili, despite popular resentment of him, the king found faithful allies. Thus the army of Babili crossed the plain in support of Sennacherib's campaign to find and capture Arda-Mulissi.

They scoured the lands east of the Diglat even to the borders of Elam. The Elamites often supported Sennacherib's enemies in rebellion, whenever it seemed likely to bring them booty or advantage in trade. On this occasion, however, Asshur's treaty with Elam held. Their agreement allowed each to pursue miscreants across their common border, so Sennacherib took his forces over the border until they met the Elamite army.

After exchanging civilities the king of Elam swore that Arda-Mulissi had never come near his kingdom. "The king of Asshur should look in Umman-manda," he declared.

"I thank you, Khallushu-Inshushinak. You are a faithful brother to me as I am to you." The two kings feasted one another for some days, parting on the full moon of autumn.

Though his armies dispersed to winter quarters, Sennacherib, with three chariots and a baggage wagon, travelled beside the Radanu north all the way to Arbail.

On the day preceding the new moon fast before Kislev the king's party set up camp a short distance from the gate of the temple to wait for a servant of Ishtar who would emerge to bring Ahat-Abisha's greetings. Sennacherib posted Aram-Suen as one of the guards at the entrance. The silence in the temple forecourt was broken by the ringing of a small bell and Ataril stepped through the gateway on to the forecourt.

Aram-Suen extended both hands to receive the sprig of evergreen, a myrtle, which Ataril presented. After blessing the camp and its people, Ataril proclaimed, "I bring the words of Ahat-Abisha to the king my lord."

Aram-Suen invited Ataril into the king's tent and waved away the other guards.

Ataril made an obeisance until, commanded to speak, he said, "The Mother of Arbail blesses the king her brother. His land is at peace, his enemies have been placed beneath his feet. If it pleases the king our lord to fast today, the Goddess invites him to keep the feast of the new moon with us tomorrow. If it pleases the king our lord, the king's request has been anticipated. Ishtar has blessed the king's endeavour."

Sennacherib, looking smug, asked the boy his name. Ataril gave his name, saying, "I know nothing of what the goddess has promised, but I hope the king's purpose has prospered."

"Go for your fast, boy. We will speak much and hear more at the feast."

At the head of the assembly hall Ahat-Abisha reclined beside the king with Aram-Suen on the other side. Naqia and three other votaries, including Ataril, faced them across the table. At first they all ate in silence but whenever Naqia looked up from her plate the king's eyes met hers. Each time she blushed, despite herself. *Will he let me stay here? As a priestess? I'd never see him then. What if he sent me back? To Qat?* she wondered, shivering a little. Her stomach felt as if it were shrinking inside her, and swallowing hurt her throat. She reached for a beaker of wine and sipped it, her eyes looking down into the depths, staring at the lamplight's reflection shimmering. The silence seemed to be a spell, but the priestess broke it.

"If it pleases the king our lord, we want news of his campaign to the east. Perhaps, too, the king would be pleased to tell us the reason for the visit here which gives us such pleasure and pride."

"Are you mocking me, sister?"

"No, brother, we want news of the world."

"Sister, I chased the rebel to Elam, even crossing the border. Khallushu suggests he has disappeared to lands north and east, to where the Mandaeans dwell. A land unfamiliar to me and from what I have heard I don't wish to go there. The king of Elam knows the reward I'll give to anyone who brings me the head of my son. He won't harbour him. There it rests."

"The kingdom is at peace?"

"Peace? I suppose so. Enemies have a way of not staying defeated. Urartans would hold back their tribute, they'd refuse to pay if they didn't have Tab-shur-Assur marching his army up and down their lands keeping the Shuprians in check. The men of Bit-Yakin threaten Nadin-shumi, little feints, annoying more than worrying. He'll not be seduced by them the way that Bel-Ibni was. But he has to be vigilant, or Tashmetu does on his behalf. Our son seems happiest spending his gold on decorating temples. But, sister, you may think that the right thing."

"My dear, only five years ago you plundered Babili of much temple treasure and still they found enough to buy troops from Elam to fight you. I don't expect you to like that. Nevertheless Babili is a storehouse of learning and worship for all the king's holy places."

"Yes, well, and you have some followers here from Babili, haven't you?" The king looked pointedly across the table.

Ataril returned his gaze for only a moment. He muttered, "My lord the king, my name is Ataril. I invited you in so you know I am here. If it please the king my lord, neither the scholars of Babili nor any other temple officials wanted to release that treasure. Furthermore, they don't seek gold from you or from your son the king. I do not wish to give offence."

"Everyone says that to me. Go ahead son, speak."

"My father, the king my lord should know, he's ... he should be temple-enterer of Nabu. When your father removed the gods to Asshur he ... Like the others, scholars and magnates of Babili, he longs for the return of Marduk and Nabu. Nabu and Marduk bless the king my lord continuously. Such is the proper business of the servants of the king my lord in all the temples."

"Thank you for your observation. Shall you serve in Babili then? Is Ishtar of Babili your goddess?"

Naqia interrupted. "We serve Ishtar of Arbail."

Both the king and the priestess frowned at Naqia's words.

Ahat-Abisha put her finger to her lips and then turned to her brother.

"The king has answered my first question. Thank you. We are pleased to learn that all is well. Now, will you tell us your business with us?"

The king got to his feet. They all stood. Sennacherib bowed to the priestess and placed his palms together in entreaty. Naqia looked at Ataril, each seeing the wonder in the other's eyes.

Sennacherib bowed to Abisha. "My sister, I believe you know what I have come to ask. The goddess herself may have told you. I have signed a treaty with the king of Judah, to marry his daughter into my house. As I have no son now to take this girl into the Succession Palace I propose to marry her myself."

With a mischievous look he returned to his couch. When he sat down the others returned to their places. All eyes watched the king and the priestess except for Naqia and Ataril who still stared at each other. Out of the corner of her eye Naqia saw the priestess's face. A cool smile played about her lips.

"The king my brother should know we have taken divination, foreseeing his request. The goddess has blessed your union. It will be fruitful. Naqia, child, what is wrong? You've become so red?"

"So everybody knew all about this except me!"

"Naqia, you have heard the king's words. The goddess has spoken; you are hers. She has blessed your marriage to the king. What else could you expect to know?"

Eyes wide Naqia gazed at the cheerful company. As her sight blurred, half in a faint she seemed to hear a song, a praise of the groom from long ago.

> My beloved is mine,
>   and I belong to him who pastures among the lilies
>   until the moment when the day expires,
>   when the shadows flee.
> Turn thyself, Oh my beloved, into a gazelle
>   or into a wild stag among the deer
>   upon the cleft mountain.

Still as if in a trance she heard the voice of Sennacherib replying to the song.

> I have entered my garden, my sister-bride,
> I plucked my myrrh and my spices,
> I eat my flowing-honey with my honeycomb,
> I drink my wine with my milk.

Ataril woke her with a whisper in her ear. "You'd better say something."

She blinked twice as she looked around the table. No one seemed to have moved or changed their expression. Though she had not, in her momentary lapse, heard, she knew the Mother had asked what she wanted to know.

"Mother, tell me, may I ask the king my lord what he means," *I mustn't lose control now.* "Uh, what he means to do with me. I have no ... no dowry, no bargaining advantage." *Oh dear, that doesn't sound right.* "Where am I going? What do I have to do? What about ..." *no, please, I mustn't cry* "... clothes?"

"My lady, my wife as you now are, I haven't yet asked what you would like for a bridal gift. What would you like me to give you?"

"Give me? I don't know. Can I think about it? I need to know what kind of life I'll lead." *Are they all laughing at me under their breath? I'm desperate. Why doesn't anyone explain? And look, there's Aram-Suen whispering to the king about me. The king's nodding.*

The meal finished, the maids cleared away the platters and brought scented water and fresh linen towels for the company. Aram-Suen took Naqia aside speaking quickly and in a low voice. She kept her eyes, full of tears, on the floor.

"He has offered you a bridal gift."

"Yes, but ..." *There's no one here to help me. They're all so quiet, expecting something.* "Aram-Suen, my brother—is that still right?"

"No, you are now my lady. You just use my name."

"Tell me, what do other brides get?" *Oh, don't just stand there. That funny smile—he's not mocking me, but he isn't liking this at all. I can tell.*

"My lady Naqia, I cannot help you there. In this the choice is yours."

"Oh ..." *He seems to be suggesting that not many other choices will be mine. What have I got myself into?* "Aram-Suen, I have no idea about anything. What sort of place will we live in? How does it all work? Can't you describe for me how it will be?"

Aram-Suen spoke quickly and softly, he described the royal palaces of Ninuwa, how the king's business was carried on, the foods and fabrics of the metropolis.

Naqia shook her head. "I want to know what I do."

"That I cannot tell."

How do I know what I need? Or even what I want? I wish I didn't have to decide. I need someone to tell me how it's supposed to work. There's Ataril looking at me. He'll know. But yes, that's what I'll do. My first decision. I'll bow to the king and just ask him.

Naqia strode back to the table and made an obeisance to the king. "The king my lord asked me to name a bridal gift. I know what I would like but not whether it would please the king my lord, or the priestess. Or him."

"Him?"

"My lord, I would like to choose my chief servant. I would like you to ask the Goddess for Ataril, my friend and teacher. I ..." *Oh-oh, he's surprised and he doesn't like it. I suppose Ataril has annoyed him. Maybe that bit about Nabu.*

"My lady, I would give you garments of silk, and oils of a rare fragrance—a kingdom's wealth I would lay at your feet. Do you ask only one servant?"

"Yes, that's all."

"Sister, this is embarrassing. It's Naqia's right to ask, but the man she wishes serves you, I think, a votary of this temple?"

"Yes, of course."

"What do you say?"

"If the king my brother desires we will ask the goddess to release Ataril. If Ishtar refuses we refuse. The king my brother knows we obey only Ishtar; you take my life if you act otherwise."

"My lady and I abide by the word of the goddess, Sister."

"Mother? What if he doesn't want to?"

"We will ask the goddess, and that's that."

"That's settled now, Sister. I must leave soon. Naqia, take my hand, stand up as I do. Now, my lady, we will not marry right away, but I must take you ..."

Naqia snatched her hand away to clutch at her throat. She couldn't speak, she couldn't even think. Picked up to be carried around like baggage from one outlandish place to another. First she thought, *No, I just can't.* Her distress prevented her from even looking at the king. No one spoke. Out of the side of her eyes she saw Aram-Suen tap the king on the shoulder, the two men moved apart from the others to speak.

Naqia sat alone beside the table, hands shaking and stomach knotted. *I must have done something wrong*, she mused. *I thought the goddess received me for safekeeping and blessing but now she means to send me away.* She heard the king's feet coming towards her.

"My lady wife, I spoke carelessly. Aram-Suen has reminded me that you are not familiar with customs here."

"But my lord. I can't just walk away." *I can't just leave them all behind, Ataril and the Mother and ... and even Annabel.* "You want to leave right away. I'm not ready ..." *Oh, he won't listen.*

"My lady, you must come now. I need you, don't you see?"

"No, I don't see anything."

"I am counting on your intelligence. I'll explain. My magnates, they need to see that I have really decided to break with Arda-Mulissi.

I don't want them to go over to that rebel. No matter how I denounce him they will still see him as my successor. You must now live in my Palace at Ninuwa to make sense of my divorcing Zaza. I've made her remarry. But, don't you see? There's a gap I have to fill. What's more I have to do that now."

"Yes, my lord." *I have to bow to him in thought as well as in life. And I have to look down or he'll see what I'm thinking. I'm a piece of baggage, someone to fill a gap. He doesn't really want me, he has a gap. He's sitting there but with his foot tapping—it's clear he wants to jump up and go.* "Thank you, my lord. I never …" *I mustn't say I never expected to fill his gap. He just wants me in his palace. But … he said 'not marry right away'. I have to ask …* "May I know when you mean to marry? "

"I can guess you are reluctant to leave. My lady—"

"I need to plan." *He's looking at me differently now.*

"You are sweet and innocent, my lady. Come, sit in my lap, we are betrothed. Not so stiffly, I'm not going to hurt you. Not ever."

"And? When …?"

"It will be before the New Year but not before the end of next month."

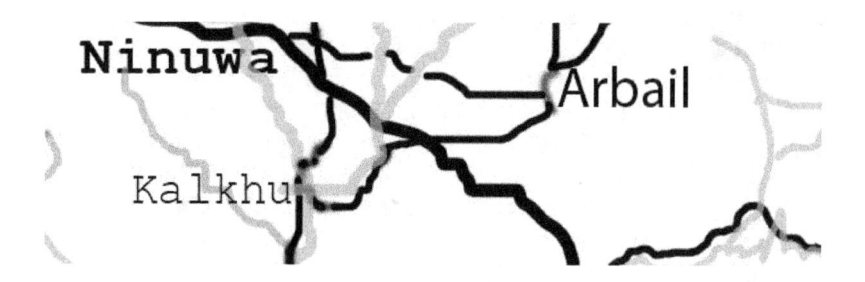

Chapter 8: Naqia in the King's Palace

The trip to Ninuwa was horrible. The king had brought no mounts for Naqia or for Ataril. Instead they bounced on or walked beside the baggage cart just as Annabel did. The autumn rains had settled the dust but in places the road's mud coated their feet, sometimes coming up their legs to the knees. *King of the world and king of the universe*, Naqia thought, *Not how I imagined marrying a king*.

At the last rest stop, in Fort Shalmaneser at the Kalkhu gate, they watched the chariot and wagon being loaded onto a barge to be towed up the river to Ninuwa. Trumpets sounded, and six soldiers appeared with tents and supplies. Sennacherib handed Naqia and Annabel over to an old woman who took them into a tent. Baths and new clothes appeared at her order. With hair dressed and skin anointed, Naqia followed the escort to the king's tent.

Sennacherib too had bathed, his skin glistening with ointment. He sat on a stool in a clean tunic while Aram-Suen dressed his hair. Naqia stood behind him, quiet, alert, waiting for someone to speak. Not turning around, Aram-Suen acknowledged her presence with a piece of advice. "Now is a good time for talk, my lady."

Naqia blushed, unable to think what to say. Even to thank him for letting her have a bath would reveal resentment. She stared at the eunuch's fingers settling each lock of the king's hair into a spiral. All that came to her mind were thoughts she couldn't say. *So this is marriage. I'm not very impressed.* The thought of marrying filled her mind. At home she could have expected to be petted and made much of. Songs, laughter and feasting would follow. Here, it seemed, you just got added to the baggage train. *What ceremony do they have?*

"My lord, when we marry will it be ... I mean, where will we be? Is the ceremony in Asshur, in the Inner City? Is there ..."

The king tried to nod his agreement but Aram-Suen held on to the king's head. Taking the eunuch's hand off him, the king turned towards Naqia, laughing. "That's your question for today? Yes, I'm joking. I know my sister rationed you. Why don't you sit over on that stool there?"

Naqia moved to where he pointed and pursed her lips, annoyed and uncomfortable.

The king sighed. "Now I will answer you. Yes, we'll celebrate our union at the New Year Festival; it must be in the Inner City."

Naqia knew that Asshur, which they called the Inner City, was the centre of worship of Asshur. She knew very little else, so she asked, "And there? Is there a temple to Ishtar? For me?"

"Yes, at the highest point of the city. Next to it is a temple to Suen and Shamash, for me."

The king thought for a few minutes. *Of course Naqia would expect to come from Ishtar's house to him.* He sighed again. Naqia couldn't know how things would be. It would be different from anything she knew. He'd have to prepare her, gently, for the public bedding during the feast.

"The ceremony proper starts down by the river in Asshur's own temple. Then we have boats to carry us up the river to the Bit Akitu. I see you frowning. Look at me, trust me. The Akitu hall where the New Year feast is held—it will be our marriage bed. That shocks you? Of course. But don't worry. We will be partly hidden, but you see, the fact of our coupling forms the climax of the celebration."

Naqia started to stand up, to refuse, to object. But then she realised her powerlessness. *In public? He'll bed me in public? Oh no. But wait. Ishtar copulates with Tammuz in public. But that ... that's a story.* "My lord, I ..."

"Naqia, your face tells me everything. No, look at me. You told me once how you wanted to know, like a sage, like Adapa. Look at me please. I want to comfort you, but you may not like some of the things you learn. You have to accept it."

I wish I had a joke now. But I can do it. "I didn't like the road from Arbail to here. You were up in your chariot. We followed in the mud."

"Quite right. Let me stroke your lovely hair. Come closer. Your bodily comforts—they'll improve. I was thinking about your spiritual comfort."

He cannot know anything of my spiritual comfort. The Mother says he doesn't know. I won't ... and now he's getting angry. "Ahat-Abisha assures me that the Goddess still keeps me. My body she has made over to you, wholly. You can drench me in mud all you like. But my spirit is all hers."

"Well spoken. I think you are going to do well." The king blew her a kiss, keeping his head still as Aram-Suen worked around him.

Naqia arrived in Ninuwa to the sound of trumpets. A corps of soldiers ushered the king's baggage through the rear gate of his old palace—Naqia and the servants too, as part of that baggage. The little she saw of the city didn't impress her. The rain drizzled down from a grey sky on grey walls, grey streets, leaving puddles and a cold damp that penetrated their bones. She shrank into the fleece cape a soldier threw over her. Annabel, she saw, shivered without any cape. She showed no eagerness to be home.

Then they passed a portico surrounding a huge courtyard As Naqia looked around to ask Annabel what that was, Annabel scowled. Naqia realised it must be Ninuwa Central, the Ishtar temple of Sennacherib's capital. *So that's the domain of Nikkal-Amat. She's the chatelaine who manages all the wealth gained by Sennacherib's mother and, I suppose, by him. All those women and treasure were headed there. And oh, we're here.* The king's party turned into the next courtyard and he rode away, leaving the servants to install Naqia and Ataril in their new quarters.

Naqia hated Ninuwa. She knew that Ataril, too, hated the place, that he felt insecure and out of place as he went about on errands. Naqia simply had to stay in the suite of rooms the king provided for them. The small palace, its rooms damp and cold, looked bare and ugly. "More like confinement," she complained. "A prison I have to share with Ataril and the women."

For weeks no letters or messages reached them; Naqia wondered whether some official of the king intercepted their messages or whether no one wrote any to them. At the approach of the new moon, as they prepared to fast, Naqia sent Ataril to enquire whether her household would worship at Ishtar's temple. After three hours Naqia began to fear something had happened to him, something bad.

At last he clumped back into Naqia's wing where he flopped on to the divan. His hands were so cold he had to clench and unclench his fingers to warm them. Naqia brought the brazier close to the divan where she hunkered down to hear his news.

"We're not welcome. The priest at the gate wouldn't even let me in. We talked in the doorway."

"Not welcome? Why not?"

"My lady, I'll quote him exactly. 'Ishtar of Ninuwa rules here. The king's sister can play games out in the countryside but here lie wealth and power. Our goddess holds them, not yours.'"

"What? The words 'our goddess' and 'yours' make no sense. Don't they know the goddess isn't the property of any city or town?"

"I'm as puzzled and frustrated as you. I want to know what's going on, what it all means."

"Ataril, I have an idea."

"When you look like that I know you're planning some mischief. You have to be careful, Naqia."

"Annabel has friends."

"Where?"

"In Ninuwa Central."

"So?"

"Gossip. We'll invite some of their palace maids here to … to teach us songs."

"I don't think the king's steward will allow that. And we'd still not know what goes on in the temple among the initiates."

"So you have a better idea?"

"I'll ask around."

When Ataril did so all he heard was the latest scandal. The chatelaine, it appeared, now fostered Sharrani-Muballissu, a son born to Sennacherib just two years before. Ataril told Naqia that everyone first heard that the boy was Zaza's but that now they doubted it. Rumours said that Sharrani-Muballisu was the chatelaine's own son by the king. Naqia, puzzled asked, "How could he be the king's son if he's hers?"

"Naqia, don't you get it? He took his wife's sister to get another son. I would not ask the king about it if I were you."

Naqia frowned with a reply in a tone as bitter as his, "No chance of that, he's never here."

From late autumn to early winter unrest in the provinces kept Sennacherib away with the army most of the time. The day he returned he told them he'd only stay one night.

Naqia, disappointed, remarked, "I don't see what good I'm doing you here. I know I'm not supposed to complain, but I still know nothing about the city or its workings. There are things I'd like to ask you." *Like why I cannot worship Ishtar in Ninuwa.*

The king gave her a stern frown. "Exactly. You don't see. I have peace and supplies from all the people of Khanigalbat because you brought good fortune to the Katmukhi people."

"I don't believe you. How could I?"

"My lady, some day you will have to learn to control your thoughts, at least the ones showing on your face. Their excellent grape harvest, they say, comes from the little Ishtar I brought riding through their area. You are doing me the very best service just being quiet here."

Oh no, now I can't stop the tears. "You don't understand."

"I don't want to hear you, you're right. You aren't supposed to complain."

"But ..."
"No, I have to go. My council is waiting in the throne room."

Naqia had only Ataril as company, and he tried to distract her by discussing his own problems. Ninuwa was a city of servants, very rich and powerful servants, all at each other's throats. Suen-Akhu-Utsur, the grand vizier, received Ataril, briefly, each day. Anything their entourage needed they got—anything except advice, that is. "Your marriage won't bring any improvement," Ataril admitted.

Naqia suggested, "Why not ask for someone to teach us?"

He shook his head. She knew that nowadays he hated to contradict her or even to laugh at her jokes. Each of them had their own fears but Naqia felt she had more to fear than he did. If the king tired of Naqia he could send her away, even divorce her as he had just done to his wife of nearly twenty years. Ataril, on the other hand, could go to his father; the temple of Nabu would always be open for him. She felt that Ataril pitied her because he knew she had no refuge. Even Arbail might be closed to her.

Ataril couldn't seem to find an answer. "A teacher? I can't ask. The way I figure it, any of the Great Magnates would try to use me to bolster their own position. Otherwise, since they each have provinces to run, they'd not see me as important enough. As for the lesser magnates ..." Ataril snorted. "Each of them hides behind his master. They work at so many intrigues of their own they'd be of no use. To us, I mean."

Naqia declared she'd ask the king to let them all live in another place, another city. Then they'd be out of Ninuwa; she could be happy and free while he would have plenty of time with Aram-Suen who could teach him how to handle things.

"You think you can arrange that?" Ataril's tone was more scornful than it should have been.

Naqia shook her fist at him and said, "You'll see."

Her first letters to her betrothed bubbled with the outpourings of her heart. Very gently the king suggested she be more circumspect. Then she realised. She'd observed his routine, she knew he couldn't read them himself. One of his scribes would read her letters out among all the other correspondence coming to the king while on campaign.

If she had to be discreet she could not write about how she wanted to get out of Ninuwa. But the goddess continued to favour her. Before the full moon of Kislev she received a letter that made her shout with joy. The king intended to reside in Kalkhu for part of the winter.

> I do not fear uprisings in my own lands, but I would not want the King of Elam to think he could make inroads against us.

I am putting on a show, but it must be believable.
So you and I will spend at least some time this winter there.

Winter seemed much too far off, and she paced restless with idleness through her rooms. For something to do she requested pigments and oils. One by one she had the walls freshly plastered. On them she and Ataril traced out and coloured in scene after scene from the Ishtar tablets.

She sketched wildly dancing ecstatics, frothing at the mouth as they bore their thyrsi. Wreathed in vines, their legs leaping high in the dance, rejoicing at the return of the Goddess, some fallen drunk on the ground. Ataril made patterns of the holy numbers, intricately interlacing the symbols for each in their place on the sacred tree. Naqia indulged herself colouring exuberant scenes from the Ishtar cycle.

"Really, Naqia, I think you've gone too far. I can hardly bear to look at it. You draw well, but ..."

"You don't like Ishtar leaning against the apple tree, legs apart, waiting for Tammuz?"

"It's not whether I like it. You've shown his phallus in the basket."

"It's not secret. And he'll have to look at these all the time or move us out."

"Or he'll stay away."

"I want to be at Kalkhu so we can get to Arbail every month."

"Every month? Are you joking? You've forgotten the mud? And do you realise they'd have to garrison the temple at Arbail as well as Kalkhu?"

"No, I haven't. So what?"

"Even now the Grand Vizier says you need more protection. Two new royal bodyguards."

"I don't care."

Throughout the autumn, closeted in Ninuwa, Naqia fretted, sulky, railing against her fate. As winter drew in and she came to understand more of the local dialect, she began to enjoy listening to the gossip of her maids and palace women. She never joined in, her dialect not fluent. *Because I can't bully them, they like me. They're free to say anything too, since they think I won't understand.*

One cold afternoon, huddled around the brazier with several of the palace maids, Naqia asked about the women from Judah who had come during the summer. Had they met any of them? A sudden quiet descended on the circle.

"They're gone." Annabel told her.

"The ones who didn't die of disease lived down south in the Aramean provinces. Nice places." One of the maids offered reassuringly.

Not long after this the king's steward visited Naqia. "My lady Naqia, I have come to be sure all is well with you, that you are safe and content."

"Thank you, Na'id-Ilu. Please sit here for a moment. I am not content, for many reasons, but concerning one in particular I want to know … I see you are worried. Don't be. I have heard of a sickness, you see, which came upon the Judaean women last summer. Have you heard of it?"

"My lady, the chatelaine sent for every healer in the city. A great loss. Some of us … some of us wondered why it took only the Judaean women and no other men and women suffered."

"What sort of sickness?"

"Oh, a sudden fever and then … well, then their bowels turned liquid and …"

"What did the healers do? What did your healer, the man I saw treating the soldiers' feet yesterday, what did he do? What did he say caused it? Were they cursed, do you think?"

"My lady, that is a hard question. I don't know about those things. The healers believe some food or drink caused it but the women ate the same as everyone else. Everyone looked forward to receiving the women as gifts, everyone knew them to be wonderful singers and dancers. Why would anyone have cursed them?"

"You haven't said what you think."

"My lady, I am only a steward, not a man of learning or a physician. In this city, though, I have observed how people born here rarely sicken so. Travellers from upriver—captives I have brought in from the north, for instance—they often sicken here. I always say many men, perhaps women too, would rather die than live as slaves. The commander's captives, from the southern provinces, don't fit the pattern. Like our own people they live on for years here in the city. Some are slaves still, in Ninuwa Central, in good health too waiting to be redeemed."

"I thank you very much, Na'id-Ilu." *That's interesting, I can think about that. Maybe no one offered to redeem any of us. And me, will I get it? The coals in the grate crackle and I hear the rain, the everlasting rain splattering in the courtyard.*

The river? When the rain stops I hear the river Diglat. The wind drives it from the west against the walls here. That water runs down south where people in captivity live instead of dying. So much water passing by the city, burbling past Asshur, lapping the shores of Surmarrati where Ataril says they have the best wine. Past so many little towns until it reaches far-off Elam.

The captives from Khanigalbat died when they were brought down the river, the ones from Babili didn't die, brought up the river. I didn't die because Sennacherib brought me up the river from Arbail. They died because they were brought down the river from Balatsu.

Unless Nikkal-Amat, unless she tortured them—that would have turned their bowels to water. Still, I'm not going to barge down to Kalkhu—I'll make him let me go on horseback. I'll begin a campaign of persuasion in my next letter.

> To the king my lord: your servant Naqia. Good health to the king my lord! May Nabu and Marduk bless the king my lord. I am well, the king my lord may be happy. I hear about many servants of the king my lord who have not been well in this city. I worry. Kalkhu will be much healthier I am sure. If it pleases the king my lord, let it be soon, the time when we will ride our horses to Kalkhu. I have all my servants and baggage ready.

"So, Naqia, did it work?"
"I can't tell. Here's the letter."

> To my lady Naqia, your lord Suen-Ahhe-Eriba. I am well, you may be happy. I am happy that you are well even though some in the city are not. You may tell your servants I am happy they keep you well. The Shubrians have ceded three more towns. Sura and Madura will become yours as a wedding gift. I think you would like a city in the south also. Lakhiru houses my weavers, twenty of them. You said you wanted tapestries to cover the walls. I too look forward to Kalkhu.

Chapter 9: Naqia and the King in Kalkhu

News of the king's gift of towns to Naqia came just after the winter solstice. Days later a commotion in the central courtyard drew Ataril out to see. The chief eunuch from Ninuwa Central had brought some of Nikkal-Amat's soldiers to the palace. Weighed down with full armour, they looked ridiculous among the statues and columns of the portico. The royal bodyguard, the troops of Suen-Akhu-Utsur, the Grand Vizier, and some of the Chief Steward's household took up a fighting position barring their way. They were holding weapons at the ready but wore no armour. Evenly matched in number, neither side wanted to force the issue.

The troops' leaders came face to face to parley. Nikkal-Amat's fat eunuch, Ruradidi, spoke first, a medium-sized tablet in his hand that he shook with every word. He thrust it into the vizier's face to make Suen-Akhu-Utsur inspect the seal. The tablet showed a decision from one of the judges that Naqia belonged in Ninuwa Central, ordering that she be transferred at once. Suen-Akhu-Utsur spoke. "Listen, you upstart, anyone can purchase a scribe, can forge a seal. Listen to me. The king's word says she belongs here. The king my lord took omens. Whose judgement overturns Shamash's? Yours, Ruradidi?"

"We have not seen the haruspex's report. We did not witness it."

"Are you here to see the report? With troops? No. You plan to seize the woman without an order from the king, don't you? Are you in league with Arda-Mulissi?"

"What?"

"Here, Ruradidi, here is Ataril, chief eunuch to the queen."

Ataril stepped forward, looking not at all certain what he should do. He was confused, partly because he hadn't before heard anyone call Naqia 'queen'. He had no idea how he was supposed to prevent armed troops from taking Naqia.

He addressed the eunuch formally. " My brother Ruradidi, my lady and I have no business with Ninuwa Central. I do not know why you are here. I shall, of course, report your visit to the king my lord. But I can say no more. My brother Suen, have you more to add?"

"No, Ruradidi may depart." He turned to the fat eunuch and said, "My troops will escort you to safety, brother."

Ataril walked away beside the magnate. "My brother Suen, did I speak correctly? I am not used to being an authority."

The vizier patted Ataril's shoulder. "My brother, you did perfectly well. I suppose this is your first time, but you are now part of the great game played out here in Ninuwa among the king's servants. And do not worry about Nikkal-Amat and her men. I can help. She needs taking down a peg. Don't worry. I have evidence."

Ataril joined Naqia to put together the letter.

> To the king our lord: your servants Naqia and Ataril. Good health to the king our lord! May Ishtar of Arbail bless the king our lord. We hope the king our lord is well. This day, 9th Tebet, Ruradidi, eunuch of Nikkal-Amat, entered the courtyard of the king's palace ordering Suen-Akhu-Utsur to hand over the lady Naqia. Ruradidi claimed he had an order sealed by your chief judge. He demanded to see evidence of the omens taken for handing the lady over to Ishtar of Arbail. Your sukkallu brought his guard into the courtyard, outnumbering the chatelaine's force. The king our lord may be happy, we are in your palace hoping for your return, soon.

Not until the full moon did the king enter Ninuwa with a large force and a wagon train stretching across the whole eastern plain. The king's forces in the city made it certain that Nikkal-Amat would make no further attempts. The king though, with only Aram-Suen at his side, came straight to Naqia's rooms. The servants scurried off, leaving Aram-Suen and Ataril to secure the doors.

As well as an obeisance Naqia apologised for her disarray, excuse after excuse. Her hands fluttered helplessly, they flapped at the writing tablets scattered over the table and passed over the pots of colour she'd been trying out.

Sennacherib, muttering about having to leave at once, stared at the wall facing the door of the reception room. In half profile the goddess lay back, her vulva a dull red lozenge in the centre of the wall. The apple tree against which she propped her shoulders sported a gnarled trunk, with pale green lichen making patterns of the eight-armed star. Fruits red and yellow hung from the branches overhead, carefully drawn and coloured. Only the face of the goddess remained blank. No eyes, no ears, no lips. A grotesque.

He took Naqia by the upper arms to give her a shake. "What have you been doing?"

"What are you doing hurting me? I've done exactly as you asked. I've been quiet here. My best service, you told me."

"I didn't tell you to wreck the place!"

"You didn't have to—we found it wrecked already. Or didn't you notice when you visited, weeks ago? So you are angry, are you? Tight-lipped. Pacing around my room like a lion. Yes, go ahead. Look in the other rooms. Cheerful, aren't they. Dark. Dusty too. You didn't provide much in the way of hangings, did you? And you can't sit in there either since there's no furniture." *I'd like to batter him with my fists, scream at him. I want to throw myself into his embrace, to weep with joy because he has come at last. He's watching me now and, no, his lips have parted. Is he going to laugh? He's opened his arms.*

"You still show every thought on your face, my lady. I see your every thought. A right pert little miss you are. You have been quiet, have you? You have been safe."

She turned away wordless. The king took her by the shoulders as if he would shake her, but she faced up to him. "So, let me look into your face then, to see what you are thinking."

"Don't mock me."

"You should say, 'Don't mock me, my lord the king.'"

"There then, you are mocking me."

"No, I have heard the reports. But you are still here, Arda-Mulissi no longer threatens. Come into my arms, my bride."

"No. I will bow to the king my lord and ask his forgiveness for my words."

"You will not. I will stop your words. Rise, lady, and don't worry. This palace is yours to use as you please. I am happy to see you safe. I am happy to see you indeed."

"At least now you are smiling."

"So they wanted you in Ninuwa Central did they? What did you make of it? Come, now, and let me kiss you."

"You are too tall, my lord. I cannot reach."

"I will help you reach, little one."

"My lord I do need to stand on my own two feet."

"No, sit down, my lady. Perch there on the couch in the corner. Good, you can look at me and smile. I like that."

"My lord, I am not so innocent as before. Not all your magnates accept the banishment of your son."

"True. And your view?"

He's sitting so close I can't see his face. But I need to reply. If he keeps on holding my hand I don't have to worry. "I'm like a parcel tossed to and fro, to be kept by the strongest. You are the strongest, the only contender as far as I know. Now ..."

"What now?"

"We're worried, Ataril and I. Not because you're not the strongest but simply because you are. It makes us ..." *Now what's the word I want?* "We're more important than we have any right to be."

"Maybe I can help with that."

"You don't know what it's like."

"Don't I? Do you think I have always been secure? No one is. Send for Ataril."

Naqia clapped her hands in the signal she and Ataril had devised.

The king motioned him to stand up from his obeisance." Ataril, your report was perfect, saying neither more nor less than was needed. Very circumspect, very diplomatic. But it came without a seal."

"My lord the king, I have no seal. I am uncertain as to my title or my role."

"You haven't one? Get one made. You are chief eunuch to the queen. Don't worry, you will grow to fill the shoes you wear. Please leave us now."

Ataril made his obeisance and left. The king smiled. "Naqia, come into my lap. Let me fondle you." "My lord, you are singing, I am surprised. And it's an Ishtar hymn, too. I recognise it.

'Clothed with pleasure and love, laden with charm and
voluptuousness.'

I like your soft kisses, my lord. And your song:

'in lips she is sweet, life is in her mouth.' "

Naqia giggled as she felt shivers going down her spine. The king put his hands on her shoulders to brace her for another kiss, thrusting his tongue into her mouth and twirling her tongue around his. She gasped, pulling away, face hot, breath coming fast. She wondered at his grin. *Does he think it funny to surprise me like that?* "Are you Tammuz then?" she asked.

He spread his arms to take her back into his lap. "I am only Sennacherib, you are only Naqia. But after only ten weeks we perform the New Year ritual. Then you will be Ishtar as I am Asshur. And we will join our bodies in the marriage. The prophetess says you will conceive. I must enter you then as you must receive me."

"So now?"

"So now I must teach you. The Mother has told me you are without experience."

"Here? Oh, please, no."

"Why do you pull away?"

"I thought we'd be in Kalkhu. I'd ... imagined us near the ... No, don't frown. It's only a day's journey, isn't it? And ..." *No whining, and no tears.* "I'm going mad shut up here. I love riding with you. Couldn't we ..."

"You do make me laugh, I just can't help it. I want to keep hold of you or I will not be able to stop."

"If you hold me so tight I can't breathe and I'll die. You won't laugh then, will you?"

"I'll keep on kissing you but you will not die of it."

She melted in his arms, content that she had finally won a point. Four days later on the nineteenth of Tebet they rode south.

Kalkhu, once the capital, languished now because Sennacherib had wanted to enlarge Ninuwa, to make it the largest city the world had ever seen. He had shifted all the government functions to his new capital, leaving Kalkhu to dwindle in importance. The old governor's palace was tiny but readied for the king's private use. Separate on the south stood servants' quarters, while on the north side of the courtyard, bordering the still lovely gardens, airy rooms waited for the king and his new queen.

Naqia was dancing happily among the date palms, but suddenly she saw the remains of another palace abutting the west wall of the Nabu temple. She went to it. In places the roof had caved in; litter had blown about into the corners of the larger rooms. As she tiptoed round the ruins Naqia found three rooms still in good condition. She stood to marvel at the walls, hardly breathing. Frescoes glowed on all four walls of each room, as if a god had taken the caricatures she'd drawn in Ninuwa but refined them into perfection. The faded colours lent enchantment, and she could see a central room with a garden laid out for the entertainment of the great gods. Varieties of fruit trees grew beside pools, courses of stone set apart bushes laden with fragrant blossom from grape vines bending to the ground with grapes whose purple sheen made her mouth water. Filled with awe and gratitude she ran back to their rooms where Sennacherib had settled himself down with warmed wine and fresh bread.

In the other wing Ataril and Aram-Suen took their afternoon refreshment to toast each other for a mission accomplished. Ataril relaxed, comforted by the ease and security of the quiet palace.

"My lord the king has ordered me to have a seal made. My father's brother has just died. I thought I might send to request his seal as a model."

"What's it like?"

"Just his name and his image, offering devotion to Asshur and Ishtar."

"Sounds perfect. They'll be merging soon, I suppose."

"Yes."

"You don't mind my little joke."

"Not at all. It has a deeper meaning too."

"Yes, the king told his council that the move to Kalkhu was a retreat for meditation, 'a chance for me to instruct the lady in ritual duties'."

"Did they laugh or snigger?"

"Of course not. Half of them are afraid they've been implicated by you in Nikkal-Amat's plot. They pretended to pay no attention, only went on with arrangements for the feast. There's no laughing in the council—they don't trust each other that much. No, they debated who should act the substitute king when the omens were taken."

"Who'd they choose?"

"The king means to bring Nadin-shumi to stand in for him."

"But ... but what if the omen is evil? If they have to sacrifice him?"

"It won't be. The astrologers of Babili love the young king. They'll make sure the omens are all good."

"How can they? Everyone will see."

"For Nadinu's son you're very naïve."

The king and his new bride shut themselves away in the royal bedchamber. Now, bathed in herb-scented water, lying on a huge bearskin with braziers making the walls themselves warm to the touch, Naqia awaited her lord. He came from his own bath, oiled with scents of myrrh and balsam, clove and cinnamon, and a strange new scent she couldn't place. He sat beside her reclining body and, dipping his fingers in a pot of rose-scented ointment, began to touch her lightly with his right forefinger. He traced the hairline above her forehead, starting from the centre. As his finger moved from right to left he intoned, "She is glorious, veils are thrown over her head."

Naqia waited for him to touch her body but he leaned over to kiss her forehead. Then he licked the skin above each of her eyebrows and kissed the lids of her eyes as they shut.

"Open your eyes," he murmured. She saw his eyes soft with tears as he breathed the words, "Her eyes are brilliant."

For a while he spoke no more. He let his finger touch cheeks and lips but he didn't kiss. He took hold of her body to shift her up to the head of the couch so he could easily reach all the parts of her.

He let his finger trail down the insides of her arms and around her palms, then lifted each hand to his lips. She felt drowsy and limp as warmth from his caresses seemed to well up within. He anointed each of her small breasts, fingering the nipples so lightly she felt she had to concentrate to feel his touch. As each nipple stiffened he took it gently in his lips as if, she thought, he might suck milk from it. "Oooh," she breathed and felt his thigh shake with suppressed laughter.

His finger lingered over her rib-cage before tracing lines from waist to crotch from different spots on the belly. She could feel the ointment in streaks as if he'd been tracing rivers coming down a mountainside. With a shiver she felt her own moisture ooze out to meet his finger as he drew it down into the dark hair between her legs. "Ah," he breathed. She recited to him.

> "For however long the king is in his bed, so long does my nard give forth its fragrance. Dripping with myrrh is my beloved for me as between my breasts he lies. A cluster of henna flowers is my beloved to me."

Sennacherib responded by lying beside her. He handed over the pot of ointment. "Your turn, O voluptuous lady."

She looked down at his face turned towards her shoulder; he smiled, eyes shut. He seemed to be sleeping through a happy dream. She sat up beside him, trying to figure where to put her feet. If a finger needed to reach him all over she'd have to put one leg on the other side. She couldn't help putting her foot above him though it seemed improper. By the time she'd got into position she found herself sitting on his stomach, one leg on either side, to begin her task, following the same tracing he had done. When she ran fingers over his lips he took them between his teeth. She withdrew them before he could bite her. The sight of his teeth as he pretended to growl almost made her laugh. She reached down to kiss his teeth but he put his tongue fully in her mouth, searching and searching her own tongue, as if he wanted to drink her dry of juice.

She drew a finger down the inside of his right arm until he shivered. When she did his left she felt him twitch. As she shifted her body further down his length so she could anoint his nipples she felt his penis stiffening and standing erect against her own pubic hair. The hair seemed so alive with electricity that she quivered, desire flooding her consciousness. She hardly noticed his strong arms lifting her on to him. She gasped as a quick pang startled her, then sighed as a pleasure greater than any she had ever known replaced the stab of pain. "Oooh." She let some breath out and wished she could collapse. Smiling and keeping very still inside her, he took her right finger and pushed it towards the ointment pot.

She continued the ritual, forced to gasp again with pleasure when she leaned forward to kiss his nipples, brown and hard on his hairy chest. She twirled the curls in her fingers and, inspired, pulled them gently to move herself up a little and down again. He moaned, his buttock muscles twitching. Her smile broadened to match his. "I like this," she sighed.

By the time their weeks at Kalkhu ended Naqia knew what she needed to do to make sure Sennacherib would be happy—happy and well able to play his part. In her bedchamber she toyed with the pots of scented oils and ointments. *They cost so much, Ataril says. He says some people would trade a horse to get a jar like this. The chants describe how the Goddess draws her consort to herself, wading through rivers of nard and cinnamon.* Naqia's thoughts drifted to Arbail, to the Goddess, to her breastplate, the source of her allure.

Ataril came to her door, to see if she needed anything. Suddenly she remembered the autumn festival at Arbail. Ataril felt Ishtar's allure, he even mated. Her thoughts trailed off but, motivated by curiosity, she asked, "Ataril, when you and the priestess—"

He interrupted, his voice hard, "You don't speak of it. We're not in Arbail now."

"Quite right, I accept that. But I want to know how you felt."

"I can't tell you that. I know that the child in Ahat-Abisha's womb, if a boy, would be Tammuz-Iddin. The omens indicate a girl."

"How did you learn that? We've been isolated, no one's allowed in or out. How did you hear of the birth omens? Did you just know, right away, still in Arbail?"

"My lady, you are queen now. Keep your own secrets, even from me. I shall have to keep some secrets, too. But don't object. 'When through the seventh gate he made her go out, he returned the great crown for her head.'"

"I asked for you to be beside me because I need you to guide me, to hear my secrets. We shouldn't keep things from each other."

"The things you asked about they're not our secrets. The omens, though, they are known even in Babili."

Everyone treats me like a child, even Ataril. Oh, he's showing me ... it's his new ring. I'll look. His new seal. The signs are so tiny I can hardly read them. "But, Ataril, it says you belong to Asshur and Ishtar. I thought you belonged to me."

"I belong to Ishtar. So do you."

He's lecturing me again. "Hmmph. Why don't I have a seal then?"

"Naqia, really."

He means don't be childish but is afraid to say it to the king's wife.

The days lengthened as winter came to an end—time for Naqia, with Ataril's help, to ready herself for the New Year ceremony. Sennacherib headed off to Asshur overland but insisted that Naqia be barged downstream during the fast. With Ataril she would enter the Inner City in a procession of the gods and goddesses as the sun rose on the first of Nisan. Sennacherib as Asshur would receive the procession that would bring them into the temple—gods and goddesses, magnates and priests, magicians and dancers. The New Year would see Naqia queen in Asshur, expected to provide Sennacherib with an heir to the throne. As Ishtar in all her glory she would wear the crown symbolising the sacred Inner City. When the time came she accepted everything they did; it wasn't the struggle she had expected.

Afterwards—as long as Sennacherib stayed with her in Ninuwa—Naqia pranced about the old palace chirping and singing. Her pregnancy was a triumph. Once the weather eased the king prepared to return to the field.

She held on to his hand as he made to leave their chamber. "My lord, I am with child now. Why don't you send me and Ataril back to Arbail?"

"Little love, I do not keep you by me just to get myself an heir. I expect to find you waiting for me each time I return."

"You are sweet to say so. And yes, I do not see you comfortable in my tiny cell in Arbail. But—"

"No buts, Naqia."

"Wait. Couldn't I go to Kalkhu? You know that here in Ninuwa there is always business. All the building you are doing here makes everything full of dust. It's not good for us, or for you."

"I see how you care for my well-being, little one, but—"

"No buts. At Kalkhu you can relax, enjoy yourself throughout the whole summer. Imagine us lying amid the trees of the orchard, smelling the blossoms, feeling the breeze refreshing our bodies. I can sing to you out of doors, at evening in the garden. Please."

"I will arrange for us to summer at Kalkhu."

"And then I can go to Arbail for Tishri?"

At his nod of approval Naqia jumped to hug him, kissed him furiously. He extricated himself and went out.

Chapter 10: Esarhaddon Born in Arbail

As Naqia's belly grew so did her household. Ataril brought his cousin from Babili to Kalkhu as steward; Naqia recruited a tall, thin woman, homely to look at but sharp-witted and energetic. Amat-Baal had come from Samaria, so her dialect was easy on Naqia's ears. As chatelaine she ran everything—not a small task since Naqia's wealth kept expanding with each gift from the king. Taken from the west as a child, many years before, Amat-Baal's long service in Ninuwa had made her shrewd and skilful. She always knew where to find the best prices for both necessities and luxuries.

The king teased Naqia about her collection of essences. She plied him with her home-made tonics, and used distillates of delicate flowers to rub his body. He enjoyed the attention. "You spoil me. I should be out surveying the defences, inspecting detachments of my armies. Instead you make me linger here."

"Don't you like being spoiled? Come, kiss me."

"It's like a foreign place. You have that Amat-Baal babbling on in your odd dialect. I might be somewhere in Judah instead of at home. Then there's Ataril and his cousin nattering on in their prissy Babili way. They're no better."

"Oh, yes? Prissy dialect? Your wife, Tashmetu, doesn't she talk prissy?"

"You're the wife I'm talking to now. Your Aramaic is good. Thanks to your maids you have a good Asshur dialect. But him, he doesn't want to sound like us. Every time I look at him I can see …"

Looking sideways at the king, she wondered how much she might tease him. The king clamped his mouth down and just stared whenever Ataril was with them. Naqia noticed Ataril swallow hard every time he had to speak to the king. She supposed her eunuch needed to swallow the bitterness and resentment all the men of Babili felt. They resented their gods being held captive in the Inner City. Everyone knew how prickly Ataril's people were. They barely tolerated Nadin-Shumi as their king, and even that only because they saw Tashmetu as one of themselves. With all this in mind, Naqia changed tack. "You're impossible. You don't feel at home unless you're away. It's not my fault! Go off to your army or your defences." She tickled him under his beard.

He put his hands around her stomach. "I might just as well go. You're getting too big now." He bent down to kiss her navel and then straightened up to pull on his tunic.

Three days later the post rider brought messages for the king. His entourage was hard put to catch up with him as Sennacherib sped off south and east. Arda-Mulissi had been sighted in the Khabkhu hills.

Naqia, alone in Kalkhu, missed the king's presence. When with her he made heavy demands, but the pressure to sense his moods and respond in the right way energised her. She gloried in having to keep her wit sharp and her senses alert. Now, stifling in the midsummer heat she found herself restless. *I must get to Arbail for the new moon, I'll just go. I'll go now, just me and Ataril.* Stepping outside the bounds, doing the unexpected, lifted her spirits. But the mood was hers alone.

Ataril and her maids rode beside her litter, none of them making cheerful conversation. There was no joking between the bearers either. Naqia knew she'd erred by leaving the walls of Kalkhu without guards; she saw Ataril looking sick to his stomach with worry. "Who's to know we're on the road?" she challenged.

Ataril bit his lip, but the tips of his fingers touched her token, the winged sun disc of Asshur embroidered on the hangings.

The procession moved slowly in the summer heat, quiet but for the soft moans of the litter-bearers. When they arrived at Kilizi, halfway to Arbail, the sun had reached the horizon, dusk falling over them. The governor of Khabruri had his palace there rather than at Arbail in order to straddle the main road between Ninuwa and Arrapkha, but the new fortifications sheltered few residences. In the days before the king's father had pacified the lands to the north of the river, raiders had crossed over to plunder. The rich landowners moved away, leaving the valley empty except for grazing herds.

In the guardroom men dozed, waiting for night and their evening refreshment. The gate wardens stared open-mouthed as the litter bearing the king's tokens drew up to the walls. They shut their mouths again as soon as they realised Ataril rode alongside, not Aram-Suen. The head guard greeted the eunuch, offering an obeisance and politely expressing surprise. "Is all well? Who is it? The lady Naqia?"

Ataril acknowledged the guard. "She is well, you may be happy. She will wish for food and lodging this night. Is your lord the governor well?"

Proud of posture, tall and looking straight into Ataril's eyes, the captain explained he'd had no warning of their coming. The governor's household had left days ago for an excursion into the hills upriver. Pointing to the dust sticking to his sweaty body, he sighed, "It's cool and well-watered around their summer-palace."

"Who then can offer us hospitality?" Ataril's voice sounded firm, but Naqia sensed his nervousness. With a pang of guilt she regretted her whim. *When I indulge myself this way he has to deal with the practicalities.* She knew she couldn't utter a word without beginning to weep with fatigue. *Next time I'll plan ahead.*

The guard offered them the gatehouse for shelter while he made enquiries. A few minutes later his runner returned. "The word of Shemahu, physician of Kilizi," he said. "I would be honoured to entertain the Lady Naqia in my small house. Tomorrow I too ride for Arbail. If it pleases, my lady, I will join the company."

Naqia's low spirits revived. "You see," she boasted in the face of Ataril's sour expression, "I told you it would all work out."

Ataril muttered she'd been lucky rather than wise. He greeted the physician—a short well-rounded man of middle age—praising his hospitality with flowery flattery: "Your house is a corner of paradise." Ataril added in a more sober tone, "My lady seeks adventure but we are all glad to see her safe and well cared for."

Later, in two small rooms off Shemahu's dusty courtyard, Ataril whispered to Naqia, "Thank your stars we're not holed up in the gatehouse, or given a tent outside the walls."

She hissed her reply. "I know what it's like in a daub hut outside the walls—you don't." Ataril couldn't imagine what she'd endured the year before. He'd always belonged somewhere, and his father obviously loved him. Her inner voice reminded her, *He's a man of Babili and you've forced him to stay in Asshur where he is disregarded and mistrusted.* Inside the darkened room she sensed rather than saw him draw back into himself. An uneasy silence fell between them.

Dinner was millet porridge and summer vegetables—beets and lettuce, fat sharp radishes, spiced with fennel and coriander. The doctor himself served her, with the state of a queen.

She played up to him shamelessly. "Your supper is perfect medicine for travellers at this time of year. Fennel to quiet our stomachs and garlic too, isn't there, in the pottage? It wards off fever."

"My lady Naqia should know—" the doctor gave assurance "—we have no fever in these parts."

"You are fortunate then, indeed."

"Has fever come to Kalkhu? You come here to escape?"

"No, my good doctor, we set out early because I must travel at such a slow pace but we want to reach Arbail before the new moon." A serving maid brought in bowls of cool melon—sweet and ripe, some orange-coloured, some pale yellow. Naqia tasted them and licked her lips. "How lovely! How do you get these so perfect? I did sow melons in Kalkhu but they went soft before they became sweet."

Shemahu beamed. Sweat stood on his brow and dripped on to his cheeks as he promised to show her his fields on their journey the next day. He told her, "As soon as they are ready, we pluck them and place them in barrels in the river. Cool, they ripen but do not grow soft."

In the morning Naqia chose to walk alongside the doctor for the first hour and a half, to see the melon fields and to exchange remedies and herb lore. As they walked Naqia told Shemahu of her coming to Arbail a year ago, arriving at evening, and how the king offered her to the goddess. "The omens then were true," she told him. "Almost the full moon. Ishtar's star was in the western sky alongside the king's star. And Saturn too, but I haven't learned what it means. No one would tell me. I was only a child then, and now, see my huge belly."

"A child? And not from these lands, I think. My lady, your name, we all know you are ... but what does it mean?"

"Naqia? It means 'innocence'. I was too. Very innocent then. How would you say it in your language?"

"I'm not sure. Maybe we should ask your servant. I can think of several synonyms." He turned. "Ataril? Your lady asks me how we say her name in our language."

"I am not sure either. But what would you say to Zaqutu?"

"Yes, I agree."

"So, my lady, shall we call you Zaqutu?"

Agitated now, Naqia spoke to Shemahu sharply, "Do as you please. But, Ataril, we are going so slowly. Will we reach the temple on time?"

"We are near. I think so. When we come into view our Mother will send someone to us, I'm sure."

Naqia strained to look forward and when she spotted the gate she stared at it fixedly. She blinked away some tears when they stopped, waiting for Ahat-Abisha's greeting or for someone else to come. Regret flooded her mind. *If only I'd been more prudent.*

Now she pulled herself from the litter to stand beside Ataril, eyes lowered. The hair on the back of her neck bristled, and her lips tightened into a line. *I should have written to ask the priestess whether we might come. Will she send us away, back over the road to Kilizi? I will get really chilled as afternoon wanes.*

Her expression showed such misery that Ataril reached over to stroke her cheek. "The Goddess guides you, looks after you and will receive you."

A wave of bliss swept through her. She looked up to see Ahat-Abisha coming towards them, smiling, hands upraised. Unbidden, Naqia's lips burbled a prayer of thanksgiving not quite under her breath.

At evening, in the little room Naqia had used before, Ahat-Abisha came in holding her sleeping infant. Naqia sat beside the priestess, pouring out worried thoughts. "But I never know what I ought to be doing. At Kalkhu I wait on him, amuse him. Fine. But he's off somewhere most of the time and then what?"

For what seemed to Naqia like hours, Ahat-Abisha kept silent, Naqia's hand held in her own, looking off into space. Night closed in on them, the air cooled. Relief from the oppressive heat—she had felt it boiling up inside all day—brought tears of relief.

The older woman must have caught sight of them. Turning to Naqia, she reached over to smooth the girl's hair, touching each of her ears. "Certainly the Goddess has chosen you, but further advice is hidden from me—what you are meant to be and do. What do the astrologers say?"

"Oh, Mother, I ... was it wrong? Ataril suggested I get the wise men to read the stars, but I ..."

"What did you prefer? Don't choke up, just answer me."

"I ... we argued about it. I refused to let him ask the wise men to read the stars. Ataril ..."

"That's enough. Ataril can't say—he has neither birth nor training for a magus."

"No, let me say. He doesn't. I know that. He tried to make me ask them, but I wouldn't."

"I see. There's nothing to say."

"But, Mother, what about the stars that ordered my arrival at Arbail last year? Can you not say what that all meant? I always feel that you aren't telling me the whole thing. As if some parts were missing."

"You mean the position of Saturn? Who knows? You'll have to wait and see what Ishtar has in store, at a loss and unprepared. Perhaps such uncertainty is your fate. You were muttering outside the gate. Were you praying?"

"Yes, I blessed you for welcoming us."

"A prayer to me?"

"Yes, a thanksgiving."

The Mother frowned, her voice hard, her words sharp. "You address prayers to Ishtar, not to me."

Naqia's huge belly prevented her from curling up into a ball. Instead she looked away, shame bringing on a flood of tears. Losing all self control she began to wail and only stopped when she stared, open-mouthed, unable to breathe, overwhelmed by a vision.

The Goddess was bending down to touch her, to take her life from her, the fingers of the golden hand poking her huge belly.

Ahat-Abisha embraced the stunned girl, petting her, making soothing noises. "So you do call upon the Goddess." When Naqia's sobs eased, Abisha continued questioning. "How do you address the Goddess? Do you ask for ... guidance? Inspiration?"

Naqia wet her lips with her tongue. "I don't think." Desperate, she tried to keep her voice from squeaking. "I tell her what's in my heart." Eyes lifted to gauge the older woman's response, she added, "I talk to her."

"You do the talking? You don't listen?"

Naqia nodded, abashed, eyes shut, her toes curled tight. Her cheeks felt red, and she imagined more heat burning her inside. She reached out to feel a spot where the baby kicked her.

"You have one day before we fast for the new moon. Spend it with the Goddess. See if she will speak to you. Listen for a change!" Standing up to leave, she kissed Naqia's forehead and spoke a spell for sleep and a blessing from Gula, the Goddess of healing.

Next day, the twenty-seventh of Elul, Naqia sat at the feet of the Goddess, straining her ears in the stillness of the sanctuary. Half in a trance, she seemed to be sinking into the stone flags of the floor, as if their chill penetrated her, calling her down into the earth. Fragments of the Ishtar liturgy swam through her brain, not in whole passages but isolated words. As she concentrated they formed themselves into part of a hymn.

> Her word is powerful; it is dominating ...
> she swims in intelligence, cleverness and wisdom ...
> she asks long life for the king, her consort.

Naqia sat upright, shocked, as the vague words ceased. The words of the gatekeeper of Hell boomed in her ears as he announced Ishtar's arrival in the underworld.

> "Be silent Ishtar,
> the ordinances of the netherworld are perfect.
> O Ishtar, do not question the rites of the netherworld."

But real voices reached her, Ahat-Abisha discussing with Shemahu the storage of his healing balms and powders.

Naqia wanted desperately to recover the words of her trance but her mind held nothing but a picture of the vials in the store cupboard. She thought about Ishtar, how her own consort gets long life, while her sister-self, Ereshkigal, mourns her consort. *Am I supposed not to question the rites?* Why would I see Nergal in the underworld, dead? Naqia wondered if the Goddess put her in that trance to tell her the king was in danger. *Should I have stopped him going east?* About to give a cry of grief, she suddenly felt flooded with tears. With a loud moan she struggled to get to her feet but swooned.

The next hours went by in a blur. Afterwards she remembered Shemahu suggesting they carry her to her room but the priestess refusing. "The Goddess wills the labour here—here it will be. You just push until we see what comes forth." When the doctor made a very grumpy reply, Naqia wanted to smile, she even started to laugh but it turned to weeping, hysterical.

"Quiet," commanded the older woman. "Draw on all your strength. Ishtar wills you to bear a son, a prince. We'll call him Esarhaddon. Get on with it."

Naqia tried to faint, to lose consciousness, to escape the pains racking her mind as well as her body. But the pain kept on. She shrieked herself hoarse, until she felt as if life had passed out of her, left her hollow and empty, as if she were a shell, like Ishtar herself in the underworld, a corpse hanging on a tree.

As she came out of her faint she heard Shemahu exclaim, "He can't suckle." She heard Ahat-Abisha's firm voice rise in pitch, "He will." *He will*, she thought as she felt hands bathing her with warm, sweetly scented water. *And I*, she thought, *I'm being prepared for burial. Ereshkigal has taken me, that's what I will hear.* She struggled to form words, reaching out to where she'd heard the Mother's voice. "Thank you, Mother," she whispered.

When she woke the next morning she could hear chanting from the sanctuary. Still dozing—it took some minutes for her mind to clear—she realised she hadn't died. She lay still in her little chamber until, peering around, she found a basket beside the bed. Annabel sat up from the pallet next to her to rush out into the courtyard to summon the priestess.

Abisha came with her own infant daughter cradled in her arms. After she had set her infant down beside Annabel she turned to Naqia with a broad smile of pleasure. Crouching beside Naqia's bed, she put one of her hands into the basket and drew something out. Now then, little mother, I've fed him but let's see you feed this tiny prince.

Naqia saw the Mother's hands enfold what seemed a tiny animal, passing it to her. Entranced, she reached up to receive it. Ahat-Abisha uncovered Naqia's breasts and placed the tiny thing against one, kneading the nipple as she did so.

Naqia's brow furrowed. "How can I ..." she protested, but the Mother told her to husband her energy.

"Just care for your son."

At midday Ataril sent off to Babili for a reading of Esarhaddon's stars. The astrologers of Asshur replied four days later.

> For twenty-seven Elul. Before the morning watch we saw the star of Ishtar and the star of the Prince Nabu rise together in the east. They rose until the sun himself appeared in the east. Before dawn this day, the last of Elul, the sliver of the moon, Suen, held the queen of heaven and her son in his palm.

"Did you ask about Saturn?" Naqia asked when he showed her the tablet.

"Saturn. As you requested.
> I note that Saturn set in the west before the queen and her son rose in the east."

Esarhaddon was two months old before Sennacherib sent for Naqia to return to Kalkhu with the new prince. She left Arbail with only Annabel and Ataril, but her return journey turned into a triumph. In each village—at each well even—crowds of villagers blew trumpets in praise of Naqia. All summer the omens had proved favourable. Peace endured throughout the summer battle season. As autumn came on the harvest promised to be excellent. The birth of the new prince seemed to be the cause. "It is our little queen," they chanted, as she passed by.

"Blessed of Ishtar, " they named her. News that the Goddess herself had suckled the new prince spread throughout the countryside. Gifts from the magnates poured into the new fortress at the gates of Kalkhu, Fort Shalmaneser.

The king welcomed her into the courtyard before the gates. "Your city of Kalkhu awaits your residence," he smiled.

"Mine?" she asked in wonderment. "How so? What about the royal tombs?"

"Yes, well, the kings' city, but I make it yours since you bring me a more priceless gift. A king to rule after me is fair exchange for the tombs of my forebears."

Naqia, Esarhaddon's basket in her arms, dropped to her knees. With a flourish she offered the child to him.

During their time together Naqia had opened her ears to Ahat-Abisha's advice. At first she obeyed the priestess, thinking only of the baby. As the round of rituals in the temple began to absorb her she asked to visit the Mother's rooms.

"My mother, I come to offer you my thanks. From your own breasts you fed my son. He is strong now, and blessed. No gift can match the gift of his life which you have given me."

Esarhaddon Born in Arbail

"I hear your words, Naqia daughter, but you are again mistaken. Ishtar ordained Esarhaddon's birth. Not I but the Goddess has blessed you—you and the king. Your road will become more difficult as a result, I believe. This year you have gotten away with behaving as a child, naive and charming, irresponsible. You trust Ataril too much. Don't let his prejudice guide you, perhaps to endanger you."

Prejudice? Ataril? How can that be? I'm not allowed to ask what she means.

"Naqia, you are so easy to read. Your face is like a wax tablet. You wonder at my words? I will explain. Ataril's people serve Nadin-Shumi grudgingly. The great gods of Babili, Marduk and Nabu remain where my father the king placed them, in the Inner City, in Asshur. The priests of Nabu, including Ataril's father, cannot perform their rites. As you increase in power ..."

"Me? Power?"

"Shh. You and Ataril both are now very powerful, you are targets, at risk. Arda-Mulissi has been driven far off into the mountains, to Turushpa, among the Urartans. Don't you know that's only one worry? The Chaldean prince Nergal-Ushezib lives in Shushan with the king of Elam, always inciting the people of Babili to rebel."

"If I can't trust Ataril then who? Who will advise me?"

"I didn't say you couldn't trust him, but you have to set your own course. He'll assist you."

Oh no, that's too much. I can't. "Mother, please, what is my course?"

"My dear, come with me; let me get my shawl. Now follow me. We'll sit here inside the doorway of the temple."

"I do like it here even though the resin from the incense tickles my nose." *She's so quiet and so straight and tall, staring into that darkness.* "Mother? Will I hear the Goddess?"

"Give me your hand. We hope so. But here is some advice. We serve the Goddess of Love, the Goddess of Beauty. Let those attributes be your ideal. Be wise, as the daughter of Suen. Your husband, my brother the king, is wise. Not to overreach. You know Adapa could have reached for immortality. He chose not to eat the bread of life."

"But it was a mistake. Ea was wrong."

"Listen to yourself! The wisest of the gods, eh? Wrong? You say so?"

"Sorry."

"Adapa in his wisdom, the wisdom from Ea, refused the gifts of Anu. He settled for mortality. That's wise."

So that's it. I must ask, just a whisper. "You want to make sure I don't get a swelled head."

"Naqia, my dear, you do make me laugh. Immortal Ishtar, being proud, commands gifts from her heroes and they give—even to their lives. My little dear, you are mortal—she is your mistress not your example."

So what does she mean? Ea refuses Anu's gift. So, ah, as I become wealthy and powerful other powers, ah, I threaten them. "I can refuse gifts without giving offence?"

"Use your judgement, listen to your heart. Ishtar will speak to your heart."

Now at the gates of Kalkhu Naqia listened to her heart. She set down the cradle. In her most confident voice she proclaimed, "He is yours, my lord. I am yours, my lord. The city is yours, my lord."

In the still autumn air the whole crowd heard her voice quivering with intensity. As she finished, a moment's silence hung in the air while the king recovered from his surprise. Brushing aside his heavy embroidered robe, the king bent down, fell on one knee and picked up the cradle where the baby slept. He stood up to hold the cradle high over his head, circling around for all to see. "He is mine," the king announced.

Then, gesturing to Annabel to take the cradle, he took Naqia's elbows, one in each hand. He lifted her up, moved the same way in a circle, holding her high. At his words, "She is mine," a cheer went up from the soldiers before the whole company went through the gates into the city.

Chapter 11:
Naqia Becomes Zaqutu, Sennacherib's Queen

Happily settled in Kalkhu, Naqia half-expected Sennacherib to ask her to go with him to celebrate the New Year festival in the Akitu Palace, that they might get another child. It didn't work out that way. She asked, "Why not? I am willing."

"That's not the point, little one. We must act to contain the disaffection in Babili."

"How? What will you do? Sennacherib, if you're holding warmed wine in your hands don't try to gesture."

"Don't order me about. I will bring my first wife, Tashmetu, north from Babili. You see, I'm setting up a bull statue in Ninuwa in her name."

"In Ninuwa?"

"Yes, the men of Babili will interpret it to mean that I will be installing Tashmetu's son in the Succession Palace."

"Instead of Esarhaddon? But ..."

"Not instead of him, and he's but a baby. No, it's how it will seem to them. And I'll bring her to the Akitu Palace."

"Yes, instead of me."

"Naqia, this is politics. And think. You will get to meet Tashmetu since she will stop here for a while."

Naqia felt close to tears, but as she glanced over at him the king's face softened. Whenever the king looked at her that way she softened too. She couldn't help it. "I know, my love. I am not supposed to fear on behalf of Esarhaddon. I don't. The Goddess has spoken."

"Exactly."

"But you, do you want another son from her?"

"If the gods will."

"And if not?"

"I can always sweeten the men of Babili by improvements to their Arakhtu canal. It's needed and they'll like that."

A week later Tashmetu travelled to Kalkhu. The two queens exchanged songs and poems, but kept a polite distance. Instead of a sense of rivalry towards Tashmetu Naqia found herself liking her, moved by pity. Tashmetu's own people treated her as a traitor, hating her son's rule, despising Sennacherib their conqueror. Naqia could sympathise. *She's like me. And maybe my people also hate me, hating the king whom I love.* With real sorrow she watched Tashmetu board a barge to return to Babili.

When the next New Year drew near Naqia had weaned Esarhaddon. Again the king didn't take her as his consort for the Akitu festival. Instead he let her go to her brother's enthronement in Jerusalem while he brought Tashmetu north again.

Naqia expected the visit to her childhood home to be a treat. She'd belong there, be one of the family. She'd be safe among friends. She took thought for her preparations. Not wanting to offend or upstage her brother, Pele, she decided to park her royal entourage at Dimashqa so that she'd arrive in Jerusalem with only one maidservant, Amat-Baal. Ataril could serve as her male servant, the only eunuch. She'd bring no more than a pair of soldiers. *That way I won't overwhelm them, won't make anyone uncomfortable.*

Her plans were unrealistic. Her years in Asshur had changed more than her appearance. Aramaic had become her usual language, and the Judaean dialect sounded strange to her. She was surprised to see how small the city seemed and how poor. The priests' regalia looked faded, the women's silks shabby. Of the old grandeur only the songs and dances endured.

More surprising still was how she was received. Well, not received really. As her gift Naqia had brought omens for her brother's kingship from the famous astrologers of Babili; she'd translated them herself from the old speech of Babili into Judaean.

She needn't have bothered. No one came to receive her gift. Naqia's party watched from the sidelines, not invited to join the dancing. Her foster parents brought her to their pavilion to make small talk; otherwise she remained unnoticed. She sat quiet in a corner as resentment boiled up in her. *Qat just wanted to get rid of me. What do any of them care?* Bile seemed to rise and burn her throat.

Her father smiled from across the banqueting field but didn't come over or send for her. She looked at his lined face, grey and sad.

Grey and sad like the feast itself. Depressed, she joined the first visitors to leave the field, glad to leave her family behind.

Astride her horse, heading north from Jerusalem, Naqia recalled her earlier journey. At each landmark along the road she grew more and more bitter. By the time they reached the gates of Dimashqa she hadn't spoken to anyone for hours.

Ataril rode up beside her. "Are you unwell?"

Her voice wouldn't come, and if it had she wasn't sure she wanted to let Ataril know how hurt she felt, how much hatred welled up inside. She dismissed him with a shrug.

A blast of trumpets from the walls of Dimashqa and an escort of soldiers accompanied the Governor as he rode out to meet them, making an obeisance and offering them anything the city contained. She smiled and let his sleekly oiled eunuch help her from her horse. She remained wordless until Ataril rode up to tell the Governor she'd be better able to respond after a bath, clean clothes and some food.

The Governor surprised her. "My lord the king still hunts in the hills. We will have the queen ready before he returns."

Naqia reeled, faint with surprise. Undiminished, her resentment fed a desire to bury herself in Sennacherib's embrace, to weep on his shoulder, to tell him everything. Meanwhile she acquiesced to the ministrations of the Governor's women. They bathed her in scented water, anointed her with soothing oils. She sat still as a cat in the reception hall with the Governor and his wife to await the trumpet call that would herald the king's return.

When she first caught sight of him she flew into his arms, so eager she made him laugh. Later, alone together, she poured out her misery. As she began to tell of the event he looked amused by the description of the poor feast and threadbare finery. His slight smile faded when she revealed she hadn't enjoyed the reunion with her own people. By the end of her tale, hearing how they ignored her, his serious expression dissolved into one of fury. She couldn't retract her words. She did her best to stop him but he remained adamant. He'd muster the whole western army against Jerusalem, they'd be sorry they'd insulted Naqia, he'd plunder them.

She tried to object. "But they didn't know. Really. I bore no tokens, put on no style. I didn't want to make a show. I didn't want to be seen as stealing my brother's thunder. Don't …"

"Don't you try to tell me what to do."

"Please, my love. Please don't leave me."

"I will avenge this insult in a way they'll never forget."

Naqia wept as he stormed out of their chamber. By morning she felt too heavyhearted to get up and see him ride off. By the king's orders the queen's entourage, escorted by two troops of soldiers with all the insignia of Asshur on display, travelled to Guzana with letters for the Governor. There they'd stop to wait for the king.

She rode through the summer heat in comfort this time, with a horse provided for her at each rest. Sometimes the landscape reminded her of the smell of the mule and the sun beating on the veils of the women. At one rest stop she showed Ataril the thorn bushes of the western desert, plants he'd never seen or heard of. She even showed him the place where the track passed between the hills the raiders had ridden down to attack the king's caravan of booty. No raiders now. Instead they met contingents of the king's soldiers marshalled to the unexpected war in the west. Those troops hurried past them. The wait in Guzana became more agonising for Naqia as the days passed.

"We get no news here, Ataril. I need to be with my baby. I want my baby."

"I don't think it will take them long. And you are moaning in part because you know it is your own lack of self-control that has caused this."

"You are so perfect, you know so well how to be reassuring. Yes, I did. But in private. I never thought he'd take it personally."

"Don't be sarcastic. We are friends. You could have spoken your hurt to me without it having this effect. But anyhow, they'll not be long."

"Not long! Last time it took them months and months of siege. How can I persuade him to let me go home?" *Home—I said home, meaning Kalkhu. Jerusalem was no home, more like a different world.*

Ataril asked the Governor of Guzana to take omens for the fate of the army and the safety of the queen. The first were very bad, even when taken again. The omens for Naqia, however, came out uniformly favourable. She observed in person, shivering at the sight and smell of the blood, unnerved by the twitching of the carcass. Nevertheless she questioned the haruspex carefully, peering at every aspect of the liver. Uneasy, she asked Ataril what the stars might indicate.

"You can't have them read from here. No wise men, no tablets."

"What do you see?"

"Anyone can see the king's star and the star of the god of war close together. Look into the sky after dark."

"And Saturn? I believe that Saturn stands for the darkness that seems to me to lie around the king when he isn't with me."

"You'll see it far in the west, nowhere near the king's star."

Within the Governor's palace Naqia made friends of the Governor's wife and daughters. They shared herb lore and poetry to make the days pass. Before the month's end the king returned. Trumpets greeted him while the Governor's household scurried around, making a great feast of celebration. At the meal, however, the mood was glum; no musicians or jesters amused them.

Sennacherib explained, "Two-thirds of the western army dead."

"My lord the king, how could this be? Have they found some new weapon? How could such a poor city defeat your army?"

"It was no defeat of arms. They didn't even have an army in the field. They watched from the walls as we died. In one night a soldier would go from fit and healthy to wretched, by the next afternoon—gone. I have lost almost all that army."

"Oh, Ataril, that must be what the omens meant."

"My lady Naqia, what omens do you mean?"

"I worried so. We asked the Governor here to take omens for us."

"I see."

Sennacherib turned to the Governor and stood up. The whole company then also stood to hear his speech. He thanked the people of Guzana, of all Khanigalbat indeed, for hosting his wife, for keeping her well and safe. "This is a place of good omens, a place of safety and good order. I will bequeath its governance to my wife. I will recommend she appoint a governor, and you—" here he bowed to the Governor who stood before him "will be the man I recommend."

In their quarters later Naqia asked the king what he'd meant by passing on to her the governance of a whole province. Would she have to move? He reassured her she'd have, as all his magnates did, stewards and governors to rule in her name. "No pipsqueak kinglet of Judah will ever write you off again," he vowed. "Oh, and you'll be pleased, I think. I've made your Abby's husband Governor of Dur-Sharrukin. She'll be able to visit you back in Ninuwa."

Naqia shuddered at his words. 'Back in Ninuwa.' *I'm safer here or home in Kalkhu.* She sighed. Yes, she had thrown herself into the king's arms in the west, comfortable and safe with him. Safe, but—the thought caused her breath to stop—*maybe even he wasn't safe.*

She knew he expected her to receive his gift with a smile, so she tried to offer him one. A failure. She saw his mouth screw up in a wry smile. He couldn't be fooled. With a sigh she moved into his embrace, clutching him about the waist with all her strength.

Naqia heard rumours; she knew the king's mother, Atalia, wielded great personal power. Many of the magnates would oppose the king if his mother took against her son. Naqia's chatelaine Amat-Baal had been very explicit in her advice. "Keep clear of Atalia's clique. She's very old. Frail in her body too. Maybe feeble in her mind, I've heard. But keep this in mind, my lady: Atalia retains full loyalty to Zaza and Nikkal-Amat. She resents the king's having chosen you."

To Naqia's mind, however, Atalia far off in the hills at the temple to Gula in Mutsatsir seemed powerless, even unimportant. Naqia was certain that danger to both her and the king must come from Nikkal-Amat who still ruled in Ninuwa. *Nikkal-Amat favours Arda-Mulissi, and both of them want his father dead.* Tears filled her eyes as she hid her head on the king's chest. She felt his hand caressing her hair, knew he sensed her worry. At his words, "Don't grieve, my sweet, I won't let anyone harm you," she let the tears flow.

Within days, at high summer, the remainder of the army and the king's entourage set out on the dry roads to Natsibina. In each place the king proclaimed that Zaqutu, as he'd decided to call Naqia, now ruled the province. The news of the good omens at Guzana and the freedom of the whole area from plague made people believe in her, that Zaqutu meant good luck, that she brought blessing from the Goddess.

No blessing fell on Naqia herself. In Ninuwa in late summer she miscarried. Throughout the winter Sennacherib stayed in Ninuwa but she would not stay with him, pleading weakness. She chose to go to Kalkhu. The fear of Nikkal-Amat's plots and the near certainty that her own luck would run out armoured her against the king's requests.

Luck was running out for the king. Without the western army pressure came on all the garrisons; his southern enemies grew bold, and his old rival, Marduk-Baladan, threatened to retake Babili.

The shortage of men among the king's western allies meant they couldn't send him troops. To compensate they sent boats so that Sennacherib could cross and recross the river; that way he might attack Elam and Bit-Yakin from their rear. As Ataril commented to Naqia, "It was a clever idea, really ingenious, but it didn't work."

Chapter 12: Challenges to Sennacherib's Rule

Naqia kept her entourage in Kalkhu, grateful for the war in the south that meant she didn't need to stay in Ninuwa. When Sennacherib returned he again took Tashmetu to the Akitu Palace. While he was escorting her there the war intensified, the Elamite king attacking across the Diglat from the south. The Elamites made impressive headway, coming through as far north as Nippur. To the nobles of Babili it appeared that Sennacherib's star had waned. Thus, during the time Tashmetu visited with Naqia in Kalkhu, the Elamite general carried off Nadin-Shumi to Shushan their capital. There they castrated Sennacherib's heir, king of Babili, to ensure he'd never be king anywhere. He remained there, captive.

In Kalkhu Naqia tried to comfort Tashmetu as she grieved for her son, castrated and imprisoned. They all waited to see whether she had conceived another son at the Akitu festival. She hadn't and her rule over Babili ended. A prince of Bit-Yakin took Babili's throne for a few months. As they celebrated Esarhaddon's fourth birthday in Kalkhu, Naqia assured Tashmetu, "I love having you here in Kalkhu."

Tashmetu looked dubious. "I can't see why."

"You can help me. I govern Khanigalbat now and I am supposed to oversee the governor and his magnates."

"What is your problem there?"

Naqia explained that she did read and reply to all the reports and got Amat-Baal to go over the accounts. "But it all seems perfect. How do I know it's true?"

"Does all your revenue come in on time?"

"Yes, of course."

Tashmetu laughed. "You really are Zaqutu. So naive. Sometimes, you know, it doesn't; then you have to act."

Naqia gasped. "Act? How?"

"At worst you go in person, and with strength."

"Otherwise?"

Tashmetu explained that her own personal servants might go first, with tokens and soldiers. Naqia tried to imagine herself commanding one of her governors but failed. *I'll never be able to do that.*

As Naqia attended to Sennacherib's comfort when he came to Kalkhu she tried to apologise. "Don't you worry about my mistakes?"

"Worry? Me? About what mistakes?"

"It's all my fault, this."

"All your fault? How can you think that?"

Naqia glanced at his face, seeing real puzzlement. "It is because I told you about the ceremony back in Judah—that's why all this has happened. Because I cost you the strength of the western army."

Sennacherib sat up and looked into her face. "My love, don't be a fool. There are always rebellions. Defeated kings don't like paying tribute. They are always waiting for an opportunity. You didn't make that situation, and besides, I chose to do what I wanted to do."

"But it was to avenge me."

"It was still my decision. You rule where you rule, in the northern province. I rule where I rule."

Naqia's expression changed. Sennacherib laughed. "You rule your province well; they are at peace and they pay up."

"So you have been checking up on me?"

"That's what I have servants for."

But Sennacherib didn't stay long in Kalkhu. He set off to attack Elam for supporting the upstart from Bit-Yakin and to drive his supporters out of Babili.

Ataril brought the news to Naqia, his face grim. "We men of Babili—I mean my people—we don't want men from Bit-Yakin ruling over us. This time we have not been fortunate enough to get rid of them. Sennacherib attacked swiftly; he outflanked them to get them from the rear. But it didn't work." Ataril noticed Naqia's eyes widen and added, "Don't worry."

Where his strategy had failed him, Sennacherib's luck now provided better news. Rebels killed Elam's king. Without that support, weak and nervous, the upstart from Bit-Yakin fled first to an eastern village and then south to his marshlands. Sennacherib moved forward against Elam and Babili. Only the rebel Elamite's brilliant general, Umman-Menanu, managed to hold Sennacherib's troops at bay. Ataril again brought the news to the women's quarters. "A stalemate rather than a victory."

With a year to regroup and bolster his forces, Sennacherib would have returned south to take Babili, except that his mother died. He was obliged to observe her funeral rites. Since the cortege would have to come downriver past Kalkhu Naqia made excuses to spend the late summer and autumn at Arbail, leaving Ataril behind in Kalkhu. The temple surroundings were strangely quiet, with Ahat-Abisha in Asshur at her mother's burial. When the priestess returned she was subdued, her expression more than usually grim. As they watched the sun set, sitting in the doorway of the sanctuary, Naqia recalled her first night at Arbail six years before. "My mother, is it only grief for your mother that troubles you?"

"Troubles?" The priestess sighed. "Throughout my mother's long life her placid nature shielded her from worries over her children, her estates, or her servants. She settled a large property and great wealth on this temple, but I wonder if we'll ever see it. My brother refused to let her see his face, snubbed her really. I believe she retaliated the only way she could, by hanging on."

"Why ..." Naqia began to ask, before remembering she'd used up her one question. Ahat-Abisha said nothing. In the silence Naqia recalled Ataril's rejection at Ninuwa Central. But the king now controlled Ninuwa Central. Surely he could get rid of Nikkal-Amat? *Perhaps I should return to Kalkhu*, she thought, but the peace of Arbail soothed her; here she felt safe.

Ahat-Abisha was right. Atalia's death did not lessen Nikkal-Amat's grip on Ninuwa Central. Just before the autumn festival Ahat-Abisha asked Naqia about her glum looks. "My daughter, you have worn a sorry face these past few days. Has someone read your stars? Have you had bad news?"

"My lord the king worries. I worry too. He's angry because I will not winter in Ninuwa."

For a few minutes the priestess did not speak. In the silence Naqia heard her own words as if for the first time. She was startled when, as if reading her mind, the priestess asked, "Are you regretting your choice?"

"No. I mean, you know how he's enlarging the city walls and bringing new waterways in."

"So? Why should that keep you away?"

"It doesn't. Some of it I suggested. I told him how I feared the river because, well ..."

"Naqia, have you been listening to the Goddess? Has she warned you about the river?"

"Oh no. The new works will divert the water away from the king's palace."

"I heard about the canal."

"His master of canals has aroused Sennacherib's interest. He enjoys the challenge of engineering the canals to best advantage. I love being with him and poring over parchments with plans and measurements. He wants me nearby while he oversees the actual works."

"I can picture him, busy and happy."

"I can too. Mother, I oblige him in every way in Kalkhu."

"But not in Ninuwa which is his capital. I think you might be tempting fate. Of course, he can command you, then you'd have to go."

Naqia thought about that. She recalled Tashmetu telling her that she wished she could leave for Babili no matter what, but that her return would mean the king had lost control of Babili. She couldn't have her own way. *If I had to make such a choice, what would I do? I cannot tell.* "I'll cross that bridge when I come to it. But you mentioned the stars."

"Yes. See here, I have a long report from the wise men at Asshur."

"It's so old-fashioned, the way they write. I can make out that the crescent moon blocked out first the prince's star and then the king's star. For days it hovered near the stars but last night it passed before them, blocking out their light. Does it signify ... they'll die?" Naqia's voice quavered and she felt a heavy weight like a stone inside her. *What would I do if Sennacherib just isn't there? If he dies ... I would have to die too. But then they'd take Esar, make him be substitute king and let him be sacrificed for the sins of the people. For my sins in fact.* "Mother?"

"All week the crescent has hovered near Marduk's star. Naturally it predicts a great battle. The gods of the dead, Ereshkigal and Nergal, will feast on the slain. But, daughter, the stars shine on everyone. We do not know which king or which prince she will take."

Naqia arrived at the gates of Kalkhu to hear only silence. Startled, she opened the curtains of her litter to peer out. The fort gaped, empty of soldiers. Her bearers set the litter down a little way inside the gate while they looked for water before tackling the steep hill up into the city proper. Naqia stepped out and walked around the litter. Up above her the city yawned, empty of noise and movement. When her bearers carried her up the hill towards the royal precincts through an empty landscape she wondered, *Where are all the people then?* Only a few household servants occupied the royal precincts. Ataril came to attend her litter and she learned he had to serve as the city's scribe; there wasn't anyone else. Later in her rooms, Ataril chased all her maidservants out so he could sit beside her to explain.

"Last year the king's Elam campaign drove the Elamites into the hills."

"I know that already, Ataril. And I want my bath more than old news. The king told me that only the hard winter snow kept him from catching that ... well, he calls him the stupid king of Elam."

"But, Naqia, now the Elamites have risen up again, killed their king and set Umman-Menanu up as their king."

Challenges to Sennacherib's Rule   113

"So?"

"Umman, they boast, can defeat the gods themselves—he's a great general."

"Hmmph. So why have all our soldiers gone? To fight the gods?"

"Naqia, sometimes you sound like a fool. I know you're not, but … Didn't you hear that Bit-Yakin has put Marduk-Mushezib on the throne in Babili? He's not as stupid as his uncle. So the king has moved south with a huge army—all the royal troops plus all the garrisons along the way. That's why we're here alone, no guards at all."

"I can hear that you are really worried, but can we not talk after my bath?"

"The king will call up the southern army too. It's a big operation."

"But they'll win. Weren't the omens favourable? Why do you shake your head?"

"No omens taken."

"Oh, now I see. Yes that is scary. Has all of Babili turned against the king?"

"Yes, Naqia, they've revolted again. This time they've even stripped our very gods of gold and jewels. They think they can buy Umman-Menanu's allegiance. My father writes …"

"Yes? So he still writes to you—he's not in revolt?"

"He fears that now Nabu will never return to his temple. The sages all have gone over to Mushezib. Sennacherib will get no more advice about the stars, no haruspex will kill a sheep, no omens at all."

"Not even in Asshur?"

"The sages have left the Inner City, any from Babili. Those are now rebels."

"You are worried, I can tell. Is your father safe?"

"I cannot know. The king calls Umman 'a man without any sense or judgment'."

"You called him a great general."

"I don't always agree with the king. Umman's the one who led the raid on Babili that captured our king, Tashmetu's son."

Naqia shuddered. Tashmetu hadn't wept when they had taken her son captive. She'd gone silent. Her grief was something Naqia had felt rather than heard. Losing her only son. As the image of Tashmetu's face came into Naqia's mind she gasped. *Oh, Esarhaddon! What if they get here?*

She stared at Ataril. "You said we're all alone here. No guards."

"That's right. I see you are beginning to understand."

Now that I'm taking him seriously. "Has the king abandoned us then? Is Esarhaddon safe here? I'd never have gone to Arbail if I'd thought …"

"I think we are more safe without troops. We could hide, we could walk to Kilizi as if we were not important."

Naqia clenched her teeth but left her chamber, unwashed, to visit Esarhaddon and Annabel in the young prince's wing of the palace.

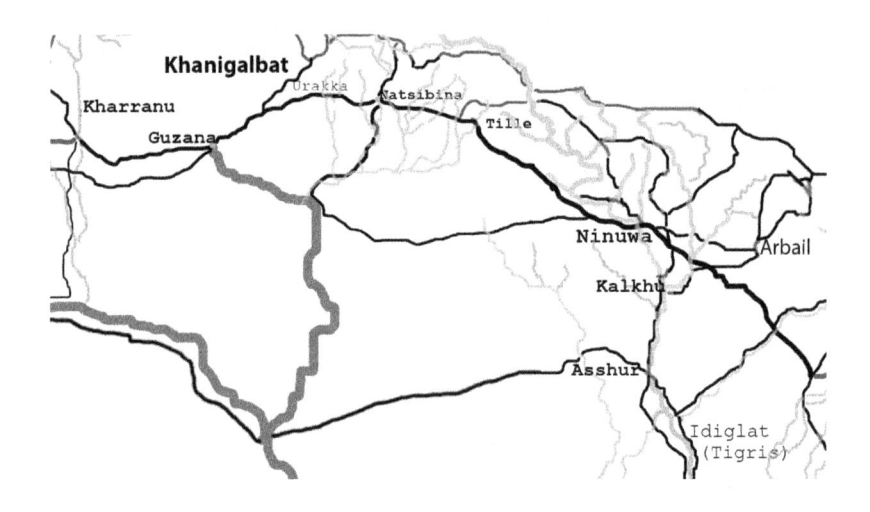

Chapter 13: The Retreat to Khanigalbat

Throughout the winter the forces of Asshur mustered from north and east to gather in the fortresses along the river. The king wouldn't use boats to carry the armies downriver this time; he left troops to garrison every important town against the men of Bit-Yakin. From the cities and temples of the north he brought trustworthy scribes to keep each town aware of the wider situation. As word spread of unrest in Elam, Sennacherib stripped the border towns of their winter food supplies. An army from the east would starve, he insisted, if they crossed the river to get to Nippur.

"Ataril? What did my lord the king do wrong? Why did the men of Babili turn against Tashmetu's son? He's of their own stock."

"They see through him to his father not his mother."

"Why do they hate Sennacherib so? He's honoured them, given them his first-born. Done the canal. He treats Tashmetu with huge respect, honours her and all."

"He keeps our gods, Marduk and Nabu, in Asshur."

"Yes. I understand that. When Sennacherib invaded our country we hid most of our wealth, but the gods, I suppose, they were too big to hide. So, the men of Babili hate the king my lord. What about you? Do you hate him?"

"He is the king; all the great gods acknowledge his rule over the whole world. What I think or feel is unimportant. I have taken the oath and for my own sake I would not fail in my duty."

"But you don't love him, do you?"

"I don't have to. I serve you and love you. I don't have to love him."

Though Tashmetu remained in Kalkhu, still mourning her son, the king chose Naqia to celebrate the New Year's coupling at the Akitu festival. She didn't conceive.

Tashmetu comforted her. "You are young. Sister, you will have more children."

"You too can still conceive. You may have another son to reign in Babili."

"I think not," Tashmetu replied.

The two women never returned to the subject.

As the spring passed the gardens' lushness mocked the sombre mood of Naqia's household in Kalkhu. The year of Mannu-Ki-Adadmilki was one of abundance, but the early fruits placed in baskets around the courtyard remained untasted. Every midday when the post rider arrived they received latest bulletin with dread. From the west came worrying news of revolt. Stripped of troops loyal to Asshur, the western city-kings had formed an alliance, Egypt supporting them, and—Naqia learned with irritation—with Qat, her own mother, prominent among the conspirators.

Just before the summer solstice, as Ataril prepared for its feast, trumpets sounded at the gate—not signalling troops but giving the full seven blasts indicating the king's approach. Though she wore only a light tunic Naqia began to run towards the gates. Before she made it halfway across the city she met the king's chariot—with all three men standing up—as it clattered up the steep track. Sennacherib shouted at his driver to stop, he jumped down to take Naqia's arm, to walk with her up to the palace.

She squeezed his hand. "How come you're here so soon? We had no warning."

"We came swiftly. Perhaps the Elamite army follows. The northern army—your army my dear—fought brilliantly. Unlike my southern forces who fled before the enemy. A pincer attack—standard, we could have destroyed the whole enemy army if they'd held fast. We turned one flank but the southerners collapsed, fleeing before the other flank. Their cowardice forced us to leave the field."

"A defeat? I can't believe it."

"No defeat. I am here, not in Elam's capital, not castrated. Well, Mushezib still holds the throne of Babili, but the year is young. I'm here to make certain you and your whole household, including Tashmetu, go north to your province; you'll stay there until I allow your return."

"But ... oh look, here he is, dragging Ataril down the path to meet you."

"Papa! Tell me about the battle."

"Not now! You can listen when I dictate the report to the scribes."

In the king's audience room with his father Esarhaddon listened to the account as the king dictated.

> With the dust of their feet covering the wide heavens like a mighty storm with its masses of pregnant clouds, they drew up in battle array before me in the city of Khallule, on the banks of the Diglat.

The Retreat to Khanigalbat

"But Papa," Esarhaddon exclaimed, "had they truly reached our river?" Naqia blushed. *If only he were more tactful.*

Sennacherib didn't sound defensive. He explained to the boy, "Yes, of course. I emptied the countryside between our land and their land to make the battle happen where it'd be convenient for us."

> They blocked my passage and offered battle. As for me, to Asshur, Suen, Shamash, Bel, Nabu, Nergal, Ishtar of Ninuwa, Ishtar of Arbail, the gods in whom I trust, I prayed for victory over a mighty foe. The gods speedily gave ear to my prayers and came to my aid. Like a lion I raged. I donned my coat of mail, placed my helmet on my head. Hurriedly in the anger of my heart I mounted my great battle chariot which brings low the foe. The mighty bow given me by Asshur I seized in my hands; grasped the javelin that pierces to the life. Against all the hosts of wicked enemies I shouted; rumbling like a storm, I roared like thunder. At the word of Asshur, the great lord, my lord, on flank and front I pressed the enemy like the onset of a raging storm. With Asshur's weapon and the terrible onset of my attack I stopped their advance, succeeded in surrounding them.
> I decimated the enemy host with arrow and spear, I bored through their bodies like a drill. Umman-Undasha, the chief field marshal of Elam, I faced down and slew, even that trustworthy man, commander of all the armies of Elam, the king of Elam's chief support, together with his nobles

> who wear the golden girdle-dagger and whose wrists are encircled with heavy bracelets of shining gold—like fat steers who have hobbles put on— speedily I cut them down and established their defeat. I cut their throats like soft fruit, cut off their precious lives as one cuts a string. Like the flush of storm water I sent the contents of their gullets and entrails flowing over the wide earth. My prancing steeds plunged into the streams of their blood as into a river. The wheels of my war chariot were bespattered with filth and blood. With the carcasses of their warriors I filled the plain like grass. Their testicles I tore off, and tore out their privates like the seeds of the cucumbers of Sivan. Their hands I cut off. The heavy bracelets of shining gold I took away. With sharp swords I pierced their belts and took away the girdle daggers of gold and silver.

"Papa! Where's all the gold and silver then? There're no baggage wagons."

"Baggage travels slowly. I wanted to get home in a hurry."

> The rest of his nobles, including Marduk-Baladan's son, my hands seized in the midst of battle. The chariots and their horses, whose riders had been slain at the beginning of my terrible onslaught, left to themselves, kept running back and forth for a distance of two double-hours. I put an end to their headlong flight.
> That Umman-Menanu, king of Elam, together with the king of Babili and the princes of Bit-Yakin who had gone over to their side, were overturned by the terror of my battle as a bull overturns an obstruction. They abandoned their tents and to save their lives trampled the bodies of their fallen, fleeing like pigeons pursued. So frightened they couldn't piss, yet they sprayed their chariots with their dung.

"Chariots? Papa, did they get away?"

Naqia rebuked him. "Esar!" *I wish he were just a little bit more stupid, not so quick to see the holes in his father's account.*

"I have to send the army to quell the revolt out west—there's no time to chase Elamites."

"What if they come here when the army has left?"

"A good question, son, but don't worry. They'll find nothing to eat in our lands. They must eat. They'll go east where their own people can feed them."

The Retreat to Khanigalbat

"We'll eat though, won't we?"

"You, your mother and your whole household will head north into Khanigalbat. No war has waged there, so they have lots of food. Travel with me and the vanguard on the road. You'll enjoy it."

Naqia stared, amazed at the king's patience, how he loved to answer the boy—teaching him to be king as his own father did before with him. She knew that in Asshur the king told the scribes what to put in the annals, so the account read as what ought to have happened. The record always contained inconsistencies.

Naqia was quite aware that the king planned to move them north because he feared an Elamite invasion, maybe as far inside his realm as Kalkhu. Since Ataril used to mock the scribes of Asshur—he'd boast of Babili's freedom, claiming the sages of Babili wrote what really happened—Naqia suspected him of taking a furtive pleasure in the king's predicament. She snapped at him peevishly, "You want the account as the Babili scribes tell it? Well, then, after the king has punished Babili you can go there, and read the account of the battle in their annals, make sure you copy this year out for me."

Ataril watched the king carry Esarhaddon piggyback across the courtyard. "I don't have to go. I know what they'll say. It'll go like this: *Umman-Menanu king of Elam mustered the troops of Elam and Akkad and did battle against Asshur in Khallule. He effected an Assyrian defeat.* My lady, I wish I could go to Babili. My father Nadinu is growing old and I should like to see him. He longs for Nabu to be returned to his temple."

"I find it hard to sympathise with you Ataril. You have observed the king's mood. Write to your father to suggest he might serve his god in Asshur. Then you can visit him."

As Naqia and her household made their way to Ninuwa—slowly because of the baggage—the king took Esarhaddon before him on his horse. Each evening at their camp the boy burbled as he savoured the details of battles and slaughter, hunting episodes and jokes.

"My lord the king," Naqia observed, "you make our son think it exciting and easy to be king. Maybe he needs to learn sayings of the wise—proverbs—and to know about all the things you call the boring bits."

Sennacherib laughed. "I like travelling with him. He's good company, doesn't try to give me advice all the time."

She pulled his beard.

When they reached Asshur the post from Ninuwa caught up with them. The king handed Naqia the dispatches to read.

"Well, now," she warned him, "here come the boring bits." She read the lists of troop dispositions on the western front, the account of levies gathered from the inner provinces, the domains of the king's magnates, and more details of provisions apportioned from the central store to the king's dependants scattered throughout the whole realm.

The Grand Vizier had sent daily accounts for the previous two months but when Naqia began to read them the king put his hand up. "I don't need to know more. He's the most trustworthy of any of my servants."

"More than Aram-Suen? "

"Yes. Aram-Suen has imagination."

The king took the accounts from Naqia's hand and laughed. "Tell me, what's in the parchment?" Naqia unrolled the scroll carefully and glanced at the heading. She gasped, her hands shaking so badly the king reached over to still them. "Who's it from?"

"My uncle Zekar."

She skimmed the letter, giving little moans, leaving the king to grunt with impatience. She blinked at him through tears but she read it to him.

> To the king my lord, your servant Zekar. Good health to the king my lord. The king my lord gave orders: "All governors must raise food and fodder from the villages to support the western army." Since the revolt of my neighbouring governors I alone, together with my brother Khizqiyahu of Jerusalem, have supplied food and fodder.
> Now the army has returned to Aram and we have no defence against our neighbours. We have recruited men from our towns to defend our cities, we are not arming against the king's forces. Whatever our neighbours who hate us may say to you, we remain loyal to the king my lord. We will not, this year, be able to maintain the levy you have laid on us. It is because we have had to support the army and now we have to feed the men who defend our walls.
> I am coming in person to your city of Ninuwa to make obeisance and to demonstrate our fealty. My brother of Jerusalem is unwell and has sent his tokens with me.

Naqia broke off with a sob. "My father is ill, and it sounds as if they are not safe. Why would Zekar come so far?"

"Just read on," the king said gently, his hand stroking her arm.

> The king my lord should know that, as I reached Kharranu I learned the king's servant, Shezibanni, has been killed by the enemies of the king. His servant has requested that I

bring to his widow the weapons and tokens which his loyal troops recovered from his enemies, whom they slew.
If it please the king my lord, let the widow of Shezibanni receive the news before I bring the tokens. I am hurrying to wait upon the king my lord in Ninuwa.
Written by Zekar, governor of Lachish, the 7th of Sivan.

Naqia dropped the parchment and slumped onto a stool. When Sennacherib took her in his arms to soothe her she grew quiet. He sounded uneasy. "This death disturbs you?"

"He doesn't even use Abby's name! His own daughter! Now she's a widow with two sons, and her third child's on the way. How will she live? She saved my life, you know."

"Now, let me kiss away your tears. Be comforted. He may not know her name, you know. Like you, they know Zaqutu as Queen of Asshur but not Naqia as Zaqutu. You expect too much of your Judaean spies. But don't worry about Abby. Half Shezibanni's lands are hers, in fee for the children. He also holds some land from you, downriver from Guzana. Kukubu, it's called."

"My lord? I wonder at you. You know all those things by heart?"

"It's part of the boring bits."

"In Ninuwa I want to see Abby. I'll break the news … and can I ask her to come north with us? And then home to Kalkhu? May I? I see you nod. Thank you."

The king remained in Ninuwa, but Ataril and Naqia rode for Dur-Sharrukin, not waiting for the baggage wagons they'd commandeered for Abby's household. Unaware of the bad news from the west, Abby was puzzled but she hugged Naqia tight, for so long Naqia could feel the child in Abby's womb move.

"It's Shezibanni," Naqia blurted when Abby released her. Tears rose up so Abby could see at once from Naqia's face that an ill wind had brought her friend to her.

Turning to Ataril, Naqia asked, "You brought the parchment?" When she handed Zekar's letter to her, she saw Abby's surprise at seeing her father's handwriting.

In a moment Abby skimmed the letter before throwing it to the floor. "He'll come I suppose, but I'll not receive him."

Naqia's jaw dropped. She stared at Abby's tear-stained face. Only now did she realise that Abby too resented being given away without regret, without ceremony. *Treated like dirt, both of us*, she thought, but kept it to herself. Aloud she said, "Come, let me see how the boys have grown."

While Naqia played with the children Ataril sat with Abby over their beakers of spiced wine, telling Abby how Naqia hoped Abby and the children would go to Khanigalbat with them.

"Ataril, I know it is a great honour, but I am still acting as Governor here."

"Abby, my sister, you can leave your steward in charge as usual."

"I have heard that there is danger coming upon all of us on this side of the river."

Ataril remarked, "There is always danger, but the king's forces are much greater than those of his enemies."

"Greater than Ninuwa Central?" Abby watched Ataril's face as he struggled to give her the answer she waited for. When it came it surprised her.

"My lady will not live in Ninuwa or let Esarhaddon stay there until Nikkal-Amat is no longer a threat."

Abby refilled his beaker. "I see. But then, Ataril, who is going to remove that threat?"

"My lady, no one knows."

INTRIGUE

690-688 BCE

Chapter 14: Shemahu Finds a Refugee

Naqia found a new excuse to remain in Kalkhu even though the king wanted her in Ninuwa. To persuade her to leave her refuge he had handed over to her the decoration of his new palace at Ninuwa. For the walls Naqia had entrusted craftsmen taken from Babili to carve in bas-relief the grand entrance and the offices opening off it. Figures of scholars and priests would fill the spaces between the upper and lower lintels, 'to inspire the king's servants.' The three-metre space from floor to lower lintel would show a repeating pattern of chariots, some engaged in war and others in hunting.

They'd carve the walls of the throne room, too, where they would put the emblems of Sennacherib's kingship and his place as chief servant to the great gods. The priesthood of Asshur had drawn up the preliminary sketches, but no one trusted the Babili craftsmen because the king had destroyed their city and enslaved them. "How will I make sure they get it right?" Naqia had wailed.

"I trust you. The king had smiled straight at her. "You'll find a way."

In Ninuwa the Babili craftsmen now took their orders from Ataril's father, Nadinu. Him they could obey with their pride intact. Ataril and his father had always been regular correspondents, and now their link allowed Zaqutu to direct the decorations. When Naqia had told the king with pride how she'd managed to ensure quality and compliance without resentment, he'd responded with no more than a sour expression, muttering something about "damned men of Babili". Ataril knew he should arrange to have duties outside the palace when the king was in residence.

For the extensive women's quarters in the new palace Naqia had decided to transfer the lovely scenes from the Kalkhu frescoes, extending them with her own designs. She stayed, then, in Kalkhu. Though Kalkhu had once been the centre of the kingdom it was now a backwater. Troops regularly visited the fortress down by the gate, Fort Shalmaneser, but few people came up the steep road to the city itself. As well, the king had ordered her to be left undisturbed. The quiet soothed her but she nevertheless welcomed Shemahu's visit. The Kilizi physician who had attended her at Esarhaddon's birth often stopped and entered the city when travelling past the fort.

"Where are you off to?" she asked.

"Don't you remember? The king gave me the village of Surmarrati, so I am on my way there."

Naqia smiled. "Bring me a flagon, then, of that wonderful wine."

"Of course," Shemahu said, then he made his obeisance and left.

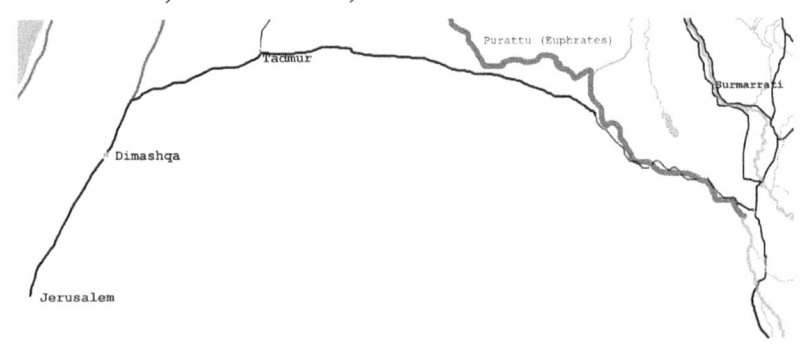

Surmarrati was a small isolated place several days' journey downriver from the Inner City. The main road to the cities of Babili followed the west bank, so the fertile eastern bank, with its prized vineyards and orchards, saw few strangers. Each spring Shemahu, as the owner of the village, came to assess the pruning, and each autumn he came to oversee the harvest and to collect his share of the produce, especially the wine.

Arriving at the gate Shemahu asked the village headman for the news and he heard of a new arrival. "How do you come to have a scribe here?"

The village headman smiled and dropped his eyes, reluctant to reply. Shemahu persisted. "I wonder how a learned man comes to live here, that's all."

The headman scuffed his sandals in the dust and looked to left and right. With a shrug, looking back at his feet, he muttered, "My lord, I do not know. You can ask him. He can tell you many things."

Shemahu frowned, but the headman pointed to the corner of the plaza. The doctor dismounted, groaning as his stiff legs hit the ground. After tying his horse to the railing outside the gate, he tiptoed across the littered courtyard. The little house, a single room but newly whitewashed, had its entrance swept and dampened to keep down the dust.

Short as he was, Shemahu had to stoop to get through the doorway.

He called out a greeting and from just inside the door an aged man, frail but dignified, returned his salutation, saying, "Peace to you," in distinct, cultured Aramaic.

"I am Shemahu of Kilizi, Father. I hear you have recently come to this village." The doctor spoke in the Asshur dialect. He understood Aramaic but rarely used it.

The old man replied in the Asshur dialect in common use in the northwest. "You heard rightly, my lord. I am Shebna ben Shaqed, newly come here from the Western Lands."

"Shebna ben Shaqed, eh? From the west? Our headman says you have tales to tell. I am fond of tales and would like you to dine with me this evening."

The old man nodded and agreed to come to the doctor's lodging at sunset.

High in the king's favour, Shemahu always found his village eager to please him. They took their best wine from store, slaughtered a young ram and roasted it on a spit. The early green herbs of the valley complemented the meat and barley simmering in the great pot on the headman's hearth.

When the men had eaten and drunk and were sitting alone in the doctor's room Shebna made a formal speech of thanks. Even using the local dialect he could be courteous and elegant, warm and yet diplomatic, not presuming on the doctor's dignity. Shemahu felt self-conscious of his own rustic manners and joked to cover his embarrassment, "So, Shebna. You have eaten and drunk. I hope now you will tell me tales to take me away from this little town to the wide lands of the west."

Shebna smiled. "All my life I have made my way by being trusted to tell only the truth, even when, sometimes, it may not please, not being what my master wishes to hear. I am no spinner of stories for amusement."

"Then tell me of your life. As a doctor I am one to learn from the truth of many lives. Please."

"You asked how I come to be here. It's an easy story to tell. Last winter, in Kislev, I set out from my own city, Jerusalem, with messages and trade goods. I brought good provision, knowing short days mean a long journey. I had plenty of water—you remember how wet it was?" Shebna raised his eyes to the doctor's face.

Shemahu lay back on the couch, eyes half-closed, ready to be amused, needing no invitation to respond and showing no curiosity about why Shebna set out in winter.

"Two days short of Tadmur my caravan was attacked; the Arabs have been …" Shebna hesitated.

The doctor stirred. "You don't have to mince words with me. Everybody knows Mushezib-Marduk couldn't keep the roads safe. Now that our king has destroyed Babili hardly any traffic passes there. Maybe in time …"

"Everyone says your king will punish all the rebels now. I heard that the king of Elam had a stroke. As soon as he stopped speaking, all the rebels he harboured took to the hills eastward. Nevertheless the western lands are still restless."

Shemahu sighed, echoing the old man's words. "Arabs are enemies and must be made to submit. They will. Their queen knows she has to give in. Those rebels—well, the king will go after them, I imagine. They say his own son is among them."

When Shemahu settled back, Shebna continued. "I had a small troop of guards, not enough. The Arabs killed some and left the rest trussed up beside the road. I've no idea why they didn't kill me. Maybe they planned to hold me for ransom—I'm too old to be sold."

"The road from Dimashqa to Tadmur is dangerous, many find trouble, not just you. For years. I know …" The doctor stopped. He wanted to hear Shebna's tale not retell his own gossip. "So, they held you for ransom. Then what?"

"As it happened I had left no one behind who could … or would ransom me. The Arabs wouldn't wait. They let me go, with a camel and a bag of food. They're not barbarians." Shebna paused, as if wondering whether he should soften his language. "Of course I know you are no friend of the Arabs, not that I know you personally. But I have written so many letters here for local householders furious about marauding Arabs."

"How did you survive? I've heard of that lonely road, and in winter?"

Shebna laughed bitterly. "As always, by my wits. Villagers don't bother to rob a poor old man, but many want charms prepared or letters written. Also I collected news of the wars in the east and worked them into songs. You, from Asshur, may not realise …" Shebna bit his lip and looked over at Shemahu.

"Not realise what?"

"The wars of these last five years—it's as if the hero Gilgamesh himself had come again to set order in the lands."

The doctor's eyes opened and he peered through the growing darkness at Shebna's face.

Shebna explained. "I mean, it's a heroic story. Asshur triumphing over the kings of Elam, one after the other, then trouncing the upstarts of Bit-Yakin. A good story. Sennacherib is a hero to the peoples of these lands and to the people of the lands northwest of here. A great hero as long as he's far away in the east, kept busy on the battlefield.

My hearers wasted no tears over the troubles of Babili." Shebna's voice remained cool and detached, free of both sarcasm and enthusiasm.

Then it dropped to a whisper. "So, I survived, slowly following the river into Suru. That's where I came to grief; in Sapirrutu my camel died. Reduced to begging for food, I gave up hope and sat in the gate of the town, waiting for death to come upon me. I've never been a religious man, never went in for prayers or omens except for reasons of diplomacy."

Shemahu sighed. "Ah! I wondered. Now I know. That's it. You've been an envoy—that explains your language and ... your cultivation. How it is that no one would ransom you?"

Shebna shook his head, looking down at his hands. "I left them."

"Oh? Why?"

"It sometimes happens. You get to a point ... I served the king's mother. She ... I had to stand by while she ... it's better to leave, find another office to hold. I've known it more than once."

Shemahu, sensitive to Shebna's reserve, smiled reassuringly. "The bearer of ill tidings gets no reward, I know that. But you were telling me of your journey."

The old man nodded and held his peace for moment, appearing to recall where he'd left off. He studied Shemahu as if trying to guess where the doctor fittted into things. But he continued. "A woman came to me in the gate, a woman from Samaria. Somehow, and I'll never know how, after more than thirty years, she recognised me. Asked my name. She'd been settled in Sippar as a girl and she'd prospered."

"A woman? Prospering? How? Hungry soldiers plunder the farms, even as far as Khallule, just across the river. The soldiers plunder because men of Bit-Yakin don't pay their taxes time and again. When the army's rations are short-changed no one prospers. So?"

"I know that. But women are able to prosper, some women anyway. Look at your Zaqutu—she has been prospering, so I hear. Maybe you disapprove, but the woman who helped me was an Israelite woman. And, yes, a courtesan. She fed me and sheltered me. When she had to return home she gave me a mule and I set out again for Ninuwa, still carrying the messages I'd started out to deliver."

"But," Shemahu protested, "you're still here. It's been six months. Why—"

Shebna put up his hand. "My mule died here, so here I am. Superstitious people would say I wasn't meant to deliver the messages. I'm more pragmatic. Soon I'll be able to afford a new mule and then I will make my way north. Meanwhile ... well, that's my story."

The doctor sat quiet for many minutes but Shebna said no more. The doctor felt moved by the tale and said, "A good story, Shebna ben Shaqed. I guess there is more, much more, you might tell. But, look here. I am riding north tomorrow, beginning as soon as they've loaded my wagon. I cannot offer you a mule but you're welcome to join the wineskins and sacks of dried fruit in my wagon."

Shebna got to his feet and straightened his back before walking up to Shemahu's couch and making a proper obeisance, his forehead touching the floor. "Your servant. I will try to amuse you on the journey, though I have told you I am no storyteller."

Chapter 15: The Two Men Journey North

The next day the men started north, the servant on the mule, Shemahu riding beside the wagon piled high with goods and the frail old man on top. They talked little on the road. In the midday heat anyone who opened his mouth to speak got a coating of fine white powder on tongue and palate.

On the third evening they reached Sinnu on the lower Zaba and stopped before dark, expecting to get across in the morning. Officials welcomed them into the caravanserai warmly, possibly because no other travellers had yet arrived. They bathed, washing their filthy tunics, and Shemahu shared his pot of ointment so Shebna could anoint his scaly, sunburned face and arms.

At the evening meal they found the table crowded. Errand runners and drovers, merchants and slaves babbled in the local dialect. Shemahu sniffed with distaste. He thought them ill-mannered riffraff, bandying crude jokes, especially about the latest Akitu festival where Sennacherib's son Shumu-Etli had made himself a laughing stock.

By now the men acted in sympathy, as friends, and in their sleeping quarters Shebna mused aloud on the stubbornness of the people of Babili, their resistance to accepting anyone from Asshur as king in Babili. "Like Gilgamesh, Sennacherib wins great victory and then ..."

Shemahu, still smarting from the crude jokes over dinner, objected. "The king had to defeat Elam to avenge Nadin-shumi his son!"

Shebna nodded, but went on, "It's not just that. If the king wars in the west, the east rises up and it seems as though Elam started the rebellion." He gestured to Shemahu not to interrupt. "I know Bit-Yakin's men think they're entitled to rule all the Mat Akkadi—they think they're safe because their marshes protect them from Asshur. Is it true that Bit-Yakin rebelled because the king gave the village of Deru to a concubine instead of to their governor? I know he has been bestowing villages and even provinces on his wife."

"Well ..." Shemahu's lips tightened. He disliked the way men cheapened everything. "No, Elam harboured the rebel, Marduk-Baladan. Our king must crush such rebellion."

"And it seems he succeeded only because kings of Elam kept dying suddenly. Does he poison them, do you think?"

Shemahu wondered at Shebna's accusation. "Are you joking? The gods punished them."

"The gods? I heard that Hallusu's rival, Kudur, sent men to murder him."

"And Kudur was killed within the year. The gods punish regicide."

Shebna made an apology, but continued, "In my telling Sennacherib is a hero, and I make the former king, Umman-Menanu, his worthy opponent, his Enkidu. Like a wrestling match, the Elamite king got a fall when he took Sennacherib's eldest son off the throne and set up a new king of Babili."

Shemahu snorted. "New king? He was useless A weakling. Running away and hiding, escaping into their marshes."

"That was the uncle. Still, Elam dominated all those years and kept their chosen man on the throne until this year. I suppose you say it's the gods who afflicted the Elamite king with paralysis, as if the gods were fighting for your king. I tell it as a tragedy—the hero loses his best enemy, the only man who could stand up to him. I think …"

"Yes?" Shemahu wanted to hear more, He was still puzzled over who Shebna might be. *He knows so much about these things.*

"I think—but this is a story—if Umman-Menanu is like Enkidu, then his death sends his friend, his Gilgamesh, mad. You may think me disloyal, but Sennacherib's treatment of Babili—I see that as an act of madness. That long siege, the plundering of homes and temples and warehouses, the destruction of the buildings, even of the walls. Even using the canal he'd upgraded for them not many years before to flood the whole city." Shebna paused and looked over at his companion.

"It wouldn't be diplomatic to tell that story in Asshur," the doctor observed.

Shebna nodded his agreement. "Often I have seen it: a great king is not followed by another great king. Sennacherib is a great king, but not lucky in his sons." This time Shebna sounded sorrowful rather than gloating.

Shemahu sighed. "As Queen Mother Atalia chose Zaza. His mother's choice but Zaza bore the king useless sons. The eldest, Arda-Mulissi, has acted like a wild man. Still, many side with him, not liking the way the king sent his wife away."

"I've heard her sister is one of them and that she rules Ninuwa."

"That's a bit strong. She has money, and power, but …" Shemahu couldn't think what to say.

Shebna finished his friend's statement. "But she hasn't got as many troops. The king rules by his army, and his wits. He's smarter than Gilgamesh, I imagine. His sons are not."

"Well—" Shemahu lifted his eyebrows "—you know they offered Shumu-Etli, Zaza's second son, to act the king at an Akitu festival. I wasn't there, but …"

"He couldn't get it up, if I understood that dialect properly."

Shemahu laughed. "Shebna, you understand all the dialects. I've noticed. But you're tactful—so tactful—I suppose it's just habit, is it?"

"You could say that."

The doctor continued, "Yes, well, I heard from a temple-warden that Shumu-Etli hasn't got much of an organ and is rather shy about it and … the priests tried to … help."

"Don't they always do that? I mean, usually they send the women to help him get the first shot out of the way so when he goes into the booth … do they have booths at the Akitu?"

"Booths? That's what you call the bed? The sacred marriage requires a bed. In the house they pile up twigs from scented trees—you know, cedar and cypress and balsam. And whatever blossoms they can find. Over it they spread drapes of scented linen. When the king and queen are … engaged … It's up on a platform. You see the movement of the branches but not the sex itself. But Shumu-Etli … I guess he wouldn't let the priests at him, or the women. He wouldn't strip off, and everyone expects the king to go naked to the bed where the goddess awaits him. It's supposed to be like Tammuz who comes to Ishtar naked and erect."

Shebna added his gossip. "The way I heard it, Shumu-Etli wore his robe all through the ritual, all the hymns and that chanting they do. But, as we heard them saying this evening, no bouncing, no crying out from the priestess, an experienced woman. So I don't think the king will set that son on a throne."

Shemahu agreed. "He'll never celebrate an Akitu festival in Babili. Even if the king sent their gods back, they'd not stand for Shumu-Etli as king. It's embarrassing all round."

"But the king has other sons."

Shemahu shook his head. "None yet old enough to become Crown Prince."

"Didn't Zaza have a third son?"

Shemahu snorted and circled his finger around his ear, "A dimwit, that one. I'm sleepy," he said and began rummaging through his pack.

Next evening Shebna opened the conversation. "My good friend, we have covered so much ground together. We have talked of so many things." He ran his tongue over his lips and went on, "Shemahu, may I ask you a personal question?"

Shemahu chortled. "My friend, you have amused me with your tales. I am filled with wonder at the adventures you have had. You have dealt with our king, and with his father, and with his father's ... cousin. I see you are old, but to think of you meeting all of them. That's four kings back. You seem to come out of one of those old tales." He laughed as he looked at Shebna. "No, you're no Gilgamesh fighting wild men and beasts. As you tell it, you talk them into submission. And I can see you're no Enkidu either—you're a smooth man, not a hairy one. Yet you play down your own part. I imagine you do yourself a disservice." The doctor's voice trailed off; he'd forgotten what he'd meant to say. "Oh—so, yes. Ask away."

Just then maidservants appeared with trays of food. Both men drew deep breaths to absorb the aromas of stewed pigeon and buttered millet. Here, at the centre of the kingdom, vast gardens of fruits and melons grew. A stew of vetches and herbs gathered from the riverbanks simmered, larded with nuts and dried summer fruits from the previous year's store. Neither man spoke for a long time. After they had filled their bellies they sipped a cool sweet wine. Shemahu looked across at the old man, so fastidious in his eating, his fingers oily only at their tips. He wiped his own hands across the napkin that had covered the bowls of food and leaned back with a sigh. "You wanted to ask something?"

Shebna shifted to his other side on the couch and curled his knees up to his chest. Looking over at the doctor, he nodded. "It's my curiosity. You have told me so many tales of the land of the Khabruri, and in your tone of voice I hear great loyalty and affection for that country."

"I have always lived there, and my father and my father's fathers."

"So I wonder how you come to be in Surmarrati, so very far south?"

Shemahu hesitated. "It's not easy to explain."

Shebna hurried to assure him, "You needn't explain. I'm curious because ... so many things have happened that seem to me as if fate plays games with me. I ... you know, I am a man who doubts every word spoken by the priests." Shebna stopped, as one who has already said more than one should. "I have seen, often, how the priest's oracle, spoken as the word of a god, so perfectly suits the priest's purpose."

"Ah." The doctor nodded. "You wonder whether someone's purpose sent me to rescue you from Surmarrati."

Shebna returned his smile with a gentle nod of agreement.

Shemahu shook his head. "No, I can't think so. It's almost eight years since I bought the vineyard." He realised he hadn't answered Shebna's question. "Why Surmarrati? That's what you want to know?"

Without waiting for a response he began, "The road that runs through Kilizi is only the way to Arrapha or into the mountains, and Kilizi is just a small town. I follow in the footsteps of my fathers to be its physician. Over the years our family's small estate became absorbed into other families' holdings. Neither rich nor poor, I held no office, only a small landholder of our town and our country. I'd never have had any estates or vineyards if it hadn't been for ..."

Shemahu stopped. *Shebna made light of the gods and showed a belief in blind chance, that it could explain everything. Fate, he called it.* "You see, I believe the Goddess Ishtar ..." He bit his lip, but Shebna waited politely. "Here's how it went. I supply medicine to the Mother at Arbail, the temple of Ishtar. Three days after the new moon of Elul, eight years ago, I went there. Perhaps you know little of the rites. At the end of Elul all the devotees fast for three days and then, at the new moon, they celebrate the old-fashioned Autumn New Year." Shemahu hesitated. "No one except the initiates know what goes on, but, over the years I've made some guesses."

Shebna observed, "I have always loved songs and poems. Many tell how the Goddess dies and comes back to life. Yet I can't imagine what part your medicine plays in that."

Though Shebna's tone remained calm and level, with no trace of mockery, Shemahu bridled. He pursed his lips and thought several minutes before he spoke. "They fast, they become faint. They mourn the Goddess so sometimes they hurt themselves. Sometimes the wounds, being serious, need simples or ointments. I serve the devotees; the Goddess doesn't require my medicine."

"You said Ishtar helped you."

"No, not me, but the Goddess surely willed what happened. I benefited." Shemahu sniffed, shifted his position on the divan. "Years ago. A woman, a girl really, from your part of the world. She came to be dedicated to Ishtar of Arbail. She'd been betrothed to Arda-Mulissi but ... the boy rebelled." Shemahu noticed Shebna nodding. "You'll know all about that."

"Not all, I suspect. We know of Arda's rebellion." Shebna chuckled. "Any rebellion in Ninuwa interests all the provinces ..." When Shemahu cocked his head, obviously hoping for another tale, Shebna smiled. "They think about not having to pay levies. I never heard about a girl."

"Arda-Mulissi stormed the king's palace to take her, not knowing she'd gone to Arbail. The king disowned him, drove him into exile. We've talked about those troubles."

"Yes, the Elamites harboured him for years. Why hasn't Sennacherib killed him?"

"Not caught him yet, not even after all these years." Shemahu gestured towards the east though Shebna, inside at night, couldn't know which way his friend pointed.

"The girl, you haven't named her. Is she Naqia?"

Shemahu nodded and reached for a second lamp to give them more light. "They call her Zaqutu in Ninuwa. It's how we say 'innocence' which is what 'Naqia' means, isn't it?"

Chapter 16: Shebna's Errand

A long silence fell between the men. Shebna's hands clenched tight in his lap. Slowly he relaxed them finger by finger. His surprise and excitement were too acute to hide. Shebna looked over at the doctor, unable to conceal his eagerness.

The doctor broke the tense silence. "You know her? You've met her?"

"I have been her mother's confidential adviser for nearly twenty-five years. So, yes, I knew her in the womb. My errand ... I seek her."

Shebna then asked the doctor to continue telling his story. "I want to know everything that concerns her. We last saw her six years ago at her brother's enthronement, heavily veiled, only one eunuch in attendance." Unable to control his voice now, he hissed, "Where is she? How is she? You mentioned Zaqutu." Ashamed of such blunt, urgent questionings, but desperate for Shemahu's information, he asked, "How does her story become your story?"

No longer the cool diplomat Shebna pressed Shemahu to continue. What little light was left in the evening concealed the men's faces from one another. Shebna relaxed only after the doctor reached over to comfort him, patting his hand.

"Zaqutu spends the summer months at Kalkhu. She has persuaded the king to let his generals fight the battles so he can focus his energies on planting trees and digging more canals and dallying with her in their pleasure garden. That's where she is." The doctor stopped speaking.

Shebna's hands twitched and his breathing had speeded up. Fearing the agitation might kill him, the doctor reached over to offer him a bit more wine.

The doctor spoke slowly. "How she is? Well, pregnant. Always, it seems, pregnant. She hopes and hopes but loses each child. Still the king loves her and treats her as principal wife. She'd be Queen Consort if ..." Shemahu stopped, catching sight of Shebna's face.

Shebna swayed as if in a faint, muttering, "Zaqutu!" He lay back against the cushions of his couch, breathing very slowly.

The doctor asked, "Are you well? What is it?"

Shebna sat forward and let out a long sigh. "We thought he'd married her to one of his lesser by-blows. No one guessed. Veiled and so quiet. None of us … we ignored her." Shebna couldn't quite recover his equilibrium. "Your news puts a very different light on my errand." He smoothed his beard before standing up and pacing from one end of the small room to the other, and back again. His steps slowed after a few turnings and he sat back down, took his friend's hand and urged him to go on with his story.

"In the third week of Elul, the year of Nabu-Duru-Utsur, I'd come to the temple storehouse with the Mother and two of the priestesses. Zaqutu, your Naqia, had come to celebrate with the other devotees. Such a tiny girl, pregnant with her first child, she looked about eight months gone but it cannot have been. Barely seven months I now believe."

"You believe?"

"You see at the previous autumn festival she was definitely a virgin, initiated into the mysteries of the Goddess. The king stayed with the army until well into Tebet so she shouldn't have given birth until a month or two after the autumn New Year.

"Right there in the storeroom as we sorted through the phials we heard Naqia gasp as her waters broke. We were in a little narrow closet next to the sanctuary where she'd been praying. Even I, having to act as midwife, and …" Shemahu stopped.

Shebna felt rather than heard the awe and wonder the doctor tried to express.

"You have to understand, Shebna, there we all were crouched on the floor, at the feet of the goddess, her image standing high above us. I—who am no fit person—knelt there holding the girl's shoulders as she moaned and shuddered, and I swear to you the Goddess bent forward and tapped the girl with her rod. The long chains of beads that she—the Goddess, I mean—wears around her neck and down over her breasts, they rattled. I heard it. Then that tiny little piece of flesh popped out into the priestess's hands and the girl swooned. I rushed into the storeroom and the other priestess there handed me cloths and one of my own tinctures to bring people out of fainting or trance. None of us expected anything other than a stillborn child.

"I watched in astonishment as Ahat-Abisha took hold of the little thing, turned it upside down and squeezed him between her hands. A gurgle came from him, a cough and then she put him to her breast. She suckled him as if on Ishtar's own breasts. So Esarhaddon has truly suckled the breast of the Goddess." Shemahu's voice grew even more indistinct with awe.

"I've since talked to several midwives. They say it cannot have happened that way. So little, so early, and nevertheless sucking. But I saw it and, I suppose you know, the boy ranks as the king's favourite."

"And Naqia? She obviously survived. Is she well?"

"How can you ask? The Goddess touched her! She blossoms like a flower, growing stronger and more beautiful every year. And wise and good, too."

Shebna murmured, "You sound fond of her."

Shemahu nodded and then shrugged. "That's my story. You must have heard about the trouble later. Arda-Mulissi's faction made out that Zaqutu had taken a lover before the king took her. Impossible! She lived in the temple, her only male companion a eunuch! A man from Babili who'd never lie. Every devotee of Ishtar knows …"

"And you? You vouched for her?" Shebna watched as the doctor gave a quick denial.

"The king favoured me because he said I'd saved the life of his son, gave me the title of physician to the boy. I insisted Ahat-Abisha had really saved the child. She did, she nursed him alongside her own daughter until Zaqutu recovered. I know Ishtar did it but the king credited me with her healing, awarded me a village in Khabruri and quite a lot of silver. I used some to buy my vineyard down south, where vines yield sweet grapes and fruits grow large and fine. I visit the village … well, you know that. That's how I found you."

Shebna stood up and bowed to his host. "Your story has thrilled me. I never thought it would be so … important. Though so many months have passed I still must get my news to your Zaqutu. Can you suggest how I might do that?"

"If she wants to see you, you'll have no problem. Tomorrow we'll come near Asshur and I'll ask the High Steward of the Inner City. You can't go directly to Kalkhu—that's forbidden—but he'll give you a passport to Ninuwa, to the Grand Vizier."

"My friend, I am already so greatly in your debt. How ever shall I repay you?"

"No need, only commend me to my lady Zaqutu, and to Ataril—he's the eunuch. It's hard for him these days; men of Babili are not well-treated in the lands of Asshur. No one trusts them now." Shemahu got up to prepare himself for sleep.

Chapter 17: Shebna Joins Naqia's Household

At the Ninuwa gate Shebna presented his passport and the guard ushered him across the bridge to the main city gate. There the wardens offered him water and bread but wouldn't let him through. Weary from five days' riding, he dozed in the afternoon sun and woke with a start when an old eunuch spoke. "Shebna ben Shaqed?"

He staggered to his feet, bowed and replied, "Your servant is here."

"The Grand Vizier sends you his compliments. He remembers your name from the Lachish dispatches, and asks me to say he feels sorry you have come out of your way. Here's a passport to Kalkhu and a letter to Ataril, chief eunuch there. Just around the corner of the wall you will find the South Road staging post. There your lodging and meals have been ordered. You will find there, as well, a satchel of leather the vizier wishes you to deliver."

Shebna bowed again, wondering at both the hospitality and the request. He had no idea what Shemahu had put in his letter of recommendation. "Your servant is filled with gratitude at your kindness and, not least, at the confidence shown in me. I shall do as your master asks. You have commended me to this Ataril?"

The old eunuch sniffed.

Shebna asked, "Is he ... trustworthy? I have heard he is a man of Babili, one of their nobles."

"His father was a priest of Nabu there,"

"Was he ... did he die when they punished the city? Perhaps I shouldn't ask but ..."

"Ataril brought news to the king, news from his father, that helped the king. The king has made a place in the Nabu temple in Asshur for Nadinu. Ataril serves the lady Zaqutu and has the king's trust. You will be safe."

The next morning Shebna left very early, to get most of the way to the village where they had arranged his stopover before the heat of the day would overwhelm him. The well-travelled road stretched

Shebna Joins Naqia's Household

level and straight before him. Every mile or so he found tents offering refreshments to travellers and displaying crafted goods. In one he caught sight of a Judaean-style amulet, crudely made but, in its way, charming. A gift for Naqia.

Then, only after he had put it in his money-pouch, did his stomach sink with dread. *How foolish to think a woman of Naqia's status, who might become queen of the world, would want a cheap bauble like that.* As he rode along, the pouch bouncing against his hip, he changed his mind. He'd be appearing as a helpless suppliant not as a rich, important envoy. He imagined saying, 'I can offer you no more than this poor thing, my lady.' His mind veered off, wondering what she'd be like. *In her twenties now. A woman of Judah, though nearly half her life had been in Ninuwa.*

As he rode on he slipped into a reverie; the mule knew the way and just kept plodding along. Nearing the end of his errand he found doubts rising up in his mind. *Did she still respect and admire her mother as she once had? Or had she? She had perfect manners, he recalled. They'd fostered her with Yoldah ... she'd not spent that much time with her mother.*

He sighed. *In no way can I hide my being a fugitive from her mother. If she chooses to have me charged with treason and killed, well ...* Tears welled up in the old man's eyes. Despite all his previous difficulties he'd not yet sunk to feeling sorry for himself, yet now he almost blubbered.

Before the sun reached its zenith and the shade of the west wall of Kalkhu disappeared, Ataril's servant took three sets of clay tablets for Babili out to the gate. When the post-horse from Ninuwa arrived he handed them over to add to the rider's bundle. Urgent, from the Grand Vizier, the rider exclaimed as he held out a fragment of parchment.

When Ataril opened the message he stared. *A Judaean diplomat to see Zaqutu in person? And alone? No, that wouldn't do. He'd have to arrange something.* Naqia paid little attention to such niceties these days. She was so absorbed in planning the decorations for Sennacherib's new palace in Ninuwa. *I had better intercept him; he cannot see her alone. And I need to know what his business might be. I wonder how he got permission to come here?*

When Shebna arrived in Kalkhu, Ataril sat him in the outer courtyard because, he explained, he must find his mistress and consult her. Shebna made an obeisance and settled himself on a low bench, his eyes closed, his chin on his chest. Ataril threaded his way through the passages to the old throne room where he knew he'd find Naqia copying the frescoes. Section by section of the walls Naqia would overlay with a stiffened fabric of fine linen mesh; onto the linen she and her women then traced each line and each colour. Ladders and rolls of cloth littered the floor spaces, everyone except her women excluded.

Ataril stood in the doorway and called her. She and Annabel each stood at the top of the highest ladders and Naqia didn't turn her head. "What is it?" she demanded.

"An audience. An old man, from Judah he says, seeks a private audience with you."

"I'm busy."

"I can see that. I cannot allow him to be alone with you in any case. What do you want me to do?"

"Bring him here. He can talk to me here. Give him refreshment and talk with him yourself until the sixth hour. By then we'll be down to the short ladders."

Ataril ushered Shebna into his own rooms. The chamber, which opened off the entrance to the women's rooms, sported two latticed windows overlooking the olive groves stretching down the slope. The eunuch's ascetic taste showed in the bare whitewashed walls that reflected the light from the windows and the plain couches covered in rough unbleached woollen cloth.

"Zaqutu has asked me to offer you refreshment," Ataril began. "We have some fine southern wines here from the Tubliash region, so highly prized that we have had to defend them from Elam for many years now." He chuckled. "Strong and sweet, they have unsettled many kings. We servants seem better able to withstand their temptation. Will you join me?"

"I will, and I thank you for your hospitality. I tasted southern wines myself, when I stayed in Surmarrati."

Ataril looked over at the thin man. His pale bald head contrasted with his face, burned by the sun, deeply furrowed with wrinkles where his white beard didn't hide them. Yet he sat straight and looked wiry and tough. His appearance didn't match his voice, low-pitched and sonorous, or his words, precise and cultivated. The man must have been a courtier yet he came without credentials. Not knowing how to place him, the eunuch spoke with polite gravity, "Were you long in Surmarrati?"

Shebna looked up, his head to one side. He turned to face Ataril smiling. "My lord, I guess that Shemahu has not preceded me here with his story."

"Quite right. No one comes here. Zaqutu occupies Kalkhu and the king makes it his summer retreat when he's not in the field." Ataril kept his matter-of-fact tone as he asked, "Shemahu? The Kilizi physician?"

Shebna nodded and then asked, "In the field? I had not heard of any battles. Shemahu mentioned that ..." Shebna stopped. Ataril saw him flustered, and wondered. *Is he afraid to talk about Shemahu? Why? Impossible to think of the physician as disloyal.*

"We're at peace, may the great gods all be praised." Ataril's lips curled at the word peace but he kept his voice level. After a brief pause he held his wine beaker up towards Shebna and they drank. "My lord the king is in the field, nevertheless. He is ... I almost said obsessed, but I mustn't be disloyal."

Shebna listened carefully to Ataril's words to guess from them how the eunuch felt abut the king. Ataril made a point of praising Sennacherib, telling how the king had turned his energies and his mathematical genius to construction and canals.

The conversation limped on, hampered because each man felt uncertain what common ground they might share. The sound of women's voices drifted in, distracting the younger man. Though as chief eunuch he managed hundreds of servants, he himself stayed attuned to Naqia and her needs.

When the men's silence grew oppressive, Ataril began, "My friend."

Shebna looked at him and replied, "You do me honour."

"We may speak of the business at hand, the errand that has brought you here. For what reason I do not know, you have come and asked for a private audience with my lady. That's not possible. I will explain that to you, but first I need to know more of yourself, whom you serve, why you have come. I need to understand how you arrived here where no one may come."

Shebna did not reply at once. "I do not truly understand myself—I mean how I got here. I know why I started out and what I meant to do, but months have passed, months when I have been ..." Shebna hesitated. Such words as these seemed pretentious for a beggar such as himself. "Not for many years have I been so disconnected from affairs. When I began my errand I thought I had a simple mission and that once I had discharged it I would know what to do next. Arabs waylaid me on the road and since then I have been tossed about by fate. Shemahu would say it must be the will of the gods. I ..."

Shebna pursed his lips and looked across at the young eunuch who sipped from his beaker. At the same moment they reached for salted almonds and sweet dates. The smell of baking bread came to their nostrils together with rattles and shouts from the servants working in the Governor's Palace next door.

"The good doctor found and befriended me in Surmarrati. He believes the gods arrange every single event. For myself I am more sceptical." Shebna stopped there.

Ataril responded with careful tact. "Our scholars, even those wise men who study the gods and their ways, are often—as you say—sceptical."

"And you?" Shebna asked.

"I serve the goddess Ishtar; my life belongs to her. Nevertheless I understand your doubt about whether fate governs everything that happens to you." Ataril paused and looked fixedly at his visitor.

Obviously the wine and the restful couch soothed him. As Ataril examined him, Shebna's face relaxed. The westering sun now shone through the lattice, making a slowly changing pattern of shapes on the bare wall. When Ataril shifted his weight on his own couch, Shebna saw he must respond.

"You want to know whom I serve. I wish I could refuse to answer, at least until I have told Naqia the news I bring." Shebna looked straight into the young man's eyes, smiling grimly. "But you can refuse to let me speak to her."

Ataril nodded.

Shebna continued, "I have nothing, no advantage to offer to persuade you. I am but a beggar and of little use. Perhaps you will decide to ask me to leave." Shebna lowered his eyes.

The eunuch straightened up and, his tone pompous, declared, "I believe every man is of use, though not every man consents to be useful." Shebna made no response. "I can reassure you that she knows you have come and that she has asked only to finish her work before hearing you. I would have to answer to her if I sent you away." Ataril shifted his weight again as if to stand up, but then leaned back against the wall, the patterned sunlight playing over his beardless cheeks. "If you know her, you know I do not lightly cross her will. I am her servant though the king's orders control me as well. You cannot see her alone, and I will certainly hear what you tell her. So you may tell."

Shebna said, "I serve no one. I served Naqia's mother much as you serve her daughter. She used me to plan and carry out most of her policies. No, all of her policies until …" At this point Shebna's voice had dropped to a whisper.

"Until she sent you here?" There was a pause.

How can I explain? Shebna thought. *He must wonder why Judah's queen didn't send a younger man. When I tell him he'll wonder, too, why I'd take such risks.* "Until I left her service." Shebna screwed up his courage to answer.

"So you'll speak about Judah's policies?" Ataril's voice wavered, he didn't conceal his doubt of Shebna's veracity and his motives.

Shebna nodded but kept silent. Ataril asked "Have you betrayed her, Judah's Queen Mother?"

Shebna Joins Naqia's Household

"I left her, without leave and without warning. I took nothing that was not my own, and that ... well, the Arabs had it all. Until now I have not spoken of her or her plans to anyone, so I believe I have not betrayed her."

"Why have you come here?"

"Outside my own country every court is subject to Asshur's king." Shebna gave a short laugh. "Except Egypt. But, in my mistress's service, I've disappointed any official of importance there." Shebna hesitated. "Since my mistress's policy has been to adhere closely to Asshur, only here am I not in danger."

"Danger?"

"Am I being too melodramatic? Yes. No, our Queen Mother makes it her business to cause offence to every one of her neighbours, most often using me as the agent of the deed or of the news of it." Shebna's eyes fell to the floor, mirroring the abject tone of his voice.

Ataril turned to the door where Annabel stood, her stained hands grasped together under her apron. "Yes? Are you on the floor yet?" Ataril asked the young woman. She nodded, so he turned to Shebna. "We're not allowed into the women's workrooms, but we will sit in the doorway and speak with them."

When they arrived at the entryway Shebna addressed Naqia in Judaean, expecting that only he and she spoke that language so what he had to say would still be private. "Peace be with you, Shebna," she replied, adding how pleased she would be to hear tidings of her family and her native land.

"My lady." He stood up from his deep obeisance. It seemed unnecessary as she stood on a short ladder with her feet at the level of his shoulders, facing away from him, busy with tracing. "I bring you news that may not seem ... that may not be welcome."

"If everything goes well, I think, we never hear news."

"A wise observation."

"Do you bring greetings from my mother?" Naqia asked coolly but politely.

"First I must tell you, she does not know I have come here. She may guess that I headed here when she found me gone, but she will have heard nothing since."

Naqia turned her face to look at him, swaying a little on the ladder, making the woman holding the base cluck with worry. "What happened? Have you quarrelled with her?"

"Not openly. I ... I sided with your father ..."

"How is he? I hear nothing of Judah, you know."

"My lady, I have said I bring evil news. But they look after your father well. He's gone to Zekar in Lachish."

Naqia faced the wall, and asked, her voice still cool, "Is the kingdom run from Lachish then?"

"Your mother has the seal, your brother Manasseh rules in Jerusalem."

"Manasseh?"

"Yesha has prophesied … a new name has been spoken for your brother, his old name lifted off."

"So Yesha still lives—that's good to hear. He must be very old now. Is he well?"

"My lady, you know that your mother had many differences with the prophet. He often pulled her up short, disapproved of her decisions."

"Shebna, I know my mother made many poor choices. Don't try to soften your words and don't try to mislead me. I am no gullible child. Qat sent me off as part of a bevy of slave women, with no escort and no means to keep up any position. I nearly died as a result. You need not be afraid to criticise my mother to me." Naqia swayed on the ladder as she coughed to get rid of the catch in her throat. "Had the goddess not chosen me and guarded me I cannot imagine what life would have brought me. I have Ishtar and Ahat-Abisha for mother." No longer cool, Naqia's voice had hardened with a bitterness that struck Shebna with force. *She might be like her mother, but she seems to hate Qat intensely.*

Shebna felt his throat tighten; speech wouldn't come. Her women, alerted by Naqia's tone of voice, had stopped working. *I don't suppose they understand Judaean. But they can't miss such bitterness. And she's far into a pregnancy too.*

Into the silence Shebna cleared his throat. "Yesha no longer lives." He took a deep breath and coughed. "Your brother the king … my lady, please come down off the ladder. I have a gruesome story to tell. You might fall. Please come down."

Naqia did not respond at once, running her hands over the pattern she had just traced and looking down. She saw she could finish the tracing now from the floor so she stepped down the ladder and signalled to her women to take it away. They leaned it beside Annabel's against the further wall. When they had pulled a stool over to the doorway Naqia sat down heavily. The women left her and went around to their own courtyard where a bath and their evening meal awaited them.

Shebna touched his fingertips to his chest and then put his palms together in his lap. He began his story in Aramaic for Ataril's benefit. He told first of the Queen Mother's policy of alienating her neighbours. "Each time Pele, I mean Manasseh, took a new wife it seemed that Judah made a new ally. Each time a son born of that marriage came along—" Shebna cleared his throat "—she deliberately alienated each new ally: Egypt, Moab, Ammon, Aram, Sidon. One after another she'd get one of their daughters for her son's wife, and then each time they bore a son she'd offer it, a sacrifice to Melek."

"Sacrificed? Didn't the people object?" Naqia spoke in Aramaic but stopped at Ataril's gasp of surprise. She turned to him and noted his puzzlement. *I suppose he's shocked by the infant sacrifice. No, probably not. In Asshur and in Babili they routinely put substitute kings to death. It must have been my expecting the people to have a say.* She opened her mouth to speak, but no words came.

Shebna replied in Judaean. "We saw to it that Jerusalem supported her. My lady, the 'people of the land' no longer matter. Judah pays tribute to ... to your husband, not to your brother."

Naqia frowned as she listened to an inner voice, trying to recall her old life. *Jerusalem, Judah, their problems, not mine.* Lips pursed, she gazed steadily into Shebna's eyes. "So," she said guessing, "the people didn't object but Yesha did—is that it?"

"Exactly so. In fact, Yesha had retired to Lachish, but he made She'ar bring him back and they rousted your father out of his cell, pulled him out of bed and—so he told me—gave him a talking to. Together they went to confront Manasseh and ..." Shebna stopped. "Oh, my dear, that's when it began."

Turning to Ataril and speaking in Aramaic, Shebna explained. "I told you, friend, how I used to be a sceptic but that things have happened to me, things I can't explain. I first noticed it just then." He turned back to Naqia and continued. "Yesha spoke in Yahweh's name, condemning Pele. He withdrew the blessing given him at his birth. Lifted it off him, gave him the new name."

Naqia looked over at Ataril to explain. "Manasseh means, in our language, lifting up or carrying away." She waved Shebna on to continue.

"No one moved and your brother just crumpled."

"What did my mother do?"

"She wasn't there or I suppose the execution would have happened then and there."

"Execution?"

"The next morning Manasseh held a court in the gate and accused Yesha of treason. He sentenced him and executed him. My lady, I am sorry to say but they tied him to a tree and sawed him in half. Your father left the city that very day. Next day—I had to make arrangements—I too left, came here."

Naqia looked down and let a few tears fall on the floor.

Ataril broke the silence. "This Yesha, you loved him? A friend?"

"He and his wife Yoldah taught me to read and to sing and to honour God.

You often admire my herb lore. Well, Yoldah taught me, she ... all over the western lands they knew of her skill." Naqia sighed.

"Yesha was not always my friend," Shebna admitted. "On the last evening of his life, though, we sat together. Your father and I, with She'ar and Yesha, in their palace. We knew we'd come to the end, though only Yesha recognised it as his end. We talked over all the old days and we came to find many points of agreement."

A long silence followed until Ataril stirred. He spoke slowly in Aramaic, "The old days are gone now, and we have to make something of the present. My lady, Shebna has no home and no property, from what he has told me."

Naqia stood up and the two men rose. She said, "Shebna, if you will serve me you are welcome to be part of my household." To Ataril she added, "Perhaps Shebna has been modest but he can offer many talents. He is a loyal servant, known by everyone to be unwilling to betray master or mistress. He served as my mother's master-spy for many years and knows all the nations over whom my lord the king rules, their language and their customs. He would be a good tutor for Esarhaddon. Find him quarters in the Governor's Palace and let him share our meal tonight. Let it be a festive one."

Shebna made an obeisance but Naqia took the hand she had held in the small of her back and gestured to silence him. She wanted no more words now. She waddled off into a side chamber, leaving Ataril to pluck the old man's tunic, get him off his knees, and lead him backwards out of the doorway.

Behind the eunuch's reception area Ataril let Shebna enter a small walled garden surrounding a pool. Steps of polished stone led down into it. Several menservants had already stripped and were lounging in the cool water. Until the others had gone he talked to the old man about Naqia's doings, the transferring of frescoes, Sennacherib's building programme.

Certain they could not be overheard but using Aramaic for further secrecy, Ataril explained that Zaqutu had persuaded the king to let his generals carry on with the army and to devote himself to improving the circumstances of the citizenry, in particular the peoples of Asshur's heartland. "She's young, but of course she's anxious to keep the king safe and well. She's wise, or seems so. I believe the goddess gives her powerful allure and the king responds to her power, though he is not himself weak or easily swayed. Not at all. I see them as two powerful figures; they sometimes clash. We who serve them feel the tension that binds them one moment and rips them apart the next."

Shebna looked down and splashed water over his legs. "What duties will you find for me?"

"I've no idea. She spoke of you as a tutor. She'll tell me first to see if I object. Then she'll tell you. Wait and see."

"Earlier you offered to explain why no one speaks to her alone."

"It's history now, or I think so. The king feels less certain." Ataril explained that when Sennacherib divorced Zaza and married her off to a nobody, all the other wives became unsettled. "Years ago now. All except Tashmetu, the king's first wife, turned on him. Up till then she and her son, Nadin-shumi, ruled Babili and things went well. Tashmetu," he added, "decided it would be prudent to side with Naqia, giving her gifts and exchanging courtesies."

Shebna splashed water on his head and smiled. "The wars in Babili and Elam, yes, I made stories out of them to entertain the men who succoured me along my way. Sennacherib won the day. I wonder …"

Ataril shrugged and shook his head. "There's debate about that in many quarters. Babili is destroyed, but Nadin-shumi still languishes in Elam, a eunuch who can never rule either in Babili or in Asshur. 'Won the day' is an overstatement." Ataril gestured to the surroundings, the little hive of activity that contained Naqia. "The king my lord has other sons but Arda-Mulissi is a rebel. Sharrani-Muballissu well …" Ataril sniffed. "Even Shumu-Etli … no one will train them either for battle or for government. My lady's son, Esarhaddon is still young, eight years old, but the king favours him."

"I see, making him a danger to many interests. But his mother? She's not his consort—I thought Tashmetu still held that honour. Why keep the world from Naqia?"

Startled, Ataril looked to see if Shebna had made a joke. The old man's eyebrows had lifted but he didn't smile. Unable to suppress a flicker of irritation, Ataril explained, "Only on account of his mother does Esarhaddon find favour with the king."

Chapter 18: A Special Role for Shebna

In the days that followed Esarhaddon spent more and more time with Shebna who had become his tutor. Shebna learned that Ataril's reading of the situation differed from Naqia's. She was utterly certain that Esarhaddon would succeed his father as king—the Goddess had spoken and there could be no doubt. Shebna, however, had seen the boy's grandfather outside the walls of Samaria, had seen his father outside the walls of Lachish. Now he had the son questioning him, hearing him, sitting at his feet. He felt he was too old for this position—and too foreign. This was his first time as teacher and he took pains to show himself equal to the task. Each time he gave the prince new problems to solve he could recall events that it had once been his task to understand and to shape. Now he was free of those cares, and was grateful. Moreover Naqia approved of his work. She invited him to accompany them to Arbail for the feast of the New Moon.

In the township outside the temple of Ishtar at Arbail the garrison detailed to protect Naqia's household practised their manoeuvres and kept the prostitutes busy. Shebna and his three servants occupied a small house behind the arsenal. There every day he received Esarhaddon. The boy was tall for an eight-year-old, and somewhat plump, but Shebna found him a gifted student, quick and easy to motivate. "Boy, you need to know north, east and south as well as west. How shall we do that?"

"Oh," Esarhaddon responded, "I can read about those places—the archives, you know, and we get copies from everywhere."

"Good. Anyone who knows about the past can get things done in the present."

"They're writing up my father's deeds now. All the battles and kings."

"You like that, battles?"

"Oh yes." His voice fell as he spoke. "The king my father doesn't fight now—he's too busy with building, you know, fixing up Ninuwa."

"Fixing it up?" When the boy nodded Shebna gave him a quizzical look.

"Why? Tell me why your father does that."

Esarhaddon pursed his lips, thinking about the question. "Gardens. Mother wants gardens or she won't go there. That's why."

Shebna lifted his hand, put his forefinger up towards the boy's face. "You can't be serious. I hear about the works in the capital, so you must too. What is being done? Some gardens, yes, but what else?"

"You mean the New Palace? I went there last year. It's huge, and he's made a big wide street out front for a promenade—you know, when they take the gods out in procession."

"The entire levy from Khabruri and the Mat Masenni? So many men and horses and oxen and stonemasons? For a street and some gardens?" Shebna's voice was stern.

"Oh, the canals. Of course. They call Paqaha my father's right hand."

"Is that a joke, do you think?"

"No, he's the master builder of canals. Papa sees more of him, they say, than of his Grand Vizier."

"Canals, right. What of roads?"

The boy nodded.

"So you say you read the scribes' words, telling of each year of the reign. Let's work our way back. You tell me, why canals?"

"The one here?" He waited for Shebna to nod. "It brings water from the mountains where it's fresh and cool. It's cool because it runs underground. Down the road they've built one for Kilizi that has to come across the river. The mason told me how they did it. It's called an aqueduct." He sketched the foundations with a stick in the sand as he spoke.

"Have you been to see the canal that comes here?" The boy shook his head. "It's only a morning's ride from the temple; you may go after the new moon, follow the water to its source."

Esarhaddon loved visiting the engineering works so Shebna sent him off with some troops on manoeuvre near the canal.

In autumn they all returned to Kalkhu. One morning Shebna and the prince sat on a bluff looking out over the gate. Obsessed now by canals, Esarhaddon asked Shebna, "Why doesn't Kalkhu have fresh water from upstream? Why do we have to get river water and filter it all the time?"

At that moment they saw chariots wheel round the corner of the city wall and heard the trumpets at the gates.

The boy jumped up and tugged at Shebna. "Come on, it's Papa!"

Shebna struggled to his feet and followed the boy down the slope to the city gate. The soldiers who'd formed up to receive the king parted to let them pass. Shebna reached for the boy and held him out of the way as the king's party galloped in. Shebna told the boy,

"I can't tell you why you filter your water, but he can."

Seeing them, the king stopped and came down out of his chariot, hugging the boy and looking curiously at Shebna. "Papa. This is my tutor, Shebna ben Shaqed," Esarhaddon explained and, without stopping for a breath, asked his question.

Ignoring Shebna, hugging the boy to him, Sennacherib laughed. "Son, only two hundred people stay here. One thousand times that number live in Ninuwa these days. They drink a lot of water."

"But Arbail? And Kilizi?"

"There's drought there—the rivers run dry. But when we finish up north I'll get water for Kalkhu from Mount Tas. Will that please you?" He put his hand on the boy's shoulder and they walked across the plaza to the entrance to Zaqutu's orchard. Shebna observed the king's easy behaviour, the obvious warmth of his feeling for his son, and wondered. *Ataril claims it's Naqia's allure alone that draws the king. He must be blind.* Shebna turned aside to his cottage and sat on the bench at his door, listening to the calls and cries from the garrison below.

While in Kalkhu the king took his son hunting so Shebna was free to dream and doze his hours away. On the third day Zaqutu—Naqia stopped using her old name after Shebna came—sent to invite him to join her and Ataril in her apartments, an evening of food and music. Shebna smiled to himself at the luxury of her summer palace. *She plays down her importance, pretends she doesn't rule here.* This evening he couldn't take his eyes off the hanging that covered the south wall of her reception room.

To celebrate the summer's fruitfulness it portrayed a bucolic scene, with flocks of sheep and vines and fruit trees up a green hillside. The foreground showed a summerhouse, cunningly wrought, lush with decorative flourishes and filled with flowers. The centre showed a table laid with Epicurean delights. The tapestry contained no signs or words, no human figures, but a sort of tree had been worked into the background. Shebna peered, squinting, to make out some of the emblems of the gods. The tapestry absorbed him utterly. So much so that neither the silence nor the attention of his hosts registered with him. He came back from the tapestry only when Zaqutu coughed to clear her throat. "Do you like it?"

Shebna shook himself out of his trance and bowed his head to her. "My lady, my liking or not is of no matter. It is magnificent. I can see that it has deep significance though I cannot understand."

Her reply seemed off the point. "Ataril and I were up on ladders, installing that hanging, when the king my husband came back from Elam. He'd been off with the army for so long he didn't even know I'd ordered it. So long! By the time he came home we had it ready to hang." She snorted. "Up on the ladders, deep in our task, we'd not heard trumpets or anything."

Ataril squirmed. "We did hear the footsteps, we just didn't recognise them."

"Not until he stood there at the foot of the ladder did I look down ..."

Ataril laughed. "Not the first time she threw herself at him."

She coloured, her face glowing with pleasure at the memory at first. When she looked down, her lips pursed, Ataril resumed speaking. "She was no little package to catch, either, six months gone."

Shebna looked at her belly and then at Ataril's face. Zaqutu insisted, "That was the last time—a miscarriage again. Not because I jumped."

"I was so happy ... The symbols—you're clever to spot them—have a purpose. You see, there in the centre, an omphalos, the navel of the world. It means Mummu, or Ishtar, the source of life and beauty.

"Ah." Shebna stood up and went over to the wall. With his fingers he traced the sacred tree. At each place where the branches crossed he touched mysterious symbols. "These?" he asked.

"Each of the great gods, you know, has a number. In the writing of Babili a number—some of them, it means ... how shall I say?"

Ataril interrupted her. "They have the power of the god in them." Shebna said nothing, but, off his guard, he let bafflement show in his face. He turned to face the queen when she spoke, breaking the spell.

"I worried over him—the king, I mean. He went on every expedition with the army, sometimes far off too—not just in the west but up in the north and northeast. In those mountains and ... the Mandaeans there are wild." She laughed. "Unafraid, I chased him into his hall, challenging him, asking why he had generals if he always had to lead the army. He claimed the commander-in-chief couldn't be everywhere. So I said, 'Why not have another commander-in-chief then?' and he ... he'd never thought of it."

Her scorn was pretend, Shebna could hear that, and he laughed. Ataril didn't join in, didn't even smile. Feeling the tension between them, Shebna asked Ataril, "Didn't it work?"

"Oh, it worked all right for her. The king has been off the battlefield. He's divided the army ..."

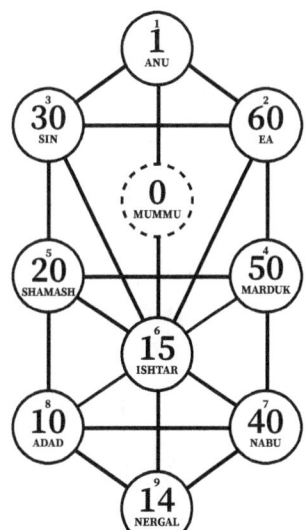

"Ataril claims the king puts all the seasoned soldiers in the north and what's left in the south …"

Interrupting again, Ataril added, "I've said they loot for pleasure, attacking friends as well as enemies. If the south remains always under pressure, always weak, they'll never accept …"

Zaqutu rushed in. "They didn't accept even when Tashmetu ruled them. They weren't pressured or weak then, but they still rebelled."

Ataril turned to Shebna. "You see we have a disagreement. I grew up in Babili—a beautiful city, rich in old stories and lore. I don't want to see it now. My father wept when he told me. We don't disagree about the king. I know he's happier to be building canals and city plazas than destroying earlier foundations."

Zaqutu brightened. "Gardens! We'll have spaces inside the city with all the plants that grow in his lands, and even some with animals, animals from far away such as we have never seen."

Ataril observed, "You complain I'm always thinking too much of Babili, but you are planning to make Ninuwa over in the likeness of Babili itself."

"Impossible. I've never been there so how could I?"

To smooth the dispute that lay under their words, Shebna asked about the dividing of the army. They disagreed about that too. Ataril's point was that when only a single army of Asshur was in the field everyone knew that Asshur fought at the head of the troops. The troops knew and so did the enemy. "Now, the divine order is … unclear," he muttered.

Shebna bit his lip, looking from one to the other. "I hear … well, the armies are both victorious."

"The king follows her." Ataril pointed at Zaqutu. "And each commander gains strength. How long will it be before they bring civil war as they compete to see who is supreme?"

"The king is, everyone knows that." Zaqutu's voice was sharp as she pulled herself to her feet and joined Shebna standing beside the tapestry, following his fingers tracing the branches of the tree. "Everything is ruled by the gods." She placed her forefinger at the centre of the picture.

"You think the hanging does it?" Shebna couldn't keep the scepticism out of his voice.

"It does." Zaqutu moved her finger to the trunk of the tree, halfway up. The background elements formed converging lines, highlighting the centrality of the point. "This is the place where Ishtar struck the huluppu, expelling Lilith, chasing off the Abzu bird and driving off the snake. Woman's power …"

"My lady," Shebna began, "I cannot doubt your words. But your power—I do know something of power. When I came here you ... you were closeted away from the world. Only your household, and but few of them, even see you. Your power draws and holds the king, but you—pardon me but I speak frankly as an old man to a young woman—you are a prisoner."

"Shebna, you are a wise man." Zaqutu laughed, fingering the double strand of beads that circled her neck and rested on the shelf of her pregnant belly, "And brave. A prisoner, while Elam supported rebels east and south, yes. Many of the king's servants ... could have joined the rebels. My son and I stayed secure in the north far from Ninuwa's magnates and from the other risks."

"Other risks?"

Zaqutu didn't reply and silence fell among them. Ataril rose and offered his arm to Shebna who stood up and made an obeisance. The men withdrew.

"I'll walk with you to the gate to clear the fumes of wine from my mind," Ataril suggested and they set out following the paths of the garden in the moonlight. "Zaqutu does not speak often about the women, the ones who came out from your country. Their deaths, unavenged, pain her."

"Deaths?"

His voice low and dispassionate, Ataril told how the hundreds of Judaean women sent to Sennacherib as tribute fell into the hands of Nikkal-Amat, the chatelaine of Ninuwa Central. "You may know how the bureaucracy grows bloated with tribute. The precious metals and stones all go into the temple treasuries, nowadays mostly down in the Inner City. But Nikkal-Amat oversees ..." Ataril couldn't disguise his sarcasm as he told the tale. "Every shipment of tribute that came to Ninuwa passed into Nikkal-Amat's hands."

"I have heard ... she ..."

"Nikkal-Amat took all the Judaeans that the king had meant to distribute among his officials as prizes. She started to market them as slaves. Before the king could intervene the women began to sicken and die. Zaqutu believes it comes from the river. Except that she sickened sooner, before she got there, she'd have been one of them."

Shebna hadn't heard how the king had rescued Naqia from Urakka, so Ataril told him. "That's why he has been endowing her, more and more each year, with villages, towns, and more than a whole province along with other northwestern towns. They are her lands."

"Ah," Shebna murmured. "I had heard he'd given them to his wife, but I didn't know which. I never ... I shouldn't have said 'prisoner' then."

Ataril reassured him that Zaqutu often called herself a prisoner, that she fretted in her safety. "She frets even more that she has not given the king another son. This child, when it comes, will be an occasion for rejoicing."

They reached Shebna's quarters and Shebna thanked the eunuch for his company.

"My cobwebs are gone," Ataril replied. "Just one more thing you may need to know. Even if the king names Esarhaddon his successor, until Nikkal-Amat is gone Zaqutu will not move him into the Succession Palace."

Chapter 19: Shebna Sees a New Prospect

Shebna dreamed alone in his rooms, little affected by the excitement of Shadditu's birth. A sister for Esarhaddon, he understood, relieved Zaqutu's despair at failing to bring her earlier pregnancies to term. He wondered what, if anything, it meant to the boy. He wondered even more that the king didn't get rid of Zaqutu's enemy, the chatelaine. In the quiet that fell upon Kalkhu after the royal family had left for Arbail, Shebna thought about Ataril's suggestion that he should write his memoirs.

Ataril had insisted, "Shemahu is correct, many of us would treasure your memories. You visited Pulu in Dimashqa, you went as envoy to Shalmaneser at Hazor. Your perspective on Sargon's subduing of the lands beside the Upper Sea would interest our older scholars, and I myself wish I could hear your tale of the king's siege warfare in the west. If you focus on the military side of things you'll give no offense. We won all the battles."

He had demurred, not wanting to make the effort, but Ataril sent to his rooms parchment and quills, scrapers and a most cunning lectern, designed so that Shebna could sit or recline and still write. To use the new piece of furniture he had begun a list of the events he could tell. He'd got no further than the capture of Hoshea when he was surprised to see Ataril himself in the doorway.

"Peace to you, Shebna," he began. "Tashmetu has asked the king to hold a council about affairs in Babili. I have been released by my lady to attend the visit in Asshur."

"You'll be able to visit your father."

Ataril nodded. "Because I will be gone, the eunuch who usually serves you will have to look after my duties here. I hope you don't mind."

Shebna smiled.

"And Esarhaddon will be yours for lessons for several weeks." Pointing to the parchment lying on the lectern, Ataril added, "Let him take your dictation. It'll bring on his Aramaic."

"Of course. But do you know how long you'll be away?"
"The king may be longer, but I'll be back after the next new moon."

The days and weeks that passed swiftly for Shebna were, for his pupil Esarhaddon, an eternity. Moaning to Zaqutu hadn't helped. She'd stroked her daughter's bald pate and, putting off her son's complaints with a snort, sent him back to Shebna's rooms.

"I'm weary, boy," Shebna muttered that afternoon. To counter the boy's boredom the old man suggested, "I've told you about the slingers. Get a sling and try some practice yourself. You'll see how hard it is to hit the target."

For days Esarhaddon practised doggedly, impressing even Shebna with his growing skill. Even so, both of them rejoiced to see Ataril and his entourage approaching the summer palace across the bleak orchard. From the west the sun lit up his face and brought out the rich colour of his new cape, dyed indigo. He walked slowly, as if weary or reluctant, and blinded by the sun's glare he jumped with surprise when they greeted him.

Later, sitting together in Ataril's anteroom huddled next to the brazier, Shebna asked, "How did things go? Your father? Is he well?"

"He is well, I am happy to say, but the temple affairs—not only in his Nabu temple, but ..." Ataril sighed. "The cities of the south are restive. When the king destroyed Babili he ..." He looked over at Shebna with eyes squinted under his frown. "The king my lord says he's king of Babili but he doesn't ... act like a king. A king would embellish temples, not strip them. A king would hold his Akitu there, not in the realm of Asshur."

Shebna nodded. "What if Tashmetu gives him another son? Would it matter if he ruled from Asshur?"

"Tashmetu grieves for Nadin-Shumi. Oh, I know he's not dead. He writes often to tell her the latest about the succession crisis in Elam. No doubt that's a great comfort to the king." Ataril let his spite show.

Shebna smoothed over the lapse. "A convenient spy. I heard that they've replaced Elam's king again. What's the new king like?"

"He's Umman, too. They call him Umman-Ha. Nadin-Shumi is certain he'll not court the men of Bit-Yakin the way the earlier kings of Elam did. But, you see, it isn't just the threat from Elam or Bit-Yakin. Tashmetu and the priests know Sennacherib won't propose Shumu-Etli as king. And, frankly, they hope not. It's hard for them. They want their gods back, they want their city restored too, but they don't want a king from Asshur."

Shebna nodded, musing, "I've heard that, like us in the west, Babili wants a grown man as king, not a boy and his mother."

"Tashmetu couldn't control Nadin-shumi—he worked against his father's interest. He was a man rather than a boy, but not very clever."

Shebna asked, "Will the king expect Esarhaddon to be king in Babili?"

Ataril's reaction surprised him. "May Ishtar not permit it! Esarhaddon will be king of the world, king in Ninuwa, to command everything. The king will beget a king for Babili on Tashmetu, whether she wants it or not." Ataril's lip curled as he added, "The king will be in the south for some months yet."

"In the meantime," Shebna asked, "what of Babili?"

"Rebellion, uprisings—I expect they'll continue."

"Is that why you don't like the idea of Esarhaddon as king in Babili?" Shebna kept his voice bland and heard, at great length, how Esarhaddon would receive the best education and become the most skilful of all the rulers that had ever been. He wondered how Ataril, from Babili, would consider Esarhaddon too good for the city.

As Ataril continued, Shebna realised that the matter wasn't about Babili. For Ataril, Ishtar had decreed it, nurtured the boy from birth. The outcome was not in any question. Shebna listened quietly. He folded his hands in his lap and regarded them thoughtfully. *Didn't Ataril know? Any son the king sired on Tashmetu would overshadow Esarhaddon, especially if Zaqutu wouldn't go to Ninuwa. Not until that chatelaine, Nikkal-Amat, was gone.* As he rose to go Shebna asked, Ataril, "Why does the king not remove Nikkal-Amat from Ninuwa? The boy should move into the Succession Palace soon, shouldn't he?"

Ataril's reply was a shock—he didn't know. "Some of his council would support him, but others ... well, maybe not. It's not worth the king's trouble, stirring up such a hornets' nest."

Shebna swayed a little, finding his balance. *Getting rid of Nikkal-Amat? Do they expect Ishtar to accomplish that?* He deplored his cynicism in silence, only murmuring thanks to Ataril as he rose to go to his own rooms.

When Shebna woke the next morning he saw his writing materials laid out. The eunuch who served him muttered something about 'clutter' and Shebna asked him to leave the chamber. Foreboding clouded his mind, his eyes wouldn't focus, and thoughts chased one another across the front of his mind. *So sure of her hold over the king, so sure Esarhaddon would succeed. Zaqutu's blind faith in the Goddess prevented her from seeing that Tashmetu's son could claim Ninuwa too. Should I speak to her about that?* So he wondered, and shivered under his heavy fleece. *If she wouldn't go and take her place, what then? She was endangering her boy and maybe didn't realise it, full of pride in her new motherhood. I've nothing to lose, I'll offer her my thoughts.*

Chapter 20: Zaqutu Sends Shebna to Ninuwa

Zaqutu smiled as she recalled Shebna's embarrassed look when she had asserted her status as blessed of Ishtar. His letter, she stopped short as she carried Shadditu to her basket. *Was he suggesting I'm blessed of Ishtar of Arbail but that in Ninuwa ... in Ninuwa I'm not? And why did he write? I see him so often—why write to ask for an audience?* She knew Shebna used court etiquette as a soldier used a sword; every stroke had to count. Her smile faded when she thought how her mother had used that diplomacy. Shebna always obeyed his master or mistress— not without question, but entirely. *If I make a wrong choice he'll carry it out. Who would stop me?* Ataril obviously liked the old man, enjoyed his civilised conversation. *I wonder if Ataril trusts him?*

She moved to her inner room, stalking around, taking a vase from stool to table, then going round the other way and putting it back. Too many things happening all around distracted her and she suspected more happened than she knew. Every change in her household upset her. Nani, her usual scribe, had gone to Asshur with the king so Baya had come from Arbail to replace him. Too twitchy to sit, she paced to the doorway and saw Baya writing in the next room. *I've got one of Ishtar's own prophets here. I'll ask Baya.* Nonetheless, as she entered the anteroom to hand Shebna's letter to the prophet a worried sigh escaped her lips.

Baya took the parchment and asked, "That's your old man, the boy's tutor?"

Zaqutu nodded. Baya read the note and gave her opinion, "I think you must hear him out. Esarhaddon will not stay a boy forever, and soon he will not be safe anywhere. Hear the old man, but keep your own counsel."

"What can I do? As soon as he is finished in Asshur—" Zaqutu smiled at her choice of words "—the king my lord will take us to Ninuwa. Will he get Tashmetu with child, do you think?"

Baya simply refused to answer, explaining that she had no vision from the Goddess. Instead she repeated the concern everyone felt. "Even if she gets a son, the people of Babili will continue to resent the king my lord for his vindictiveness. Some priests from Babili, I hear, court the new king of Elam. They call him Humban-Haltesh. I hear too that Zaza's son has been sighted in Elam. If Arda-Mulissi gets support from Elam and from the nobles of Babili he could be unstoppable." Baya shook the parchment gently and sighed. "I'll write a reply."

> To Shebna ben Shaqed: Baya of Arbail. May Ishtar bless your thoughts and words. My lady has received your letter and hopes you will join her women at the time of the evening meal. Bring your pupil with you.

The setting sun made a yellow reflection off the bark of the trees that lined the path from Shebna's rooms to the summer palace. For seven winters Zaqutu had resolutely occupied the old capital of Kalkhu instead of accompanying the king to Ninuwa. *She'd regret leaving*, he supposed, *a place full of happy memories*. With a wry smile he felt a softening within, as if tears would come soon. The paths wound between shrubs from all over the world. She'd gathered flowering bushes, trees and fruiting shrubs, transforming the royal enclosure. He mused on the meeting to come. *Qat's daughter, like her mother, strong-minded ... how to put the case?*

She stood to greet him, held his hands in hers so he couldn't even make an obeisance. "This is a war council. We will eat." She looked behind him. "Where's Esarhaddon?"

"Forgive, my lady. He preferred to go out for a ride with his new chariot driver. Here's his message." After he had passed over the wax tablet, Shebna greeted Baya and the women.

Zaqutu chortled as she told them, "So the boy's not afraid. Of course he isn't. He knows nothing about it."

"Perhaps, my lady, I too know nothing. But I have been visited by gloomy thoughts. You don't seem to like the idea of living with the king in Ninuwa but you do want Esarhaddon named as his successor. A choice faces you. I wonder ..." He stopped when she put her hand up as if to block his words.

While a palace maid ladled soup into their bowls Zaqutu laid out the situation as she saw it. As long as the chatelaine of Ninuwa Central held all the power, Zaqutu and Esarhaddon were at risk from her. Everyone knew Nikkal-Amat favoured Arda-Mulissi and most believed she would do anything to have him crowned king in Asshur.

As Zaqutu spoke the others nodded agreement. She finished by asking Shebna directly, "Tell us, then, what you think needs to be done and how you think it can be done. Skip the polite details. I want to know what you think."

"You have said yourself what needs to be done. Before you go to Ninuwa you must get Nikkal-Amat out of the city." Shebna elaborated. "Central's chatelaine controls most of the troops in the city. She has great wealth of her own, but even more power because most of the city's trade passes through the hands of her traders." Shebna stopped and spread his hands wide. "You cannot unseat her by force of arms."

"I would not stoop to using force." In the silence that followed they ate. Zaqutu turned to Baya. "Isn't that right?"

Shebna's hands, perhaps rising to his head in a gesture of despair, stopped halfway. He sat with his chin in his hands, to wait for the prophet's reply.

Zaqutu pursed her lips together. "I follow the Goddess, the source of love and beauty. Surely she can't mean me to join her in battle?" Zaqutu swayed, shaking her head to clear the thought from her mind. She looked over at the prophet for assurance, hoping she'd taken a wise position.

Baya touched the double string of lapis-lazuli beads that Zaqutu wore. "Think of the third gate, those _me_—Ishtar carries those for a purpose."

Zaqutu put her hand up against Baya's mouth. "Let me explain to Shebna," she begged. "Among the _me_ that Ishtar gets from Ea are intrigue, the education of the child, and the necessity for fighting rebellion. That's what Baya means." She nodded for her scribe to continue.

"My lady, you would use force. If rebels came to this city your guards would fight. You would stoop then, wouldn't you? Well, Nikkal-Amat has rebelled, she appears to be the one paying her nephew's troops and all his expenses to help him to muster an army against the king."

Zaqutu shook her head. "Baya, by your mouth Ishtar spoke saying 'Do not trust in man; lift your eyes, look to me.'"

"Ishtar has promised you victory. Perhaps a man, even Shebna, prepares the way." Baya turned to Shebna. "What could you do?" her deep voice asked.

Shebna outlined his plan. He knew all the tricks of espionage; it had been his whole life. He would infiltrate Nikkal-Amat's household to get evidence that would compel the king's magnates to act.

Baya stirred. Zaqutu, sensitive to the body language, signalled her to speak.

"I don't see how that would help," Baya objected. "Compel the magnates? The chief eunuch, not Nikkal-Amat, controls the royal army, certainly. But most of those troops are south with their commander, many days' journey distant. Nearly all the soldiers in Ninuwa are hers to control. She likes to control things, I think. Very much."

Zaqutu said nothing, her eyes on the beads she wore, her fingers twisting over one another, her lips pursed. When Shebna didn't respond, Baya added, "Is there more? Things you haven't told us?"

Shebna turned to the scribe, his mouth slightly open as he tried to find a correct form of address. Baya of Arbail spoke sometimes as priest, sometimes as priestess. "My lord, I mean my lady, there's risk involved. I must shake the loyalty of the chatelaine's most powerful supporters. I must be subtle. It must seem as if I never came here or as if I had been sent away in disgrace. Also, it may not work."

Zaqutu quivered. She had always despised her mother for using underhand methods for getting her own way. And now, here, she herself needed Shebna. Desperately she thought, *I mustn't turn into Qat*. She could hardly get words out of her mouth. "We all know, even with your help, that things might go wrong." Zaqutu cleared her throat, constricted by fear. "I do not want to bring the king's wrath down on my head."

Shebna kept still until she pushed her bowl away and stood up. They all rose but she motioned them back down. She'd decided. "I'll feed Shadditu and return."

As she left she pointed to the lectern in the corner—all she had to do to tell them her decision. Baya went over to make a list of what Shebna would need.

When the list was finished Baya sighed. "My lady imagined supplies and money. What you ask is far more complex. Once anyone could expect straightforward honesty from a person who swore by the name of Asshur. Not any longer. How can we find you a conduit to the king's magnates?"

Zaqutu overheard the question and answered, "The Grand Vizier, Suen-Akhu-Utsur, is on our side, wholly. He hates Nikkal-Amat and has stood up to her before now. No one could be suspicious if I wrote to him, he's Grand Vizier."

"He's old!" Baya exclaimed.

"So am I," Shebna retorted.

When Esarhaddon complained to Zaqutu about Shebna's leaving, Zaqutu said he'd been offered a home with friends in Ninuwa.

"Why?" he asked.

"He is old and wants to be with men who share his language and his times. He will be happier there."

"I thought he was happy here. He always said so."

She reassured the boy he'd see Shebna again when they went to live in Ninuwa.

As months sped past she began to doubt her own confidence. The vizier claimed to have heard nothing from 'my lady's elderly friend'. Ataril returned from Asshur with news, but no comfort. Tashmetu had conceived but had not brought the child to term. "I will write to her," Zaqutu told him. "I know how she feels, poor woman."

Both women, so different in age and experience, shared the same hope. *We both want peace, a secure future for our children, and we want our babies to live.* Tashmetu called Zaqutu 'the lucky one'. Zaqutu remarked to Ataril after reading Tashmetu's latest letter, "I'm sure Ishtar of Babili is like Ishtar of Arbail, not that perverse image in Ninuwa."

Ataril interrupted her to insist, "All Ishtar's manifestations are true, but your narrow prejudice blinds you. No, I have to say it, you don't want to see everything. Ishtar of battle drinks the blood of the slain, she is Ereshkigal and demands the death of Tammuz. Holder of the *me*, all wealth and power stem from her. Without that she is the corpse hanging from the tree."

Before he could continue she snapped. "Ataril, don't play games with me. Asshur, in the name of all the great gods, calls for justice and truth, not lying and greed."

"I'm not playing. Cruelty repels you, I know. The heavenly *me* are not all justice and truth. From Ea Ishtar brings oversight of the underworld. Alongside lovemaking and kissing of the phallus she brings stabbing weapons and prostitution. Alongside speaking truth she brings flattery and slander, the boasting of the tavern."

"Ataril, I know, I can recite the *me*. Art of the hero goes with treachery and plundering, lamentation with rejoicing."

"You want the heart-soothing counsellors but not the strife-kindling." Her fingers tapped the table in impatience, but he persisted, his voice raised. "Nonetheless, my lady, wherever you walk strife is kindled."

Another year passed before Sennacherib returned to Kalkhu to hear his daughter's first words and watch her learn to walk. "You'll all come to the new palace after the autumn festival." He pointed his finger straight at Zaqutu's open mouth. "Shadditu can be devoted, but only if she comes with you to Ninuwa afterward. Otherwise I ..."

"Otherwise you what?" Zaqutu stormed. "Shall you have me executed? Who will protect your little prince then? I suppose you think it's self-indulgent to want to stay here. Don't pretend to me that Ninuwa is safe. You know Nikkal-Amat is plotting to give Arda-Mulissi your throne; everybody knows she has all the troops and all the money."

Drawing in her breath, she tried to hold it but words burst out. "Don't treat me like an idiot. You know the proverb, 'Let me lie with you! Let the god eat your ration.' Nikkal-Amat beggars you. What your magnates owe you, she collects. You're just ..." Zaqutu stopped herself. They were alone in the garden and no one was listening, not officially. But anyone could hear.

The king's face had flushed a deep reddish brown and his fists were clenched. "Yes? Just what? Finish your remark."

Her mind raced to find a word. Unrealistic. *It wasn't good enough.* She could see she'd wounded him. He'd had no chance to boast about the success of his latest campaign and she couldn't now show how glad she was, in fact, to see him.

He'd grown pale again but his eyes flashed. "You're the realistic one now. So, tell me of your realism, of your greater knowledge of affairs." His jaws worked to and fro. "Street gossip! They have another proverb in Babili: 'The discreet whore slanders the peasant wife.' You've turned into a ..." He snorted. "The gossips have told you that I am weak, is that it? And you believe that? Instead of the omens I have taken? Their word over the will of Shamash?" He looked away and, briefly, appeared to doubt his own words. "Have you had this from Arbail? From whom? A prophecy?" He raised his face to hers, and she knew she had to speak truly.

"No prophecy. But ..." She stopped. The rest of the proverb 'At Ishtar's command the noble's wife gets a bad name'—came too close to the bone. "Nikkal-Amat is your ..." She'd heard the gossip about Sharrani-Muballissu—that not Zaza the wife but Nikkal-Amat the sister bore him to the king. "Your enemy," she continued. "You can't deny it, can you?"

"My mother installed her. You will someday wish Esarhaddon to behave well towards your servants, to Ataril and Annabel, to Abby and Amat-Baal. There's another proverb that says, 'Slander no one and then grief will not reach your heart.'"

She reeled in fury. That sounded like a threat. *How could he?* "I respected your mother as much as you did. Your mother chose Zaza whom you divorced," she snapped. "Why be balked by her sister who hates you now and will do anything to increase her power and decrease yours? She supports Arda-Mulissi. You keep defeating him and he raises new armies. Where do you think those soldiers come from? They're mercenaries not hill-dwellers! She weakens you, keeps you from securing the eastern borders, keeps you from gaining ..."

Zaqutu's voice stopped as her courage seeped away. Sennacherib now stood facing her, close enough to touch and he towered over her. As she gazed up into his face the thought passed through her mind,

Esarhaddon will be this tall. I hope ... and she smiled. The words they had spoken faded before her helpless love of him, his presence, his smell, the timbre of his voice.

Her face gave her away and he reached forward, put his hands heavily on her shoulders, and laughed softly. "I've always known that you are clever and brave, from our first meeting. To you I may seem weak before the chatelaine you hate, but I am clever too. You've been up to something, I'm certain. Suppose you tell me what and then I'll tell you my plans." As she turned to oblige him he added, "The wise men say also, 'Eat no fat and there'll be no blood in your excrement.' You hide in Kalkhu or Arbail but that doesn't solve the problem."

"Look here." Zaqutu offered him the reports she had had from Shebna via the Grand Vizier, as always forgetting he had never learned to read.

"Just tell me," he said.

"Here, see he's used the old signs, so they'd be hard to read, and we've invented a sort of code."

Shebna would use the code word 'extra rations' to send names of servants in the New Palace who were on Nikkal-Amat's payroll. The word 'short rations' came attached to names of servants from Ninuwa Central he'd recruited to supply him with information.

The king followed her finger with his eyes. "Your old man gets these? How?"

"That's his secret. But you see? Each dispatch of supplies from Ninuwa Central comes a month before one of your army's engagements with the rebels. And look at the locations of the battles." She recited the names: Dur-Asshur, Zibia, Mutsatsir. All places where Sargon won victories and settled his veterans. Nikkal-Amat ran the brothels during those campaigns. She knows your fathers' veterans, subverts them, pays them to side with Arda-Mulissi. They don't do it because they like him, but because—" the scorn in her voice made her words thick "—Nikkal-Amat pays well." She felt him looking at her back as she turned away to set the wooden crate of tablets down on a table.

"Zaqutu, you think I don't know all that?"

Both of them had calmed down now and her voice softened. "If you know all that then you know I won't be safe in Ninuwa, and nor will Esarhaddon. Worse than bloody turds. We can't stop her."

"Yet your old man is trying. It's bizarre. Why did you try that ruse?"

She lowered her head. "If she pays a high enough price she will get her way. Shebna has proved it." Hesitating, not wanting to speak of anything connected to Arbail, she hedged the truth. "I dreamt a special dream. I saw Shebna's hands around Arda-Mulissi." She grunted. "I've never seen him but I think that's who it was. Shebna held him by the balls and cut them off with a sword, not with a knife. It wasn't at Arbail."

Zaqutu, as she lifted her eyes to his, saw that he knew she was lying. She stiffened, but before she could draw back from him Sennacherib took her in his arms and kissed her forehead.

"What has happened to you? Have you forgotten the promise the goddess made at our son's birth? Ishtar wills him to become king in Ninuwa; it will happen. No person, however mighty, can overcome her." He dropped his voice. "Now I must tell you some news."

His tone warned her to expect pain. She let him take her hands and pull her into his lap; she leaned into his chest and murmured, a sound without words, only seeking solace and hoping for comfort. Before he had finished tears came into her eyes; her father had died and Pele—called Manasseh now—ruled alone. "I wonder whether my mother has had the grace to weep for him," she whimpered. "So much joy in life and so much energy, shrivelled by the wife he loved." Qat's face came to her mind and she shook her head. She lifted her dripping cheeks to gaze straight into Sennacherib's eyes. "To Ninuwa, then. If that's what you want."

She felt his relief and saw on his face a weird sort of joy. "Still, my lord, my love, you must promise me to stay in Ninuwa yourself while I am there."

He shook his head, his arms tight around her. "You cannot dictate my comings and goings."

"But I won't be safe!" she wailed.

"You'll be fine. My Chief Eunuch cannot be bought—not by Nikkal-Amat, not by anyone."

She snorted, but the despair she had felt slowly ebbed away. In his presence she felt herself melting even when she tried not to.

The king promised, "I shall ensure the royal army will be quartered near you."

First she took a deep breath and then she repeated, now in a whisper, "I'll go if I must. But you know how I love it here in Kalkhu. It's ... well, it's peaceful."

"But you must go. Besides," he stroked her hair, "You haven't even seen the New Palace—your own designs graven in stone. They cannot be erased just as your name cannot be."

In mid-autumn the roads were firm and the long train of wagons made its way north. Zaqutu's household and the king's bodyguard were towed on barges, safe from attack. Secretly Zaqutu hoped that a miracle would happen, that they'd arrive and find Nikkal-Amat had been murdered. She kept her thoughts from the king but not from Ataril.

His response surprised her. "My lady, I cannot tell you how, but I am certain you will prevail." He spoke with more assurance than usual.

Since that trip with the king, she thought, *he thinks he knows everything.*

His next words surprised her. "You will be set up in the Succession Palace with your son and the wife we have chosen for him."

"Chosen! I thought I got to choose my son's wife."

Ataril grinned as he gripped the barge's railing to steady himself. "Too late. Esarhaddon met her on his trip south a couple of years ago. They were just children together, but they liked each other. She's two years older than him."

"I see you and the king have chosen without any thought of me. Why? Why her?"

"Esharra-Hammat is the only daughter of the Bit-Yakin rebel, Mushezib-Marduk, and thus the only living descendant of Marduk-Baladan. Makes her an obvious choice."

"From Bit-Yakin? Why was she in Asshur then?"

"When the king defeated Mushezib six years ago they devoted her to Ishtar of Asshur. She has remained there in the temple."

"What does she look like? Is she ... well, is she pretty?"

Ataril laughed so loudly that the king came to hear the joke. "She is very tall and, I think, fasts only when she has to. Healthy, but not what I'd call pretty."

The king looked at Zaqutu, reading her expression. "You must be talking about Esharra. You're not much of a judge of female beauty, Ataril. I was impressed by her." The king faced Zaqutu, "She has grandeur, walks like a queen, straight, a bit stiff. She's light-skinned, too fair for my taste, and her hair is very long but straight. An Egyptian woman got into that line somehow." Zaqutu's expression hid nothing, and the king went on. "Looks aren't everything. I liked her, so you will too. She's just a girl, but to my mind she's a bit like you. She's lively and confident."

Zaqutu fumed at their high-handed disregard. "I should have a say. I'm going to be the one living with her." She paused. *How will it be? Living as queen in the succession palace?* "What if she doesn't like me?"

"I'll order her to and she will obey," the king joked.

Zaqutu's first days in the New Palace were uneventful, even boring. The chilly rain and grey fog kept her indoors so she explored all the roofed-in parts of the complex. The women's quarters were entirely enclosed but could be entered from the courtyard on the northern side or from the courtyard shared by the king's quarters, her own rooms and the strong rooms. From the kitchens and service areas only two small doorways opened into the main corridor. She paced the corridors and studied the doorways and gates. When the king had laid out the palace he might not have been thinking about defending himself and his servants from rebels, but the layout served that purpose.

On the other hand Ataril had brought her a plan of how the Succession Palace was laid out. She would move there when Esarhaddon was named successor. Sargon had liked things square and all four sides opened into courtyards. No thought of security for the inhabitants showed in the plan. When Zaqutu complained about it the king just shrugged. "Look at the city walls. We have guards to keep enemies out."

"Not if the enemies are already inside," she muttered.

Meanwhile life in the New Palace pleased everyone else. The throne room opened on to a portico a hundred metres long. The palace children set up foot races and shooting games when the council wasn't in session. Esarhaddon, backed up by Abby's oldest son, Banba, led the other children in games through the short winter days.

Zaqutu found Addati, the chatelaine of the New Palace, reserved. In the hope that it might be only the manners of the capital, Zaqutu tried to charm her, to make her a friend. From cool, Addati's response went to chilly. The noise of the children and the wear and tear on the earthenware tried her patience to its limit.

"Look here, Addati," Zaqutu complained, "I know you wish we'd all stayed living in Kalkhu. You probably know that I wish the same." Zaqutu sighed, partly from regret for her freedom in the summer palace and also partly because she hated having to plead. "Neither of us can afford this stand-off. It could lead to ..." She stopped, unable to find the word she wanted. Addati's frigid look froze her mind.

Drawing herself up to full height though her head barely reached Addati's shoulders, she forced herself to speak firmly. "Our servants must know that they cannot play us off against each other." She looked up into the older woman's face. "I have to trust you so I must be sure that you won't undermine me. Sit down, please."

Futile to expect any words from her. No matter what the question Addati answered only a 'yes' or 'no', never volunteering information. Zaqutu couldn't ask straight out whether Addati was informing on her to Nikkal-Amat so she tried subterfuge. "You will know that the king has made over to me several estates, and I plan to appoint chatelaines for them. Can you not advise me? If you'd suggest names, or even tell me whether someone I fancy would be a good choice ... please, will you help me this way?"

Addati nodded and kept her mouth shut. Zaqutu stood up and paced across her reception room to the frescoes she had worked so hard for, tracing a figure with her fingers, remembering her days in the ruins of the burnt palace. She knotted the shawl around her hips tighter, her lips drawn into a grim line. Addati stood, impassive, waiting for her to speak.

"How do you manage? I mean, when you have estates and you want to appoint someone to look after them. What do you do?"

Zaqutu's genuine frustration and the implied flattery had an effect, though slight. "I have no estates, my lady. None of my own."

Without any conscious thought, Zaqutu blurted out, "Haven't you? Nikkal-Amat has just bought that huge estate in Ekallate, made her son the headman of the town! How come?" By accident—she later felt Ishtar had inspired her—she had found the vulnerable spot in Addati's façade.

Addati left her stool and stood. "I manage the king's property in the king's interest, my lady." She looked down into Zaqutu's eyes. Her own eyes glittered—with rage, or perhaps with spite.

Zaqutu dropped her gaze, wondering whether to apologise. "Nikkal-Amat manages in her own interest; that's what you mean, isn't it?" Addati nodded. "I need to get someone like you and not someone like her. Shouldn't I ask you?"

"I try to find the best people to manage the king's affairs. Your own business is your affair."

The conversation had reached a standstill and Zaqutu knew she had not found an ally. As the sound of a troop of children turning the corner broke up their talk, Zaqutu smiled. *Not an ally, but at least not an enemy. Addati could be trusted.*

"One more question," Zaqutu said, her voice raised to be heard over the growing clamour, "the month is ending. I will fast and then I will want to keep Ishtar's feast. Do you hold a festal meal here as a rule? Or do you take your feast with Nikkal-Amat, at Central, in the Ishtar temple?"

"My lady, in the king's absence we attend the Ishtar temple. Suen-Akhu-Utsur has told me that you are a priestess of Ishtar of Arbail. I expect that you will order the fast here and that we will feast here. This month, of course, the king will officiate with the army at the Shamash Gate."

"Yes." She nodded. "That's how it will be. Years ago Ataril was denied entry to the Ishtar temple. As though Ishtar of Ninuwa were somehow not the same as Ishtar of Arbail. What do you think?" Zaqutu hushed the children and took Shadditu in her arms to still her whining.

"You need to ask one of the scholars that question, my lady. Try Zarri—he loves those puzzles." Addati smiled at her own words and Zaqutu smiled back.

No answers to her questions but she felt more certain that Addati's stiffness made her unlikely to succumb to bribery. *Someone I can trust, even if I can't like her.*

As the winter wore on to spring Zaqutu left her quarters more often. She found the library and came to know the scribes and scholars who kept the king's records and—for amusement—debated the rationales for new customs and the justifications for old ones. Zarri, she found, was the son of a priest of Shamash. He seemed more frivolous than the others, often joking, loving puns. He teased her from time to time—"Let our Ishtar priestess decide," he'd say in the midst of a debate on some trivial issue of protocol. The library was no place for serious discussion.

The full moon of Adar was only a day or two away when Zaqutu sent a palace maid to invite Zarri to join her and her women in late-afternoon refreshment. It was a favourable day and Zaqutu's companions had set out decorated cakes and warmed spiced wine. Abby was teasing Akhi-Tzalli—a woman Zaqutu had taken into her household as a harem woman—about her embroidered shawl. The shawl, perhaps chosen to flatter Zaqutu, displayed luscious gardens full of summer blossoms and fruit. The women's laughter drowned out the sound of footsteps, so the women didn't hear Ataril usher Zarri into the reception area. The women were flushed with warmth and ready for witty conversation, and for most of an hour they traded gossip and banter with the young scholar.

By Zaqutu's arrangement the children came in and called the women away, leaving her alone with her eunuch and the young man. "Zarri, I have heard that you are well-versed in the stories of the great gods. Ataril and I have been schooled, too, but in Arbail where … I don't know how to say it. Maybe we are rustic in our understanding. In any case, we are not only ignorant but curious."

Ataril interjected, "You need not answer if the knowledge is unsuitable for us, just as we would not if you inquired of us."

Zarri shifted on the bench where he sat. "What sort of things do you want to know?" His tone had become uncertain.

Zaqutu hastened to reassure him. "The finer points of interpretation are not for us, we know that. And—"

Ataril interrupted her. "We are speaking in confidence. You will not, I hope, make my lady's questions items for gossip."

"Nor jokes!" Zaqutu laughed. "Now listen," she began and asked about the different aspects and characteristics of Ishtar in her different cities. "Ataril tells me of Ishtar of Babylon, and I recognise her but not Ishtar of Ninuwa." Zaqutu stopped, feeling the tension in the air. "Of Ishtar of Asshur I have heard no tales."

Zarri looked from one to the other. "You are both devoted; you must know more of the Goddess and her rites than I do. I may not have the answer." He looked uncomfortable. Zaqutu thought he feared to appear uncooperative. After a pause he asked, "How can you expect me to know anything?"

Zaqutu exchanged glances with Ataril before she answered. "I made my choice with some care. You see the service of the gods from outside, as it were. Perhaps you can say why Ataril, Ishtar's devotee in Arbail, is treated as a stranger by Ishtar of Ninuwa."

Zarri leaned back and looked at his toes, raising both legs off the floor a fraction and then putting them down and leaning forward. As he began to speak they saw him lose his diffidence; he warmed to the task. He gave them a full description of Ishtar of Ninuwa, concluding, "Here Ishtar is Belet-Nina, Sharrat-Ninuwa. She is Sherua, daughter of Asshur. We call her Anunitu, the goddess of war. Her nature … ah, I'd say her nature was money and power."

At his words Zaqutu looked at her feet, finding that she was unwilling to say anything.

Ataril spoke softly, as if to himself. "That is a mystery indeed. We know Ishtar of Arbail as the Goddess. Her nature is love and beauty. She shines in the evening as Agushea and lights up the morning as Dilibat."

Zaqutu stood to signal the visit's end and the men stood with her. She took Zarri's hands in hers and pressed them, with fulsome thanks. After he'd gone she observed to Ataril, "We still don't know why Ishtar of Ninuwa will not receive you."

Next morning the Grand Vizier sought an audience with Zaqutu. He brought bad news. A prostitute from the brothel where Shebna had lain hidden, spying, had sent a parcel containing a few tunics and all his writing tools. Within the parcel were a sheaf of parchments, small pieces with tiny letters. "My lady, I cannot read them. The messenger told me that your friend was found buried in a dung heap. Soldiers … er … discovered his body."

"Her soldiers?"

The vizier nodded. "Took him from his bed; he'd been asleep. Took all the large items off his lectern. But they didn't take these scraps."

Before accepting the parchment fragments from him Zaqutu put her finger to her lips to silence him. She ran her fingers over the writing tools, remembering Shebna's expressions, the words he used, the flickers of amusement that lighted up his eyes when he'd caught someone out in a lie. She ought not to weep—he had lived more than half again as long as most men. He had served different masters and yet had kept his own honour intact. *How very sad*, she thought, *there is no one to mourn him.* Then two tracks of tears fell down her cheeks and she showed the vizier a rueful smile. She reached out to take hold of the dusty bits he had set on the table.

Thick parchment, like that used for official correspondence, but the writing was Judaean and it seemed like doggerel. She carried one of the sheets to the window and peered at it. Tears still trickled down her face but she laughed and then wept freely. She wept over Shebna's horrible end. A tide of soothing relief welled up and she wanted to laugh wildly at the same time. She stared at the piece of parchment and tried to control her breathing, to control the hysteria in her throat and the emotions stirring in her bowels.

When she had brought her feelings under control she turned to the Grand Vizier, who stood silent beside her at the window. "He was perhaps the cleverest man I have ever known, worthy of Adapa himself. You see these." She pointed to the pile. "Of course they're hard to read. He's scrawled proverbs and bits of poems in Judaean script, see? But look underneath, there's Aramaic. Here, this one is a bill of lading consigning chariot wheels to—" and Zaqutu hooted in triumph "—Arda-Mulissi. Look, it includes the date, twenty-second Tishri, year of Suen-Ahu-Eriba. This year. We've got her!"

The vizier took the parchment from her and peered at it. "How did he get such writings? Perhaps he pretended he wanted them for scraping," he mused aloud.

"Or he had someone raiding the rubbish heaps for him. I suppose he'd select some to use for the letters he wrote for people. He posed as a scribe down on his luck. But when he got a good one he overwrote it in his own language."

Tears welled up again and she wiped her nose, her voice more like a sigh. "Even if his room had been searched thoroughly they'd not have spotted it. He probably knew they'd come for him, expected to be betrayed sooner or later." She took the rest of the parchments. "What will you do now?" she asked. "We have proof of her rebellion."

"The council meets tomorrow to plan for the Akitu festival in Asshur. I was planning to ask you what arrangements you want us to make for your transport. By river?"

Zaqutu, distracted from any misgivings by the coded notes, nodded in agreement.

"We'll keep your part in this quiet. I came to see you about transport; that's true now. Tonight I will send a note to the king that I want to lay a charge for the Chief Judge to hear."

"If the king speaks to me of it," she promised, "I'll play dumb."

Chapter 21: The Fall of Nikkal-Amat

Faithful to his word, the Grand Vizier took Shebna's evidence to the council of magnates, a proper act but one that stirred up the predicted nest of hornets. Holding Zaqutu at arm's length, the king told her, "Your old man has certainly forced my hand."

"It cost him his life," she replied, defiant.

"It may turn out for the worse, you know," the king warned.

After the Grand Vizier, Suen-Akhu-Utsur, was found strangled in his bath Sennacherib ordered Zaqutu and her children off to Arbail, along with an escort of two cohorts of the royal army and a dozen bodyguards. He wanted them away at once.

As soon as she'd set everything in order, she came into his reception room and found him there alone, placing black and white stones into holes in a game board. The board held three rows of holes, the outer ones of three holes each and the inner one of four holes, the pattern of the sacred tree. She realised, as she watched him, that they stood also for the positions in his council of magnates.

"What are you doing?" she asked.

"Before we lay Suen-Akhu-Utsur in his grave—it'll be the one next to your Shebna—I must promote someone to his post. I want to make sure I don't elevate anyone implicated in the murder."

"Why do you …" she began, but stopped herself. He assigned the positions of the chief magnates to mirror the sacred tree. The Grand Vizier served as the purity and wisdom of the council, just as the moon god, Suen, served the council of the great gods. Not easy to choose a successor. She gazed out the window towards the row of graves that stretched north from the palace.

They'd turned over the dung heap outside the Ishtar palace and removed Shebna's body. Zaqutu hadn't allowed them to follow their customary practice, where sorcerers would manipulate the corpse in their attempt to provoke and identify its murderer. "He'd have hated that worse than anything else," she insisted. Even without such evidence, the king had exiled Nikkal-Amat from the city and banned her. Anyone who communicated with her would share her banishment. Zaqutu's triumph and feelings of relief remained muted by her grief for the old man who had died to bring it about. *My made-up dream has come true. Shebna has cut off Arda-Mulissi's balls, in a manner of speaking.*

Few of the officials who had kowtowed to Nikkal-Amat in her power dared to leave the city; all feared coming under suspicion. So none reached her estate in Tarbitsu, where the king's guards kept the gates and sent details of her visitors to Ninuwa.

To the Grand Vizier's palace, east of the new palace, only senior magnates and their deputies ever came. Tab-Sar-Asshur, the treasurer, and several of his deputies went to audit the bills of lading Zaqutu had found. Using that evidence, they disembowelled two of the vice-chancellor's deputies, men who had sealed off on supplies to Arda-Mulissi.

Zaqutu knew the king expected all such decisions he now had to make to be ratified by the gods, so she was puzzled by his preoccupation and by the worry that transformed his face into that of an old man. "Surely you've ordered divination about Suen-Akhu-Utsur's successor?" Zaqutu asked, but the king merely shook his head. "Why not?"

"My dear, all the magi, every haruspex in Ninuwa … they hedge their bets. You must see how it is. I got 'no reply' from every one of them. It'd take six days to get advice from Shamash in the Inner City and I have to call the council now." Her mouth opened to ask, but he shushed her. "Asshur-Natsir will take charge of your troops. He's certain to be loyal; Nikkal-Amat killed his parents and castrated both Asshur-Natsir and his brother so there'd be no one to claim their land."

"But what about you?"

"Don't you worry. I'm keeping my Chief Eunuch and the royal army. I'll be safe."

It took the wagon train four days to reach Arbail. After the longest day—when they started before daybreak and arrived at Kilizi by torchlight—the royal family, including Esharra-Hammat, stayed in Shemahu's palace.

Zaqutu held Shemahu's hand as she told him of Shebna's death and all that had followed. "The king my lord knows you saved the prince at birth, and now it turns out that you have saved us all." When Shemahu shook his head, bewildered, she explained, "You brought Shebna to us."

"My lady," Shemahu stuttered, "I liked him, that's all. I wanted to help him." He withdrew his hand and drew out a piece of linen to wipe his brow, sweeping it across his eyes as well. "Your Shebna could tell a good story and he'd seen so many wonders. What a life."

"We tried to get him to write his memoirs but, among his papers, nothing."

"That's a pity."

"Shemahu," she promised, "when I return to Ninuwa you will come with me and we two shall make offerings at his graveside."

"When will that be?"

Naqia smiled at him but shook her head. "It all depends. The king will send for us when it is safe."

PATRICIDE

685 BCE and Following

Esarhaddon as Crown Prince

Chapter 22: Esarhaddon is Made Crown Prince

The time Zaqutu had been living in the New Palace in Ninuwa felt like a distant memory. Her entourage had come to Arbail safely, and, at the temple gate Zaqutu had sent Ataril to ask the Mother to welcome Esharra-Hammat as a devotee. Abby and her children had to live outside the enclosure but most days they would come into the main courtyard of the temple to play. In Arbail they were safely out of the way while the king made the arrangements for a change of leadership. Older counsellors who had sat in their posts since his father's time were replaced, the new men tested. The process took far longer than Zaqutu had expected. Peaceful and uneventful days slipped away. When, from time to time, letters came she learned the details of the king's purge of his council. It surprised Zaqutu to find herself now chafing at being so far from the capital, *as if I no longer exist.*

Her letters included correspondence with Tashmetu who remained in the Inner City; the two women found comfort in their shared concerns. One winter day, though, the news from Asshur dismayed her. Tashmetu's scribe, Bel-Lei, had prepared a tablet. Tashmetu's health worried them all, he wrote. Zaqutu checked her interpretation with Ahat-Abisha. "What does he mean by that?" she asked, pointing to the name of the apkallu demon.

"We cannot be sure. Perhaps she's bleeding to death."

"She says she's informed the king she is unable to do the Akitu festival next spring. I know he'll expect me to take the role of the king's consort at the next festival." Dread swept over her and she tried to hide it. Tried, but she couldn't.

When she raised her eyes from the tablet to the priestess' face she saw that the older woman had read her feelings. "Zaqutu, you know the king cannot let the people of Babili hold an Akitu since there is no one to act as king in Babili."

"I know they cannot have a separate festival for Babili. I know that since he holds their chief gods in Asshur he expects them to come to the Inner City. I can't go."

"You must go, and you haven't seen the beautiful new Akitu Palace the king has built northwest of the Mushlali gate."

"But Tashmetu always accepts the annual excursion—she doesn't mind the king's efforts to beget another son on her. If her illness will make that impossible ..."

"You will have to take her place."

Zaqutu set her mouth. "I won't go. It's less than a day's trip from Tarbitsu downriver to the Inner City. The Akitu Palace, like any open plaza right beside the river, would be too easy to invade."

Abisha warned, "Daughter, if my brother takes another woman and she conceives, you and your son will gain a whole new set of enemies."

I've got enough already, she thought, but she promised to reconsider. *Once Esarhaddon marries we could bring forward his naming as Crown Prince, his moving into the Succession Palace ...*

From her bench in the late winter sun, Zaqutu watched the children playing; they'd started a slinging contest. Esharra-Hammat came to sit beside her. No one in either Babili or Asshur used slings to cast stones as a sport. Esharra couldn't compete and was too proud, or too wise, to try. Shadditu at six years old could play. Abby's son Banba came ahead of Esarhaddon one time in three, but Shadditu never won. She whined that she never had a chance.

"I was a better slinger than my brother," Zaqutu observed. "I remember once a hawk circling overhead, threatening the doves in our garden. I got him, with one cast, before Pele had even loaded his sling. "

Shadditu had come over to her to demand a lesson but stood listening. Zaqutu and Ataril continued their earlier conversation.

"My lady, I have never said you needed to cast stones with a sling to accomplish your purpose."

"My purpose? You mean my survival?"

"The new chatelaine has charge of Ninuwa Central, but she is like one of the doves in your garden. The hawk ..."

"I know, Nikkal-Amat."

"Until you arrange for her to be strangled ..."

"We've been through that, Ataril. The king hasn't ordered it and I won't."

"Then your servants in Ninuwa will shiver in the shade of some tree or roof until they starve. They won't act, they won't serve, while they are menaced. Like doves, with no slinger to protect them." With his hands he drew in the air a crown over her head, murmuring the traditional description of the <u>me</u> associated with Ishtar's crown, a queenly incantation.

"It's the king's role to protect them, not mine." She saw, out of the corner of her eye, Shadditu's mouth dropped open. *I wish she hadn't been hearing that.* Zaqutu shooed the girl off to continue casting. Full in their sight, Shadditu shoved Banba at the crucial moment, giving the match to Esarhaddon. She and Ataril watched the boys square off to fight each other before, thinking better of it, they rounded on Shadditu.

"Are you sure Esarhaddon is old enough to marry?" Zaqutu asked absentmindedly, her eyes still fixed on the two boys. "Will he be ready, do you think? It's only two months from now."

Banba, a month older, was smooth-faced and his voice still a child's. Esarhaddon's voice hooted and growled by comparison, and a few whiskers had sprouted over his mouth. Zaqutu's heart seemed to stop when she thought of him and Esharra-Hammat being obliged to perform the ritual in the Akitu Palace.

Ataril followed her eyes and, since he guessed her mind, suggested, "Ahat-Abisha could let them marry here, now. You might ask her." He added, "She's wiser than I am and even much wiser than you."

Zaqutu coloured. "But would he be … you know, able?"

Ataril laughed. "Have you noticed Esar's chariot driver, Hussani?"

Zaqutu shook her head.

Ataril continued, "I have heard that he is very skilful with women."

"You mean … to teach?"

Ataril meant exactly that and promised to arrange some "lessons."

As she nodded in acquiescence Zaqutu heard rustling behind her and turned to Esharra-Hammat, who had brought a tray of warmed wine and barley-cakes. Zaqutu supposed the girl had overheard. "Would you be happy with that?"

Esharra looked puzzled. "With what?"

"Marrying, here, soon." Zaqutu turned and searched the girl's face. Surprise and, yes, relief preceded her smile and a barely noticeable obeisance. They all turned to watch the boys taking turns at a target set far outside the open gate.

"Careful!" Ataril shouted. "Someone may be coming."

The courier who appeared showed commendable caution. He had a side view of Esarhaddon so he dashed to the gatepost and waved his arm before asking the gate-warden for permission to enter. He smiled as he held out to Ataril the leather pouch clinking with clay tablets. Messages from the Babili priests in Asshur. Conservative to a fault, the scribes from Ataril's home city wouldn't use Aramaic.

Zaqutu—imagining hawks and doves—visualised the youngsters in the Akitu Palace.

Ataril held out a tablet for Zaqutu. "Not good news."

She stood and reached for the tablet. Holding it away, he shook his head. "Tashmetu has died." Zaqutu gasped but he reassured her, "Not murdered, it was a sickness. But I must leave you. The governor has asked ..."

"Leave!"

Ataril handed over the tablet. While Zaqutu puzzled out the message, littered with scribal abbreviations, shortcuts and missing words, Ataril stood shifting his weight from foot to foot. When she handed the tablet back with a frown he offered to explain. "As temple-enterer of Nabu, my father is next in line to oversee the worship of Nabu and Marduk. The king wants me to go ..."

"To Asshur?"

"As the king's representative." Ataril reassured her, "It's not to stop rebellion—the priests think they're letting Sennacherib off the hook."

Zaqutu turned away. She couldn't bear to meet his eyes, her heart swelling with bitterness. *Ataril belongs to me, my bridal gift. What's it to me whether they are minded to do the king a favour?* Her voice curdled with the sour bile that rose into her mouth. *Nobody cares about me— just something to use and discard, that's what I am.* When Ataril tried to comfort her she went into her chamber and drew the curtain. *Now I've lost everything.*

For three weeks Zaqutu hid herself away, refusing to receive any messages that came from the king. She knew as she did so that her sulking did her no credit. *I'm digging a pit to fall into.* Self-pity tasted sweet, and she brooded on how unfair everything was.

She presented herself for the fast pale and wasted, grim-faced and sorrowful.

"Zaqutu!" Ahat-Abisha was severe. "Who asks you for this self-sacrifice? Not the Goddess. She has not abandoned you. Tomorrow we feast and celebrate your son's marriage. Will you still lurk in that underworld, being eaten away by the kurgarra and the galatur?"

Zaqutu kept still. *If I let any words out they'll become flames burning away the priestess.* The flames in her mind's eye became kurgurra and galatur. The sexless beings Ea created to distract Ereshkigal in the underworld. She crouched down as if possessed by Ereshkigal, huddled in the darkness, uttering groans of pain as kurgarra and galatur ate away at her. *They might as well.* With her face contorted she looked straight into Ahat-Abisha's face and began to tear her rough tunic down the front. "No linen was spread over her body," she chanted. "Her breasts uncovered, her hair swirled around sprouting from her head like leeks in springtime."

Abisha joined her in the chant. "Ereshkigal moaned, Oh! Oh! My inside! Oh! Oh! My outside! Oh, my belly, oh, my back, oh, my heart, oh, my liver."

As if enquiring of the demons, Zaqutu asked, "Who are you, moaning—groaning—sighing with me?"

Her words came now like a real question, not part of the chant.

The Mother answered from the ritual, "If I were a god you could bless me, but I am mortal so you may give me a gift."

Zaqutu smiled and replied, almost without willing it, "I know you don't wish water or grain. The corpse belonging to Ishtar, that's what you want." She felt her sour resentment fade.

Abisha's reply completed her return to reason. "You are that corpse, belonging to her, her beloved. Come, fast. Later you will wash, dress in fine clothes and celebrate the marriage of your son."

At Arbail, four days after the wedding feast, Sennacherib stood at the gate waiting for his sister's greeting. The chariot driver Hussani brought him Abisha's words.

"May Ishtar of Arbail bless the king my brother, may Suen and Shamash strengthen his wisdom and power, let Asshur and Nabu maintain his everlasting kingship. Great Mummu and Ishtar of Babili guard in the womb the son who will be born to your son."

The king's whoop of delight and laughter could be heard in the temple courtyard. Zaqutu rushed into his arms, forgetting all the reproaches she had rehearsed. She smothered him with kisses, holding tight to his beard. When he could speak he asked, "Beloved little one, I am happy to see you, so well and cheerful. How do you like your daughter-in-law?"

"Don't be silly. You know I like her. More important, Esarhaddon likes her very well indeed. I cannot pry them apart! It worries me that they don't eat much." With happy laughter she escorted him to the Mother's hall where food was laid out.

Sennacherib looked around for the young couple but, as Zaqutu had warned him, they were nowhere to be seen. At dinner the king gave Zaqutu a worried look but she reassured him with an old proverb. "Has she become pregnant without nakimi? Has she got fat without eating?"

After their meal Ahat-Abisha signalled for the king to join her and Zaqutu inside the sanctuary. In the cool darkness they waited many minutes before she spoke.

"Brother. Shall you choose Esarhaddon as your successor?"

"Of course."

"You expect him to move into the Succession Palace? Soon?"

The king nodded and peered at Zaqutu's face in the darkness. Zaqutu kept silent.

Ahat-Abisha pressed him. "Will you tell us what plans you have, what measures you mean to take regarding him—them, that is."

At his sister's words Sennacherib turned to Zaqutu. He said softly, "He's your son. Will you tell me what plans you have?"

She shivered a little and replied, "They should live in the Succession Palace. That is clear. I have taken thought for a chatelaine for them. I want a woman from Babili."

"Why?" the king wanted to know.

"Esharra-Hammat has lands there. I mean to bequeath my villages there to her, Lakhiri and the others. So Remutu, her chatelaine, should know—"

"How did you find a woman from Babili capable of …"

Zaqutu put her hand across and laid it on his knee. "Are you angry? I'm trying to answer you."

He put his hand over hers and squeezed it. "So, who is this woman?"

Before she could reply, the Mother stood up and announced, "Be alone here. Let the Goddess watch over your choices."

Sennacherib reached over and placed Zaqutu in his lap. "I am not angry with you but you are angry with me. Tell me. Is it Ataril?"

Zaqutu stared up towards the crown of the Goddess without answering him. The silence between them lengthened. It grew fully dark and she shivered again in the chill. In a whisper Zaqutu confessed. "When Ishtar has to find a substitute for her body in the underworld she chooses Tammuz. He is sent to appease the appetites of Ereshkigal. But Tammuz has a sister, and her tears rescue him."

While the king waited for her to say more she only snuggled close to him for warmth, drawing slow breaths. The king asked, "My beloved, I do not understand you. Asshur is not the underworld."

Zaqutu stirred. "It's nothing to do with Asshur," she insisted. "Listen, I want Arda-Mulissi in Ereshkigal's realm and I want him to stay there. While his aunt sheds her golden tears for him he escapes that fate."

Sennacherib pondered her words. To him they seemed to have little to do with finding the right staff for the Succession Palace. As he held her close, savouring the smell of the incense that lingered in the sanctuary, a vision came into his mind. He spoke, "I see."

Zaqutu's body began to shiver and she jerked like a puppet on a string. She sat up to peer at his mouth. "You see?"

"I'm not sure what I see. Maybe it was that handsome charioteer driving in a chain of chariots and wagons, far away, in the hills. Snow-covered, they looked like the hills of the Mandaean country, off in the northeast. And Esarhaddon in the chariot, a lance at the ready as though hunting. He stuck a lion, killing it—but the lion was Arda-Mulissi. In the country of the Mandaeans!" As his words echoed in the sanctuary he suddenly understood the vision. *Yes, both of them.*

He hugged his wife and murmured in her ear, "Just for you I will exile Nikkal-Amat from all my lands, send her to the Mandaeans. She cannot buy them—they are robbers. They just take and don't cooperate."

"But Arda-Mulissi?"

If she couldn't see the sardonic smile on his face she would hear it in his reply. "He'll go to her, you'll see."

Never had Zaqutu enjoyed living in Ninuwa as she did that year. Even Addati had softened, coming forward with gifts and luxuries for her to take with her when she visited the Succession Palace. In Elul, almost on Esarhaddon's own birthday, Esharra gave birth to a full-term and healthy son, Shumukin.

The ceremony where Ishtar of Ninuwa gave Esarhaddon his new name, Asshur-Etel-Ilani-Mukin-Apli, was the first occasion when Ninuwa's new grand processional avenue filled with people—thousands of them. Flowers came down the river from Zaqutu's provinces. The people brandished branches laden with fruit, symbolising the fruitfulness of the Crown Princess, and the prosperity her son would bring to the kingdoms. "Shumukin, son of the Crown Prince! Blessed of Ishtar! Son of Asshur!" the crowds chanted.

At the entrance to the temple courtyard Sennacherib proclaimed the terms of Esarhaddon's succession. Heralds repeated his words line by line until they had echoed across the royal precincts and throughout the wide streets of the capital.

> The treaty of Sennacherib, king of Asshur, son of Sargon, likewise king of all the peoples—rulers of cities and rulers of kingdoms, all the men, young and old, from sunrise to sunset, over whom Sennacherib, King of Asshur, exercises kingship and lordship, with all their sons and grandsons who will be born in the days to come after this treaty—concerning Esarhaddon, the great crown prince designate, son of Sennacherib, king of Asshur, on behalf of whom he has concluded this treaty with you, which he has confirmed, made and concluded in the presence of Asshur, Anu, Illil, Ea, Suen, Shamash, Adad, Marduk, Nabu, Nushku, Nergal, Mulissu, Ishtar of Ninuwa, Ishtar of Arbail, the gods dwelling in heaven and earth, the gods of Asshur, the gods of Sumer and Akkad, all the gods of the lands.

As the heralds finished, in a perfect stillness, Sennacherib announced the order for everyone to swear, each individually, by Asshur and in the same way by each of the gods of the lands. The oaths echoed in the morning air and continued until the sun was almost at its zenith.

> This is the treaty which Sennacherib, King of Asshur, has concluded with you on behalf of Esarhaddon, the Great Crown Prince, son of Sennacherib, King of Asshur, whom he has named and appointed Crown Prince:
> When Sennacherib, King of Asshur, passes away, you will seat Esarhaddon, the Great Crown Prince, upon the royal throne and he will exercise the kingship and lordship of Asshur over you. You shall protect him in country and town, fall and die for him. You shall speak with him in the truth of your heart, give him sound advice loyally and smooth his way in every respect. You shall not depose him nor seat any one of his brothers, elder or younger, upon the throne of Asshur instead of him.
> You shall neither change nor alter the word of Sennacherib, King of Asshur, but serve this very Esarhaddon whom the King of Asshur, your lord, has presented to you.

At this point Esarhaddon—seated on a gilded, carved wooden chair, that was decorated with scenes of hunting, warfare and banqueting worked in deep relief—was carried slowly by four bearers from one end of the processional avenue to the other and back again. The crowds milled about the dispensers of chilled wine, grabbing dried fruit and handfuls of sesame wafers. When the presentation was complete and trumpets were blown, the crowd grew quiet and the king continued.

The next part of the ceremony ensured that no one would harm the Crown Prince.

> If you should hear improper things, you shall speak out—coming to Sennacherib, King of Asshur, your lord; and totally devote yourselves to the King your lord; you shall protect Esarhaddon, the Crown Prince designate whom Sennacherib King of Asshur has presented to you otherwise:

Now the priests struck great drums repeatedly, in a slow, steady beat until goose pimples travelled down the spine and knees grew weak. Then the king prayed, in concert with all the priests assembled from cities as far south as Uruk and as far north as Karkhemish, hundreds of them chanting together, the curse from all the gods that would fall upon them if they violated their oath.

The long day, a series of ceremonies that seemed never to be ending, finished with the king's family sprawled out on couches, ignoring the musicians and dancers. Outside in the city they could hear the sound of revels.

"Father," Esarhaddon ventured, "as Crown Prince can I …"

"You'll do as you're told."

"But," he began to object until Esharra reached over and put her finger on his lips.

Sennacherib, impatient, asked, "What have all of you been doing? Hasn't anyone ever taught this boy anything?"

Zaqutu looked up in alarm. This was no time for the king to have a temper tantrum. But Esharra's chatelaine, Remutu, turned to the prince. "The king tells you the truth. As Crown Prince that's just what you do. Whatever they tell you to." She shook her head, her solemn expression dissolving into a grin. "Tomorrow we'll come to Ekul, Asshur's temple, and your elevation. Before the priests crown you you'll experience every form of exorcism anyone knows, just in case you have ever disobeyed." As if he were king, she explained, he'd fail in his duty if he didn't maintain a perfect harmony with the gods.

Esarhaddon showed no enthusiasm. "What does that mean?"

"You know how your father has to stay in on unfavourable days, to avoid actions that have not received positive omens?"

"Sometimes he goes ahead anyway," Esarhaddon insisted. The king stirred and Zaqutu saw by the look on his face he was going to object. But Esarhaddon gave his father an ingratiating grin. "Oh, I know, then he makes atonement and gets purified."

Zaqutu felt she had to say something. "And you will too, from the moment Asshur makes you Crown Prince and then forever."

Silence followed while the prince digested her words. "I didn't have to take any of the oaths or utter curses. Why not?"

"That was just the treaty," the king explained. "You'll make your vows to Asshur in his temple, in Ekul. Then you'll obey, even as I do. I don't 'go ahead anyway' if I can help it."

Zaqutu stirred herself again. "Esarhaddon …" she hesitated a moment and looked around at them all. "I'm not going to use your new name. It's much too cumbersome." She turned to the king, "I know it's the right name, all that, but it takes so long to say it. I think everyone will use his boy-name, and why not?"

They all looked at the king and there was some embarrassed laughter, but Zaqutu shushed them. "My son the Crown Prince, you know the hanging I have in Kalkhu, the garden one?"

He nodded.

"Think of that river, the source of all life. It's Ishtar's navel and she is born of the earth itself, and she is the earth itself. So, you and your father are like Ishtar and her mother, one and the same."

"Her mother?"

"Mummu, she whose number is zero because she is the mysterious depths."

"I never heard of that before," Esarhaddon complained, to laughter from the others.

"There's a lot you've never heard," Remutu joked, "Maybe you never listen." Before he could object she turned to Zaqutu. "What is this hanging?"

"My weavers in Lakhiri did it. The tree of life and the river of life are displayed in the garden."

"Which version of the river of life did they use? Does it show how Ishtar as daughter of both Ea and Enlil?"

Zaqutu laughed. "Enlil's penis is not floating under the water in my hanging. The tree is elaborated with every detail." She turned to her son and said, "You should think more about the tree. It's your emblem now. It means Asshur rules the world, that he and the goddess are one incorporating all the gods and ruling over all the lands. Just as the tree is perfectly balanced, left and right, male and female, good and evil so you are now. Like Asshur himself you are to be the Shamash of justice and the Marduk of mercy. Wise as Ea and true as Suen. Careful as Nabu and fierce as Adad."

He looked down at his lap where Esharra's head rested as she dozed. A silence followed, broken by the prince. "So, all I'll ever do will be what the wise men say the gods have ordered."

The king reached over and stroked his curls. "Then you won't go wrong, and if things go amiss you make atonement."

When they left for the Inner City Zaqutu travelled overland; she hated the sense of being swept away by the river as the barges went downstream. The ceremony itself was almost incomprehensible. They had used those chants in the Inner City for hundreds, maybe thousands, of years. To her ears they didn't make sense. *I wonder what I have let my poor boy in for.* Ataril seemed to be more aware of the ritual. She whispered to him to explain, but he only put his finger over his lips.

The feast afterwards was easier to understand. Esarhaddon sat between her and the king, and every magnate, governor, high official in the army, head of any of the colleges of the priests or magi came and made obeisance to them. Zaqutu enjoyed that part of the affair. Now she could see the faces and persons of the many men and women whose names she had known only through reading the king's correspondence. Suddenly it dawned on her. *Now they can see me. I'm no longer in the background.* The thought disturbed her. *I have to be more careful now. I mustn't put a foot wrong.* She turned her head to catch sight of Ataril who stood behind her and to the side. *I must ask him to take special care to watch my steps.* He saw her gesture and smiled at her, quietly letting his hand rest on her shoulder, but not so it could be seen. She let go a little sigh of relief. *With Ataril I'll be safe. If only the king won't keep him in Asshur or send him off to Babili!*

Chapter 23: Another Son

When the time came for the Akitu festival, Zaqutu felt Shumukin was still too little for Esharra to keep the feast with Esarhaddon. Not wanting Esarhaddon to get a child with some other woman, Zaqutu proposed that this time she would go with Sennacherib. She looked at the tablet in her lap so she'd not have to meet his eyes as she read him Ishtar's oracle.

> I am the Lady of Arbail.
> To the king's wife: Because you implored me saying: "Make my son king after his father" now, fear not, my queen! He will be faithful and will rule, he and his sons and his sons' sons.
> By the mouth of the woman Ahat-Abisha of Arbail.

"I will get another son, a son you can send to Babili to be king there, to serve Marduk and Nabu in their own cities."

"I see. You've resisted before … "

"Never resisted you," she teased. "I hear the news, though. The rebels are now far away, starved of funds. Nikkal-Amat languishes in the far east, whether because you are so clever or because the Goddess inspired you. You were right, Arda-Mulissi no longer nibbles away at your peace since he has followed his aunt into exile." Zaqutu stopped to think. *He wants me to say why I've changed my mind.* She continued, "Besides, now you've told Paqaha you'll send water to Kalkhu. I'm so pleased." She sat herself down next to him and put her hand on the inside of his thigh, gently stroking.

He held back his response. "You'll come to Asshur now? Because I'll water your city or because you feel safe?"

She smiled and shrugged, caressing him, but made no reply.

He grumbled, "You know it's called the Inner City because it's the best fortified place in the whole world."

"I feel safe in Kalkhu," she started, her voice strident, "but ... I suppose it's because it's my true home."

"Aren't you safe here in Ninuwa? In the Succession Palace with your son the Crown Prince? What more do you want?"

She looked up at his face, smiling, luring him on, teasing. "I want to be with you, always with you."

He harrumphed. "You go off to Arbail most of the time. Live like a beggar. Maybe it's safe but it's damned uncomfortable."

"I don't think the Bit Akitu is either. Not safe and not comfortable." He shrugged but she pressed on. "Anyhow, if the Inner City is so well-fortified, protected by all the great gods, you don't need the gods from Babili in there. Send them back."

The king shook his head. She didn't have to look at him; she could feel his resistance. Not angry, but not cooperative either. *He can tell I'm only pretending.* Her resentment of Ataril's absence stood like a pillar between them.

After a deep breath he laughed and took her in his arms. He put his lips to her ear to murmur, "What if only by coming forth to you from their presence can I get you with child. What then?"

She laughed as she fondled him. "You don't need any gods for that."

Zaqutu refused to barge downstream to the Akitu festival so she arrived on horseback before the king's entourage reached the Inner City. She played her part in the ritual proudly, confident, mother of the Crown Prince, Queen of Asshur.

When summer came drought lay heavy on Asshur. Water levels in the river fell so low that when Zaqutu traveled from Ninuwa to Kalkhu in late autumn the barges went aground twice. They transferred her swollen body to a small coracle for the trip up the Zaba to Arbail. She lay back in the tiny boat surrounded by cushions, buried in fleeces, and stared at the leaden sky. At Arbail she observed the devotees as they fasted, danced and feasted, not a participant but a remote pair of eyes. Her heart felt as withered as the dry foliage and bleached landscape.

At the following winter solstice Zaqutu gave birth to a son whom she named Shibanu saying, "The only descendant poor Shebna will ever have." The king, overjoyed, gave the gods of Babili all the credit. To Zaqutu he sent a heavy necklace of lapis-lazuli, large enough to be worn by the Goddess herself. Too large to wear. Holding it in her lap, she stroked the cool stones, polished to an aquamarine that rivalled the winter sky at sunset.

Entrance to Asshur

Chapter 24: Impasse

At the full-moon ceremony after Shibanu's birth Sennacherib unveiled special barges to carry home from Asshur the gods of Babili, Marduk and Nabu. He offered the restoration as a token of his gratitude for the new son, but his plan to pacify the southern kingdom misfired.

In the king's council on the fourth day of Shebat, Sulmu-Bel, palace herald and commander of the eastern forces, spoke before the king. Many minutes, a speech well prepared and memorised, correct in form, he made his points precisely. At the end the council sat in stunned silence.

Though Arda-Mulissi no longer threatened the eastern borderlands, trouble nevertheless loomed. Sulmu-Bel had received reports. The veterans whom the king's father had settled east of the river were furious at any proposal to send the gods back to Babili. They'd fought, and their comrades had died to win that booty from Babili and Elam. The king heard the speech through but left the council so that no decision could be made.

In the New Palace braziers filled the women's quarters with warmth. Sennacherib stood beside one of them to warm his hands. Though Zaqutu saw only his back she could imagine his face contorted with fury. She heard his voice, high-pitched with irritation. "Don't you see? If the statues leave Asshur the southern army will mutiny."

She looked up as he turned to face her, "You know for sure?"

"Yes. Since your Ataril is in Asshur to oblige the priests from Babili, they have provided me with an oracle." Sarcasm and a grim smile transformed his face. "Oh yes, 'Your rebellious sons will take arms against you. All your enemies will gather behind one of them. You will be overwhelmed.'"

She sat with the new prince at her breast, her hand passing lightly over the soft hair of his head, and looked away from the king to stare at the coals. "So—" she pitched her voice low and quiet "—until this lad grows up Ataril is lost to me."

Sennacherib laughed. "You need not wait that long. As soon as Shumukin and Esharra go to Asshur to honour their gods, then Ataril can come back to you."

She looked up from her suckling child into the king's eyes. He was serious. *Barge them downstream? What if ...* She imagined Esharra sickening. Saw her convulsed with vomit and diarrhoea, dying. *Shumukin, my darling grandson.* She imagined him being seized and mutilated by the Elamites. She asked the king, "Shumukin too? Won't he be in danger? Esarhaddon needs a successor!"

"You sound like a fool. You know the prophecy. Esharra will bear another son, soon, and we'll call him Pulu. He's the destined successor. Don't you believe that?"

"The oracle came to Esarhaddon and isn't easy to interpret." Zaqutu recited:

> Fear not, Esarhaddon! I am Marduk who speaks to you, who watches over the beams of your heart. When your mother gave birth to you sixty great gods stood with me and protected you. Suen the moon-god was at your right side, Shamash the sun-god at your left; sixty great gods were standing around you and girded your loins.
> Do not trust in man. Lift up your eyes. Look to me! I am Ishtar of Arbail; I reconciled Asshur with you. When you were small, I took you to me. Do not fear; praise me!
> What enemy has attacked you while I remained silent? The future shall be like the past. I am Nabu, lord of the stylus. Praise me!

"It came 'By the mouth of the woman Baya, son of Arbail', and is like the earlier prophecies. The goddess loves Esarhaddon. I have no fear for him. Yet Ishtar reveals herself as Marduk. Why didn't the oracle say 'I am Asshur'?"

He echoed her last words as he searched her eyes. "So. Do you fear for yourself? Because Ataril is away? Do you believe Ataril would undermine your son?"

She shook her head but her lips stayed clenched, her face grim.

"You want to keep Esharra here?"

She looked down. After a moment she nodded her agreement.

He sighed, muttering at first and then saying out loud, "My love, I cannot oblige you. While the gods are in Ekul I have peace south and east. If I send the gods back it means civil war and then ... If anyone other than your eunuch could serve I'd send him back to you. The gods stay in their temple in Asshur, in Ekul."

Zaqutu put Shibanu to her breast and refused to answer him or even to look at him.

He started to walk away but turned back. "Will you celebrate the Akitu with me? It's two months away."

She refused. He tried again. "Esarhaddon and Esharra can't."

She shook her head. She didn't even follow him with her eyes as he strode out, shouting for his chariot. If she had known ...

Chapter 25: Zaqutu Sinks

That winter the cold froze the sides of the river, fires shrivelled and food grew short. Zaqutu sickened; no potions could warm her. She watched as the son she cradled against her chest stopped sucking and then, like her, chilled. Two weeks after Esharra bore Pulu—lusty, healthy and large—Shibanu slept and did not wake.

Winter settled in Zaqutu's heart, and the coming of spring brought no thaw. She cared not that the king had taken a new wife, Tebua. Before, when she had grieved for the lost babies or Ataril's absence, her sense of abandonment had been hot with rage and resentment. Now, cold, she felt nothing. Everything that had been her joy had slipped away—not all gone from the world but gone from her. Even Annabel, her most constant attendant, had stayed behind in Ninuwa with her husband and newborn daughter.

Zaqutu hid herself in Arbail until speech and writing deserted her, even worship of the goddess dimmed. She observed rituals as if smothered in a cloud of foam. Her dreams grew vivid in contrast. At first she was outside looking in. The underworld churned with demons torturing the damned. Shades of the dead drifted alongside the two rivers, the river of memory on the right and forgetfulness on the left. She seemed trapped on the right, unable to leave behind the world of the living, hungering for the left-hand stream but bound tight, immovable.

As the particulars of Ishtar's true rites faded from her sight, her dream life took over. She moved among shades, feeling light and young, bearing a palm branch that shed gold drops, the fee for her passage across the river. There she found Ataril, naked and golden, piping sonorous notes that eased her pain and drew her after him.

The king visited her in late spring, describing the Akitu feast and his new bride. "They found me a very young girl, Tebua, not trained at all. I'd much rather you had come. But you will be interested in the oracle." Her eyes met his, though the lethargy that afflicted her prevented any words from coming forth. " 'At the summer solstice Shamash will decide for Marduk and Nabu, whether they will leave Ekul to enter again into their own city.' "

Roused, she asked, "Will you do it, if Shamash gives the sign?"

Sennacherib stood up and walked a few paces away and then back to her. "I have never disobeyed an oracle. If that word comes to the priests of Asshur, to the wisest scholars of the world, how could I not do it? The men of Babili will have to find themselves a building. I'm not establishing anything in that rebellious city."

"Your veterans?" she asked. "How will they react?"

"Ah, yes, that I do not know," he sighed. "Esharra wants to return along with the gods, with Shumukin, to rule in Babili. The men of Babili love her and Bit-Yakin will never unseat her. I hope my veterans will love my grandson in whose name she will rule. Pulu will stay in the Succession Palace with the Crown Prince. They will need you. Won't you join them? Aren't you Queen, mother of the Crown Prince? I would ..." The king hesitated.

Just one of her shoulders twitched. "You will do what you like, and with whomsoever you choose. It's nothing to me."

He came and stood before her. She made no move to rise, and his face grew hard. She looked up into his grim mouth, those hooded eyes. Her mouth felt stiff, her whole body paralysed as in her dream. Without a word the king stalked off. *I'll never see him again,* she thought, and felt only a chill. She shivered.

With summer's warmth Zaqutu began to sleep more than she was awake, dreaming instead of thinking. She saw the goddess moving about the temple enclosure, entering and leaving sanctuary and storeroom, picking up and dropping items one by one. The images dissolved and reformed until she saw the goddess at the top of her ziggurat, naked to the wind that blew her hair swirling about her head.

In her delicate, long fingers the goddess lifted the shugurra-crown, turreted like a city wall and bedecked with gems over each of its twelve gates. She placed it on her head, subduing the coils of her hair. One by one she added earrings with dangling pendant emeralds, lapis lazuli beads on long chains. Across her breasts she strapped the alluring breastplate and around her hips she draped the girdle of birthstones. Balancing on one foot, she lifted the other high so her hands might fasten her anklets, one at a time. On her arms she placed torques, while gold bracelets studded with gems surrounded her wrists. Finally she slipped a richly embroidered cloth under the girdle in front and then in back. She descended the ziggurat sleepily, as if drugged, a single step in a minute.

In dreams Zaqutu endured torments worse than any she'd imagined. The gnat demon and the scorpion, kurgarra and galatur, lunged at her. She cried out for Gula to come with her dog, to chase them, to save her from their poisoned stings. Her head seemed to flame with outrage.

Awake she grieved for her dead boy. Asleep she saw his lifeless corpse hanging from Ereshkigal's arms. The full moon of Elul came but still she slept or sat entranced all day, all night. The food they brought her stayed in the bowl; she never spoke. She dreamed herself as the Goddess mourning, drinking the sacred brew of forgetfulness. She tasted the malted barley, the sharp mint, the sweet honey. Awake she refused all food. Asleep all the great gods sought to comfort her. My boy, my golden boy, was always her reply.

Two days before the three-day fast for the autumn new moon Ahat-Abisha came into her chamber and took both her hands to lift her up. She floated to her feet and, drawn by the priestess into the presence of the Goddess, began to stumble until in front of the statue she fell headlong.

> I am the Lady of Arbail, she heard.
> To the mother of the Crown Prince: Because you implored me, saying: 'You have placed in your lap them of the king's right and them of the king's left, but my own offspring you took from me. He roams the steppe as a shade of the underworld'—because you said that I say to you 'Now fear not, my daughter. The kingdom is yours, yours is the power!' By the mouth of the woman Ahat-Abisha of Arbail.

Zaqutu stirred and pulled herself into a sitting position; she felt the cold of the polished stone floor, smelled the incense and the musty odour of the ceramic figurines. Awake now, she turned her head from side to side and gave a moan.

"Daughter. We will begin the fast and the rites of the goddess. You have been teetering on the brink of some abyss. Lest you mean to offer yourself as a sacrifice, stop and consider. The word of the goddess is against that course."

"I heard you," Zaqutu answered in a toneless monotone, struggling to frame words. "Mine is the power. What if I don't want it?" As she asked her insides boiled over. A torrent of unspoken words that welled up inside her began to pour forth.

Ahat-Abisha listened in silence. She heard the pain Qat, Zaqutu's power-obsessed mother, had caused. Hours passed because night fell and they sat in the darkened, chilly chapel, neither moving, letting the words emerge, drift around the goddess and fall empty to the floor.

Finally the priestess uttered a long sigh. "Only a scholar would find some saying of the sages of old that would soothe or direct you.

Nevertheless, you are not meant to open your ear to the Great Below, though that is where your dreams lead you. Your hatred of Ishtar of Ninuwa is misplaced. You, Naqia, you hate the misuse of money and power there. Well and good, but every evil or discomfort you have ever imagined you believe comes from Nikkal-Amat."

Zaqutu stirred, first at the mention of her childhood name and then at the name of her enemy.

"In you lives someone you hate; call her Ereshkigal. When you hate that aspect of the goddess in you then—" Zaqutu straightened up and tried to wave her hand front of Ahat-Abisha's mouth to stop her words, but the older woman continued, "You see her outside. In Nikkal-Amat for instance."

"I have seen the goddess heading for the underworld, forsaking the *me*. I am inside her. She weeps for her boy, I weep for mine."

"Nonsense. You are Naqia, her devotee, you are not the Goddess herself. In a few days the goddess will set her mind to the land of no return, the realm of Ereshkigal. She will enter the darkness, where dwell those who eat dust and clay, wear wings for clothes, sleep in the dust. She goes in love, not mourning. I'm asking you. Will you throw your life away or will you mourn her as we do, beseeching the gods to bring the water of life to anoint her corpse, to order the kurgallu to bear her up, back through the seven gates? Will you mourn or will you die?"

"I will do as the goddess commands."

Ahat-Abisha put her lower lip between her teeth. "You will do your own will. You are angry—angry because your baby died, angry because your husband has taken a new wife, angry because he rejoices in a son who is not your son. You are jealous, Naqia, and that jealousy eats you inside like a worm. Your flesh is decaying. You are not a fit offering for the goddess."

A light of anger burned in Naqia's eyes. "Jealous?"

"You act like you're playing Tsarpanitu to Tebua's Ishtar."

"Tsarpanitu? Marduk's wife? And why do you say 'Tebua's Ishtar'?" Zaqutu roused herself to ask again. "Why is Ishtar hers?"

Ahat-Abisha showed surprise at Zaqutu's ignorance and Zaqutu blinked in response. She felt Ahat-Abisha sit back down beside her and take her hand. "Don't you know the lament of Tsarpanitu?"

When Zaqutu shook her head Ahat-Abisha sighed and told the story.

"Ishtar came along to Marduk and poured forth her powerful allure. Her power drew him away from Tsarpanitu, his wife, and he went off to make love to his sister on their palatial bed. Tsarpanitu, totally dejected, lamented, 'She was preferred to me, so I heard, to make love with.' She asks why she sleeps alone in a little cell while her husband frolics with a rival on the roof. Isn't that what you're doing?"

Zaqutu, lips pursed, shook her head.

Ahat-Abisha continued, "When the sulking queen learns that Ishtar is her rival she exclaims:

> 'So it is none other than you, the mother, Ishtar of Babili, the pretty one ... you, the mother, the palm tree ... most beautiful among the most beautiful, whose appearance is just so alluring ... You.'

"So she curses her, curses Ishtar, goes down the ziggurat and into the garden, seeking maybe to poison her rival or to gather magic herbs to make herself again full of sex appeal. Again and again she curses Ishtar."

Zaqutu, interested now, exclaimed, "I saw Ishtar going down, not Tsarpanitu!" A moment's doubt and a moment's interest exhausted her. Her voice still fogged by drowsiness, she asked, "She curses the goddess?"

"Oh yes indeed.

> 'You, you're quite used up! Into your vulva, by which you set such great store, I shall make a fierce dog enter and tie shut the door. Into your vulva, by which you set such great store, sharp fangs instead of jewels. "O vulva of my sweetheart why do you keep discharging?" Ha! Oh vulva of your sweetheart, all Babili seeks rags to wipe up after you. From your vulva, by which you set such great store, sniff there the smell of cattle, the stench of something not worth a tailor's mending, a thing no laundry man would soak.'

"She threatens to send a bird to nest in Ishtar's vagina, a spell to make Ishtar's armpits reek. Then, she says, let them flock around to call Ishtar 'beautiful one, queen, a palm of carnelian'."

Zaqutu clasped her arms around her chest and shivered. "It seems more likely that Tebua has been cursing me, not the other way around."

"Naqia! It's no one else's problem. It's yours. Your spite will turn the king against the Crown Prince and still you don't act. Not because Marduk and Nabu remain in Ekul and Ataril remains with them, but because you cannot control the hatred and bitterness inside yourself."

"Let my death appease the goddess. I don't care."

"It won't." Ahat-Abisha stamped her foot.

Zaqutu looked up in alarm as she sensed the priestess's departure. *Would she abandon me, her own protégée?*

Her voice quiet but hard, the priestess continued, "If they go to Asshur, you know, and receive the oracle, then soon will come preparations. Don't you see what will happen? If the king even starts building ... or once new barges are built for Nabu and Marduk and they ride to Babili, maybe it would be at low water this winter. Whenever they set off, it means war, civil war. Don't you know that?"

"He needs Ataril. No one needs me—they'll all go on as they would do anyway."

When dawn began to break Ahat-Abisha left the sanctuary. "You heard the word of the goddess. Yours is the power."

Zaqutu shut herself up in her room and refused to keep the feast, the first time in seventeen years that she had held back from the mourning and from the rejoicing. Messages came to her with news of the war to come; that Shulmu-Bel had abandoned the army of the south and joined the eastern army in rebellion. She refused to read them.

At the full moon of the winter solstice Esarhaddon came to Arbail and entered his mother's quarters uninvited. "Mother of the Crown Prince, see, here I am. I need you. The wife you gave me and our sons, we need you. The temple of Arbail is no longer sanctuary, no longer safe. The king my father goes this month to the Inner City to set the gods of Babili on their barges. Asshur will be safe, but east of the river there will be rebellion, war. Esharra and Shumukin will go with the statues. I want you to take Pulu to the Succession Palace. Will you not come?"

Roused, Zaqutu asked, "Are you going to Asshur?"

"No."

"Why not?"

"Politics. The king's magnates don't … they don't believe the gods of Babili brought good fortune to the king. They resent his plan to rebuild the temples of Babili."

"So? Why does that keep you away?"

"Because the king wants to mollify the nobles of Babili. The magnates of his council, he says, blame me for the whole policy. He 'favours Babili' they say. Then the king became angry with me for some reason." Esarhaddon hesitated. "In front of the whole council he declared to me, 'You're the problem.'" He's acting like I'm a danger to Tebua and her son. I suppose that's why he's sending me off to Khanigalbat to muster the northern army, so I'm not able to stay in Ninuwa. That's why I need you to live in the Succession Palace with Pulu. The gods have said Pulu will be Crown Prince when I am king. Come to Ninuwa, please."

Part of Zaqutu's mind paid attention despite her feelings. Esarhaddon's explanation rang false. "I will stay here until the Goddess expels me."

Esarhaddon pleaded, "Mother, please. We have all heard the oracle. Ishtar of Arbail says that you hold the power. If you just sit here doing nothing …"

She paid no attention to the plaintive tone of his voice but slowly formed the words of her reply. "From your own mouth: I have the power—the power to sit here and do nothing." She heard him sit back on his haunches but would not look at him.

But he spoke, "The wise have many sayings. I have heard them. You can do wrong by doing nothing."

News came to Arbail of the son born to Tebua in Ninuwa. After the birth the king travelled down the river to Asshur to give thanks, to oversee the transfer of Marduk and Nabu from Ekul to Esagila, from Baltil in Asshur to Babili. He seemed so absorbed in his plan no one dared to interfere. Like Tammuz lounging under a tree while Ishtar suffered, the king followed his course. Despite his advisers' reservations he proclaimed his intention to all the lands south of Asshur, ordering the project like a military campaign.

As the king's control over the south loosened, his officials became uneasy. They noticed preparations for war in towns along the eastern shore. Two of those officials—spies, Tsilla and Nabu-Shumu-Ishkun, wrote to warn the king. No answering reply came to them, no words from their king, no deeds to obstruct the preparations. They opened a correspondence with Arda-Mulissi.

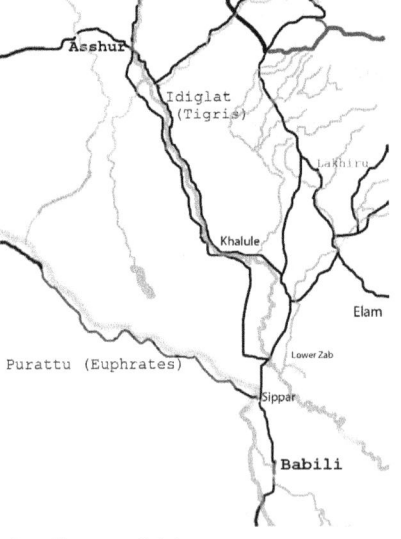

During the last three months of that year Zaqutu sank deeper into the dream-world, her soul exploring the depths. In her waking moments being supplanted as queen meant nothing. In dreams she saw herself headless, unable to speak any priestly incantation, having no mouth. Awake she merely huddled in her room. When she slept her body walked the porticoes of Ninuwa Central, traipsed through the storerooms, searching for her missing ears, seeking the pendant earrings. She forgot how Esarhaddon had begged her to live in the Succession Palace, forgot being dressed richly and hung with necklaces, remembered nothing but mourning, able only to mourn her lost child. She dreamed herself naked, lying among the dead with Shibanu sucking at her breast. Where her alluring breastplate would have been she could feel the chill air of the underworld.

Chapter 26: The Patricide

While Zaqutu slept in Arbail, Arda-Mulissi led the eastern army of Asshur in rebellion. Late in Tebet they crossed the Lower Zaba, getting hold of both banks of the Diglat. News of this failed to reach Arbail. It failed also to come to Ekul where the king and Ataril set about readying the gods of Babili for their journey downriver.

When the eastern army had set up its encampment, as dusk fell and while no moon lit the evening sky, Arda-Mulissi with his two brothers and three oarsmen rowed upriver. The boat landed at the dock below the Shamash tower. While it was still night, the three brothers crept up the steep embankment. In capes of dark-dyed wool and their hands free of any weapons they made their way furtively into the storerooms of Ekul. There they left their cloaks and sandals.

Arda-Mulissi sent the youngest of his brothers, the half-wit Sharrani-Muballissu, to climb the ziggurat. Sharrani was to shout and scream when he could no longer see his father on the promenade that linked the palace with the temple. An otherwise harmless idiot, he'd draw off the king's bodyguard. Etli would get rid of Aram-Suen, Sennacherib's third man, chief of his bodyguard. Arda-Mulissi reserved the killing of the king to himself.

Years on campaign had given Arda-Mulissi a good head for tactics; he had planned the assassination well. Three resourceful and determined men could have carried off the project, both the murder and the seizure of the Inner City. But Arda-Mulissi's brothers were not resourceful or determined.

It began well. When his brother's shouts rang out in the early morning air, Arda-Mulissi picked up two votive statues—a winged, eagle-headed apkallu figure and the fish-skinned image of the divine sage, Adapa. Standing behind the huge statue of Marduk, he waited until the king came close. With Adapa's image he smashed in his father's head, striking blow after blow with both hands in a berserk rage. He stopped only when Etli's screams echoed in protest. Panicked, sick at the sight of so much blood, Etli had let go of Aram-Suen and fled out of the temple and down the embankment to the boat. Aram-Suen, bleeding where Etli had knifed him in the back of the knee, tried to follow.

Alone now, afraid to be cut off from his retreat, Arda-Mulissi sped after them out of the sanctuary, threading his way through the storerooms. The guards, massed in the front of the temple, missed the assassin's escape from the back. Only Aram-Suen saw Arda stumble and fall headlong down the cliff. Just before he fainted from shock he saw Arda make it into the boat before the oarsmen obeyed Etli's command to push off.

In the temple, among the shouts and tumult of the soldiery, Ataril knelt weeping as the king tried to take his hand, tried to speak, tried to swallow the blood that flooded in his throat and out his nose. The guards, holding Sharrani-Muballissu captive, found the queen's eunuch shutting the king's eyes, his own tears coursing down his cheeks.

Once Sharrani had babbled out the whole story, the royal troops learned more than just information on how the plot against the king had worked. The rebels lay encamped only a day's journey away! The Chief Eunuch ordered, "Bury the king at once. He will not lie in state as his fathers have done but he will sleep with them outside the old south tower. Have boats outside the Crown Prince's palace. Send messengers to have chariots and extra horses brought to the nearest landing stage north of the city."

It was the second day of Shebat when Ahat-Abisha swept into Zaqutu's chamber, tears streaming down her face, wailing her grief.

At first Zaqutu thought the apparition part of a dream. The noise woke her but, light-headed, she felt too weak to stand.

"Get up," the priestess demanded and Zaqutu struggled to obey.

The two women faced each other without a word spoken. As if she were swimming up from deep underwater Zaqutu left her dream world. At once she noticed the older woman's torn robe, the ashes on her head.

"My lord the king?" she asked, but without waiting for a reply she made to tear her clothing. She was naked except for a breechcloth and some jewellery. The clasps had seemed too hard to undo and she had not allowed herself to be washed or anointed for weeks. Tears came then, gushing forth, and she wailed with a wild abandon that had never taken her when she mourned the death of Ishtar. "Let me go to him," she cried.

"You're too late," Ahat-Abisha sobbed out. "He's been hurriedly buried. They have sent messengers to the Crown Prince, your son. He's with the army of the north. Part of the southern army is on the march from Asshur, and some will come here to protect you."

"Me?" Zaqutu had quite left the world of dreams now. "Why?"

Ahat-Abisha shook her head, her voice grim. "Daughter, you act in folly. Believe me. Arda-Mulissi will want to take you as wife. You know the Goddess did say 'Yours is the power'?"

Zaqutu laughed wildly, growing hysterical. "Oh, my mother. How funny." She drew off the breechcloth and pointed to her vagina. "I cannot oblige him—I have not that power."

The priestess blew her nose and sniffed. "You're ill! Why ...?" As if her grief had been forgotten she took hold of Zaqutu and pushed her back on to the bed. She unclasped the queen's torques that had crusted over with the pus from the scratched sores. Muttering about the way Zaqutu's servants had let themselves be dismissed, leaving her unattended, the priestess sent for medicine and cloths, and dispatched a runner to bring the doctor.

"I will die," Zaqutu told her, calm and rational. *I understand what I must do.* At the sight of the Mother's lifted eyebrows she explained, "See, I have come to the seventh gate. Crown gone, earrings gone, beads gone, breastplate ..."

"Naqia, you never had the breastplate. You drew the king to you without it."

"I am no longer able to invite ... to lure a consort. With this ... this red itching, painful and putrid body I am fit for nothing but to hang from a tree to satisfy the new life that will come from the Great Below."

"You suppose you're accursed, do you? Not at all. You quarrelled with your husband, and not for the first time. He went off and took another woman. You couldn't face that. All that has happened, you have done."

"Me?" Zaqutu looked at herself, seated on a stool over a straw mat, her body dripping with oil that smelled of crushed juniper. Now, remembering her widowhood, she hunched forward, rocking a little, and wept.

Helped by servants, the priestess dressed her in a rough tunic and laid the Queen Mother on her new bedding. Zaqutu took the sleeping draft without protest and turned to the wall to sleep, hoping the goddess would bless her, and that she would not wake again.

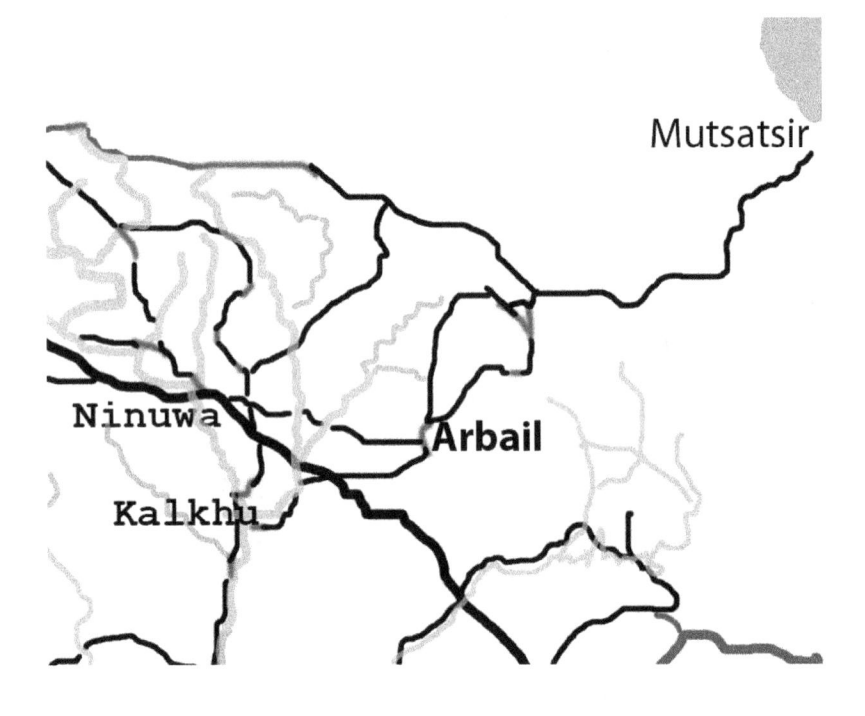

Chapter 27: Zaqutu Reaches the Temple of Gula

While Zaqutu slept in Arbail the power she held set all the armies of Asshur on the move. Much of the southern army had not gone over to the rebels; they had formed up under Esharra-Hammat's chief eunuch. They called themselves the army of Babili and marched against Arda-Mulissi's rearguard at Asshur, forcing the rebels to fight on two fronts. They harried the stragglers but could not prevent the rebels from moving north.

Unopposed, Arda-Mulissi's army marched to take Asshur, Kasappa, Kalkhu and Ninuwa. Until they reached Ninuwa, on the eighth day of Shebat, they took whatever they needed and moved on. In Ninuwa the royal army fought to save Tebua and her infant son, to no avail. Arda's rebels had far superior force. Sennacherib's youngest son and his mother were slain.

The rebel army looted the royal palaces and Ninuwa Central, an enormous plunder of food and wine, women and gold. Glutted, overwhelmed with plunder, the soldiers broke ranks. More than a week passed before the rebel generals could regroup their forces to push further on. Arda could not rule until he had found and defeated Esarhaddon.

The Crown Prince, however, led all the forces from the northern and western provinces—troops raised from Zaqutu's provinces. They were loyal and well-supplied as well as being supported by the governors and headmen.

At the new moon of Shebat an army corps from the Inner City arrived at Arbail. Ataril left the soldiers at the gate, and entered the sacred precincts alone. Inside, he went straight to Zaqutu's room. She sat on the floor in one corner, draped in a rough tunic, torn and sprinkled with ashes. Her hair lay loose over her shoulders and clumps of hair she had pulled out lay about her on the floor.

At the sound of his footsteps she raised her tear-stained face to him and broke into a new paroxysm of sobbing. "Ataril, weep with me.

Weep for me—my own sin is grievous to me. I cannot be comforted."

"My lady, I have wept for my father who perished in Asshur, slaughtered in front of Nabu his god. I have wept also for Sennacherib, the king, my lord. No days now remain for mourning." He reached forward and took each of her hands in his. "Come, my lady, come out into the daylight."

He took a fleece from the table by the door and put it round her shoulders, then half-carried her emaciated body outdoors. Since she was too weak to sit he propped her up on a bench and held her close to him. "Your own sin? What have you done?"

Zaqutu felt a stirring of interest, more from the sound of his voice and his nearness than from his words. When he asked again about her sin she let the tears roll down her cheeks, and sobbed softly, unwilling or unable to put her shame into words. "My lord the king," she murmured. "She says I had it in my power to save him. I let him go. I didn't even speak. I never kissed him." She faltered and fell silent.

Ataril stayed beside her, holding her upright. She could feel him looking at her. At last he said, "I heard that you were ill—samanu sickness they say. You need the healers."

"I cannot be comforted," she repeated.

"I will comfort you but we must leave. We'll go to Gula's temple in Nagir, you and I—with Annabel, of course."

At the mention of Annabel's name she roused herself, just to try to catch his drift. *Why?* she wondered and heard herself asking him aloud.

He sounded urgent. "If you stay here you will fall into Arda-Mulissi's hands."

Still dazed and heavy with a lassitude that came from her sickness—but also from the drug the priestess had given her, she declared, "That doesn't matter."

"My lady! The northern army stays with Esarhaddon because of you, they are your men."

She shrugged and waved his words away.

Ataril sat shivering, watching her face. She looked up at him to read his thoughts, saw him looking at her the same way. Servants who crossed the courtyard saw the two as they leaned against the sun-warmed wall, silent, staring into each other's eyes. Finally Ataril put his arms around her so he could whisper into her ear, "Tell me what so grieves you, what has kept you here long before the king went to Asshur?"

Stirred by the sun or by his closeness she rested her forehead on his shoulder. At first she whispered in a dull monotone, but her voice rose in pitch as she came to feel the shafts of her poisoned regrets; she recited how she had blundered. "I used my allure, my sex appeal, to pull the king away from the army. You yourself warned us about having two armies, a recipe for civil war.

"We should never have gone to Jerusalem or at least I should have told the king I had a good time. He lost most of his veterans from the northern army in that affray. My fault, all of it. And then, if that hadn't happened he'd not have lost to Elam at Khallule. That's what made the veterans in the east hate me—and hate him because of me."

Ataril held her as she began to weep, not wildly but in exhausted frustration. "Oh, Ataril, if only … I ought to have given him many sons, to rule many provinces—sons of the same mother who would hold everything together, branches of the one tree, Ishtar's tree."

"You cannot be at fault for not trying. Many seeds sprouted in your womb. Is it sin to miscarry? None of the wise have ever said so."

"Our mother says it's my fault, that it all comes from my hatred of Nikkal-Amat. The troubles in the east—she fomented them. All her provinces were there. Now you want to take me to Nagir." Her voice rose in hysteria. "We mustn't go east, we mustn't."

"I assure you, my dear, you must go east in order to go anywhere. Arda-Mulissi holds both sides of the river from Asshur to Balatsa."

"Oh," she wailed, "see what I've done." He shook his head but she persisted. "No, really, I sent him away because he made you stay in Asshur. I nagged him endlessly to ship the gods back there so you could come to me. You, my bridal gift," she sobbed. "He gave you to me."

Stroking her back through the fleece coverlet, Ataril murmured, "I am yours. Both of us owed our service to the king. You are …" he hesitated. "You were his. I was too. Now your son will be king." He shut her opened mouth with one finger under her chin. "The Goddess speaks only truth. So now you will be—you must be—Queen Mother. You have no choice."

"I told Esarhaddon, if I have the power I have the power to refuse."

"The power is hers, Ishtar's, not yours. She won't let you refuse."

"Ataril, she should. She should let me refuse. I make bad choices. If I hadn't nagged him to make him send the gods back he would be alive and—"

"And we'd have civil war anyway. Babili and Elam would come in against Asshur and might again prevail. We'd have had civil war in any case when Tebua's son strove to oust Esarhaddon from the Succession Palace."

"Don't you see? It is all my fault," she wailed. "I should have gone to Ninuwa Central in the first place, taken my punishment, married Arda-Mulissi. Maybe I was being a fool then."

Ataril opened his mouth to reply but she fainted, slumping against him and then falling to the ground.

"We'll be safe, first of all because no one will expect us to go that way," Ataril reassured Ahat-Abisha. "I'll rig a litter so she can lie in it asleep all day, I'll need to drug her."

"Yes, you will. She's quite mad and won't agree to go. The ashipu will come down to Mutsatsir or to the Upper Zab. At night you must let her wake, you will have to stay in lonely places. Gossips and spies are often the same."

"The herbalists up there—have they …?"

"You need not worry. A runner has gone already. Tomorrow Shemahu will be here; he will want to come with you."

"Oh no. He's too old—he'll hold us up."

"Someone has to help you carry the litter. Annabel will walk alongside carrying Pulu. You'll be going quite slowly."

"Pulu?"

"You must keep him with you—Annabel is his wet-nurse. And anyway, Zaqutu must have one maidservant."

The lands of Nagir Ekalli could be reached in two days by barging up the Zaba, but in late winter the waters were too low. By road the journey took seven days. Each night they found a secluded hut and Ataril walked to a village to buy food. They left the baby beside Zaqutu's pallet; she would babble nonsense to him from her drugged dreaming and he repeated the sounds back to her cheerfully.

The temple of Gula stood apart from any villages. It lay where a stream went off towards Topsawa. Upstream the river curved sharply northwest. People of the hill country of Urartu and its huge lakes took no interest in the politics of Asshur. A good harvest, with storehouses still full of food, cheered them. They would sell their surplus to travellers and ask no questions.

The temple enclosure was less than a quarter the size of Arbail, and dusty. Dogs roamed everywhere, clustering about the door of the room next to the sanctuary where they held bread rituals. Their noise and smell became oppressive in the damp mist that covered the area at night. Ataril found a small hut not far from the stockade, next door to the potter's workroom. Waking from her stupor, Zaqutu could hear thumping as the potter mixed his clay, and could smell the smoke of the fire in his oven. Ataril commissioned five small pottery dogs as an offering to Gula, one for each of them.

Chapter 28: Healing

For two days they kept Zaqutu awake, tending her sickness and chills, binding her tightly as she thrashed and shivered. Annabel wept at the queen's pitiful cries for more poppy. She would sit outside the door of their hut ready to put her hands over the baby's ears so he should not hear.

A barrage of loud barking announced the arrival of the ashipu, an exorcist who dwelt most of the time far off in the hill country. Shemahu left their hut and entered the sacred precincts to greet Zakir. Years before, the exorcist had come to Kilizi for Shemahu's uncle, possessed of a demon.

"Peace to you, Zakir. The Queen Mother has needed your help for a year now but has not been willing." Shemahu wondered at the grizzled face and thin arms of the healer. He looked to be at death's door himself. He also looked wary and puzzled.

"The Queen Mother? My lady Atalia is long dead." The ashipu's voice came surprisingly strong, but Shemahu realised that the old man must not have spoken to anyone on his journey, that he knew nothing of the civil war.

He beckoned the old man to a seat on the bench outside the stockade and told of the king's death, of the war raging throughout the land between the rivers and eastward. "The Crown Prince is now king, and his mother needs your help."

"Is she truly possessed?" the ashipu asked Shemahu. "May it not be but a wife's grief? And why have you come here?"

"We will speak of these things later. I will take you to the lady and then say what I have tried to do. It is no mere grief. Samanu sickness I think, but she has seemed slowly to die to the world. Sleeping long and eating little, dreaming terrible dreams, forsaking her duties, even withdrawing from the Goddess."

"From Ishtar? She's a devotee? Oh, of course, I knew that. Let me see her. Are her servants—" he spoke hesitantly "—aware that I must see all of her?"

"We have been anointing her body with juniper paste. She is kept wrapped but not clothed." As they walked Shemahu explained how they had drugged her for the long slow journey. She was now demented from being kept awake, and Shemahu urged Zakir to ignore anything she said.

"Friend, I cannot ignore what she says. I have to name and find the demon in her. In Gula's presence she will speak true."

"And the priest?"

"He stays away."

When Zakir arrived at her hut Zaqutu was dozing fitfully, emerging from sleep only to utter cries of pain. Her poppy withdrawal was almost complete though she had not begun to show any interest in her surroundings or in any person except Pulu. If he woke she petted and tended him, and watched silently when Annabel nursed him.

The old man stood in the doorway, sniffing, but did not enter. He asked Shemahu, "Who are they in there? There's a baby."

"The new king's younger son, Pulu, and his wet nurse. My lady, the Queen Mother is ... well, not just fond—she seems bound to him. He comforts her."

Zakir asked the others leave the hut before he would go in, and made it very clear they were to stay away when he brought her into the complex. "No one but the Queen Mother comes with me."

"But she cannot walk—she's too weak."

"I will carry her."

Ataril had heard the exchange as he came around the side of the hut. "Greetings, my brother Zakir. I am Ataril, Chief Eunuch of the Queen. Must I leave her too? Her illness has been brought about by ... well, partly by my leaving her. Her distress ..."

The healer only shook his head in furious denial, but Ataril added, "May I not even carry her in for you? You are ..."

"I am old, not weak."

The exorcist had his way and Zaqutu's servants huddled in the doorway of their hut, straining their ears. A deep stillness settled on the entire temple complex.

As Zakir went to enter the hut Shemahu began muttering under his breath, saying he wished he had treated her against her will, wondered if maybe it wasn't samanu, maybe he'd used the wrong medicine. "Do you know," he asked Annabel, "if she hurt herself in her wanderings? I wonder if that might be it?"

Annabel stirred and shrugged. "My lady has always been one to keep her thoughts and hurts to herself. I wasn't with her the whole time, either." After a silence she added, "I think she hasn't been right in the head for a long time. Even before the red skin and the pain. Even before her boy died, she ... I wonder if some demon was already seeking her death. Only it got her baby first."

"Perhaps you're right," Ataril commented. "I feel Pulu is the only one of us she thinks is real."

Inside, in front of Gula's statue, Zakir had set up pots filled with coals. On them he sprinkled pieces of resin and dried blossoms. Zaqutu lay full length on the floor, wrapped in sheepskin, whimpering, tense, her teeth tightly clenched with pain or fear.

"My lady," Zakir began, "you and I will learn the name of the demon who afflicts you."

Zaqutu found herself unable to open her mouth, unable to move, unable to resist the old man who took a small pot of sour-smelling ointment and rubbed his hands in it. When he reached forward to remove the sheepskin that covered her she tried to turn away from him, to find Gula's image. Instead her head moved in the opposite direction and she saw them, the dogs, slavering at the doorway. Her breath hissed in her nose.

"They are Gula's servants. Your sickness will pass from you to them. Gula ordains that they remain unharmed."

Zakir lifted the covering and peered at Zaqutu's flesh. His oily fingers probed at her armpits, at her groin, then he parted her legs gently and bent down to sniff her vulva. "Juniper, ah, for the evil eye? Has any enemy looked at you?"

Zaqutu found she could move her head from side to side to deny it. Still her lips were clenched tight and she couldn't open her mouth. The ashipu then began feeling her upper arms, rubbing at the scabs where her torques had been. The pain opened her mouth and she moaned, feebly trying to push him away.

"That hurts?" He placed his long fingers around her upper arm and stared at her legs, bony with knobs poking out at knee and ankle. "You have lain still for a long time, unhappy woman."

With a grunt he pulled himself to his feet and rummaged in his satchel until he found a bronze canister with a tight-fitting lid. He took from it some seeds and sprinkled them onto the incense pots. Once he had brought them up near her nose she gave a cough and sputtered. Drawing breath with a gasp, she inhaled the sweet-scented smoke that curled about her head. *Hemp*, she thought, *of course*.

A smile rose to her lips unbidden and she sank into a reverie. She felt him cover her body and smelt the oil of his hands as he squatted beside her on the floor. She saw, perhaps only with her mind's eye, quiet coming forth from his head in rays. Her hearing caught every nuance in that silence. She heard the dogs lie down too, quelled by the stillness that radiated from the exorcist's brow.

Zaqutu closed her eyes and let the spell take over. Coloured lights flickered and clouded over. Shapes danced before her, clothed in brown linen, like Gula herself. She knew they were sweet-tempered and merciful. A smell of healing balm—a balsamic odour blended with the smoke from the braziers—and her vision went dark. A dull red light streamed from her eyes, lighting up the face of the exorcist. She could hear him chanting, a hymn to Nergal, his lord, king of the underworld. She struggled to move but all her limbs felt paralysed.

Maybe she slept, if only for a moment, but she knew she waked suddenly to hear Zakir's gravelly voice command her to speak. A river of words came out of her, an incoherent babble. With a power of quiet he listened—patient, dreamy, nodding from time to time. After a while he began to tap his bronze bell in a rhythm that made her drowsy.

Her words began to make sense. She could hear herself singing love poems, praises of the bride's sex, hymns to the glowing of her eyes, boasts of her lover's prowess. To her husband she addressed praise, "Your lovemaking is sweet, the allure of your love is sated with honey." Her eyes opened and she saw, clearly, the statue of Gula and she shrieked. Shivering, yelling, she felt herself sinking into darkness. At the same time her eyes sprang open. Her body rigid, pupils dilated, she struggled to move, her neck throbbing, she gagged.

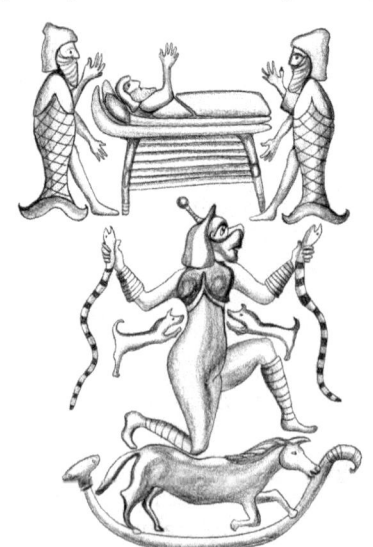

Now held by a sort of vice squeezing her, she felt Zakir's breath on her face. He had leaned forward, was peering into the depths of her eyes. All she could see was his mouth. "Name him!" he commanded.

Under his spell she uttered the name, "Lamashtu."

Ah," he sighed. "Yes, it would be." He moved closer to the incense burners and inhaled deeply.

Zaqutu heard the clang of the bell, the monotonous thrum of his voice, but she couldn't make out any words. The chanted nonsense went on and on until the flames in the burners sputtered out. The air cleared. Now she could make out some of the words. Names of demons. Each one he ordered to come out—male demons, female demons, galatur.

A thirst came upon her and she tried to form words. Her lips moved and she took a deep breath. "Water."

Zakir stopped his chant and clapped his hands. The priest of Gula came from behind the sanctuary with a beaker of sweetened water and a basket of stale old bread. He handed Zaqutu the beaker with a bow and left the room.

Zakir waited while she drank and then he uncovered her body again. Over every part of her flesh, reddened parts and healthy parts, he rubbed the crumbs of mouldy bread.

"Now, lady—Queen Mother of Asshur, daughter of Ishtar—you are free."

She lay still, a warmth suffusing through all her limbs—a warmth that came from within, not from the chill air of the sanctuary. She sat up and looked around. Zakir was rummaging in his satchel and took out a small broom. He ordered her to stand and shake out her fleece and she found herself able to stand, to walk around.

"Now, lady, wait while all these crumbs are fed to Gula's dogs. Every evil from within you will pass out into them. You will find peace and they will love you."

"Love me?"

"The dogs will try to follow you. Does it still hurt? I saw you wince."

Restored to herself now, she replied, "You haven't told me your name." She took his hand and repeated his name. She wondered at her manner, how suddenly she had changed. "I am, you say, cleansed." She touched the inside of her arm. "This is still sore, and my groin too. Your balm—I thank you—has made me whole but does not take away the pain."

"Ah, I will talk to your good doctor. You sit here at Gula's feet and thank her."

Ataril stood when he saw the ashipu coming towards them and went to meet him. "Is she ...?"

Zakir brushed him aside and gestured towards Shemahu, that he follow him.

"See how it hurts her when I rub the skin here? The demon has left her but the pain stays. What do you suggest for that sort of thing?"

"The Queen Mother has been indoors—not only this winter but in summer too. Hiding herself from the sun might cause her skin to redden. They say she has eaten little, and that too may harm her skin. Fish, I would think she should eat."

He turned to Zaqutu. "My lady, you didn't tell us of the pain. Vinegar and water compresses we need to put on you. You need to move about during the day."

When he had taken the ashipu aside he continued. "You know, we must somehow find our way to the king's forces, to my lady's provinces. She must walk since we must appear to be ordinary travellers. How soon …?"

"Obviously you must leave at once. I believe you should take one of Gula's dogs with you, a sign of the goddess's favour. Along the way people will know you have been to this place and will think you on the way home. Also, the dog will let you know if enemies approach—not only demons, but ordinary thieves or spies."

Shemahu thanked Zakir and took Zaqutu's arm to pull her to her feet. The dogs milled about them as they walked, snuffling at her knees and licking their chops. At the sight of the dogs, Annabel took up the sleeping infant and disappeared inside the hut.

Zaqutu looked up at the sky. In the west the sun neared the horizon and she blessed Shamash, squinting at the light that seemed so bright though evening mist shrouded the sun. "I am hungry, very hungry. Annabel, what have you got? Are there any dates?"

"My lady, your grandson is hungry too so I cannot serve you. That leather satchel in the corner. In it are parcels of food. One has some dates. Eat, my lady—oh, do eat."

"Annabel, I thank you. For everything. For staying with me when I have been so harsh on you." Zaqutu hesitated. "I realise we must travel as humble people do. You must not show me too much respect. Let us be as we were when we worked together on the frescoes. Forget 'Queen Mother'. I was happier as 'mother of the Crown Prince' anyhow." She rummaged in the pack and found the fruit, two handfuls, and stuffed them into her mouth.

She smiled at Ataril as he came in but continued speaking to Annabel. "Happier then because my husband was alive." She sat down in a huddle on the floor and began to weep softly. "Oh, my husband, my dear." She clasped the water flask to her lips to stop her words. After drinking she greeted Ataril with more thanks.

"My lady, it rejoices us to see you well, so well. You will be in pain still and that saddens me. We must leave here tomorrow. I've bought a mule …" He stopped at the horror in her eyes. "No, not to ride, but we must carry provisions—plus medicine for you and food for your dog."

"Medicine?"

"Not just chickpeas or lentils nor wheat for your compresses, your son has sent us a new thing—rice. I'm to make it into a paste. We'll eat the other things. We'll need vinegar too, quite a lot. Compresses every night, the doctor says."

"Why tomorrow?" Zaqutu asked, still in a dreamy haze.

"Arda-Mulissi is coming. He will be travelling fast, looking for you—looking for Pulu too, I shouldn't wonder."

"Ataril, she asked, "he murdered the king his father, so why hasn't Shamash struck him down?"

"It may already have happened. We have had no news."

Just then they heard hoofbeats outside the door, a single rider by the sound. Ataril put his finger to his lips and went out to see if he could gather news.

Chapter 29: Behind Enemy Lines

"My lady, you must come out of mourning for the king."
Startled, she asked why.
Ataril relayed to her the news he had gathered. "Sulmu-Bel has let his soldiers sack Ninuwa. They'll be looking for you, searching any young-looking woman dressed as a widow. You must go in disguise." His voice pleading, he ordered, "Bathe and dress in these new clothes."

Zaqutu couldn't hide her dismay from him. She couldn't decide on a response. *Should I accede to his reasoning or should I stand up for my feelings and for the proprieties?* She chose the first, bowing her head.

"No matter what your hurry," she insisted quietly, "I have one last thing to do before I can end my mourning." Using the writing desk that belonged to the priest of Gula, she took his quill and parchment and penned a lament. It followed the formula everyone used, but as she wrote out the letters she finally felt them in her heart.

> O my husband, why are you cast adrift like a boat in midstream?
> Your crossbars broken, your tows cut;
> Your face shrouded, why did you cross
>   the river of the Inner City?
>
> Oh my wife, how could I not be cast adrift,
> How could my tows not be cut?
> On the day I saw my son, how happy I was!
> How happy was I, happy my wife.
> On the day of her labour pains, my face was overcast;
> On the day she gave birth, my eyes brimmed over.
>
> Oh, my husband, my hands were opened as I prayed to Ishtar,
> Ishtar, Mother, save his life, bring him back to me.
> When Ishtar heard this, she veiled her face:
> "You faithless wife, why do you keep praying to me?"

> I cried out: "Do not rob me of my charming husband, my king!
> He cherished me over all the years,
> Guided me in safety through lands full of misdeeds,
> Took me with him from the Inner City,
> Brought me with him to the House of Joy."
>
> Oh my husband, now you sleep forever in the Inner City,
> I hear your voice as you scream in woe.
>
> Ever since those days, when I was with my husband,
> As I lived with him who was my lover,
> Death has crept stealthily into my bedroom.
>
> Death sent me from my home, separated me from my lover,
> And set his feet towards a land from which he will not return.

When he had purchased supplies and packed the mule Ataril came to the doorway, calling her, "Now, you must come."

She turned away from him to face the statue of the goddess, wordless, breathing slowly.

After a moment's pause she turned back to face him. "I am well now, I think, truly well. Even so, I feel as if I will be going to ... no, not my death—not that any longer. But I see myself stepping out of my old life into a new one."

She followed Ataril outside and then touched his arm to stop him. "It's all so strange here in the hills, not like any people's home. It's a wild land, isn't it?"

"Yes. It will be rough going, but you will manage. The healers say you are to be in compresses every night until your pain is gone. In case we find a fireplace I've loaded a cauldron so that you may get pottage."

Zaqutu hitched her tunic up into her girdle so she could make big strides and went forth from Gula's presence with a smile, the first for many months. After an hour's walking across the rough tracks, heading towards Shiru her smile failed. Travellers would usually walk the trail in one day, but Zaqutu soon felt so weak she could not keep on.

"In that case," Ataril said, "we'll find shelter when we're halfway."

Zaqutu stroked Pulu's head to still his grizzling. *More than two days to Shiru and that's such a little way. Can we find Esarhaddon in time?*

That night, their first without walls or a roof, Zaqutu slept deeply and without dreams. Ataril and Shemahu sat late, tending the fire, sharing their anxiety.

"We met no one after midday. I'm sure we are safe," Shemahu reassured him.

"Safe, yes, for now. If we are being pursued by post riders, they will have reached Topsawa. My last news said Dur-Sharrukin had not fallen. If so, then our pursuers will come north, just as we have."

"For myself," the doctor observed dryly, "none of the rebels have ever seen me."

"I cannot say the same."

"If we meet anyone, then, let me greet them. Keep your head down. we'll tell the women to keep their heads covered and huddle around the baby." The dog—they'd named him Ben-Zakir—stirred in his sleep and the doctor reached out to stroke his fur.

Ataril watched the firelight flicker on the doctor's moving hand. He mused, *My lady, she isn't used to walking.* He sighed and asked the doctor, "Travelling in this fashion. Can she ... will she be able to keep on?"

Shemahu put Ataril's hand on the dog's head. "We'll see tomorrow."

The full moon of Shebat glowed in the east when they reached a tiny hamlet. Ataril was carrying Pulu. Annabel and Shemahu supported Zaqutu, who could hardly stand. A boy saw them and ran to fetch the headman.

"Who are you and what is your business here?" the headman asked when Shemahu stepped forward to speak with him.

"I am Shemahu, a doctor from Kilizi. The sick woman is a merchant's wife from Kharranu, named Belet-Adad. I am escorting her home from Topsawa."

"Kilizi to Topsawa? That's a long way." The headman scratched his greasy curls. "You say she's from Kharranu?"

Shemahu nodded.

"The others?"

"They're her servants—a eunuch and the child's wet nurse."

"We're a poor village. What do you want?"

"My lady Belet-Adad is not poor. Would a family in your village offer us lodging? We could pay. I want to offer my patient cooked food. Some meat and a fire. We can pay for that too."

The headman peered closely at Zaqutu's clothing, but when he made as though to test the quality of the cloth with his fingers Ataril stepped between them, the tall eunuch towering over the squat villager. The headman stepped back, hesitated, but then volunteered, "My brother's widow has a room. Wait here, I will send for her."

Zaqutu slept as soon as they showed her a bed and they had to wake her in the night to take some food. As she munched the ash-covered loaf of bread they explained her new name and history. She grunted, sceptical. "Would a merchant's wife go from Kharranu as far as Topsawa? Why?"

"If she wanted Gula's help she'd have to. Clever of your ashipu to give us this dog. The villagers will be doing bread rituals all night. Ben-Zakir will be well-fed from this village." Ataril handed her more dates. "But you, how are you?"

Zaqutu took a deep draft of beer flavoured with crushed mint. "I will keep going, have no fear." She lifted her eyes to explore the damp clay walls of the tiny room, the smoke-stained ceiling. She sniffed the odour of the long-unoccupied space—rats' urine, droppings, mould. In her mind she pictured the light coming into her suite from the courtyard. She longed for the green balsam smoking in the brazier, the soft hangings. *Oh, to have a cushion! Ataril must be wishing for the same things. Poor Ataril. I believe he's never been in such places—always in a palace or temple.* She remembered his panic at Kilizi before Esarhaddon's birth and a smile fitted across her lips. She grew serious at once, thinking, *I have brought him down to this. It's all my fault.*

She turned to him and clasped his hand. "Ataril, you know Esarhaddon came to me at Arbail—came himself to bring me to Ninuwa, to keep Pulu there when Esharra left for Asshur. Why didn't I do it? How much better it would have been. How long ago is it? When would that have been, when he moved north?"

"Six weeks, I suppose. It's been nearly three weeks since the king's death."

"I just hated the thought of being in Ninuwa. I suppose I always have. And now I've killed Sennacherib, haven't I, with my stubbornness." Zaqutu kept her voice level but felt inside that she'd started to say something wrong.

Ataril answered her unspoken thought. "Why do you think your faithlessness killed him? Esarhaddon grieves too, I'm sure. Like you he was distraught. He probably thinks it's his fault—that he should have been there to kill his brothers before they took the king's life."

Zaqutu looked at him in surprise. "He wasn't there?"

Ataril told her how the king came to be murdered. Then he added, "Had he not been sent away, Esarhaddon would have died too." Ataril began to pace back and forth. The light from their brazier dimly lit his face. While the others slept he told her the gist of what he had learned about what had happened after the killings in the temple Ekul. "We'll pretend for a while, but you are no merchant's wife, or widow. You are Queen Mother; Ishtar's prophecy is stronger than your feelings."

Zaqutu listened. On her pallet she moved only to breathe. "I recall he told me—Esarhaddon did—how the king was angry with him, rebuked him in front of all the magnates. I don't remember why."

"I think it was a ruse, a pretend quarrel. Sennacherib was acting to flush Arda out of hiding. He was trying to provoke the rebellion. He succeeded in that and he saved Esar."

Zaqutu found Ataril's reasoning unbelievable. "Wouldn't the king my lord have known how dangerous that would be?"

"He knew. My lady, the king your husband heard Ishtar's oracle. He trusted the Goddess entirely—enough to put his own life at risk. He must have believed her powerful enough to convince you to rule with your son, to rule Asshur and, through Esharra and Shumukin, to rule Babili. Yours is the power."

"Mine is the power, yes." Zaqutu felt despair rushing up from her stomach. She wanted to shriek her defeat and despair but, fearing to wake Pulu, she stuffed the panic fear back down her throat. She reached out to the sleeping child and let her hand rest on the fleece that covered him. Her voice quiet but taut with agony she whispered, "Oh Ataril, even if I knew what I had to do I still wouldn't be able. I am weak—not just in body. I'm not fit to be Queen Mother. You know that—you must."

"No, I don't. Think, my lady. Right now Esharra-Hammat rules Babili, from exile in Asshur, with only a boy-king. We'll help her and I'll try to help you, but you—only you—can take the power. Think of the _me_, how Ea gave them to Ishtar, how they adorn her. They belong to Ishtar but she asks you to show them forth." Ataril touched Zaqutu's girdle to remind her of Ishtar's girdle of birthstones, of becoming the king's bride.

Zaqutu began to weep softly, tapping her bosom and whispering, "The alluring breastplate? I have no husband. I am no wife."

"You are mother still, Esarhaddon's mother and, these past days, Pulu's as well. Ishtar's allure—it's not only wife to husband, you know. The mother, Mummu, she draws all her children into her. You have that allure."

They sat in silence a few moments before she went on, "I see how I need a perceptive ear, that's clear. And the crafts—I have no problem there. In my breechcloth though, are fear and dismay. How can I awe anyone?"

"On your own, I suppose you cannot. Yet everyone can see how Ishtar favours you, you and Esarhaddon. Ishtar is the awesome one. Just remember her earrings."

Zaqutu told him how in her dreams she wandered Ninuwa Central looking for the earrings—for truth, kindness and secure dwelling. She giggled as she gestured around the tiny room where they had to whisper not to wake the others.

"Zaqutu, my dear, you know the descent to the Great Below and the Ascent. You know deceit with rebellion. Rebellion is all about us—we have no idea who this village supports. Arda-Mulissi could find us at any moment."

As she fingered the necklace of beads she thought *intrigue, fight rebels, educate son*. A wave of her hands preceded her next words, "I begin to see, Ataril. How will I ever find the wisdom?" She touched her wrists and pointed to her ankles. "You say I'll be in control, responsible for all the king's servants. It's too much."

"It cannot be. Your head will wear the crown; you will make the queenly incantation. And Zaqutu, you do know how. When Sennacherib lived you bent him to your will."

She stirred and started to object. "No, your own ravings convict you. You can't moan about being guilty of his death and then pretend you never did anything."

She clasped his hand, accepting his words in silence.

The next day they set out for Shiru where they negotiated larger quarters. They stayed two nights since a dreary, cold rain had come up.

Zaqutu overheard Ataril and Shemahu laughing as they came back from the tavern, full of the news they'd got from the headman. "What's so funny?" she asked, She stood at the doorway and peered out into the courtyard, damp and fogged so thick she couldn't hear their words though she heard their steps before she saw them. "Doesn't seem the weather for jokes."

Shemahu explained how Ataril had asked in the tavern whether they'd had news of the war.

Zaqutu frowned. "So? Is that supposed to be funny?"

"The headman told us—" Ataril sniggered "—there wasn't any war. 'The king has routed that brother of his' was all he would say."

"I'm still not laughing."

"Don't you get it? It would work well whichever side he's on."

Wind swept through the courtyard that night, chill but with no frost, and next morning the weather brightened. Two more days they travelled, tenting each time. After six days they hadn't even reached

Tille because they left the main track to go northwards to skirt Talmusa. At the crossing of the Diglat they heard that Arda-Mulissi had reformed his troops after the looting of Ninuwa and had sent them towards Tille almost a week before.

"I'm glad we didn't catch up to them," Ataril commented.

On the 18th of Shebat, while the rebel army fought Esarhaddon's troops at Simme, Zaqutu and her party traipsed across the Mat Masenni—only three or four days' journey behind them. Rumours reached them, many tales, not always consistent. Ataril supposed Esarhaddon had fallen back to Natsibina in Zaqutu's province of Katmukhi. They heard that Arda-Mulissi's army had rolled forward, that he had forced Esarhaddon to retreat towards Guzana.

Zaqutu despaired. "We'll never make it. Soon we'll blunder into Arda's rearguard and then it will all be over."

By the time Zaqutu's party reached Tille they learned the battle had been fought four days before. They were still behind enemy lines. Zaqutu and Annabel stayed in the temple enclosure where they hoped to be safe from prying eyes while Ataril and Shemahu went for news. Their luck held; none of Arda's troops had lingered in the city. The tavern-keeper, however, who titled Arda-Mulisssi as 'king', had reassured the doctor that Tille didn't want any trouble.

This is it, she thought when she heard. *We've reached the end of the line.* "Ataril, find us a little house. We'll have to stay here until we're sure where to go. Tell the tavern-keeper that I've become too sick to move on, I need cooked food—something. But get us out of here. There are too many people who pass through here. I'll be recognised and ..."

"Yes, I'm worried too. People here say you are already with the Crown Prince, even that you are the one who makes him retreat." Her jaw dropped but he went on. "Should I go and see what I can find? No, I'll get Shemahu to do it. I think the whole town is still on your side, no matter what the tavern-keeper says. Shemahu can use his own name—he's physician to the Crown Prince so a local official will want to oblige him."

"You think? What if you're wrong?"

Ataril raised his eyebrows. "Shemahu is a much less attractive hostage than either you or me." His mouth was grim and Zaqutu realised the wisdom of what he said.

Shemahu managed to get a house, one that belonged to a merchant who had left before the war. On the 25th of Shebat they settled in and Zaqutu showed Ataril she knew more of the *me* than he'd thought.

"Of course I can make soup," she insisted, sending Annabel to the market for a chicken and some leeks. Annabel grumbled about 'lowly tasks' but Zaqutu reminded her she was only a wet nurse to a far-off merchant of no account. "Look at you. Or at me. No one would think we belonged in even a minor governor's household."

Annabel snorted and babbled to Pulu how he wasn't any Crown Prince, just a merchant's son, so he'd be carrying squawking birds all round the town in no time.

Zaqutu wouldn't even watch as Shemahu killed the bird but she did the plucking, clicking her tongue as the skin tore and she scattered feathers all over. "Don't just stand there," she ordered. "Get the broom and sweep up." Next she scoured out the cauldron. Into it she put the lungs, liver and heart, but she sliced open the gizzard and washed out all the grit. When she'd added the flesh she heated the cauldron very hot over the charcoal brazier and waited until it smoked.

"Ugh," Ataril complained, "you're making a right mess of that."

"No, I'm not." She took the cauldron off and put an earthenware bowl of water and milk on to heat. After wiping the bird carefully she returned the singed meat and innards, salted, to the cauldron. To the fat from the chicken's skin she added cinnamon and leaves of rue.

"Where'd the rue come from?" Shemahu asked.

"I picked it up along the way."

"I never spotted any, I always collect rue when I find it."

"Umm." She stripped the leaves and put them in the mixture. Once it boiled she added the leeks." I found these too," she said as garlic bulbs slid into the pot.

"That's why you're so damned slow walking," Ataril fumed. "You stop to pick flowers."

"Don't be silly—there aren't any flowers until the spring rains. Even a city man like you should know that." Zaqutu smiled to hear herself speak as if she really were a merchant's wife. *I fit very well into that role.* She stopped for a moment to think. *What would my life have been like if I'd been such a woman, married to some merchant of Dimashqa? I'd never have met the king.* She gasped and saw them turn to look at her.

To cover up her unease she snapped, "You should be grateful first that I'm well enough to gather what we need and second that I'm clever enough to cook it." In the back of her mind lingered a shocking thought. *The Goddess! I'd never have* ... A vision of Arbail, of Ahat-Abisha as Agushea, filled her mind and brought a bliss that shone in her face.

"My lady, I rejoice in your good health. Even more in your good humour."

As evening deepened they sat around the brazier, their thoughts bent westwards to where, soon, the two armies would clash.

Ataril spoke. "At the tavern some said Esarhaddon had drawn his forces back from Natsibina without a fight. Others said they had a big battle. No certainty at all. There's a rumour that Arda-Mulissi isn't with the army, that Sulmu-Bel leads the rebels, and that all of them are his veterans from east of the river. Some say Arda's holed up in Balatsa, others that he's left his Mannaeans in Balatsa to guard his rear from the southern army but that he drives the rebels to face up to the Crown Prince. We just don't know where he is."

Zaqutu shivered and couldn't keep her eyes from searching the shadows in the corners of the room.

Ataril took her hand. "He's not in Tille, that's sure—we'd know it if he were."

"When was the battle at Natsibina? That's my town; I put the governor there. He's always been so good." Tears welled up but she focused on the soup pot, not minding if her tears added salt to the meal.

Ataril reassured her, "If one happened it would have been two days ago, the men bringing the news had left two mornings ago." As they sat around the brazier she served up the delicious meat, broth and dumplings. Ataril muttered with his mouth full, "This is really good."

"Don't sound so surprised. I lived on a country estate and our cook taught me, I even copied out scrolls of recipes."

Ataril sat back chewing. "I wonder what Arda-Mulissi finds to feed his army. It's the wrong time of year to be in the field. He hasn't a whole lot of money, they say. Last week when they passed through here he just took the supplies he needed, not even writing a scrip. The villagers complained openly. It seems they don't fear that he will triumph. I imagine Arda's desperate now. He has to kill Esarhaddon and Pulu,because he's alienated towns and cities both sides of the river. That's my guess. Plundering isn't good strategy."

"Well," Shemahu commented, "as a rebel against his father he may feel he has to show his ways are different. He'll be a cruel king—as cruel as his father was kind. Takes after his grandfather, then, maybe."

"Was Sargon cruel?" Zaqutu asked.

"My father said worse than that," Ataril replied. "My father regarded Sennacherib as cruel too, wiping Babili off the map."

"What do you say?" she asked, her voice light as if joking.

"My lady, the months I spent in Asshur showed me the king's subtlety and his courage. I've told you how he meant to test the oracle, to risk everything. He even spoke to me, saying he believed in the oracle and would do so despite the risk."

Serious now, she asked, "Was he cruel? Answer my question. You said subtle; that can mean crafty and cruel or it can mean to be wise, like Adapa."

"My dear, I would say wise, for your comfort. You will rule now and you couldn't do better than follow your husband's example. The king made Esarhaddon Crown Prince very early. He'd held off marrying Arda to you and so delayed making him Crown Prince. But he figured that as soon as your son entered the Succession Palace Arda-Mulissi would make a desperate move and take risks that would make him easier to catch and kill."

Zaqutu closed her lips tight; she'd stopped eating. *So to be wise is to plot to kill your own son. I don't want to be wise like that.*

Ataril chewed a lump of meat. "So Esar went in and nothing happened. Then Sennacherib went even further. As I told you, he deliberately provoked the eastern veterans—a ploy to bring Arda out where he could catch him. He wanted Arda disposed of so Esarhaddon would have an easy succession."

Zaqutu remained sceptical. "Or did he want an easy time for Tebua and her son?"

Ataril held a piece of leek in his fingers. "I think from what he told me that she too was being used to flush Arda out." Zaqutu gasped but Ataril continued, "The king expected something to happen at the ceremony of the barges."

"Was he pretending to send the gods back, then? Is that why he wouldn't restore the temples? He told me ..." Zaqutu stopped. *He asked me to leave Arbail and go to Ninuwa. Was I being used as another bait? Or did he want me safe?*

Chapter 30: Zaqutu Reaches her Own Province

After the skirmish in Simme on the 18th of Shebat, Esarhaddon's army—led by the commander of the northern forces, Bel-Emuranni—had found quarters in Kharranu, Guzana and Natsibina. Men and supplies to support a long campaign came forth readily. The local governors and populace supported Esarhaddon. They felt no loyalty to Zaza's sons. As well, Zaqutu's habitual policy of calling her governors to strict account for honesty and justice made her and her son well-liked. She never exacted excessive revenue, and when disputes came to her attention she was fair. Now her popularity brought its reward. When Esarhaddon came up with his rearguard to join the main army volunteers streamed into the camp.

For his military strategy, Esarhaddon took Bel-Emuranni's advice. Each time his troops met the enemy he deployed only a small portion of his forces, then would draw back in apparent defeat. Arda-Mulissi's forces were tempted further and further into territory that would be hostile to them.

As Zaqutu and her party travelled through the quiet countryside they heard nothing and saw very little. They didn't know that Arda's troops had rioted. Tired, hungry and frustrated, harried by small bands of archers along the wayside, the rebel troops broke formation. They roamed over the countryside of Singara seeking food and looting. In small bands, like brigands, they became easy prey for the local guards. A huge slaughter of Sulmu-Bel's soldiers took place just outside Guzana and a detachment of the Crown Prince's troops turned the survivors back towards Urakka. Sulmu-Bel's army had shrunk from an overwhelming force to a demoralised remnant. Bel-Emuranni now pursued them with his whole force.

As Zaqutu and her party moved from Tille to Natsibina they passed a few bodies, stripped of weapons and clothing, tossed in the fields or beside the path. Just to see their bloody wounds tormented Zaqutu's mind. She had to keep walking though her stomach churned.

I wonder if they're my soldiers? Her thought surprised her. The soldiers from each army were dressed and armed alike. *We're fighting each other, and it's my fault.* Tears welled up and her stomach tightened.

To gather strength she let herself breathe in through her nose. The bodies, recently killed, didn't yet stink. "They don't even smell," observed Zaqutu to the others.

Ataril said, "No, but I can smell danger. If those bodies are that fresh the armies are close by. At any moment we might pass through the enemy lines." He wrapped a woollen shawl around his head and face and stumbled along behind Zaqutu, letting Shemahu hold the mule's bridle in the lead. The countryside lay silent, wrapped in death.

On the 26th of Shebat Zaqutu arrived at evening in Natsibina to find the gates open, and the guards come out to greet her and escort her into the city.

The governor heard the trumpets and came rushing out, recognising the Queen despite her travel-worn clothing and reddened face. "My lady the Queen, we had no word of your coming. Things have been ... the runner has just come from Urakka. They will defeat those rebels tomorrow," he hesitated. "Or the day after." The bedraggled appearance of the queen and her party suddenly made him mute. He stood open-mouthed and had to shake himself.

Zaqutu smiled and came forth to greet him.

Reassured he could continue. "Come, I see you have been through adventures." He peered around, scanning the countryside. "Where is your escort?"

"Peace be with you, Governor. We are the whole party. In wartime it is safer to travel incognito. I cannot hide here, in my own city, but I am Belet-Adad, wife of a merchant from Kharranu, at the moment. So, since there may be spies, don't treat me otherwise. Not where others can see. I remember that your women's quarters have ..."

He laughed. "A bath—of course. I will speak with your servants as if I wanted news of the road." He clapped his hands and sent them up to his palace to the women's entrance.

Zaqutu and Annabel played with the baby while serving women filled the sunken pool with warm water. As they lolled back in the water Zaqutu remembered her first visit. "You won't remember, Annabel, but I was so young then."

"I do remember, my lady, very well. You were headed for Ninuwa Central and I had hoped to stay in Natsibina. I never wanted to be sent back to Ninuwa."

"Is that why you told me about Nikkal-Amat's tortures?" Zaqutu looked at her maid, smiling but worried. "Were you lying? Or exaggerating?"

Annabel shook her head. "Neither. Why would I? Abby was your maid then."

"I do hope she's safe. And Banba. He'll be with the army. My poor Abby."

Annabel responded, though not to the point. "Tonight I'll dress you and do your hair. It won't hurt. When we're on the road the dog will still protect you even if you're clean and sweet smelling."

"He'll be stuffed full if they do bread rituals here—Natsibina is a big place."

Chapter 31: The Humiliation of Ahat-Abisha

As when a drowning man clutches too hard at his rescuer and both sink, so Arda-Mulissi—grasping after power—brought himself to ruin. Against the will of the gods, on the 18th of Tebet, he had murdered his father. Rather than take his army of rebellion north to seize Ninuwa and usurp the kingship, he fell into a madness. He did send his army of rebels off to take Ninuwa, but as the moon of Tebet waned he himself headed for Kalkhu. Despite knowing that Zaqutu belonged to Ishtar—that only the goddess herself could give her, he had set his heart on taking her.

He told his general, the rebel Sulmu-Bel, "Marduk and Nabu give us victory. The Great Gods fight for us." In his heart he added, *I can forget Ishtar.*

When Arda entered Kalkhu he found it empty. With only his bodyguard he rode in haste upriver to Arbail. Thus, on the day when Sulmu-Bel entered Ninuwa—when the invaders overpowered the guards at the New Palace, when they found and killed Tebua and her son—Arda drove his chariot through the gates of Ishtar's sacred community. While Sulmu-Bel and his officers lost control of the rebels, while they plundered the wealth of Ninuwa and all her temples, in remote Arbail Arda stormed into Ishtar's temple enclosure

The ninth of Shebat was an unfavourable day and at Arbail neither rituals nor work outside the walls occupied the devotees. Hoofbeats broke the silence and Ahat-Abisha emerged into the courtyard to stand alone looking up at the chariot, challenging the men.

Arda-Mulissi's third-man and his driver leapt down from the chariot and seized the priestess's arms, pinning them roughly to her back.

Arda-Mulissi snarled, "Now listen to me, my lady, my aunt. I want her—the wife my father stole from me. Now. No excuses. Have her brought out from wherever you have hidden her."

"Let me go."

"Not until I have her."

"Then you will hold me long; she is not here."

"You have spoken. I will." To his charioteer he said, "Take this woman, do what you like with her—but hold her, hear?"

"My lord the king, have I heard you rightly? She is your aunt. Would you have me dishonour her?"

"I said so. You saw me ... no, you didn't. Look, I struck down my father with a mortal blow. What matter if you rape his sister?"

The chariot driver dragged the priestess over to the chariot and bound her hands and feet with thick leather thongs. He hoisted her up into the well of the chariot and crumpled her up at Arda-Mulissi's feet.

"Now then, Aunt, where have you hidden Zaqutu? It will go ill with you unless you tell me."

> "I am Ishtar, the Lady of Arbail," Ahat-Abisha spoke in a voice strangely firm for someone bound and cramped. "To the son of the king: 'Because you despised me you will roam the steppe as a shade of the underworld. Be fearful of my wrath. Never shall victory be yours, never shall you prevail, never shall you rule. By the Great Gods above and the Dark Ones below I curse you, Arda-Mulissi. Cursed of the gods you will stumble from folly to folly until you are killed by one whom you pursue.' By the mouth of the woman Ahat-Abisha of Arbail."

For one instant Arda-Mulissi frowned but then he laughed. "A fine curse, Aunt. I do not fear. You have told me what I needed to know. She's not here. I can guess where she has gone and we will follow her, to Khanigalbat where her silly son has fled. We'll go there, and you too. To Ninuwa first."

"Since you know where she is you don't need me," the priestess observed.

"Oh, yes, I do. You will watch me as I humiliate her."

He shouted to his bodyguard to stuff their saddlebags with provisions from the temple store. Of course they looted the treasure as well. Even so, within the hour they were on the way to Imgur-Bel, heading for Ninuwa.

It took longer than they'd planned. Two horses went lame but because Sulmu-Bel's troops had stripped every way-station of horses and mules Arda's bodyguard couldn't find any. At Shibaniba Arda-Mulissi shed his guards, going on to Ninuwa with only his chariot.

By day Ahat-Abisha huddled in the well of the chariot, bounced and jostled, desperately thirsty but too miserable to feel hunger. At night, left to lie in the cold with no covering, she shivered, straining to hear the men's talk, able to decipher no more than their mood—obviously elated. Arda-Mulissi boasted that he had overrun Asshur's heartland without a fight.

For their arrival at the gates of Ninuwa Arda-Mulissi had made his third-man prop the priestess up so everyone would see Sennacherib's sister as his prisoner. She stared dumbfounded. Sennacherib's pride—the great avenue and its exotic plantations, the new palaces of the magnates, the fountains—lay littered with broken wagons, pieces of smashed furniture and shattered wine jars. It looked like a toy city smashed by an angry infant. Even now, about the eighth hour, no citizens could be seen—the market devoid of traders, even the tavern across from Ninuwa Central empty.

"So, nephew, where are all your subjects? No cheering multitudes?"

"You are not to speak," he said, threatening her with the back of his hand.

The chariot pulled up at the entrance to Ninuwa Central beside its broken gates. An uncanny stillness gripped the city; no sounds of carousal reverberated from the walls. Arda and his men entered the temple precincts, having left the priestess propped up in the chariot.

I suppose I could take the reins and drive off now, Ahat-Abisha thought, *except I cannot think where I might go. Arbail? They'd come there first and ...* Feeling faint, she leaned against the side of the chariot well and sank to her knees. *I will wait for whatever fate the Goddess has in store.*

Within two days Arda-Mulissi had located enough sober officers to police the city and discipline his troops. Ahat-Abisha slept or dozed in a cell in the New Palace, having as company only the four-days-dead corpse of Addati, Sennacherib's chatelaine. On the eighth day of her captivity Arda's man came for her, tugging her tied hands and hoisting her onto a wagon loaded with supplies and treasure levied from the plunderers. The wagon bounced along behind the chariots until they reached the barge-crossing to Balatsa. There Arda's troops set up quarters in the city for themselves, saving the Governor's palace for Arda-Mulissi.

"Well, Aunt, stay here while I capture and kill your favourite, the so-called Crown Prince who hides away in the hills. Ha! You'll be here until I find your pretty little protégée, my betrothed."

Perhaps because she was his aunt or because he only pretended cruelty, Arda-Mulissi did not watch her humiliation. The men of his bodyguard turned the women's quarters of the governor's palace into a bordello, with Ahat-Abisha as sole attraction. Food she had, and baths and clean clothes, but no serving women or eunuchs to wait upon her. Despair took her and she cursed the *me* that adorned Ishtar. Her throat dried, she croaked and couldn't sing, but they beat her until she forced out the sacred lyrics:

> She is clothed in pleasure and love.
> She is laden with vitality, charm and voluptuousness.
> Ishtar is clothed with pleasure and love.
> She is laden with vitality, charm and voluptuousness.
> In lips she is sweet; life is in her mouth.
> At her appearance rejoicing becomes full.
> She is glorious; veils are thrown over her head.
> Her figure is beautiful; her eyes are brilliant.

Tears rolled out of her eyes as the men mocked her, forcing amorous dalliance upon her, raping her again and again.

After a week she began to forget who she was, where she slept, what might lie outside the modest palace of the governor of Balatsa. The life of a whore took over her daytime thoughts. In sleep she dreamt of solitude, dark and quiet. Death—her spirit willed it to come soon.

While Zaqutu travelled across the Mashenni lands and while Ahat-Abisha underwent her ordeal, Arda-Mulissi headed across Khanigalbat. Wild abandon took him. Not even mustering his troops, he led them like bandits against Esarhaddon's forces, regardless of the odds. Certain of victory, not suspecting Esarhaddon of toying with him, he followed each feint, moving further from his support base. He saw only himself crushing his enemy.

A month earlier, following his raid on the Inner City and the murder of the king, it might have been so. Arda-Mulissi then commanded an overwhelming force. If, after taking Ninuwa, Arda-Mulissi had assumed the kingship he might have ruled all Asshur, squeezing Esarhaddon and the troops loyal to him further and further westward into a nest of hostile vassal kingdoms.

Instead, the gods themselves defeated Arda. Unreasoning, unrestrained, driven by madness, Arda-Mulissi threw his victory away. Such madness came like a judgment from Shamash, swift retaliation for patricide. Defeat, but not death, became his fate. Of Arda's transgression against Ishtar, of her revenge, no one spoke.

Ahat-Abisha's ordeal of harlotry did not end in the death she willed. The end of her suffering as a whore came from one of Arda's soldiers, a Mannaean from the hills, ignorant of civilised ways. No matter what she did he drooped. Furious, he raged like a bull. To show his manly strength he picked her up and slammed her down on the stone floor.

The pain from her dislocated hip drove out the last of her wits. She deafened the men who came to abuse her, screaming and weeping every time someone tried to open her legs. Silence came only when, exhausted, she fainted and could not be revived.

Now useless to the soldiers, she was 'awarded' to the Mannaean and sent her off to his village. By some chance they took the tapestry that had hung behind Ishtar's statue in Ninuwa Central and used it as her wrapping for the journey.

Tied to the top of a loaded wagon by day, left to sleep on the open ground at night, she received water but very little food. The day the soldiers arrived at Dur-Sharrukin besiegers had surrounded the walls. The Mannean could not move on until messengers rode in from Arda-Mulissi.

The captain told the Mannaean he could not take the Priestess. "The king wants this captive held. We have orders."

The Mannaean shrugged, mumbling that she wasn't good for anything.

"That's not what the scribe has written." The captain read from the scrap of parchment; "From the king. The woman Ahat-Abisha is to be kept alive and secure. Take her to my stronghold outside Mutsatsir. She is hurt, you say. I say, Zakir will heal her." The captain overrode the Mannean's objection. "You'll do it. I'll send two men to help you guard her."

The captain walked over to the wagon and peered at the bundle tied to it. "My lady, aunt to our king? Have you been given bread and water?"

"Yes, but no bath these many days, no clothing, no woman to tend me."

"My lady, I cannot provide you with a bath but the women with our camp have clothing. I will send someone to tend you now. However, when you continue your journey ..."

"Where to, if I may know?"

"The king has ordered you kept alive and safe. He is sending you to the healers at Mutsatsir."

The priestess took in his words and sighed in resignation. They brought water for washing. In a clean tunic she sat inside the empty wagon, hoping they'd not wrap her again in the soiled tapestry. Men arrived with sacks of flour and lentils. As they piled the supplies around her propping her up she might have been no more than another bundle; they ignored her.

For four days her wagon trundled across the hills of the Mashenni lands, past tiny villages wet with the rains of early spring. Ahat-Abisha heard little from her captors, hill men from Urartu, who were dispirited, saying little even to one another. Her mind drifted to the stories her old nurse had told her as a child. She looked up at the hills for the tower of Adad, but barrenness was everywhere. She wondered if she might disappear into the fearsome tunnel Gilgamesh used to reach the ferryman. Perhaps he could carry her with him over the waters of death. Bitter bile welled up in her throat—fear and desire, but not of death. *It's my only way to thwart my nephew, to see my revenge—I must not die. I will not die, I know it.*

The aching in her hip kept her awake at night; during the day she tried to doze but hunger pangs gnawed at her. Visions of revenge on Arda-Mulissi filled the corners of her mind at first. After a week, when they neared Mutsatsir, she feared she had lost her senses. *I myself will actually need Zakir,* she thought. Then, with a lifting of her heart, she remembered; *He will tell me how Naqia is. Maybe he knows what is happening.* She focussed on that thought, and on the Goddess, seeing her figure as it had stood in Arbail but obscured by shadows. Tears rose in her eyes as she recalled the plunder of her sanctuary. *I will not die! I will see him die!*

At the plaza in Mutsatsir they hauled her out of the wagon; there was no guard, just the stupid Mannaean who had injured her. Most of the men of the town had followed the army, leaving behind old men, women and children. Ahat-Abisha's wagon contained but the second shipment of plunder from Ninuwa to arrive, and the villagers found its contents disappointing.

"What's this? What's the use of one woman? She's not even young!" The elderly headman ordered her to get up but the priestess sat in the dust of the gate. He tried to grab her arm but the soldier grunted and got between them.

"It's the king's aunt. She needs the healer."

"King's aunt? That's not Nikkal-Amat, looks like a filthy whore to me."

The soldier shrugged but went into Arda's quarters and rummaged around for a litter. He found one, dirty and too small, more for a child than a grown woman. He shouted to the serving men in the kitchen and made them come and carry the priestess into the women's quarters.

Ahat-Abisha looked around. A chair, for Arda's use when visiting, stood against one wall. She signalled to the men to place her in it and signed that she wanted water.

The headman stood in the doorway and asked if he might enter.

She felt relieved. "You can speak Aramaic? Please come in."

Uncertain whether to make obeisance, the man shifted his weight from foot to foot. "My lady, by order of the king I have sent for Zakir, the exorcist. You are not possessed, you do not seem ill. Have I done well?"

Ahat-Abisha drew a deep breath and tried to think. *The headman holds me in his power, certainly, yet he seems to fear me as well.* "My nephew's instructions specified Zakir. Surely you have done well." Though doubt took her and must have showed in her face. *Is Zakir in Arda's camp?*

Did I send Naqia into danger? I will have to be careful. "There has been much fighting. Has the healer been busy? Is he nearby?"

"Our own women heal the wounds and sicknesses we suffer. Zakir is sent for only when they cannot manage. He is not far."

"Will one of your women be able to come and help me? My legs do not hold me up."

"Can you pay?"

"My nephew will pay," she retorted, smiling as she considered her deeper meaning.

The afternoon's silence had lulled the priestess into a half-slumber broken by excited women's voices producing a clamour in the marketplace. *Someone important has arrived,* she thought. *I wonder who it is?* The priestess could hear the women but their dialect sounded strange to her. She thought she heard them calling "Zakir". When the voices died down she could hear steps approaching her, slow and heavy. With a start she looked up and saw a tall woman, draped in ragged cloaks, dragging a heavy cauldron.

The woman peered around the room and then, roughly, pulled the shroud off the lattice, letting rays of the evening sun enter the stuffy room. She tutted at the filth and shouted to someone outside. Other women entered to sweep and tidy the room but none even looked at the priestess. One woman brought a bench for Zakir, another a brazier to heat water in the cauldron. When all was ready the large woman—clearly the chief healer of the town—ordered her servants to undress and bathe the priestess.

Two more braziers were brought and set alight, the flames at first making shadows flit across the wall as dusk fell. Zakir himself, carrying lamp and satchel, came in and shooed all the others out of the room and away from the women's wing. Ahat-Abisha couldn't make out his words but his insistent tone suggested he'd ordered them to go away, and stay away. He flapped his hands at the stragglers.

When they were out of earshot he turned to the priestess and said, "My lady, high priestess of Ishtar of Arbail, it distresses me to see you here at all, to see you captive, and to see you hurt. I don't know the truth of what they say has happened, but I see that—"

"May all the gods bless you, Zakir, my brother, exorcist of the borderlands. The pain is great, my legs in need of healing. Perhaps, too, your particular skill can ease my burdened spirit."

"The women say you are bruised severely. They say you cannot move. Will you show me?"

With a shiver Ahat-Abisha removed the sheet that covered her and lay naked while Zakir looked and then touched every part of her. As she spoke of what had happened he sat beside her pallet and breathed softly, continuing silent when she finished speaking.

"What will happen to my legs?" she asked, "will they heal? Will they hold me to stand and walk?"

A slow movement of his head from left to right answered her.

"So I will never again stand before the Goddess," she acknowledged, tears falling over her cheeks.

"If they had found a healer for you that day, or even the next, perhaps. But now—no. I cannot imagine why ... how ... they just left you like that."

They sat in silence until she replied, "Zakir, my brother, the gods will our fate. Most of what happens we do not understand, not if we are wise. I can never be high priestess again, but if she wills it, the Goddess will speak with my mouth. If you keep me alive then I can still ... I think I will not die until I see her revenge."

"I don't understand."

"Why has my nephew ordered me to be kept alive? He wants me as bait for the trap he has set. He wants to get Zaqutu." She hesitated, "Or he's hoping to find Pulu. The oracles have said Pulu will rule in Ninuwa."

Zakir made no response; he looked sympathetic but not involved.

She steeled herself to make her voice calm though her own words, "never be high priestess" pierced her heart. She touched the healer's hand and said, "Why did death not come at my will? Ishtar wants me alive for another reason. Now, tell me, did Zaqutu reach you? No news of her has come to me."

"I chased away her demon. I sent them on their way with Gula's blessing and one of her dogs. Beyond that, I have heard no news of her or of the war."

Chapter 32: Victory

On the 27th of Shebat, the same day the Mannaean knocked Ahat-Abisha to the floor, Zaqutu and her party left Natsibina heading west. Only four weeks were left before the spring equinox. The corpses beside the road told them how near they had come to one army or the other, Zaqutu's stomach still turned at each sight of one. Her spirits sank as guilt clouded her mind. *So much slaughter.* By midday Zaqutu's heart had sunk all the way down and she felt herself about to give up. *Am I even on the right path? Will we get there only to witness Esarhaddon's defeat?*

She winced to stop tears from falling and Ataril put his hand on her forehead. "Are you in pain?" Beside a stream she watched the dog, Ben-Zakir, and the mule—each lapping greedily. She wouldn't look into Ataril's face.

He urged her, "My lady, Shemahu can give you ..."

From somewhere she felt a rush of strength buoy her up. "I'm very well, thank you. You said the rebels went off raiding to the south."

Ataril murmured assent. "So why are there all these bodies? Are we walking into a trap?"

Ataril's shoulders lifted in a half-hearted shrug. "What else can we do but try to bring you and Pulu to safety? No matter what has happened to them, to your son."

"How much further away are they? Have you any idea?"

Ataril shook his head but gestured to the stream. "If we knew what river this flowed into we'd know more."

"All the rivers here flow into the Upper Khabur. Oh! Look!" She pointed to the horizon where a stockade could just be seen. "It's Urakka—you know, where I met the king, where they left me to die. Just a tiny village, but they keep a post station. We can go there."

As they came up the opposite bank they caught sight of an army, the encampment quiet and orderly. Men and women bustled about at one end, while smoke from an altar rose from a point near the centre. A diviner's chant broke the silence. An army, but which one?

"Shall we find the enemy tomorrow?" Esarhaddon asked the haruspex.

"Tomorrow is the fast before the new moon," came the reply.

Esar looked across at Hussani, his chariot driver standing guard beside him. "I am worried."

"My lord the king," Hussani reassured him, "all the army, all the people, know the oracle of Ishtar. You will surely rule in Ninuwa. Your father set you up in the Succession Palace."

Esar objected, "All the army knows, and all the people also, that Sulmu-Bel's troops have sacked Ninuwa."

"All know that they plundered like brigands, not like soldiers. Brigands take their loot home when they are laden. You, my lord the king, have used your wits."

"I have listened to my generals, you mean."

"You are your father's son. Sane and calculating as he was. Arda-Mulissi, on the other hand—"

Esar interrupted, "Is also my father's son. And he reaches for his father's throne. Risking all. He is venturesome, I am cautious." Hussani went silent as the king turned back to the haruspex. "You will need to offer up another ram. I want to ask Shamash about my son Pulu. Is he safe? Is he even alive?"

The young king told Hussani, "I am hoping. I want to see a cohort of soldiers, bearing the insignia of the Succession Palace, coming along the road escorting the refugees from Arbail."

"Refugees?"

"I have had word that some of Arda's men raided and looted even as far as Arbail."

"Why would he send men there? The battle will happen here."

"He wants my son, to destroy my son."

The chariot driver spoke freely, as he had become accustomed to do in the field. "My lord the king, you are no fool, even if he is. No cohort bearing your insignia can come along the road. All your men are here, massed for battle." Hussani's voice was soft, his tone apologetic.

No words were spoken while the haruspex chanted his invocation, while he made his incision. Esarhaddon drew his breath in as the warm blood oozed out of the carcass on to the stone altar. He peered close as the haruspex cut out the liver and laid it on the tray of stained wood. "Is it favourable?" the king asked.

"Not unfavourable," was the reply.

As Esarhaddon turned from the liver his cohort commanders approached to ask his commands for the next day. *Not unfavourable,* he thought. *I wonder what it means.* Ushering the commanders towards the plaza just inside the town gate, he saw a mule and four travellers coming towards the camp along the road, heads bowed. As they neared, he saw a baby's basket of rushes tied to the mule's back.

Something familiar about the travellers struck him. His hands reached up to his eyes to stop the sun's glare. Just then he recognised his mother's gait. He shouted for two chariots but made his way alone on foot out the gate, Hussani and his third man rushing to keep up with him. "'The queen and my son, at last," he panted. "Bring them here." Trumpets rang out and soldiers came away from their tents and tasks to line up and salute Zaqutu's party.

Later, inside Esar's tent, Zaqutu and Ataril lounged on divans, licking their lips. Kharranu and Guzana had not been touched by the war so Esarhaddon and his troops ate well.

When Zaqutu complimented him on the meal, he replied, "Our spies tell us that Arda's troops have mutinied. He couldn't or wouldn't feed them so they went on a rampage throughout Singara. I had your governor in Guzana send his own troops to protect the villages along the Khabur. Now I am waiting for them to return with a levy from those villages. We'll field twice as many men as Arda-Mulissi can muster."

Tall and strongly muscled, still a youth but impressive, Esarhaddon chewed thoughtfully as he told them, "I don't understand it. Either he's been very foolish or there's something he knows that I don't. Every day I have good news from the southern forces. They have retaken the Inner City and are working their way upriver, harrying the rebels' rearguard."

"So, my son, what will happen now?" Zaqutu smiled fondly.

"Tomorrow we fast for the new moon; it is the will of the gods. After a modest feast I'm going after the rebel army—even if I have to chase them all the way back to Ninuwa." He laughed, merry and confident, pleased to be showing off his skills at war and kingship.

"You will find them nearer than that. We saw bodies all along the way from Natsibina. They must be very near."

"You, Mother, I hope you will take Pulu west to your palace in Guzana. Take Ataril with you, and your dog, but, I beg you, leave Shemahu my physician with me. He will have work to do with us."

"As you wish, my son."

The first day of Adar dawned clear and crisp. On horseback Ataril and Zaqutu rode at ease to Guzana while Annabel and the baby came riding on the empty supply wagon. As evening fell they approached the town, just in time to be overtaken by a post-rider with news of the day's victory.

It was no glorious battle; in fact only Esarhaddon even claimed it had been a battle—they'd not got round to any fighting before Arda-Mulissi's troops defected. To have something for his annals, Esarhaddon made up a better story of how he came to the throne of Asshur. As Zaqutu later read the parchment scroll she laughed.

> In a propitious month, on a favourable day, I happily entered the palace of the crown prince, the highly venerable place where those live who are destined for the kingship. Once my brothers knew it they abandoned godliness, boldly planning an evil act.
>
> First they sponsored slander, false accusations. Displeasing the gods, they spread evil rumours behind my back, even alienating from me the former favour of my father's heart. I worried whether this was the will of the gods and—by prayers, lamentations and prostrations—inquired of Asshur, king of the gods, and of Marduk the merciful. Baseness appalls them so they answered me, uttering the oracle of the great gods my lords, that my brothers acted according to the decisions of the gods. Nevertheless they spread their sweet protective shadow over me, hiding me from my brothers' attack, preserving me for the kingship.
>
> After their hideous attack on the king my father, my brothers went out of their senses, doing, in their evil machinations, every thing wicked in the eyes of the gods and mankind. They drew weapons in the midst of Ninuwa, which is against the will of the gods, butting each other—like kids—in their disputes. All the gods—Asshur, Suen, Shamash, Marduk, Nabu, Ishtar of Ninuwa and Ishtar of Arbail—looked with disfavour upon these doings of the usurpers which had come to pass against the will of the gods, and they did not help them. Instead they changed the rebels' strength into weakness so that they would bow beneath me.
>
> The people of Asshur, who had sworn the oath of the great gods to protect my claim to the kingship, did not assist my brothers. But I, Esarhaddon, who never turns around in a battle, trusting in the great gods my lords, soon heard of these sorry happenings and I cried out, "Woe!" rent my

princely robe and began to lament loudly. I became as mad as a lion, my soul was aflame and I clapped my hands to let the gods know my intention of assuming the kingship, my paternal legacy. I prayed to the gods and they gave an oracle-answer—a trustworthy omen from the ram's liver: 'Go, do not tarry! We will march with you, kill your enemies!'

I did not even wait for the next day, nor for my army; nor did I turn back for a moment to muster contingents of horses broken to the yoke or battle equipment. I did not even pile up provisions for my expedition, I was not afraid of the snow and the cold of the month Shebat when winter is at its hardest. No, I spread my wings like the swift-flying storm bird to overwhelm my enemies. I set off on the hard road to Ninuwa, difficult to traverse though short. In front of me, in the territory of Khanigalbat, were arrayed the best soldiers my brothers had, trying to block the advance of my force, sharpening their weapons for battle.

The terror-inspiring sight of the great gods, my lords, overwhelmed them and they turned into madmen when they saw the strength of my battle array. Ishtar, the Lady of Battle, who accepts me as her high priest, stood at my side—breaking the bows of the enemy, scattering their battle array.

Then the enemies thought: "This is our king!" Upon Ishtar's lofty command they went over in masses to me and rallied behind me. Like lambs they gambolled and then prayed to me as their lord and king. The people of Asshur who had sworn by the life of the great gods to act on my behalf came to meet me and kissed my feet.

Seeing that, the usurpers who had started the rebellion, deserted by their most trustworthy troops, fled to an unknown country.

At dinner in Guzana with the governor and his wife, Zaqutu stood and made a speech of thanks to her provincial officials, praising their loyalty and promising reward.

"Thank you, my lady. No, I should say, my lady the Queen Mother, for so you surely are. We are honoured to belong to you, favoured by the gods and treated honestly by your scribes. Many towns envy us. What will happen now, do you think, to the rebel, your stepson, Arda-Mulissi?"

"If I knew, I would tell you. It is hard to predict what such a man may do." Zaqutu felt confident and secure. "We shall all be well. He ... I have no pity. The gods will have their way."

The gods spared Arda-Mulissi. When he saw his troops lay down their arms he ran to the baggage train and loosed one of the horses. His third-man, seeing him go, followed after, both riding hard, heading upstream. Not for many years did anyone learn where he had gone or how he lived.

ISHTAR'S REVENGE

Chapter 33: Esarhaddon Assumes his Kingship

At Guzana, Zaqutu and her party waited quietly while Esarhaddon and Bel-Emuranni dealt with the prisoners of war. From each man they took an oath of allegiance in return for a pardon. After three days the trumpets sounded. As ruler of Khanigalbat, Zaqutu stood in the gate to receive her victorious son, smiling as he shielded his ears from the fanfare.

Bathed and dressed, the Crown Prince joined the queen and her officials. The fourth of Adar, a favourable day, betokened springtime. Local nobles outdid each other with hymns to the gods and with dances enacting the battle. Later, in her own quarters, Zaqutu received Ataril and Esarhaddon with sweet wine and almonds.

"Mother, I have heard troubling news from the east."

"The east? Arda?" He nodded.

"Well? I can hear your voice and see your face. What troubles?"

"While the rebels looted Ninuwa the king's son went to Kalkhu and thence to Arbail. Looking for you."

"For me?" She drew in her breath. *Ahat-Abisha said he would come for me. She must have had a word. She knew.* "Ahat-Abisha," she breathed out. No other words came. A shiver shook her, dread choking her throat. She raised her eyes to his face and saw him look ashamed.

Softly he continued, "We hold Kalkhu now, and Arbail. We have the victory. But Mother I am so sorry, we do not have the priestess."

"What do you mean we don't have her? Is she … did they murder her?"

"Worse." His voice strained, Esarhaddon told them how she had been taken prisoner, held, prostituted, and then … "He 'gave' her to one of his henchmen as a prize. A sarcastic gift since, according to my messenger, they'd hurt her badly, left her unable to walk or even to stand. No use even as a whore."

"Where has that man taken her?"

"We don't know. East is all they could say."

"Have you sent troops to find her? "

Esarhaddon shook his head, explaining he couldn't send any part of his army off on a wild goose chase to look for a woman who might be dead and buried, who might be held in any hut or settlement across the Mashenni lands, or in Urartu, or in Manna. "Troops need orders, clear orders, and I have none to give. I couldn't go myself. I had to take the rebels' oaths in person. We've had enough of civil war, I think."

Zaqutu looked at the beaker in her hand, at the coals in the brazier, at the faces of the two men. Esarhaddon seemed still a boy now, soft and young, vulnerable to rebuke or insult. Ataril let his slow tears roll down, his hand trembling a little as he reached for the flask to pour more wine. The silence seemed to go on forever. *I cannot weep—I brought this on her. I must ...* Her thoughts broke off as Ataril put his hand over Esarhaddon's.

"My lord the king, for so you surely are, what are your plans now? What will you do? What do you want us to do?"

"Right now I need your help. Messages are pouring in from the cities of the south, on tablets, and the scribes here are all used to scrolls in Aramaic script. Help me sort these out."

Zaqutu snorted. With a rueful smile she observed, "We have all come through danger, worried out of our minds, to be your scribes! Of course we'll help. But—"

Ataril interrupted. "I meant not tomorrow or the next day. What do you plan to do?"

"My plans? I must return to Ninuwa and set everything to rights—and soon. I hope you will come, all of you, to the New Palace. There are appointments to make, officials and chatelaines to install."

"What about avenging the king's murder? Doing a son's duty at the grave? And now his aunt's as well as his father's murder." Zaqutu's voice rose in pitch but she tried to keep calm. "Arda-Mulissi? You're just letting him go?"

"He's on the run, and will keep on running until he reaches the limits of the known world. No ally of ours will dare to harbour him, but he's strong and skilled—he'll find someone who needs a mercenary. He's a soldier and he can kill." As he spoke the last word Esarhaddon's voice sank to a whisper, quivering as he repeated the phrase. Looking at Ataril, he added, "I heard that you were there."

The light from the brazier dimmed. Ataril seemed to have to force his words out. "Yes. It plays over and over in my mind. Why didn't I ... but if I'd given an order the guards wouldn't have obeyed, not soon enough. I tried to catch up to the king and my father."

He turned to Zaqutu to explain. "Nadinu was carrying the sacred vessels, hurrying forward to be at the east door before sunrise. We heard the shouts, the men behind me—most of them behind because I'd hurried too—and I turned back to check it out, but Shumu-Etli grabbed me from behind. With one arm round my waist he tried to ... well, I'm taller than he and I smashed at his hand. But he held me tight and I saw it—saw Arda dart out from behind the statue of Nabu, something in his hand. Aram-Suen ..." here Ataril's voice sank to a whisper "tripped over me. Etli had pushed me and we had fallen headlong together. I screamed, I remember that. Then he let go—Etli, I mean. I rushed over to the king; my father lay beside him, stabbed in the back, his lifeblood ebbing away. The tramping of the whole troop of guards startled me out of ... I guess I was stunned. They rushed past me, chasing the killers." Ataril swallowed. "I sat down beside the king, holding his head."

Zaqutu, tears flowing, reached out to take the prince's hands which were wiping away his own tears. *He's not a boy any more, but still soft, vulnerable.* After a moment she asked her son, "His funeral rites? What should ... what are we to do? Shouldn't you ..."

"Go to Asshur, make libation at his tomb? Of course. I asked the diviners."

"And?"

"I have to go to Ninuwa first." He looked down shamefaced.

Zaqutu thought, *He's afraid he'll seem wicked, an ungrateful son.* For an uncomfortable few minutes no one spoke.

Esarhaddon retrieved his hands and looked at his mother. "His last words to me I didn't understand then. He stood there in his chariot, ready to leave for the Inner City, and ordered me away. 'You take charge of the troops in Kharranu.' That's all he said. Then he handed me a parchment, a letter for me to take to the governor there."

Zaqutu, noting the quiver in his voice, asked, "What tone of voice? Was he angry? Taking out on you his spite ... was it ..."

"Your fault, Mother? No." His voice was hard, yes, but it seemed businesslike. "Perhaps he feigned disfavour, wanted the council to believe I wouldn't succeed. Maybe he saw what was coming. I don't understand why no one, none of the governors or magnates, reported to him of Arda's troops mustering and moving north."

Ataril shifted on his stool. "Perhaps they did." Seeing Esarhaddon's start, he added, "No, I heard nothing, but I was with the priests of Nabu not with the king's scribes."

Esarhaddon stirred and rose to cross to the doorway where he had left his cloak. "I've just remembered." From a secret fold inside he drew out a tightly folded piece of papyrus, shredded from frequent handling. "Mother, years ago, sorting through the plunder from some bandits west of Kharranu, Bel-Emuranni came across an amulet.

Hanging around a ruffian's neck he found a leather pouch containing this papyrus. It uses the script of the west but I cannot decipher it. I could make out only one word—your name. Have a look."

Zaqutu took the folded message and held it close to the candle as she opened it. She peered at the superscription, To Naqia bath Yekhizqiyahu, and puzzlement filled her mind. Quickly opening it fully she peered at the colophon. From Shebna ben Shaqed, your servant. She looked over at Esarhaddon. "The commander? Bel-Emurrani? He found this? When?"

"He has worn it for years, believes it has protected him from harm in battle and given him promotion in the army. In camp together I asked him about it. Only to the king would he hand it over. He offered it to me when we heard of the king's death. He told me, 'All I am and all I have are yours, my lord the king.' So I took it, meaning to hand it back. But then I saw your name and have kept it for you."

As Zaqutu read through the letter the only sound came from the fire in the brazier, which Ataril fed from the pile of trimmed branches. "I cannot make it all out, but I know where it came from. Shebna wrote this letter when he ran away from my mother. He is asking for refuge with me, says I'm the only person who can shelter him." She blubbered softly.

Esarhaddon asked, "What's the matter? He wanted to go—you didn't send him away."

Puzzled at her son's naïveté—sometimes so adult and then, as now, like a child—Zaqutu sniffed and put her lips together. "I didn't shelter him very well, did I? The poor man, he has no one. No one to make libation at his tomb, to remember him for the service he gave."

"Service?" Esarhaddon asked, but Zaqutu turned away from them, weeping.

Ataril stood and motioned to the young king to accompany him outside the room. In whispers he told how Shebna had put himself at risk to save Zaqutu from her enemies. They stood talking quietly until Zaqutu called them. She had regained control, having obviously told herself not to indulge herself in grief while there was work to be done.

Esarhaddon bowed to her. "Mother, I know you wished your own son, named for the old man, to fulfil the duty of son. My son lives. When he is older, Pulu will make libation on Shebna's tomb every year of his life."

She made a small bow of her head in return. "That is very generous of you, my son the king. I would like you to return the letter in its pouch to Bel-Emuranni with my thanks for the use of its magic power."

"Thank you. With your tears you will have enhanced its worth, and I shall tell the general so."

Zaqutu blushed and seemed unable to muster a reply. She touched Ataril's hand, a signal that she wanted him to answer. He stood and made a proper obeisance. "I don't know whether you're correct, my lord the king—you know we do not question the rites of the netherworld. But I think, yes, Pulu should do a son's duty to Shebna."

As he walked to the rooms he shared with the governor's chief steward Ataril thought, *Zakir has cured my friend of more than her demon—he seems to have cured her of her pride.*

Next morning the governor's scroll room was crowded, messengers handing in bags of tablets as each post rider came through. Esarhaddon hadn't exaggerated. News of his victory—in some cases even news of Arda's difficulties—had persuaded governors from the south to side with the Crown Prince. Most of the tablets were letters containing oaths of loyalty to the new king. Most, but not all.

Zaqutu fingered a roughly written small tablet and frowned. The message didn't make sense; certainly no governor's scribe had prepared it. "Ataril, look at this."

He came to look over her shoulder. For a moment he said nothing, and then turned the tablet over to finish reading it.

"My lord the king, hear this letter," he shouted across the bustling servants.

> Our brothers in Babili, they heard, messages came to them. Shalamu-Eresh was in the house, he heard of the treaty the rebellious cities made with Arda-Mulissi. He said, "I must go. I must tell the king's servants what is planned." Our brothers summoned the king's servants, Nabu-Shumu-Ishkun and Tsilla. After they came they asked him "Whom does your word for the king concern?" After he had answered 'Arda-Mulissi' they covered his face with his cloak and took him before Arda-Mulissi himself, saying to Shalamu-Eresh, 'Look, here is the king himself, speak up!' So he said, 'My lord the king, Arda-Mulissi your son is going to kill you.' After they had uncovered his face and Arda-Mulissi had interrogated him, they killed him, him and all his brothers.

Zaqutu reached for the tablet and reread it, both sides, her lips pursed. "So, my son the king, here are two officials who conspired against the king your father, caused his death. What will you do?"

"What would you have me do? Let Shamash judge since they violated his oath?"

"Is that how you will treat traitors in your reign?"

"Can I trust even the Chief Judge? If the writer of this letter speaks truth, then Nabu-Shumu-Ishkun and Tsilla betrayed my father the king, betrayed the oath he made them swear when I was made Crown Prince. Perhaps their betrayal left Arda free—free to threaten you. If so, they made the way for him to defile Ishtar's sanctuaries and ..."

"And to capture the priestess, yes."

"So, what do you think I should do?"

Zaqutu felt as though Sennacherib himself stood behind her to observe her decision. She sighed. "They killed Shalamu-Eresh and all his brothers. Kill them and all theirs."

Later that day Ataril and Zaqutu watched Esarhaddon pack up for his triumphal procession to Ninuwa. Ataril spoke for them both, "My lord the king," he said, "it will be weeks rather than days before you have settled the city. They say the rebels looted every quarter." The young king nodded.

"May I have leave to go into the east, to seek our Mother, the priestess?"

Esar gave Ataril a suspicious look. "You are my mother, the Queen Mother's to command."

"The king my lord honours us both," Ataril replied smoothly, "but Ishtar rules us all. She has made the kingship yours."

"Asshur hands over the kingship, whatever the prophet Baya said. My father the king drew oaths of loyalty to me from everyone. They ally with me or provoke the all gods to wrath."

"My lord the king, perhaps the king does not know—Ishtar is all in all. No god is god apart from her. Asshur and Ishtar are one. Did you not know?"

"I remember well the oaths that all the people of all the lands took when I became Crown Prince. I can recite the names:

Asshur, Anu, Illil, Ea, Suen, Shamash, Adad, Marduk, Nabu, Nushku, Nergal ..."

Ataril put up his hand. "I too remember. Your father invoked all those gods to witness the oaths. But the kingship—that is the gift of Ishtar. When kingship came down from heaven ..."

"From heaven?"

"My lord the king is learned in all the lore of Asshur. But kingship came first to the cities of the south, to Eridu. Think, my lord, of all those stories you know. Of Etana, Gilgamesh, Lugalbanda, all those kings."

"Ataril, I do not doubt your lore. Yet why are the gods of Babili in the Inner City? Why did my father lose his life when he sought to shift them? Marduk is the dispenser of kingship. That's what they say in Babili itself, isn't it?"

"When the day comes that you take the crown of Asshur in the Inner City, the day of your covenant with Asshur, who will give the oracles of salvation? Ishtar. Who invites the gods to the covenant feast?"

"Ishtar, I guess," the prince muttered.

Zaqutu interrupted. "I know how the word will come—no, it's not my prophecy but it's how it will be, I know it. "The word of Ishtar of Arbail to Esarhaddon, king of Asshur: 'Come, gods, my fathers and brothers, enter the covenant banquet prepared for you'.

See, she invites the gods to her ceremony. She prepares the bread that is broken, the water they drink. When she gives it to them she says:

'In your hearts you may say "Ishtar is slight," and go to your cities and districts to eat bread and forget this covenant. But when you drink from this water you will remember me and keep this covenant which I have made on behalf of Esarhaddon.'

Make no mistake, my son the king. Your kingship comes from Ishtar of Arbail. It is she who will prophesy the events of your rule as king of Asshur, she and no other."

"How do you know what they'll do? The priests of Asshur decide."

Ataril made an obeisance to Esarhaddon. "My lord the king, for so I hold you to be, listen to your servant Ataril. I observed when the king your father made Nadin-Shumu king. Marduk made a feast in his temple. Tashmetu, mother of the new king, stood beside him holding his arms as he lifted the crown of Marduk and the weapons of Mulissu. They offered the sacrifice, burning the incense and anointing the pillars—they did it together. Your ceremony in the Inner City will be like that."

"So what will happen?"

"That's when they'll make the covenant. First they'll proclaim your victory—I assume they'll do that, it's the right thing. Then you'll call out to Asshur for help and he'll answer you with a salvation-oracle."

"Does that always happen?"

"I think so. It recounts your troubles, the coming of Asshur to succour you, you know, slaughtering your enemies. It always finishes something like, 'I am Asshur, lord of all the gods, let them praise me.' They bring the oracle out, on a cushion, and it's treated as the covenant between you and Asshur. They'll anoint it, make sacrifices to it and burn incense before it."

"Doesn't anyone say it aloud?"

"Oh yes—it's read out and then set before Bel-Tarbatsi and all the gods."

"Does it stay there?"

"Until you die, yes."

"So, my father's covenant—it was there, in the temple, right where ..."

"I would imagine that by now the priests will have taken it and buried it beside him."

Zaqutu stirred, standing before her son who bowed to acknowledge her. "My son, we must find your aunt, the priestess who fed you when you came forth from the womb, she who is more truly your mother than I who bore you. It must be. When you see the seal that Ahat-Abisha bears you will see that Asshur and Ishtar are one." She looked straight at him and spoke with authority.

She lost that assurance as she turned to Ataril, feeling hesitant and afraid. "Ataril, Ahat-Abisha ..." Before she could continue she licked her lips, then she changed tack. "During my illness she spoke to me, I think—I am not sure—that it's Ishtar of Arbail who will offer the feast for Esarhaddon, her foster-son. She will make the covenant, neither Ishtar of Asshur nor Ishtar of Ninuwa."

"My lady, here we touch on secret things, but the reason I want leave to go in search of our Mother is because someone must bring the word of Ishtar of Arbail to the king at the making of the covenant in the Inner City. If not ..." He stopped as she reached up to put a finger on his mouth.

"Ataril, we shall both go. I ride as well as you—you cannot deny it. And you know I can endure hardship as well as you." She smiled as she saw the expressions pass across his face. First he looked startled, then unsure, then resigned, and finally he seemed glad.

He turned to the king. "My lord the king, you have heard your mother. What do you say. Have we your leave?"

"Might as well advise the South Wind not to blow up a storm at sea. But without her ..."

"We will come with you into Ninuwa—all the officials will see her beside you in the chariot. No one will imagine Zaqutu doesn't stand behind everything you do." Ataril touched his forehead. "We'll need to send messengers on ahead to prepare the way-stations for our coming."

The young king rose to his feet as if to make a pronouncement.

Zaqutu stood up too, because he was king and she shouldn't sit in his presence but also to give herself authority. "You don't need me. Your Grand Vizier, Inurta-Nadi, is faithful and will expect to help you. I will go with Ataril." Her words were brave but she searched their faces for any sign of disapproval. *I'm well now and this is right, what I must do.* "Until last week, as Belet-Adad I travelled secretly. I'll leave Annabel and Shemahu with Pulu in Ninuwa. Just provide us with good horses and enough supplies. We'll hear more gossip as simple travellers than as officials; tavern-keepers always know a lot more

Esarhaddon Assumes his Kingship

than they say. And their wives will often say more to another woman"

"You can't go like that! As if you were ..."

"A harlot? Like Ishtar? I'm too wealthy for a common whore—they'll take me for some rich man's sekretu. And I'll be going to Gula's temple to return Ben-Zakir. It's logical."

Ataril objected. "The dog! Oh no My lady, he'll slow us down. I want to get into the eastern hills as quickly as possible. We want to find a warm trail."

"I'll carry the dog in front of me. He won't hold us up. And he makes a good topic for gossip everywhere. You said so yourself."

Esarhaddon's distress showed, even after they both insisted that travelling in a time of peace would be easier than their journey into the west in the midst of war. He must have known he'd lose the argument but he pleaded, "What will people say?"

The journey to Ninuwa showed Esarhaddon the answer. Joyous songs and dances greeted him. His party came with few soldiers and no demands for supplies. All spoke praise of Esarhaddon's wisdom and Zaqutu's beauty. In his annals he described the reception in properly pious terms:

> In the month of Adar, a favourable month, on the eighth day, the day of the festival of Nabu, I entered joyfully into Ninuwa, the town in which I exercise my lordship. I sat down happily upon the throne of my father. The South Wind, the breeze directed by Ea, blew at this moment. The blowing of this wind portends well for the exercise of kingship, it came just in time for me. All the omens were favourable and made my heart confident.

Confident in heart indeed, the new king proceeded to discover the officials who had conspired against him, discover and punish them as well. In his annals he had the scribes record his firm vengeance.

> The culpable military leaders who schemed to secure the sovereignty of Asshur for my brothers, I named them guilty.
> I meted out grievous punishment to them;
> I even exterminated their male descendants.

Chapter 34: Rescuing the Priestess

An easy day's ride brought Zaqutu and Ataril to Dur-Sharrukin where Abby's son Banba had just been installed as the new governor, ruling in the fortress where his father had been a steward. The city had withstood the siege well and Abby received her royal cousin with celebration. While they feasted, singers and dancers regaled them with praises of the new king and comic skits mocking the rebel soldiers.

When the time came to depart Zaqutu wanted Abby to come with them.

"My dear, I can't," she exclaimed. "Leave the city in Banba's hands?"

Zaqutu laughed. "How funny. I've left the rule of all the world in Esarhaddon's hands and he's younger than Banba."

"Oh, well, he's got every magnate in the world competing to serve him. No one would rush to help us. No, I'll stay here and hold the fort with my son. Look here," Abby reassured her cousin, "I can let you have four horsemen from our garrison, a bodyguard for the Queen Mother. We've received some new horses, really good ones."

Zaqutu thanked her and, her voice partly choked by sobs, added, "Abby, if we find Ahat-Abisha alive she'll need the best healers and nurses. You'll have them ready?"

"Of course."

Zaqutu insisted on stopping at every caravanserai or tavern they passed on their journey east. They sat to listen to gossip, but no one spoke of local events, not even about strangers who might have been passing through. Instead the talk was about how the new king was rooting out any officials who had supported Arda-Mulissi.

"They deserve what they get," Ataril was told at one well where they watered their horses. "The old king made everyone swear to be loyal to that boy. They're still calling him Esarhaddon, I hear."

"The other name is too long, don't you think? But will they catch all the rebels?" Ataril asked. "I hear they haven't found the rebel prince yet."

"Him!" the man snorted, but added no news of the fugitive.

Travelling upstream, they soon reached the same trail they had followed coming from Gula's temple. News of the war's ending preceded them even there on the margins of the empire. Each village was alert for travellers; people came to the roadside to gape at the riders and ask Ataril and Zaqutu for news, eager to tell how they themselves had weathered the crisis. Stopping for such talk delayed their progress. and not until they reached the steep hills separating the Diglat tributaries from the Upper Zaba did their enquiries bear fruit.

"The last wagon with booty came through nine days ago. They hadn't got much: one woman—an old cripple—and lots of hangings. No tools, no silver, no furniture even. They'll be sorry, those hill-men, wild fellows from Manna. They went with the king's son and for all they got for it—" the old woman snorted "—they'd have been better off in the hills fetching firewood for their grannies."

Ataril nodded in agreement before asking, "Where do you suppose they were going?"

The townsfolk debated among themselves. Some thought they'd go to Zikirtu. "Izibia, perhaps. Far from everywhere. Even men of Zamua won't go there."

A shifty-looking youth sneered. "Nah. Them sons of Sargon's veterans, they hang out in Mutsatsir. Half barbarians they are."

A chill settled on the crowd. Before Ataril could ask any more questions the headman alighted from his mule beside Zaqutu. "You're Belet-Adad, aren't you? I see the dog. You've fallen on better times but the dog looks much the same." His eyes flicked over the fittings of their horses, the respectful guards hanging slightly back but watching everyone in the square. "Where do you plan to lodge this night?"

Zaqutu looked over at Ataril but he had turned back to speak to one of the guards. With some trepidation she answered, "We have provisions in plenty for ourselves, sir, but lodging we would gratefully purchase."

The headman cleared his throat. "Ha! You can't do that. There's a rich Gimmiran noble in my sister's house. They call him Bartatua and he's been very generous."

"Is there nowhere else?"

"My own house is full at this time of year but we can add a pallet or two. Your men—guards are they? You didn't need guards during the war and now, ... well, it's funny, isn't it?"

Thinking quickly Zaqutu laughed, shrugging her shoulders. "When war faced my town I wouldn't take soldiers away, but now they can be spared." A silence met her words and she realised "my town" wasn't how Belet-Adad would speak. *Maybe he won't notice,* she thought.

The headman stood facing her, not meeting her eyes, but slowly taking in each detail of her new bridle, the luxurious blanket, the horses' well-tended hooves and her quality shoes. "You two come with me. Your soldiers? Let them stay at the gate."

After they had settled in an hour's daylight remained, and wandering among the stalls of the market Zaqutu met the visitor from Gimmira. Bartatua, not much older than she, was pale; even his eyes seemed drained of colour. His hair fascinated her. It hung straight down to his shoulders and stopped there as if he had sliced it off.

Bartatua hovered over her, flirting, assuming her to be a tavern-keeper or some man's concubine. "Belet-Adad? From the west, they say? Speaking the language of the west?"

"I can and do speak the language of the west, but when in the east I try to be understood. Here, so far from civilisation, I am surprised to meet a man with such a good ear. Where did you learn to speak the languages of the Diglat people?"

"My home is far, far to the east, beyond the lakes of Urartu. You call my land Zikirtu. Fugitives from the south come to our hills and over them. They make good servants, loyal only to the man who feeds them, immune to bribes from his enemies. They speak their language among themselves and ... well, I am their lord. I want to know what they are saying." He spoke the words as banter—first looking straight into her eyes, then flattering her by running his eyes up and down her body. "Since we understand each other, perhaps you will dine with me this evening. The hut I stay in is humble, but ..."

"I know it. I stayed there myself last month on my way home from the temple of Gula."

"Will you come?"

Zaqutu turned around to see if Ataril agreed but he had stayed gossiping with the headman. She assured the man, "We will be pleased to do so, my servant Ataril and myself."

Jesting, he replied, "Bring the dog too."

"Ben-Zakir accepts your invitation with pleasure."

Bartatua insisted on accompanying her back to the headman's gate where Ataril waited for her, bursting with news. "My lady, I ..." he began but stopped, seeing the stranger holding Zaqutu's arm. "Are you unwell?"

Zaqutu winked at him. "I'm fine." But she introduced the Gimmiran and sent him away with the promise they would come to his hut after nightfall.

Once in their quarters—the headman had fingered their silver thoughtfully and given them his own pair of rooms—Ataril grabbed

Zaqutu's wrists and shook her. "What are you doing to us? Can't you be trusted on your own for one hour?"

Shaking herself free, she hissed, "What's got into you? He's from the east. He just thinks I'm Belet-Adad."

"A real Belet-Adad would not go into the streets looking for a one-night lover. I saw the look you exchanged."

"You imagine things. And so what? I might take a lover some day, you know."

Ataril sank on to his pallet with a groan.

"What is the matter with you?" She watched him shrug his shoulders looking disgusted. She asked again, in a different voice, "What's wrong?"

Ataril snorted into his bedding before he sat up and looked at her. "Zaqutu, we have been friends for many years. I am your servant and cannot be otherwise. But how can I serve you if you ... if you kick against the pricks, over and over again. Take a lover? You are Queen Mother. Anyone who shares your ... who shares your body, shares your power."

Zaqutu echoed his words with a sigh. "My power." Plaintively she added, "What about me? I'm not an old woman."

"True. You could have a child. That would really set a cat among the pigeons. A rival for Esarhaddon's throne? Is that what you want? Someone to kill Pulu and take over?"

"That's impossible," she snapped. His expression remained grim, so forbidding that she went on, "I think it was while I was at Arbail and not in my right mind, but I heard her say ..." She looked hard at his face as she spoke, seeing a flicker of doubt in his eyes, "Our mother's voice, not Baya."

> I am Ishtar of Arbail. Esarhaddon, king of Asshur! In the Inner City, Ninuwa, Kalkhu and Arbail I will give long days and everlasting years to Esarhaddon, my king.
> I am your great midwife, I am your excellent wet nurse. For long days and everlasting years I have established your throne under the great heavens.
> I watch in a golden chamber in the midst of the heavens; I let the lamp of amber shine before Esarhaddon, king of Asshur, and I watch him like the crown of my head.
> Have no fear, my king! I have spoken to you, I have not lied to you, I have given you faith. I will not let you come to shame. I will take you safely across the river.
> Esarhaddon, rightful heir, son of Mulissu! With angry dagger in my hand I will finish off your enemies.

O Esarhaddon, cup filled with lye! Axe of two shekels!
Esarhaddon! I will give you long days and everlasting years in the Inner City. O Esarhaddon, I will be your good shield in Arbail.
Esarhaddon, rightful heir, son of Mulissu! I am mindful of you, I have loved you greatly.
I keep you in the great heavens by your forelock. I make smoke rise up on your right side, I kindle fire on your left.
The kingship is strong in you, I will not fail you.

Ataril digested her words in silence. She looked across at him, her anger dying away as she saw tears in his eyes. "I believe the Goddess will see that Esarhaddon shall rule and that his son shall succeed him on the throne."

"If that is Ishtar's word by Ahat-Abisha then we must find her—we must."

"I believe that nothing I do can overturn the will of the Goddess. What I do or don't do, it's no matter."

"The will of the Goddess is hers. She doesn't put the fates in your hands; she holds them tight in her own. Power you have nevertheless. I wonder about your good sense."

Conceding his point, she reached up to stroke his smooth cheek. "Perhaps you are right. Tonight for certain I will take no lover. You may stick close and knife him if he tries anything."

"It's nothing to joke about, my lady."

She stared him down, her mouth set in a grim line. *He'd better see I'm not joking.*

In Bartatua's hut they had a pottage of lentils and meat that must have come from a very old ram that hadn't lasted the winter. He'd found no wine and the local beer tasted muddy and a bit stale. They laughed over the hardships of travel and Zaqutu kept up her flattery by asking the Gimmiran many questions about the roads eastward. "Would we find better fare east of Gula's temple, were we to travel into your country?"

"Mutsatsir, in Urartu, has a hostelry but—"

Ataril interrupted, "I am interested in Mutsatsir. We seek the healer who cured my lady, who gave us the dog …"

"It must have been Zakir the exorcist! I met him just four days ago. You named the dog for him?"

"He cured me. He is a very great healer. Was he in Mutsatsir then? If we went there would we find him?"

"Mutsatsir is not a good place to be. It's Arda-Mulissi's headquarters. The traders and landholders have all fled, fearing the new king.

I expect the new king will send some troops there soon to clean up that nest of vipers."

Zaqutu looked horrified. "They wouldn't hurt Zakir would they?"

Bartatua smiled at her. "They won't have a chance. He'd already gone a day's journey east when I met him. He's moving slowly, caring for a crippled woman, taking her to his hideaway in the swamps." His eyes fixed on Zaqutu, their host didn't see Ataril stiffen but Zaqutu noticed.

With a come-hither grin, she looked up at their host from under her eyelashes and teased him. "I thought no one knew where he came from. Swamps, you say. Do you also come from the swamps? And where are they?"

"My lands lie north of the Nairi waters. Zakir hides somewhere in the swamps south of those very waters."

"Do you pass his home on your way home? I would so like to see him again. He's not only skilful but kind too."

"I would be pleased to take you there but, as you ride horses and I walk beside my cart, I would hold you up."

Ataril broke in. "We know you are on your way to Ninuwa. We wouldn't ask you to interrupt your business. What day was it when you saw Zakir?"

"Ninth of Adar, five days ago. I know because he gave me these." Bartatua showed them his pouch. Ten pieces of linen, five of them still tied with a woollen thread, five carefully smoothed out. "I have made good progress, I will be in Ninuwa before five more days are up." He turned to each of them in turn saying, "Perhaps you yourselves will stop off at Ninuwa before returning to your home far in the west?"

Ataril's eyebrows rose at the man's tone of voice, knowing and a little mocking. "My lady seeks Zakir. If he's gone east, east we shall go."

Zaqutu nodded at his words and turned her most alluring smile to their host. "My lord." She hesitated. "I know not your rank or even the land from which you come. Can you not tell us more of the east?"

"I rule in Zikirtu, so my people come from far north of Urartu. I go to Ninuwa for the crowning of the king at the new moon. We are rough hill people, but we breed the best horses in the world. I will ally myself with the king and sell him all our horses. This will starve the Urartians, Mannaeans and Medes of horses. Your king will have peace and I will have good prices." The man smirked. "I saw your horses at the gate. They did not come from Kharranu."

"Oh, Ataril, see how wise is the stranger I met in the marketplace. It wasn't my beauty that drew him, but our horses."

Bartatua stood and bowed. "You praise my wisdom too highly. Your guards came from Dur-Sharrukin. I know, I sold those horses to the governor."

Ataril rose, and with exaggerated politeness bowed to the Gimmiran. "I believe you." With a nod to Zaqutu he went on, "I will trust you, too, because you may be able and willing to help us. The crippled woman with Zakir—do you know who she is?"

"All Mutsatsir knows that Arda-Mulissi captured his aunt, the Priestess of Arbail. I wonder why no army but a woman—a very beautiful woman, more alluring than all the horses ever spawned—rides in pursuit. I wonder how she comes by the horses of Dur-Sharrukin."

Before they returned to the headman's rooms Ataril had a map of the villages they would pass through from Gula's temple to Zakir's hut. Three days' journey followed over hills, along the ridges and finally down a steep slope in sight of the inland sea. A few shepherds saw them pass but they met no one on the road. On the third evening they saw a large fire in front of a wooden stockade. Zakir's enclosure looked welcoming and he greeted them without surprise.

More wonderful still, anticipating that Ahat-Abisha would be returning to Arbail, he had built her a padded saddle with a framework she could hold on to for balance and to keep the horse's footfalls from jolting her painful hip. He told them he had nearly readied a standing frame she could use for prayer.

"Where is she?"

"I have no women here. Even you, my lady the Queen Mother, even you must stay outside. The Mother of Arbail is asleep now, with women from the valley. My servant will lead you to her. Please leave her to sleep. She has terrible pain, so I have given her medicine."

Zaqutu walked beside the servant, praying silently, so absorbed she stumbled on the rough flagstones of the path. At the entrance to the women's compound the dogs came up to sniff at Zaqutu's pet but did not bark. Voices came from the courtyard, sounding placid and soft. The calm of Zakir, the healing peace that seemed to float over him, operated here even at a distance.

"The high-priestess, which is her place?" Zaqutu asked in a whisper.

A very young woman, heavy-set and limping, motioned her toward the northeast corner of the enclosure. At the door Zaqutu hesitated. Cloths had been hung around the window openings, her eyes needed time to adjust. Stepping inside, she saw a footstool beside the pallet where Ahat-Abisha lay in motionless slumber. Zaqutu sat down to wait. *This is how her brother, my lord the king, sat beside my pallet in Urakka. He didn't even know me then. I wonder why he bothered.* Her thoughts gathered and dispersed as she felt her past sorrow fall away. Only the priestess, Ishtar's chosen servant, occupied her. She watched the older woman's chest rise and fall with her breathing.

Slowly she thought she could hear something, as if the priestess's thoughts were coming into her own mind. Then Ishtar herself, girded for battle, appeared to her, the mouth of the Goddess forming the word, "revenge". In a whisper Zaqutu repeated the word over and over until she herself fell into a doze.

She started awake when a girl came in with a basin. The priestess stirred as well and, perhaps smelling the herbs soaking in the hot water, lifted her head, nostrils flaring.

Zaqutu reached out to take her hand. "Mother, oh how glad I am that you are here, well cared for. We feared he had left you for dead."

Ahat-Abisha tried to speak but her words were slurred beyond understanding.

"Shh," Zaqutu whispered, "don't speak if it's too hard. Perhaps you want news. Esarhaddon has defeated the rebels, been acclaimed in Ninuwa. He awaits us there in the New Palace."

The priestess moved her tongue across her lips. She tried again to speak but let her head fall back to her pillow. She brought her other hand up to Zaqutu's and stroked the younger woman's palm. They stayed so until a woman pulled aside the curtains and entered. Zaqutu moved away so the servant could bathe the older woman's body. At a gesture from Zaqutu the woman gave her the jar of ointment. Zaqutu gently massaged the swollen and bruised body.

After a day's rest at Gula's temple the party made their way overland to Arbail. The hilly countryside, ridged and now wet with spring rains, made for slow riding. During the days and at their rests Zaqutu and Ahat-Abisha told each other their adventures and then ventured on speculation about the future.

"My daughter will be priestess until," Ahat-Abisha began, "Shadditu succeeds her."

"But you, my beloved Mother, what of you?"

"I cannot serve the Goddess—you can see that. Zakir says I will never mend."

Zaqutu felt tears rise in her eyes at the sight of the priestess's face twisted in pain and misery. It seemed too hard; the older woman was innocent, really innocent. *How could that be her fate?* Doubt filled her. *How does he know?*

The priestess read her thoughts and assured her, "Zakir is a servant of Nergal, you know that. He has seen me in the realm of the dead, bent and crippled as now. Don't worry, in my dreaming the Goddess has spoken. She will continue to speak through me. You will have the oracle for the crowning ceremony at the new moon."

"What of me, then? What use will the Goddess have for my devotion?"

"Zaqutu, my dear, you know the answer to that. You are Queen

Mother. From what you say you are also mother to the new Crown Prince. Pulu will move into the Succession Palace and you will be with him."

"As his mother? Shouldn't Esharra come to Ninuwa?"

"You still let your gut emotions speak instead of your intelligence. Your heart, Zaqutu—doesn't it tell you that Esharra must rule in Babili? You must rule in Ninuwa."

To Ataril Zaqutu exclaimed, "In Babili! That's your idea, isn't it? I am stuck in Ninuwa so your Babili can get its own king." She snorted but, looking up, saw Ataril's pained expression as he answered.

"My lady, the stars predict that Esarhaddon himself will rebuild Babili."

"I haven't read that report," she fumed. *Ataril cares more for his stupid city than he does for me.* The thought began to torment her. "You'd better fetch the Mother's drug now," she ordered him.

Alone with the priestess, she took her hand and stroked the dry skin, reminding herself to anoint Ahat-Abisha when the drug had put her to sleep. "Mother, the Lamashtu demon," she whispered. "It visits me still." She squeezed the hand of the priestess more tightly. "I want to wail my misery even when nothing is really wrong."

Searching Zaqutu's eyes, the priestess asked, "Is it the thought of Ninuwa?"

Zaqutu couldn't speak; her mouth felt frozen shut.

"Daughter, it's not Ninuwa, is it? It's that you don't want to rule. Do you know why you don't want to be Queen Mother?"

Zaqutu let go of the priestess's hands. "Don't want to be Queen Mother?" she echoed. *Is that it?* As if her whole torso had taken flight she felt emptied out, dead inside. Transported back into her childhood, she heard voices, bitter quarrels. Her mother's shrill protests. *Qat wanted to be Queen Mother, desperately. She'd murder her own children for that power. She did, too—her grandchildren.* At this thought the sound and smell of her baby, her Pulu, rose up in memory. She smiled at the thought of him.

Ahat-Abisha stirred falling into sleep, her movement recalling Zaqutu to the present, to the words she'd just repeated. *Why don't I want to be Queen Mother? Is that why?*

Into the silence Ahat-Abisha murmured, "Yours is the power."

Zaqutu sighed. She turned back to the Mother, who now breathed slowly in her drugged sleep. "Esarhaddon needs me—that's what you're telling me."

They spent only two nights in Arbail—a sorry place, its walls undermined and the looted buildings filthy. On the third day they set off for the slow progress to Dur-Sharrukin, where Banba showed them his correspondence from the Crown Prince .

Zaqutu screwed up her mouth as she read of the executions. "He'll have no magnates at all if he goes on like this," she complained to Ataril. "Enemies will multiply. Why can't he learn kindness? The king his father ..."

"My lady, don't let your grief cloud your vision. The king your husband was not kind to your country or you wouldn't be here. He was not kind to my country either."

"But he gave your gods the credit for his good fortune."

"Or he pretended to, so he could bring Arda out into the open."

Zaqutu looked hard at Ataril and turned to Ahat-Abisha, who reclined beside them, dozing but neither drugged nor asleep. "My mother, do you think he never meant to send the gods down to Babili?"

"Probably he meant to. It would have been good policy. At each station along the river he'd appear to each of the cities as a proper royal king of Babili, adorning the gods' images, building ..."

Ataril stiffened. "Maybe he never planned to build. Maybe he meant to send the gods back to the heaps of rubble he ..."

"My son, you punish enemies but rebels you must crush. Your people, the nobles of Babili, they swore allegiance to the king of Asshur and then betrayed him to Bit-Yakin, to Elam—to anyone who offered them troops they could use to challenge the king's forces."

Ataril snorted. "Crushed indeed. Nevertheless, Mother, maybe my lord the king did intend to rebuild Babili someday. 'The lands of Akkad are rich and make Asshur rich,' he told me. Akkad's chief city remains Babili, even now. The new king should rebuild its walls before he tries to win the allegiance of the nobles by returning their gods."

Ahat-Abisha pulled herself to a sitting position and faced him. "Shall you be among the new king's magnates then? Is that your programme?"

Ataril could not return her look and lowered his head, eyes half-closed. "Esarhaddon has already shown us that he takes his own counsel." He smiled up at the priestess, pointing to the parchments that lay scattered around their divans. "What we don't know is what he means to do about Esharra-Hammat and Shumukin. If Shumukin is to be king of Babili, then there needs to be a Babili for him to be king of."

"The king my husband," Zaqutu observed, "chose her to gain Bit-Yakin's loyalty. But I have heard that her cousin, the governor down there, courts Uruk and Nippur. With Esarhaddon slaughtering magnates ... well, they could set up a rival kingdom. As Ataril says, Akkad is rich."

The others stared at her in surprise for a moment and then

Ahat-Abisha smiled. "Ishtar is wise indeed and speaks truth. Since you are wise, you have sources of information other than your beloved Ataril. Yours is the power. You must see to the shrine of Ishtar in Ninuwa."

Zaqutu looked down and they sat silent. *Ataril among the magnates? Did Ishtar of Arbail permit him to become my servant so that ... surely not.* She looked up into his face, but his gaze was far away. "Your thoughts, my friend?"

Ataril frowned for a moment. "I was wondering ... a procession, very slow, the king seen worshipping the gods of Babili—you know, in the fashion of Babili."

"Oh, no! Ataril, all those magnates who supported us—Tab-shar-Asshur, Asshur-natsir, Nabu-zeru-leshir—they'd not put up with it! That the king should praise Marduk for all his victories! They'd hate it."

Ataril grinned. "My lady, our mother says you must see to the shrine of Ishtar in Ninuwa. You'll hate that, won't you? But you'll understand that Ishtar has established your son's kingship and she requires you to do things you hate. Any magnates who have survived Esarhaddon's purge will have a strong interest in keeping him on the throne, in Ninuwa."

Zaqutu snorted, but Ahat-Abisha reached over and gripped her shoulder. "The Goddess speaks only truth. You have seen that. You wanted to give up and die, and now ..."

"I was possessed by a demon—you know that. You sent me to Zakir. And Gula healed me, her dogs ..."

"My child, who was in Gula to heal you? Who gives the gift of healing, of exorcism? Who holds the *me*?"

Esarhaddon's journey from Ninuwa to Asshur for his crowning was a slow progress. At each landing stage along the river crowds gathered, an altar was set up and offerings made. The praises of Asshur rang out, all his attributes chanted: 'Creator, the one who defeats Tiamat, the Light of the World, the sun himself,' and on and on.

On their barge Ataril paced to and fro, frowning and impatient.

"What's the matter with you?" Zaqutu asked.

"I don't know whose idea it was, but I don't like it. The way they have applied all Marduk's titles to Asshur. He can't mean to insult the gods, so why does he take their titles for Asshur?"

"My friend, he is king in the sight of all the gods, or will be when he is crowned. He will do what he pleases then, not what I like or what you like."

"Not what I like certainly—but you, my lady, yours is the power. All the wealth of Asshur now passes through your hands. Whatever you withhold, it is held back."

Zaqutu shook her head. "No, Ataril, he will do what he likes, I know it. It belongs to the Goddess, not to me, that power and wealth. She holds no weapon for me to wield, least of all against my own son."

Ataril shrugged and changed the subject.

In the temple of Asshur, she who was once little Naqia from Jerusalem gripped Esarhaddon's wrists as they lifted the diadem on to his head. He winced at the weight and bit his lip. But each of them stood silent and unmoving before the crowd as the priests of Asshur chanted his praises and read out the covenant given Esarhaddon by Ishtar of Arbail. As Zaqutu returned to her seat beside the young king's throne Ataril, behind her, whispered, "It is done as promised, your son will rule Asshur. I pray that he will be diligent and good."

She smiled and muttered so softly that only he could hear, "He will do what he pleases, I am sure of that."

Chapter 35: The Prophecy

In Arbail Ahat-Abisha observed the monthly rites of Ishtar, conducted by the new priestess, her young daughter, just a year older than Esarhaddon. At other times she lived in Kalkhu rather than Arbail. Arbail was too isolated and she wanted to give her daughter independence. In Zaqutu's comfortable and spacious palace she had a suite specially fitted out for her. The Queen Mother's servants competed to serve her.
When asked why she chose Kalkhu instead of Ninuwa she replied, "I can prophesy here in the Ishtar temple. Here Ishtar of Arbail speaks through my mouth."

All the messengers passed through Kalkhu going from Ninuwa to Asshur and Babili, and so also all those returning. While Ahat-Abisha waited for the Goddess to take her revenge on Arda-Mulissi she kept her finger on the pulse of Esarhaddon's rule. She herself wrote little, unless in reply to Zaqutu's questions, but she enjoyed the summers, when Zaqutu and her whole court always shifted from Ninuwa to Kalkhu—for peace and to enjoy the gardens.

"So, daughter—I suppose I should say 'my lady the Queen Mother'," she laughed. "I see that you have the power and that you use it sparingly."

Zaqutu grinned. "Yes, Mother, or should I say 'my lady, Prophet of Ishtar'?" She gave a big sigh as she looked out over the date palms and flowering almond trees. "It is lovely here in spring and I am exhausted with the folly of my son the king. He fills the New Palace with bevies of women who quarrel and feud and come running to me in the Succession Palace, trying to make me intercede with him." She snorted. "Hopeless."

"The king your son doesn't obey you? It's no surprise. His father disregarded our mother's wishes most of the time or you wouldn't be here." Ahat-Abisha kept her voice humorous in tone but between the women lay heavy memories, like stones that each stumbled over in their talk. *It's no good even thinking about it; "what if" was never wise. If Arda had been allowed to rule perhaps my mother would have been happy, but he proved too like his grandfather—impulsive, wild and over-confident.* But her thoughts no longer stayed so much in her control. *If Zaqutu had simply done what the king asked, even if she had paid more attention to Esarhaddon when he became Crown Prince.* They sat together in silence.

Ahat-Abisha looked over at Zaqutu. *If she'd not charmed Sennacherib at the outset ... but even then Arda might have refused to wait patiently in the Succession Palace. If Zaqutu had married the son instead of the father ... but maybe Arda would have murdered the king anyway.*

Against her wishes, she saw Arda before her eyes and felt churning in her stomach. Arda's dismissal of her to be tied up by his guards. She could hear the clanking and smashing of the looting of Arbail. Wincing with pain, she saw Zaqutu's face melt with compassion.

"Oh, Mother, do you want more poppy?"

"No, not now. I want a clear head to hear your news—not just about your son's palace women but about all that is happening, how things are going."

"It's changed little, really, since the beginning. He decided his policy and he follows it. Really that's all."

"Is it?"

Zaqutu shrugged. "I think he finds being king of the world less and less like a pleasure garden. Oh, the army is loyal and the magnates support him in the council. But, you know, nothing seems to please the nobles of Babili."

"He has made Esharra Queen Consort and they seem to have accepted him as king of Babili more than they did when my father tried to be their king."

"And he's spending a fortune founding new walls and repairing the canal. He's promised them so much. But Bit-Yakin is restless and Elam takes an interest in that."

"I heard that Elam's promised gift was delivered."

Zaqutu nodded. "Everything goes the king's way. They say he has a charmed life." She paused and Ahat-Abisha noted the frown cross her brow. "He has won every skirmish, but ..." She sighed.

"And so, you sigh and frown, my dear. Tell me why you worry."

"When Esarhaddon was growing up my lord the king loved regaling him with tales of battle. Always the battles were victories the way he told them to his son." Zaqutu looked up to see if the older woman was still listening. "A lot of them weren't, but Esarhaddon never knew that. No king wins all his battles."

"Are you telling me you're afraid of what he'll do when he loses?'"

Zaqutu shrugged. "His magnates and other counsellors are very complaisant. They say 'yes' to everything." She stopped and silence again fell between them.

Ahat-Abisha began to doze off until, in her half-sleep, she heard Zaqutu say, "I think my son and his proper wife should be together more. Maybe get another son. His Ninuwa women produce nothing but daughters. How am I going to get rid of all those daughters?"

Ahat-Abisha made no comment. She wondered at the younger woman's remark. Another son would surely become a source of trouble. *Why would Zaqutu worry about daughters?* She observed idly, "I hear he plans to add more provinces."

"More provinces! More battles, and the army of the north yet further away. More and more expense, but less security at home!"

"My dear, think of all those cities far away towards the Great Northern Sea. Don't you want to send daughters there? They will take with them all the arts of civilisation, all the *me*."

"Only if they are taught. The king my son is so much away and his women—well, you know, they come from everywhere. They seem to know little and care less about the *me*."

"Zaqutu, it isn't his duty to ensure his daughters are fit for princes' wives. It's yours." She saw the look of irritation pass across Zaqutu's face. Her lips in a hard line, she stared away towards the orchards.

Only a sigh came from her for a while. In a plaintive voice she cried, "Oh, Mother, I don't really like them. Neither the wives nor their daughters. They're all so petty."

"But if you ignore them," she replied, "I wonder how those youngsters may learn the arts of civilisation." She said no more.

Ninuwa Central had changed under Zaqutu's hands. The chatelaine had a policy of promoting eunuchs and fewer women served Ishtar. Fewer to teach and so very few to learn. Ahat-Abisha kept her voice low, as if thinking to herself, "Perhaps your son the king should devote some of those daughters. If he did so, then you might be less troubled."

"The king my son is off with his army all the time, winning those provinces." Zaqutu's voice had risen in pitch. She was clearly frustrated but also, it seemed, frightened.

"My dear." Ahat-Abisha felt sorry now and reached out to take Zaqutu's hand. "Are you afraid for your son the king, afraid because he is fighting?"

Zaqutu shook her head. "No, he's pretty careful when he's on campaign, not likely to plunge headlong into danger. He's always taking omens before doing anything and that makes him seem even more cautious."

Not plunging headlong. Not like my father, thought Ahat-Abisha. And then the thought hit her. *Esarhaddon is cautious like his father.*

"Always taking omens, you say. Why? Is he sick? That's the gossip."

"Not sick in the body. He's frustrated and irritable. I don't know why, or why he takes omens all the time. Maybe he's afraid of the future."

Keeping her voice well under control, Ahat-Abisha asked, "Does he worry that his father's death is unavenged?" She looked straight into the younger woman's face, trying not to let her own pain and frustration show.

Zaqutu looked down and shifted in her seat. "I've asked about that. I'll tell you:"

> In the temple of Shamash at Ninuwa the king and I stood watching the haruspex as he examined the liver carefully.
> "The king my lord should know," the haruspex began, "the question you asked is many-sided."
> "Yes," he muttered. "What's the reply?"
> "A grief to my lord the king. You will not be happy. My lord the king, the god has answered so. It's not my fault."
> "Make another offering then."
> I searched his face, "You will ask more questions?"
> Even though he knew the priest standing by the sacrifice could hear us he answered, "Unfinished business. The king my father ..."
> I put my hand up to his mouth to stop him. "My son, you have not avenged the murder of your father. It is months since you even did a son's duty at his grave. How do you expect Shamash to answer you?"
> "Mother, my father told me that as king I should do nothing without inquiring first of the gods. He told me he always obeyed the omens. I honour him by doing the same."

Ahat-Abisha listened to Zaqutu's account with her own eyes closed, in silence—a silence that continued after the younger woman finished.

It lasted until Zaqutu whispered, "So, since the king gets no reply I've had omens taken. I asked about the rebel, whether the king should find and take him. They always answer 'no'."

The old woman turned away to relieve a crick in her neck and remarked, "While Arda lives death will not take me. Daughter, I do so want to die. The omens are not to be doubted, but perhaps they suggest it isn't to be the king who accomplishes my wish. Whoever does it, Arda's head comes to me on a platter. Ishtar sent me that vision so it must happen. She keeps me waiting. I don't care who brings me the head!"

"Mother, I would seek him out myself and kill him for you if I could. But even if I caught him I don't think I could kill anyone. You know how squeamish I am about blood."

The prophet laughed and the atmosphere between the women lightened. "So, now, tell me of little Pulu. How is he coming along?"

Zaqutu spoke more sharply to Pulu than she intended. "Pulu, we will celebrate the feast with the others and you will attend."

"I don't want to."

"That hardly matters. I don't want to do many things that I have to do, and so do you."

Pulu, four years old, objected, "Grandmama, I'm not Crown Prince so I shouldn't have to go. Shumukin is. He should have to go."

Zaqutu stopped short, surprised by his reasoning. She dropped the hand she had gripped to drag him along and turned to face him. "Pulu, the goddess has named you as successor to your father as king of Asshur. You know that—you've always known that. Shamash-Shumu-Ukin is to be Crown Prince in Babili."

He looked up at her, grinning. *The little imp, he was just trying to get a rise out of me.*

Ahat-Abisha savoured the harmony that seemed to flow from Zaqutu's closeness to her younger grandson. She wondered how the king felt about it. He needed Zaqutu to be the Queen Mother, handling the vast commerce of Ninuwa, but he needed her, too, as Queen since Esharra almost never came to Ninuwa and had begun to direct his rule of Babili.

She also wondered whether Esharra could manage what Tashmetu had found so difficult. *My brother never even sought to be king in Babili, I suppose he hated them too much, and of course they knew it. But Esarhaddon has managed to be accepted as king there.* She patted Zaqutu's hand. "And so, my dear Zaqutu, what of the intended Crown Prince of Babili? Do you think he is clever enough?"

"He's so young! How can we know what he'll be like?"

"You seem to know what Pulu will be like. Clever and manipulative too. Does his brother wind himself around Esharra that way?"

Zaqutu stiffened. "You think Pulu manipulates me? A boy who hasn't started to wear a proper tunic?"

"Well? What happened? Did he go with you?"

"He argued about it—he likes to argue." Her voice softened again. "He likes words, likes playing with them. So he told me, 'You say Shumukin is too young to be Crown Prince. So, Grandmama, I'm too young too.' Of course I laughed and petted him. I like wit." Zaqutu fell silent.

"You didn't answer my question. Did he go?"

"Of course. I told him he wasn't too young to do as I say. As we made our way to the feast I thought about what he said about being too young, and thought about how great wisdom could come from such small mouths. Esarhaddon has many children but all are too young to be useful."

"You sound uneasy. Your son worries you?"

"I sometimes wish the king would settle on one of his Ninuwa women for pre-eminence. Then she'd have to order the others around." She stopped for a moment. "But his treasury is full, I've no worries there. He will have to plan to spend some, and not just in Babili. And he should act to secure the succession."

"Don't you know? I have had a word for him from Ishtar of Arbail."

"When?"

"Just before you arrived, perhaps you missed it."

"Tell me."

> I am the Lady of Arbail. O Esarhaddon, whose bosom Ishtar of Arbail has filled with favour! Could you not rely on the previous utterance which I spoke to you? Now you can rely on this later one too.
>
> Praise me! When daylight declines, let them hold torches! Praise me before them!
>
> I will banish trembling from my palace. You shall be safe in your palace. Your son and grandson shall rule as kings on the lap of Ninurta.

"What does she mean 'on the lap of Ninurta'?"

"That each will succeed through the Succession Palace, an unchallenged succession."

"So, is that why he has no more sons, do you think?"

Ahat-Abisha shook her head and gestured for Zaqutu to hand her the beaker. Her pain made her dizzy and the conversation had not eased her mind.

Chapter 36: Esarhaddon's Ambition

At the end of Esarhaddon's fifth year as king he returned from the council of magnates to Zaqutu's wing of the palace. The days were still short and the evenings cold. Braziers blazed in every corner and incense pots smouldered before the lectern where the Queen Mother squinted, initialling the inventories.
"Greetings, my son the king. Your treasury is full, your people are at peace, your son will rule as Crown Prince in Babili and they keep the peace well."
"Esharra does, you mean, and she will do so still after he's installed as Crown Prince."
"I'm being polite. Truthful too. You have been very prudent, using the armies sparingly and to good effect. Your household is large, but well-supplied."
"Large, you say. I have heard that in the land of Egypt there are women of surpassing beauty—Nubian women. I have it in mind to take some to add to my collection."
"More women! My son, you are fit and young, I know. But needing more women? Certainly not—not here. As it is I get nothing but complaints that you never visit your wives. What's the point?"
"I fancy some Nubians. Anyway, I'm going against Egypt." He smirked. "Trust me, it's not just for the women. Egypt produces so much grain they can buy my vassals in a year of poor harvest. I will put my own viceroy on their throne or—" his voice rose "—die in the attempt."
"Speak no words of ill omen."
"I must go and subdue Tsurru anyway. I'll just keep going south. Perhaps I'll stop by and see my uncle, your brother, when I'm there."
"Take my advice, son, leave them alone. Go straight down the coast. They pay, let them be. Why stir up trouble?"
"He's always writing to me, styling me 'nephew'. I thought he could provide forage."

"They pay, let them be."

"As you wish, Mother. I will do as you say—I will stick to the coastal route. I'm glad you approve of my plans."

Zaqutu sighed. He'd tricked her again, but this might be an opportunity. "My son, you have many daughters cluttering up the New Palace. Have you given thought to getting some of them settled? If you expand westward, think about securing the eastern lands with some well-chosen alliances."

"Ah, to whom do you want to give one of my daughters?"

"The Gimmiran, Bartatua, who came to your accession five years ago. Your eldest daughter is only nine. She need only be betrothed. We won't sent her off to Zikirtu for a while."

"Go ahead."

"If you add more wives, there will be yet more daughters to get rid of."

"Ha. I'll just keep on adding more provinces—one new province for every new wife. We have received envoys from some strange peoples who sail the Great Northern Sea. They like our weapons so much they might like Shubria and Urartu. So I might take some cities on their borders, just to be safe. What do you say?"

"I say no."

That summer Zaqutu was in Ninuwa until late in the season. Ahat-Abisha could imagine why. The king campaigned in the west undefeated. He added two new provinces.

Reading Zaqutu's letters, she thought, *They're not getting on. He's like a little boy, going farther and farther away against her wishes to see when she'll pull him up. And her? She won't. Too proud to stoop to using the power of the purse. She lets him go though she knows it's folly.* Ahat-Abisha sighed and picked up a parchment.

Writing was slow work these days and what she wrote cost her precious concentration.

> To the Queen Mother my daughter, your mother Ahat-Abisha prophet of Arbail. Good health to you and to the king your son. May Ishtar bless you and keep you in her arms.
>
> You say the king your son has won many victories in the region of the Great Northern Sea. The gods favour him. Now you say he will not finish his campaign but is heading south, to Egypt.
>
> Of course you cannot recall him, but you never want to cross him directly. You are never willing to deny him resources for any of his projects, and

this is no time to begin. I am sorry you have no opportunity to summer here. Of course I miss you and Pulu. He will soon need a tutor. I hope you have been thinking about that.

She sat wondering what to add. *I will really miss her of course. Esarhaddon does seem to have a charmed life. His magnates eat out of his hands like dogs. Even his policy in Babili has made an end to the ever-present rebellion in the south. Well, not his policy. When my brother chose Esharra for the king's wife he did it. She's much more clever than Tashmetu ever was. And keeps her boy on a tight rein, I hear.*

As the autumn festival approached Zaqutu did come to Kalkhu to assist Ahat-Abisha on her journey to Arbail. On the road Zaqutu spoke softly, "My mother, your advice was excellent but I did not take it. Oh, how I wish now that I had said no to his Egyptian adventure."

"Why?"

Zaqutu gritted her teeth, an angry frown distorting her face. With a sigh she raised her voice. "Ataril showed me the entry deposited in the Nabu temple in Babili:

The seventh year: On the fifth day of the month Adar the army of Asshur was defeated in Egypt. In the month Adar Ishtar of Akkad and the gods of Akkad left Elam and entered Akkad on the tenth day of the month Adar.

"He had memorised the whole entry, that was it, that's what they put for the whole year. I was so annoyed. Those chroniclers of Babili are really silly."

"Silly?"

"They put a procession of statues at equal importance with the whole kingdom."

"They do, and for them it is. Still, as soon as they suspect weakness in the north they'll be conspiring against Esarhaddon, you mark my words."

"My dear mother, I always mark your words."

So Esarhaddon's eldest daughter did not go to Bartatua after all. After the troubles in Babili, Bel-Etir stirring up unrest throughout the southern lands, Esarhaddon gave his eldest daughter, not yet ten years old, to Urtaku of Elam.

"As a guarantee of good behaviour," he told Zaqutu. She sniffed but he added, "You wanted me to get rid of daughters. I'm doing it."

"You twist my words." She thought of reminding him that he'd promised to 'die in the attempt' on Egypt but held her peace. *It's not modesty,* she told herself, *or compassion. I'll not pick on him because we have to share the power and he knows that I have it.*

In truth Esarhaddon had been troubled by ominous dreams. Zaqutu heard rumours, filtered back to her in devious ways, that the sages in the New Palace made jokes about how often the king sought advice from the gods. *His father had instructed him always to take omens, and to follow the decisions of Shamash. I remember that well.*

Zaqutu sat still, idly watching the sun sink below the walls of the royal enclosure. The sounds of the city became quiet—murmured orders, doors shutting, the occasional clatter of iron on stone. Sennacherib always called for bread and sweetened wine at this time of day but she'd left off that peaceful custom. It seemed to her unfaithful to his memory. *What does a king do if he's not conquering?* She laughed at her thought. *The boring bits.*

For two more years Esarhaddon enforced his peace on the Urartians and the Medes. Ahat-Abisha spent those years hoping his campaigns would lead him to Arda-Mulissi's hiding place. As the eighth year of his reign drew near, he himself came with Zaqutu to Kalkhu.

One evening as they sat beside the dozing priestess they looked back over their year. Esarhaddon remarked, "My mother, we have peace now throughout all my dominions, even in the south."

"An expensive peace," she replied.

Perhaps it was the tone of her voice, but the older woman stirred and woke up. They weren't emotional and the topic seemed almost to bore them. Nevertheless she kept her eyes closed and listened closely as Zaqutu spoke.

"I don't think you can any longer leave the whole province of Babili free of tax and free of imposts. The army protects them too—they must help pay for it."

"You told me that last year, Mother. I heard you then. But ..."

He stopped speaking and Ahat-Abisha tried opening her eyes a slit so she could see their faces. He looked serious but not upset.

"Esharra isn't willing. Is that it?" Zaqutu asked.

The king just shrugged and looked away.

Ahat-Abisha stirred and moaned and gave them warning that she was waking. "I fell asleep. Please pardon me, children. I am old and I am so tired of living. I sleep and wish to die."

They fussed over her and left. She wondered if they were going to continue the argument. *Maybe tomorrow I'll raise the subject myself,* she thought.

But the next day brought news that drove that thought from her mind—that and many other thoughts. In late evening, almost full dark, a rider arrived, passed the challenge and came into the courtyard. She heard raised voices and wondered.

Zaqutu came in softly and asked if she were awake.

"Yes, I'm awake."

"May we come to you, the king and I and Ataril?"

"Is Ataril here? From Babili?" She sat up and motioned for lamps to be lit.

"Esharra-Hammat can no longer rule in Esarhaddon's name on the throne in Babili," Zaqutu told her. "She fell ill. They brought healers. No good."

Esarhaddon sobbed and Zaqutu held him in her arms. Ataril stood aside, arms folded and head bowed.

When silence fell among them Ahat-Abisha expressed her sorrow and then asked the king, "What will you do now?"

"I will mourn my beloved consort—not because it is my duty, but no other woman has ever been so ..." The king faltered.

Weeks later Ahat-Abisha sat looking over the damp gardens in Kalkhu. She felt strong today; she'd refused two doses of poppy and her mind swirled with words. Words of old prophecies and some that she heard were new words. A vision of Zaqutu herself, on a throne of lapis-lazuli, her hands folded in her lap, was followed by the sight of her robed as a priestess of Ishtar, hands outstretched in prayer. But the words and the vision didn't fit together. She mulled over the words. Revenge, retribution, recompense. As she pondered she saw a different vision—streams of camels and oxen, carts laden with treasure, piled high and spilling over along the wayside, to lie there for anyone's pickings.

Footsteps behind her signalled an interruption. Uribelit came in to announce that the king and his mother wanted to speak with her if she were willing.

"Bring them in, my dear, and we could use some refreshment. They have been under strain, I imagine."

After he had received her nod of obeisance the king came to sit beside her. "Foster-mother, you succoured me at birth and I ask you to help me now."

She frowned. Such a request wasn't what she expected. "My lord the king, how can I help? I am very old and crippled with it."

"When we heard of Esharra's death you asked me what I was going to do. I brushed aside your question then, in my grief, but I have come to see whether any idea of what I should do was in your mind."

She looked over at Zaqutu, eyebrows raised in a silent question, but Zaqutu shrugged and shook her head. "If you are asking whether I have had a word from the Goddess, then the answer is no. I am sorry you have come all this way to ask. You might have written."

"But you are still wise, even without the word of Ishtar. We have to decide something for Babili. Until Esharra died they agreed to my being king of Babili, with my son set to become their king after me."

"So, what change to that arrangement have you been considering?" Ahat-Abisha moved on her divan to ease the pain in her side. *Why has he come? I wonder what's really bothering him? And why hasn't Zaqutu spoken about this to me before?*

"I don't know. Shumukin is only ten years old. He can be named Crown Prince but he can't rule, certainly not in Babili."

"You'll need to find someone to act as regent." They all looked at Abat-Abisha. Her voice was clear and strong, the old authority apparent. *Am I the only one who sees?* she asked herself. "Regents are often used when a king is too young to rule alone. That's what Esharra was, a regent."

The king's eyes sharpened. *Thinks I'm bitter and cynical. I suppose.* "So, you need to call your council. You can make them recommend a suitable person, can't you?"

Esarhaddon said as if to himself, "Shamash-Shumu-Ukin cannot really be crown prince at his age. He's not very quick to learn. In five years I could let him rule, but ..." He looked over at Zaqutu. "I could send my vice-chancellor to act as regent. He's a man of Babili, knows their ways. Asshur-Natsir would recommend him." He stopped there.

Zaqutu put her hand up towards his face. "You're looking at me for a special reason. What is it?"

"Can't you guess?"

"No, you may not take Ataril from me. All the decisions rest with me. Endless petitioners, magnates, governors—they all come to me in Ninuwa and even here. You aren't ever around to receive them. I must have Ataril. You cannot believe that all your gifts to the many temples of Babili appear by magic, that none of them have to be paid for?"

It didn't seem a good time for them to quarrel and the older woman pulled herself up to a sitting position, wincing. "My daughter, I can very well imagine you yourself might know someone who could assist the vice-chancellor."

Zaqutu looked at her in surprise. "My mother, will you ... ?"

She shook her head. "No, I am no part of your decisions. I only believe that when you next travel to Babili your party should include men of experience whom you can trust." She saw the thoughts passing through Zaqutu's mind. She'd never quite learned to keep them hidden.

Not frowning any longer, Zaqutu mused, "Our mother is right. I do know someone. One of your scribes, my son the king—Zarri. He has wit and long experience. He, too, is a man from Babili. Ataril, what do you think?"

"The men of Babili expect Shumukin to become their king. They won't make trouble. I worry more about Asshur."

Chapter 37: Esarhaddon Sickens and Dies

Esarhaddon's subjugation of Egypt had to wait two years. Medes destabilised the northeast borderlands, and Esarhaddon's treaty with Bartatua necessitated his intervention. Once peace came to the east Zaqutu insisted Esarhaddon formally install his sons as his successors. "I'll name Shamash-Shumu-Ukin Crown Prince of Babili, my mother, but I will make all men of Babili swear oaths of allegiance to Pulu, who will have his full name, Asshurbanipal."

"Shumu is the eldest. He will expect …"

"I don't care what he expects."

"Your sons should be equal—they have the same mother."

"Mother, I have decided, it is my decision. Anyway, you favour Pulu—always have. Why do you complain?"

"I don't complain." Zaqutu pointed to the chest in the corner. "I have a tablet," she began, but stopped seeing him close his eyes, hearing his sigh. "Don't sigh. Your foster-mother is old and weak, but she speaks the word of Ishtar."

"I know."

I am your great midwife; I am your excellent wet nurse. For long days and everlasting years I have established your throne under the great heavens.

"Those are the words Ahat-Abisha spoke before your crowning. You are king with no rival. Where are the words for Pulu? Won't the prophets of Babili have words for Shumu? Only when they are both made crown prince can you venture forth again."

"Is that your command to me?"

"My son, listen to the words of the goddess." Zaqutu went to the chest and took out the tablet, a copy of the one that now lay in the temple of Ishtar in the Inner City.

> I watch in a golden chamber in the midst of the heavens; I let the lamp of amber shine before Esarhaddon, King of Asshur, and I watch him like the crown of my head.

Esarhaddon Sickens and Dies

> Have no fear, my king! I have spoken to you, I have not lied to you; I have given you faith, I will not let you come to shame. I will take you safely across the River.
>
> Esarhaddon, rightful heir, son of Mulissu! With an angry dagger in my hand I will finish off your enemies ... I will give you long days and everlasting years in the Inner City ... I have loved you greatly. I keep you in the great heavens by your curled topknot, I make smoke rise up on your right side, I kindle fire on your left.

"Don't you see? Ishtar makes you great. Act with greatness. Choose. Decide."

"Yes, Mother. You say, 'choose', but you tell me to make your choice, 'decide' and you mean 'do what I want'."

"Do what is right."

Esarhaddon took a deep breath and, making an obeisance, turned to leave, saying only, "Since all the gods are Ishtar I will consult the oracle of Shamash."

In the tenth year of Esarhaddon, the oracle of Shamash proclaimed a favourable day for the formal naming of Shamash-Shumu-Ukin as Crown Prince of Babili. Not until the eleventh year did the oracle find a day for the accession of Asshurbanipal as Crown Prince of Asshur. This time Zaqutu moved with Pulu into the Succession Palace with a heavy heart.

For a little over a year after Esarhaddon's accession had she lived there with him as mother of the Crown Prince. The death of her baby, the murder of her husband, and the war had taken the time from her and now she wondered, *How long will it be before Pulu is old enough to marry the princess they've betrothed him to? Esharra was so good, so easy. That woman ...* Not only was the Egyptian ugly, she could hardly make two sentences fit together. Pulu hadn't even looked up at her during the betrothal two years ago. He never spoke of her. It wasn't going to be easy. She sighed. *I suppose I'll manage somehow.*

As she contemplated the move her thoughts drifted back to those first days in Ninuwa. *How frightened I was! To have the favour of the king was a curse more than a blessing.* She pulled herself up short. *No, that wasn't true. Whenever the king and she had been together it had been bliss, except for the quarrels. I never thought how horrible it must have been for the others when we quarrelled, for Ataril and*—a sob escaped her—*for Ahat-Abisha.*

Zaqutu sighed. The daily work of being Queen Mother, ruling in

Ninuwa whenever Esarhaddon was gone, left her little time for thought. Whenever she did get to think, problems surfaced. Pulu's new wife was not competent at doing anything in the household and Remutu, the chatelaine, came to Zaqutu for every little decision.

All the magnates considered Zaqutu the important power in the empire. Scrolls and tablets poured in each day, mostly from people too important to dismiss. *I can do this—I can juggle all those 'boring bits' the way my lord the king did. But he was better at being sure who he could trust than I am. I long to be a simple woman again, a nobody who could come and go at will.* She sighed. Ataril was a good judge of character and often advised her, but the more that happened the more everyone seemed to know and he was lobbied from every quarter. He'd come to her and complain about it.

In his twelfth year of rule Esarhaddon gathered a mighty army and returned to Egypt—"To crush rebellion." he said.

Zaqutu doubted the rebellion, she'd seen no messages, heard no reports. *He's only a boy, really. He wants to get out from under my tutelage, wants adventure, wants to outdo his father and grandfather as conqueror. It's a kind of madness.*

In truth, Esarhaddon's ominous dreams were no longer mere rumours, his frequent requests for omens had become worrying, not a matter for jokes, even among the younger sages. Zaqutu worried that he'd start an unnecessary campaign just to get away from his dreams.

"Ataril, why do you suppose the king is going back down to Egypt? I cannot believe his generals tell him it's necessary."

"His oracles tell him it is. They speak of a mighty fate."

"Ataril, you showed me what even the men of Babili wrote in their chronicle. Two years ago they proclaimed his victory as a massacre:

'He conquered Memphis, their royal city, chased out their king,
took all the man's sons prisoner. They sacked and plundered.'

The soldiers came back with so much money we still haven't recovered from the high prices."

"What more could he do? "

"He's being foolish, Ataril, I'm sure he is. The magnates from Sennacherib's time, even the loyal ones, got so up themselves they tried to throw off his yoke and had to be murdered. Now most are new appointees. Mannu-Ki-Asshur, the treasurer, is unused to the work. And the generals! Killanni and Sharru-Utsur are ... well, they know warfare, but as counsellors—"

Ataril interrupted, "The king rules: he chooses his magnates as he will. What worries you so?"

"The youth of them all. With their predecessors murdered, only young men advise him. No one thinks ahead. I don't like it. What will happen when the king comes back with yet more wealth, and more women?"

"No one knows, least of all me. My lady," Ataril sighed, "he has marched off. They're many days journey away. If anyone thought of a reason to call him back they'd not be able to reach him. You can't do anything. Stop fretting."

"There must be some way to stop him."

The chroniclers' entry for Esarhaddon's twelfth year read:
The king of Asshur marched to Egypt but became ill on the way and died on the tenth day of the month of Marchesvan. For twelve years Esarhaddon ruled Asshur. Shamash-Shumu-Ukin and Asshurbanipal, his two sons, ascended the thrones in Babili and Asshur respectively.

The death of Esarhaddon, so unexpected, halted life for Zaqutu, at least briefly. They waited a whole week for the young king's body to arrive at the Inner City for the funeral rites. Both Crown Princes did the duty of a son, taking it in turn. Zaqutu remained secluded in the Ishtar temple, rocking to and fro on the pallet she had placed at the feet of the Goddess.

"Goddess, Ishtar, Mulissu, Queen of Heaven, Mighty Ishtar, receive thy son." She repeated this incantation over and over until her voice could not croak any longer. She slept and woke in fitful bursts. Ten days she spent until she could no longer bear the sound of her own prayers. Abby brought her a beaker of sweetened wine flavoured with spices. Zaqutu's nose drew in the scent and she thought of the myrtle-infused burial shrouds, the bitter draft of hyssop, the purification ceremony that must happen soon.

She went forth leaning on Pulu's arm, wailing and shredding her clothing. She wished she had the ritual knife to slice at her arms and legs, to bleed for her son, her only son, to let him serve as Ishtar's ransom, an offering to Ereshkigal, to slake her thirst for death. Out of duty more than inclination, she washed her body, anointed herself with oil, and proceeded from the temple of Ishtar to Ekul, to declare the end of the period of mourning for the king.

"Here now and from old, long ago, are the tombs of the kings and queens of Asshur. Yet many kings were buried in Kalkhu. I want Pulu to put at least one of his palaces there. It will be dedicated to Ishtar and will absorb all the _me_." Ataril and Pulu listened in surprise. The priests of Asshur did not look pleased.

Zaqutu turned to the company and flung one arm out in a wide circle. "Here in the Inner City are the temples of all the gods.

Asshur rules and holds sway over all the earth. But all the earth is enriched in every city by the _me_ which Ishtar holds. The new king shall have a new palace and a new temple for Ishtar."

Ataril smiled. "My lady, you have brought joy to my heart. Not just because I agree with you but—" and here he hesitated for a brief glance at her face "—I have been worried lest you, like last time, were to descend again as if to the underworld."

"I cannot. The Goddess has placed me in her hand, just here—" she motioned to her seat in the temple forecourt "—to govern. Mine is the power and I cannot escape it. I know that now."

She felt her face changing its expression as if she had no control over it and she froze in her steps. *That's Qat's voice! I sound just like her.* She shivered, unable to control the tremor though she knew Ataril was looking at her in alarm. *I don't want to be like that.* A sob escaped her and both men turned to face her. *Pulu ... he's so young, he has to obey me. But I want him to rule, not me. Oh, Goddess, help me please!* She raised her tear-stained cheeks towards the sky, swallowed hard and tried to manage a smile.

Ataril said "I'm sure our Mother also fears for your health at this time. The messenger you will send to Kalkhu can reassure her."

Chapter 38: Ishtar Has her Revenge

The full moon passed before news of Esarhaddon's death had come to Ahat-Abisha in Kalkhu. She had wakened from a drugged sleep to find Uribelit shaking her. Even before she could open her eyes she felt the maid's tears fall on her cheeks. She had to struggle to wake from her trance, but she drew breath, coughed, and sank back into the fleece that lay on her divan.

"Oh, my lady, please—wake up, wake up," she heard the maid beg.

Uribelit's hand grasped her wrist and Ahat-Abisha pulled herself into a sitting position. She tried to find her eyes with her fists so she could rub them free of the crust that formed in them when she lay drugged. The effects of her dose hadn't worn off so she could sit without pain but it was hard to fix her mind on what Uribelit said. "Show me the message," she ordered.

Death from illness? Esarhaddon, that young and vigorous king? The parchment shook in her hands as she peered at the writing. It was Zaqutu's hand but unsteady. *Oh, let the great gods pity us,* she thought. *What will she do now?* As the old woman came fully awake she remembered how the death of Shibanu had taken all reason and self-control away from Zaqutu, how she had ignored and neglected her husband and her son, had even spurned the rites of the Goddess.

She sent Uribelit to prepare a pottage for her and to get someone to bring her parchment and quill. "Don't let that messenger leave without my reply." Her thoughts ran wild, hopping from one idea to the next. *Why did this happen? Shamash? Because he failed to avenge his father's death? Or, no, it can't be, but maybe Ishtar has waited too long for her revenge. Zaqutu? Has she taken a lover who hopes to get rid of her sons, to father his own on her? Was it poison? Has the king held a viper in his own bosom? All the wives? Was there a quarrel?* When the scribe arrived with parchment and quill she calmed herself. *All that is folly and empty dreaming.* "Thank you. I'll dictate the reply."

She praised Zaqutu for her foresight in bringing on Pulu's treaty of accession earlier than everyone else had thought wise. He had served three years as Crown Prince, most of the time in Ninuwa where the magnates sat in council and where Zaqutu acted in the king's stead.

"Now you must recall the army if you have not already
thought of it. Worse fate can befall than a rebel as far
away as Egypt."

The scribe looked at her, his face expressing a mixture of query and surprise.

"Don't worry, the Queen Mother will not take offence. I worry only that she will take no notice at all."

The scribe looked down at the parchment and waited for her to continue.

The reply came in only three days. Zaqutu was already in the Inner City.

"To the Prophet of Ishtar, Ahat-Abisha,
your daughter Zaqutu. I have heeded your advice."

Zaqutu asked Ahat-Abisha to come in person to Asshurbanipal's crowning, to speak the oracle of the covenant in person. The temples of the Inner City strained to hold the multitude of vassal kings, governors, allies and officials. Afterwards, on the barge going upstream to Kalkhu, Zaqutu said, "No other king in all the world has ever ruled so vast an array of nations. So much wealth, so much power. Ishtar of Ninuwa is great indeed."

"Ishtar of Arbail is great, my daughter, perhaps greater still. The kingdoms and the wealth will pass away. The beauty which you and your grandson will bring into this land will be imperishable."

"Have you seen that? Has Ishtar spoken so?"

The priestess nodded and shifted her weight on the divan, looking over the edge of the barge at the sluggish current. Leaning further, she searched below the surface for signs of fish, headed upstream like them towards their spawning grounds. "My death should come soon, daughter." When she saw Zaqutu's face contorted she softened her voice. "Not too soon; you grieve still for your son and you are prone to let grief drive off your reason. You must know my pain can end only with my death—have you no care for that?"

"My mother, I grieve not only for my son but for myself. Something precious, more precious than a son, has been taken from me. Ishtar promised, by your very mouth, long days and everlasting years in the Inner City. Yes, in the tomb they prepared for him. How can I rely on her words?" Zaqutu looked away and covered her face with her hands. "No, don't answer. If only I hadn't gone with Ataril to be healed. Arda would've found me in Arbail and taken me and then—"

"And then the kingdom would have had twelve years of dissension and weakness. Pulu would rule a few towns along the sides of the river here and little else."

Zaqutu frowned, puzzled. "Why?"

"You rule the lands where your grandson is now king—and my dear child, you rule well. You have learned to control your passion, to keep your own counsel, to plan ahead." She laughed softly. "My brother said he loved you because he only had to look at you to know just what you thought. He saw your love of him in your face."

"I see. No one will love me now because I am too hard to read?"

"Sennacherib as king, always wary, doubted everyone. Felt each wanted something from him, would try to get more than his fair share. With you he relaxed because he saw your purity and innocence. How can you say no one loves you? So vast an array of nations you say. They love you—they see in you the guarantor of their peace, of their justice. They see in you the one who will bring love and beauty into the world. They see you as an earthly example of the Goddess."

Zaqutu returned her laugh. "And our goddess, she too sometimes complained of being unloved, abandoned, left to rot in the netherworld." For some moments they watched the movement of the light on the water, listened to the squawking of the wading birds, heard the rustle of small animals in the reed beds at the curves in the river. Zaqutu spoke softly. "I do not want you to die."

"Thank you, that is pleasing. The death I seek will not come until the head of Arda-Mulissi is brought to me. Your grandson the king must bring that about." Her voice, soft and even, rang firm.

She saw Zaqutu look hard at her face, but she let no emotion show. She merely returned the younger woman's gaze and saw how the vision from her own eyes made itself known to Zaqutu. Her little Pulu slaughtering his uncle.

The first years of Asshurbanipal's forty-year reign were peaceful, almost without incident. His wives cared little for him, or he for them. He formed the habit of visiting Zaqutu's suite to take his morning meal. They would talk over the day's plans, or sing, or read advice from the sages of the past. Zaqutu shaped the boy's sensibilities more than she guided his actions. "Get good advisers, trust them, but set them to oversee one another. They'll let you know soon enough if any of the other counsellors are ... er, straying into disloyalty."

"Grandmother, if I take your advice I will do nothing at all, just sit and watch others carrying on the government. Do you advise that? It is not the way of my father the king."

"Nor the way of your grandfather the king." Zaqutu laughed.

"But you are not exactly like either of them. Half of you is like your mother's people, Babili to the core. You love music and poetry, the old stories, the wise sayings of the sages." She stopped and took some millet stew into her bowl. "Your grandfather, though, the first thing he did when I met him was to tell me the story of Adapa. It has followed me through my life. We make mistakes, the gods make our lives out of our mistakes. I regret …" She broke off and sat in silence, not even swallowing.

"I won't have any regrets when I reach your age if I don't do anything," the king mumbled.

Zaqutu looked at him, her eyes soft with love. "There is something you have to do, but I have put off telling you of it." At his raised eyebrows she added, "For my own reasons."

"What do I have to do?"

She pursed her lips, her eyes fixed on her hands clenched in her lap. She pushed away the tray of food, stood and walked over to the window, hiding her face, struggling to control her tears. "Many things. Protect your vassals, keep peace among them. Protect your own household and the ever-growing tower of wealth that builds up in Ninuwa. Find ways to spend your wealth to enrich the people who will come after you have gone.

"Your grandfather made this city large, knowing how great your estates would be, how many powerful tribes would do homage to Ishtar of Ninuwa. Your father adorned Kalkhu with palaces and gardens to honour the kings of old.

"You will, I think, bring into this city artisans and scribes, scholars and masons. You could, if you wanted, make a treasure-house that would house every song and story ever known. Yes, that would be something you could do.

"But, my grandson the king, there is something else you must do first. I cannot see how you will do it but, it will be done and you will do it. Ishtar of Arbail has spoken the word. My beloved Ahat-Abisha," she sobbed, "Wishes it done soon. She will die then, I will lose her, and my life will seem to me nothing but a drifting fringe of threads dangling from the Goddess's shawl."

"Spoken the word? A prophecy that hasn't been told me?"

Spoken long ago.

> 'By the Great Gods above and the Dark Ones below I curse you, Arda-Mulissi. Cursed of the gods you will stumble from folly to folly until you are killed by one whom you pursue.'

Zaqutu caught the sob rising in her throat and swallowed it. "Dear Pulu, Arda-Mulissi pursued us—you and me, Ataril and Annabel your nurse. Ataril cannot be expected to kill a man hardened by banditry and cunning. So who will fulfil that prophecy? Ishtar is Arda-Mulissi's enemy; she will defeat him, but it must be by your hand."

"You want me to go into the wild lands, among Gimmirans and wild men, to find an outlaw? Me? King of the world, king of Asshur, king of all the lands?"

"Why not? Your fathers went out into those lands, or places like that, hunting. You won't be hunting for lions or deer but for an outlaw. It will be good for you, too, to see something of those places. Sennacherib took Esarhaddon on expeditions but you never ..." She bit her lip. Esarhaddon had been too careful with Pulu and not careful enough with Shumu. "Your brother, Crown Prince in Babili—he has made expeditions into the Sealand to capture and kill outlaws. This one, though, I want you to bring him alive if you can, to Arbail."

"To Arbail? A sacrifice?"

"The priestess will decide that. Obviously it depends on the state he is in when you bring him. But bring him you shall; the Goddess has spoken."

For seven years, at the end of each summer Asshurbanipal ventured forth with his bodyguard and a company of the royal army. They rode far eastwards through the country of the Medes to the borders of Bartatua's domain. Later they scoured the Urartian lands and penetrated to Mushki and Luddu. At last one year, as they happened to pass through the city of Tukhana on their way to Tarzi, they stopped at a tavern. Suddenly weary of riding, the king decreed that they would stay two weeks.

"You'll miss the autumn festival altogether," his third-man complained. "We cannot get from here to Kharranu in time."

"We'll miss it. Our journey is blessed by all the gods; Ishtar has spoken. We will find him only if we keep on looking. I, for one, cannot go further right now. We'll stay here."

"We are many and this is a small place. How will they find food?"

"We'll pay and they'll find it. This country is hilly and desolate, but not empty. They can always send out merchants and those merchants will bring food, have no fear."

The king spoke truth. Throughout the region of Tabal word spread that harvested food brought a good price in Tukhana. The mayor invited the king and his bodyguard to a feast for the full moon of Elul, an unfavourable time in most places. "My lord the king does me great honour," he murmured.

"Mayor, I am pleased to do you honour as your city has provided well for us all. In Asshur this day is not a favourable day, but here you are having a feast. Can you explain?"

"The king your grandfather decreed it. The daughter of the moon—you call her Ishtar—is honoured here. This province all belonged to the king's sister, your great-aunt Ahat-Abisha. She released us when your father was born, but we honour her Goddess, and feast at the full moon."

Asshurbanipal lay back on the divan, thinking. *So this was Ahat-Abisha's province. And I felt I had to stop here.* Then he remembered. One soldier of his bodyguard could understand the talk of the men in the tavern. He'd mentioned to the king that the traders had been joking about one of their number, nicknamed Hideaway. Hideaway never came to town for full moon or new moon, they joked about how much money he saved by staying away from the crowded tavern. Even though business would be brisk, men would get carried away, a thief could get some good pickings. Now the king asked the mayor, "Do all your people observe those feasts or only some of them?"

"Men like feasts. They all come. My servants go to the taverns and listen to the gossip and jokes. I keep an eye on things that way. Everybody does. Our country is wild lands, as you know. Horse-breeders must stay weeks in the hills so when they come to town they make the most of it. The market is brisk, since all the merchants have come."

The king grinned. "I hear that Hideaway doesn't."

"Oh, him. He's a mystery. A brigand, I think, but he doesn't steal from me. He brings ore to the smelters, we've no idea where he gets it."

"Why does he hide?"

"We don't know. Perhaps there's a price on his head, someone he might meet if he hung about in the crowd who would know him and turn him in."

"What does he look like? How old is he?"

"Not young. My age maybe. Less than five times twelve I'd guess. A hard man. You look at him and don't want to get too close, if you know what I mean. Why do you ask about him?"

"He may be just the man I seek. Suppose I put a price on his head, a very large one. How soon could you bring him to me?"

The mayor looked down, scratching his forelocks, tugging at his beard. "I'd have to make it very quiet or he'd never come. He's wary. If he has a favourite at the tavern ... I don't know. It might be a while."

"Twenty minahs of fine silver if I have him within ten days. Forty if it's five days."

Three days later Asshurbanipal paid the mayor forty minahs of silver and chained the fugitive hand and foot in a wagon provided by the mayor. Pulu chose to risk all on his instinct. He forbade his soldiers to force the man's name from him.

On the day of the fast before the new moon the king's party reached Guzana. At evening the king stood beside the wagon, gazing at the miserable wretch held in the sitting position he had endured for ten days. They had doused him with water when crossing rivers but the man smelled ill, perhaps ill unto death. Suddenly the king shouted, "You! Uncle! You know you cannot now escape. Do you want to die in the wagon or tell me your name and be treated as your father's son?"

The man's sneer faded. "How did you know?"

The king walked away to order clothes for his uncle, food, straw and a fleece to sit upon.

At Arbail, Uribelit rubbed fine oil of almond over the prophet's brittle skin. "My lady, does that soothe you?"

Ahat-Abisha made a real effort and opened her eyes. Her dry lips and sore throat prevented any words from passing her lips but she nodded and then passed back into the swoon that now held her many hours each day. Her sight had dimmed but her hearing remained acute. She now heard footsteps coming to her suite and she forced her eyes to open.

"A message for the lady, Prophet of Arbail."

Uribelit had brought in a parchment, so scribbled they couldn't read it.

"Fetch my scribe," the aged woman ordered.

"Greetings, my lady," the scribe said when she entered. She took the scroll from Uribelit and looked at the colophon. "It's from the king!" she exclaimed. "Written by himself—I can tell his hand."

"What does he say?"

"I don't understand it."

> Even with new oxen every rest stop I will not reach Arbail
> with the iron cage the men of the northwest made for me
> in time for the new moon.

"That's all it says, my lady. There's no greeting, no blessing, no signature, but it is the king's seal."

Ahat-Abisha struggled to pull herself up, to touch the scroll, to peer at it. Uribelit supported her shoulders as she held the parchment to her nose. "It's fresh still," she said. "He took a fresh parchment." She smiled and a sudden swelling of joy filled her torso. "Send for the Queen Mother. No matter when they come they must proceed to Arbail and she herself must see, she must be here. I know she must."

Ten days after the new moon of Tishri was an unfavourable day. The whole compound at Arbail had made a fast and were at prayer in the sanctuary when Asshurbanipal's trumpeters reached the gate. Zaqutu signalled to the prophet's litter-bearers to come with her outside. Shadditu, who had been named high priestess at the feast, followed them out.

Ahat-Abisha marvelled at what she saw. Even her dim sight could make out the cage—iron bars set into heavy beams. The beams were borne up by axles, and great wheels trundled the heavy contraption along. Her heart fell. *Was it some bear or lion that he had captured in the hunt?* The king's autumn hunting expeditions had become the stuff of storytelling in all the taverns.

As the procession reached the entryway she saw that a man sat on a chair inside the cage. His face was hidden in his beard and a leather hood and cape covered him. *It's him all right, still proud he is, sitting up so straight. I know well how painful it is, being jounced in a cart for miles in the waste places.*

The king approached her litter and made an obeisance. "Your servant, Lady of Arbail. I have brought to you the murderer and the miscreant who dishonoured the Goddess and you."

Her voice came forth strongly, and clear. "May the Goddess send upon you such blessings as no king ever enjoyed, my lord the king."

While Asshurbanipal ordered his troops to set up camp outside the gates Shadditu arranged for him to join them within. They broke their fast quietly in the lofty chamber where the High Priestess kept court.

"My lady, I wish you could have seen his face when we drew up to the walls. He remembered only the poor wooden palings of the earlier enclosure, not the carved and painted walls of this temple site."

"He knew nothing of your father's refounding of the sanctuary?"

"Nothing. He has lived for years—many years—on the fringes of the civilised world, among people who cannot speak. Well, they cannot speak our languag— not any of our languages. Once he realised how long he would be travelling with us he spoke to us and heard our tales. He did know of my father's death but nothing more."

"What sort of people were they?" Zaqutu asked.

"They are like the barbarians with whom we treated, my father and I, on the shores of the Great Northern Sea. Pale faces and pale eyes."

"Gimmirans?"

"Not the same people as your friend in the eastern meadow lands. A different language but like appearance. They mine silver and gold as well as iron, valuable to us for trade. And now they have yielded up this brigand I have brought you. What should I do next? Will he be an offering to the Goddess?"

No one spoke for a time. Ahat-Abisha realised she had not thought about this, had not planned for it. She didn't know what she wanted. They all waited for her to answer and she could not.

"My mother," Zaqutu broke the silence. "You have envisioned this

Ishtar Has her Revenge

event, haven't you? Hasn't the Goddess shown you the proper course?"

She shook her head and closed her eyes for a moment. "You cannot die until you see his head on a plate." "That's what the Goddess said. She didn't say how it would come about." Then the prophet recalled the first prophecy she had uttered outside of Arbail, the one she had repeated to Zaqutu. She spoke it now.

> "To the son of the king: Because you despised me you will roam the steppe as a shade of the underworld. Be fearful of my wrath. Never shall victory be yours, never shall you prevail, never shall you rule. By the Great Gods above and the Dark Ones below I curse you, Arda-Mulissi. Cursed of the gods you will stumble from folly to folly until you are killed by one whom you pursue.' By the mouth of the woman Ahat-Abisha of Arbail."

She drew a deep breath. "The Goddess spoke truth when she cursed that man. He has wandered like a shade of the underworld. He has stayed cursed and now he must be killed by one whom he has pursued." They kept still, waiting for more from her mouth. "I have had a vision. In it I saw the man's head presented to me on a wide flat dish. But the head was of a young man—shaven, smiling a cruel sneer. This head is not like that as far as I can see."

"My mother, more than twenty years have passed and even then Arda was not young."

"It was a vision, that's all."

The king stirred, seeming troubled by the nervous silence all about him. "My lady, I shall have him cleaned and shaved, stripped and bathed, dressed in a fresh tunic. But shall you sacrifice him to the Goddess?"

"The time for sacrifice is past—we are nearly at the full moon."

"Where I found him they celebrate the Goddess at the full moon. They say my grandfather founded the sanctuary to Ishtar there at a full moon."

"We'll enquire of the gods," she said and asked Shadditu to give her leave to take her rest.

Next morning the king came to Zaqutu's rooms with a gloomy face. "The priestess of Arbail rejects him. That is, Ishtar of Arbail will not accept him as a sacrifice. She says that, nevertheless, if he is to die, it must be by the hand of a priestess. Of those whom he pursued, Grandmother, you are the only one who can kill him. Ahat-Abisha wants you to come to her."

Beside the litter Zaqutu stood looking down at the sunken face of the old woman. "Why? Why me?"

"He pursued you. You are to kill him and you are to bring his head to me. That's been decided."

Zaqutu's dismay was so obvious that the others showed signs of wanting to laugh. "How? I mean, with what weapon? Am I supposed to pierce a chained man with a sword? Like Ishtar? What do you expect?"

Ataril intervened. "He killed your husband with one of the statues of the Guardians of Asshur. The Adapa one, I think. You could take that statue from the Inner City …" He stopped and waved his hand in front of his face. "No, take Arda to the Inner City, to his father's grave. There smash his head in with that same statue." Ataril put his hand to his mouth as if he'd forgotten something. "Two statues were used. I'm not sure which one killed the king and which one crushed my father's head after he'd been stabbed."

The old woman looked hard into Ataril's face. He looked as though he might weep. "My dear Ataril, it is of no matter. But I suggest that you too, as one of those pursued, take the other statue and use it to stun Arda as well. Both of you can crush his head but I am certain it is Zaqutu who must actually cut off his head—she must be the one to kill him. She'll use the knife that she received at her first devotion."

A long silence followed the old woman's words. Zaqutu stood, head bowed, breathing slowly and heavily.

The strained silence broke suddenly. Asshurbanipal spoke. As if his words came from some distant source he announced, "I am determined to follow the prophet's vision. It will be in the Ekul temple in Asshur."

They all turned to him in surprise.

"Yes, very well, after the winter rains have come. The statues will stun him and his head can be cut off afterwards as you say." He hesitated, shaking his shoulders and then in his normal voice added, "When it's done we'll all barge upriver to Arbail to bring the head to Ahat-Abisha. Yes, on a plate too, one of the offering platters of Asshur. After it's done we'll barge back downstream. Except you, Grandmother—you could stay in Arbail until she dies."

Ahat-Abisha saw Zaqutu looking her way, her eyes pleading. *She doesn't want to do it, of course. I can see that. She hates any violence or cruelty, though it's really the blood.* "Ataril may be right, you know. There won't be much blood and they can drug him first. We'd be showing him more mercy that way than he showed to either his father or to me."

Zaqutu looked at each of them until her eyes came to rest on the old woman's twitching head, those old eyes rheumy with yellow crusts. "So all they have to do is stun him? I have to cut the head off?"

The old woman shut her eyes and pity welled up in her. Her mind's eye saw the stunned young girl who first stared up at the Goddess and meekly took her vows. *A long road.* Her voice low, she murmured, "You don't want to cut off his head?"

"No."

"Daughter, I wish it."

On a grey morning the king led Zaqutu and Ataril into the enclosure where the kings of Asshur had their tombs. Two soldiers flanked Arda-Mulissi who sat, hands bound to his sides.

Standing beside the tombs, Asshurbanipal read the sentence of death, the priests of Shamash sounded their drums, and then all fell silent. With both hands Ataril gripped the Adapa image and swung it at the side of the captive's head. Zaqutu shivered at the thud.

"You murdered my father who had done you no wrong," he stated as he set the image down.

The king echoed the words as he swung the Apkallu statue hard into Arda-Mulissi's skull. "You murdered my grandfather who had done you no wrong." The man fell sideways onto the ground and lay still, blood streaming from his nose and mouth.

Zaqutu shivered again. The smell of the blood recalled the smell of that first sacrifice Sennacherib had made her watch. She felt the knife leave her hand, her grip nerveless. She thought of the blood that had poured from the rapist's neck that long-ago day in the wilderness. She wouldn't look at the man's body. "Is he dead now?" she forced herself to ask. Ataril took her chin in his hand and looked into her eyes. He shook his head.

Into her mind came a scene from long ago, from her earliest time at Arbail. She'd asked the priestess why she expected Sennacherib to come back to Arbail. She could picture the temple enclosure as it had been before. *Before this man came and destroyed it.* She remembered her dismay, almost disbelief, when Ahat-Abisha had told her the king would come to "offer his son as a sacrifice to the goddess." *She'd said, "A sacrifice, his very life, to slake the appetite of the Dark Sister." And I thought, I remember, I thought, "Will he do it? Will Arda-Mulissi be offered to Ishtar just like a ram?"* The image of Ishtar with the knife to slay her children again flashed across her mind.

As if some other person inhabited her, she stooped to the ground and picked up the knife—the one she'd received at her first devotion. For the first time she looked directly into the face of the man who might have become her husband, blenching as the blood still flowed from his mouth, though slowly now. He was dying, she had to act swiftly. With one hand she gripped the hair at his forehead and with the other passed the knife across the skin of his neck. Too lightly.

It didn't cut. Desperate to get it over with, she brought her hand up and sliced at his neck with all her strength. The blood gushed forth, soaking the front of her tunic and flowing onto Sennacherib's grave.

She stood up and handed the knife to Asshurbanipal. "Take it," she said. "Strike a blow." She smiled as he looked back at her, nonplussed. "Then in your annals you can say:

'I performed this. I made quiet again the hearts of the great gods my lords.' "

Illustrations

drawn by

Rachel Brand

Loaded Mule

Arab Raiders

King Sennacherib

Royal Horse

Village Scene

Adapa

Musicians

Soldiers Killing Sheep

Ishtar with Devotee and Gazelles

The King in His Chariot

Traveling by River

Courtiers

King Hunting

Battle of Khalule

Esarhaddon as Crown Prince

Gula, Goddess of Healing

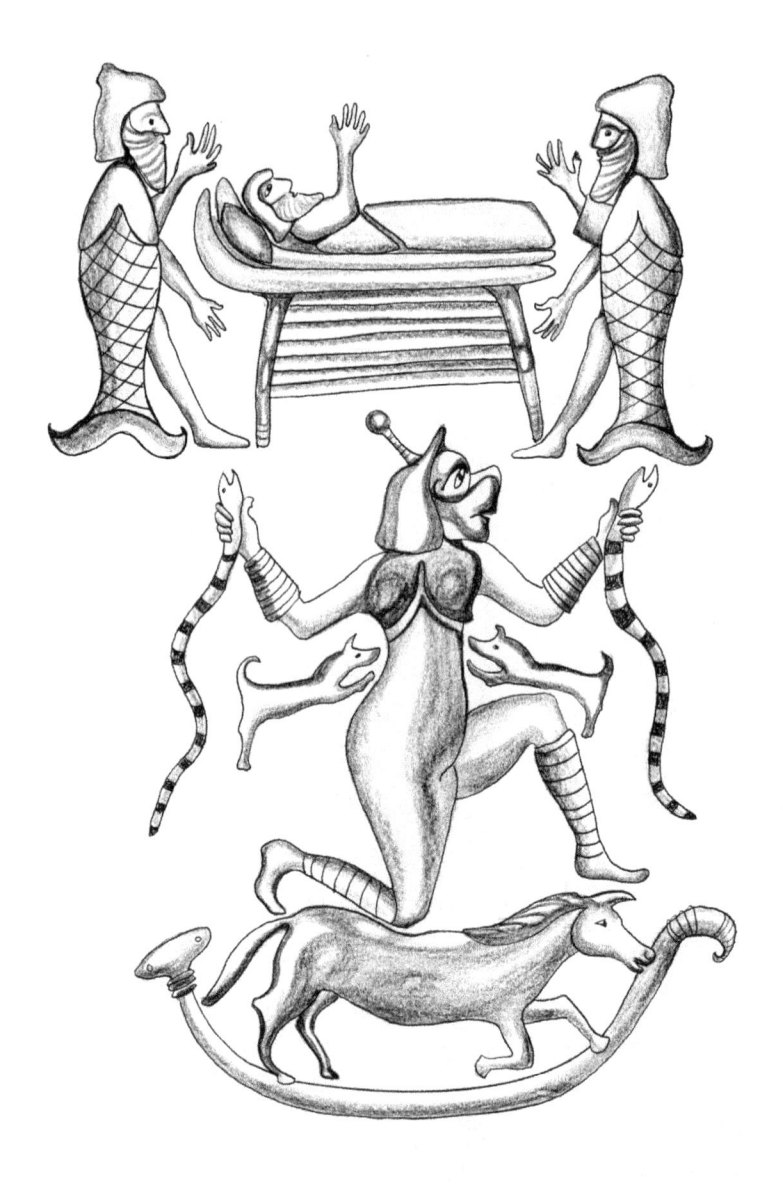

Exorcism of the Lamashtu Demon

Esarhaddon Crowned

CPSIA information can be obtained
at www.ICGtesting.com
Printed in the USA
BVHW071635040221
599249BV00004B/550

9 780473 511005